THE ALIEN EFFECT

by Cary Neeper

Penscript®
PUBLISHING HOUSE

Publisher's Cataloging-in-Publication
  Neeper, Cary.
    The alien effect / by Cary Neeper.
    p. cm. — (The archives of Varok ; 3)
    Includes bibliographical references.
    SUMMARY: Raised on the Jovian moon Varok, the young human woman Shawne returns to a ravaged Earth with her mother Tandra and alien fathers. Can their message of hope convince the surviving population?
    LCCN 2014911366
    ISBN 978-1-62222-011-3 (hardcover)
    ISBN 978-1-62222-012-0 (trade pbk.)
    ISBN 978-1-62222-013-7 (small format pbk.)

    1. Human-alien encounters—Fiction.
    2. Extraterrestrial beings—Fiction. 3. Sustainability—Fiction. 4. Science fiction. I. Title. II. Series: Neeper, Cary. Archives of Varok ; 3.

First edition, 2022 revision
Published by Penscript Publishing House
San Jose, California.
http://www.penscript-publishing.com

This book is dedicated to all
who care for the future of sentience,
wherever it is found.

Acknowledgements

The re-discovery of *The Archives of Varok* series was made possible by the enthusiasm of friend Sarah Jordan and her appreciation for all things remotely elllonian. I am also deeply grateful for her keen editing eye and those of my daughters, Indra Frank, who thoroughly enriched the story, and Shawne Workman. This book could not have been what it is without Shawne's dedication, expertise, incredible attention to detail, and hours provided so generously as my editor/publisher. It also could not have happened without the technical advice of my husband, physicist and defender of Earth's vadose zone, Dr. Donald A. Neeper.

I give sincere thanks also to John Barbieri of the Natural Resources Corporation, who supplied detailed information and a video tape of his Marine Transport Demonstration Project; Larry Gardner and Kurt Kidman of the San Diego Water Department; Charles Graham and the Scripps Institution of Oceanography; my cousin Ann Marie Haney, who devoted two days to showing me around the California coast from La Jolla to Point Loma; Rev. Dale Arnink and the Philosophy Club at the Unitarian-Universalist Church of Los Alamos; geologist Kim Manley; and Mary Zemach for her Sunday School course in environmental awareness, in which it is shown that white stuffed animals soaked in crankcase oil never come clean.

Special thanks to extraordinary teacher and artist Jerry Yarnell of the Yarnell School of Fine Art for his help painting the cover for this book.

Finally, for providing a thorough and thoroughly credible nonfiction presentation of the steady state and all the reasoning that makes it necessary, I thank Brian Czech, founder of The Center for the Advancement of the Steady State Economy (CASSE) and steadystate.org. His book *Supply Shock: Economic Growth at the Crossroads and the Steady State Solution* was released just in time to provide detailed information as a reality check for this story.

A related title, *Enough Is Enough: Building a Sustainable Economy In a World of Finite Resources* by Rob Dietz and Dan O'Neill was released for review just in time to provide a nonfiction reference for *The Alien Effect*'s prequel, *The Webs of Varok*. I have also referenced Laurence C. Smith's projections of current data in his book *The World In 2050*. My sincerest admiration and gratitude goes to these authors for all that they do, providing us with wisdom that will secure a safe and pleasant future for our great grandchildren and for all the Earth.

.

CONTENTS

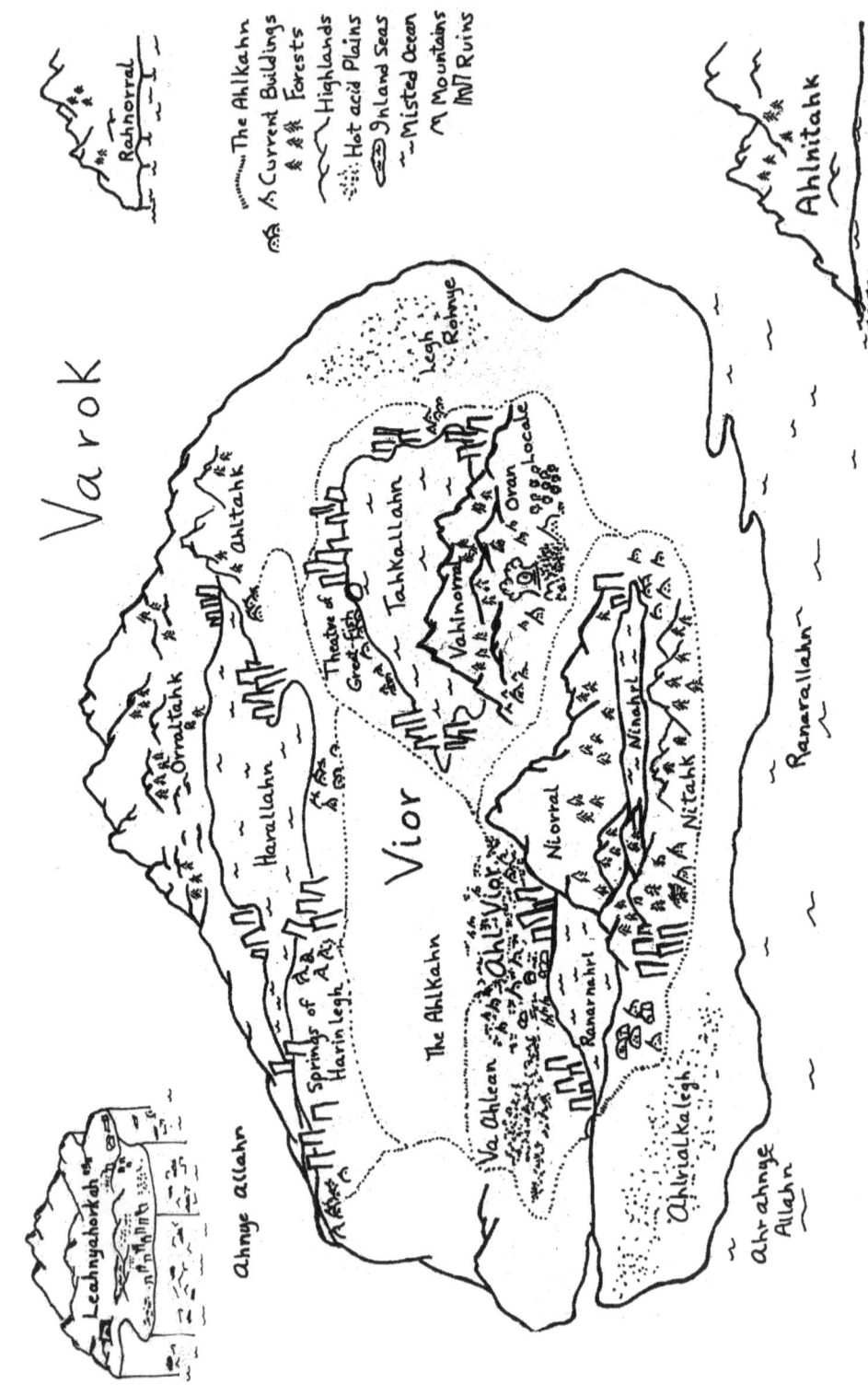

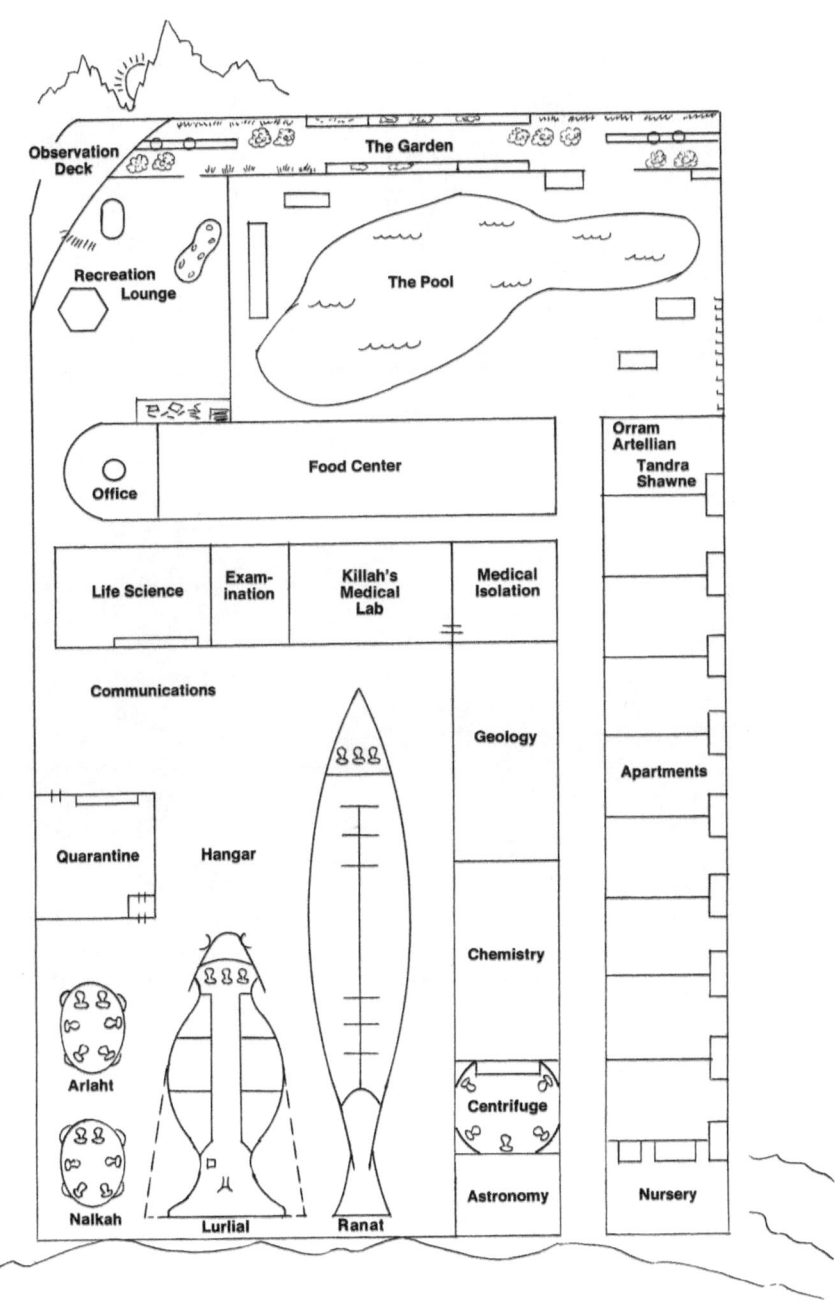

E111-Varok Observation Base

I. DECISIONS

"It must always have been seen, more or less distinctly,
by political economists, that the increase in wealth is not
boundless: that at the end of what they term the progressive
state [economic growth] lies the stationary state."

—*John Stuart Mill (1806-1873), quoted in Supply
Shock: Economic Growth at the Crossroads
and the Steady State Solution by Brian Czech.
Canada: New Society Publishers, pp. 68–69.*

Two Messages

Shawne sat on the edge of the algae pool upstairs in the Oran family home, looking beautiful and strong, her golden brown waves framing the delicate sculpture of her human face. She kicked water in the air over Conn's partially submerged sonic melons. I felt a touch of amusement as the elll's amphibioid marble eyes appeared, and his lengthy tongue unrolled to catch a shower of droplets flying past his nasal gills. I moved back a step on the stone deck to stay dry.

"I'm serious, Conn," Shawne said. "I need to go back to Earth. It's too beautiful . . . we can help salvage what's left."

Conn voiced a gill-muffled response in his favorite English slang. "No way. We're doing all we can from here on Varok. You don't need to do anything but finish Integration at the Concentrate."

"Which will be no problem for you." I spoke in Varokian. "You've done very well there, Shawne."

"Thanks, Orram. I appreciate your confidence, but neither of you is hearing me." She switched from English to Varokian to make her point. "Earth is my biological home. I can't just watch humans make the same mistakes—"

Conn's son Stringer interrupted. His rich elllonian tones soared up to the pool from the garden below. "Get down here, Shawne. Our rides are waiting."

"The train for Ahl Vior leaves in the last quarter of this light-period," I said. "You can just make it."

She sprang to her feet. "Goodbye, Daddy-O's. Don't forget to gather the eggs while I'm gone. Make Conn do some of it, Orram. Be sure the *kaehl* have enough *hoat* grain every morning. They also like—"

"I know, Shawne," I said, scanning her thoughts for concerns. "We'll also take good care of the garden. Good luck finishing your Integration Projects. You'll enjoy them."

She smiled. "I love you, *dara vahns.*"

Then she disappeared down the stones to the great porch embraced by the giant mineral tree that defined our Oran Locale lodge, my ancestral home. We heard the daramont Pork Belly snuffle as she climbed aboard the big racer's broad shoulders.

"Goodbye, Shawne Love," Tandra called. "Be good to yourself. Get some sleep."

"Wait a minute, Mom. I forgot to pack my—"

"Let's go!" Stringer hollered.

His daramont, Markup, bellowed and took off, and Pork Belly followed with a loping start.

"Wait!" Shawne protested. "I don't have—"

"Conn finished packing the saddle bags for you," Tandra shouted.

"Oh no-o-o! I won't have anything . . . "

Her voice faded as Stringer whooped a long elllonian ear-splitter, and both daramonts raced across the fields toward the closest train stop. The Ahlkahn was infamous among Varok's ellls for being on time.

I met Tandra in our downstairs office. She stood at the large window, looking out over the lush garden to the web fields beyond. "Have you heard from Bob Carliano yet?" she asked. "Do we have an invitation to go to Earth?"

"Not yet," I said, sensing the dread in her mood.

Tandra had divorced herself and three-year-old Shawne from Earth eighteen Earth-years ago, when we first bonded and became family. She did not want to go back.

I took her hand and led her through the garden, past the egg-layer's pen and into the web fields that stretched toward the valley embracing the foothills of the Vahinorral. Oval berries hung from the web bushes in graceful swirls of light blue.

"They will ripen soon," I said.

"Yes." Tandra looked out toward the valley. We waved at the tall young elll and his human sister, still visible racing across the first meadow. Stringer's green tunic plumes, ruffled by speeding through the moist air, gave his sleek aquatic figure the illusion of deep fur.

"Oh no. Stringer has forgotten to wear his wet-sweater again," Tandra said. "Let's hope Shawne will notice and nag at him."

She stood in the new light, her dark hair glowing with silver lights, its fine strands brushing the soft turn of her cheek. "The mists on the *llaoon* grass—how perfectly beautiful, Orram, how they reflect the colors of the auroral lights."

"Look how the blues frame the yellow, and a hint of green. Jupiter will be rising soon."

"Then it will all turn a golden glow at mid-light. I love it here, Orram, so much. How could we possibly think of leaving, even for a single Earth year?"

She looked at me as if there could be a solution for her dread. "Have I thanked you lately, for our life here, Orram?"

"Tandra, please—"

"We can't leave," she said. "We have a contract for care of the Oran Locale, for eggs for the locale, for this web field and its good forage for the daramonts."

"That will not be a probem, Tan. We have good neighbors who will gladly take a temporary contract."

"Look, Orram. The locale daramont pack is coming in." She laughed. "How can such big fur balls look so awkward with their huge haunches and still run so beautifully?"

Beneath Tandra's foreboding, I read another concern she was suppressing. To accept the invitation we expected from Carliano could mean losing our human daughter to her native planet.

We had stayed in close contact with the former human astronaut since C.E. 2050, when Carliano's spacecraft crashed on Earth's moon. We had used the opportunity to introduce our alien selves to Earth, while his crew recovered at our Elll-Varok Observation Base there.

Now, in 2068 C.E., our Moonbase served as a transmitting station for EV Science. We made regular broadcasts, but other contact was minimal. With Earth's global population thinned disastrously in the 2050's—thanks to climate change disasters, rampant disease, and resource or ideological wars triggered by density stress—human nations and space business ventures no longer afforded the luxury of visiting the moon.

Tandra and I walked slowly back through the web field, and took a moment to check on the bird-like *kaehll* that had been under Shawne's care ever since she was a small child. Under the cover of the mineral tree, we paused on the front porch for another colorful view of the ever-changing sky.

"Bob has sounded more hopeful lately," I said, as we entered the lodge. "The students we hosted here on Varok are now young adults. They're convinced we have workable solutions. They listen to Conn's broadcasts."

"Surely there's no chance—"

"Mom, Orram, pick up." It was Shawne, calling from atop her daramont.

I tapped the office landcom. "Orram here. Go ahead, Shawne."

"Stringer got a call from his Waterfalling lead. He says I've been accepted to be on the team. You've got to come out to Ahl Vior for the games."

"Congratulations," I answered. "You'll be the first human to compete in the ellls' Waterfalling."

"That's silly, since Mom is the only other human on Varok, but thanks anyway, Orram. Please come. Orticon says he can't make it. He's too busy."

"He has his hands full with Earth's satellite data, surveying water resources, but Tandra and I will be there, and I'm sure Conn and Lanoll will come."

Conn had walked down from the family pool, tracking water over the stone steps. "Good work, Shawnoon. Just be careful. Don't underestimate the currents."

Conn is not a schooling elll, not dependent on swimming with a larger group for his social and physiological needs. Though a loner, he provides a sort of fatherly schooling that has made a powerful and sensitive human mermaid of Shawne.

"Good luck, Honey," Tandra added. "We'd better sign off now. There's another call coming in."

Conn took the new transmission, giving Tandra a sympathetic glance. As we listened to the recorded message, his wide elllonian eyes grew wider and blacker. He put a reassuring hand across Tandra's shoulders, and she reached up to stroke the tough web between his fifth and sixth fingers.

"Message received," he said, turning to face us. "We have our invitation, from the United States Southwest Coalition."

Tandra looked disappointed. "I'm surprised it's not from Cascadia," she said.

"They probably encouraged it," I said. "We may attract some attention. Cascadia is hoping to stem the flood of people moving north."

Conn was more cynical. "The southern U.S. has more recovery money right now."

Tandra's face skewed with exasperation. I loved the way her long dark hair swayed when she shook her head, but I didn't enjoy her gloominess. "There must be other ecological coalitions also behind it. Aliens to the rescue, is it? So they'll have someone to blame?"

"At least, maybe someone will believe us now," Conn said.

Elll-Varok Science had been broadcasting arguments promoting no-growth policies for nearly twenty Earth years, confirming the economic theories developed on Earth in the 1970s by the humans Herman Daly and Donella Meadows. After Carliano's recent tour of Varok to study our recovery from Mahntik's treason, more people began to listen to full-Earth economic ideas from us aliens. On Earth such ideas had been called "ecological economics," "no-growth" or "steady state economics," "complex economics," or "full-circle economics." It came in many varieties—all focused on not depleting critical resources.

Another message came through, this one from from Bob Carliano. "You've got it, Orram, old buddy," he said. "The invitation to come to Earth and teach is wide open. You design the project. They'll go for anything reasonable. Your project name is 'Hope-for-a-Stable-Future.'"

"Thanks, Bob," I said. "You understand that we might not get approval from Global Varok. Travel to Earth is costly."

"I understand all too well."

"We'll inform them about the invitation after we take a short vacation. Shawne is on Stringer's elllonian water-sport team."

"Tell that beautiful daughter of yours, 'best of luck, and don't let their fins get you down.'"

It was good to hear Tandra laugh. "Thanks, Bob."

"Don't kid yourself, my friend," Conn said. "You'd better tell the Southwest Coalition we won't be coming to Earth. Thanks but no thanks."

INTEGRATION AND WATERFALLING

Shawne—At the Concentrate, many light-periods later

Begin transmission. Shawne Oran-ElConn-Grey to Elll-Varok Science on Earth's moon, for next broadcast to Earth:

Integration is not a favorite time for Varokian students—mostly ellls and varoks, a few ahlork, and me. When the hard wiring is over, the information force-fed by electronic hook-up needs to be made useful. Groan.

Luckily, my Integration was interrupted by a fantastic opportunity—I was selected to be on my brother Stringer's Waterfalling team. Hang on. I'll tell you about that soon.

First, Integration at Varok's Concentrate: "Mashing and dumping brains," we call it.

I had to pass Ellasonian studies, Varokian studies, do general Earth studies, then use biological parallels found on all three inhabited planets in our solar system. Nothing made sense at first.

I wondered if I had the brains for this Varokian education, until I thought of Nidok. He's the ahlork whose scar our family has taken. I think Conn has told you about that. It's old history now, how he got his flock to become more friendly with us bipeds.

In order to help the ahlork species learn the Varokian legal system and become responsible players (after all the damage they had done to the steady state working for Mahntik), Nidok had taken electronic information impression at the Concentrate. Conn tried to warn him that ahlork intellect was marginally qualified, but he managed to earn a Technical Pass, which made him eligible to vote and participate in decisions about Varok's future.

With the incentive of Nidok's example, I cranked out essays, worst-case scenarios, and a summary of solar system history. Then, when the grueling "Analysis" was done, I began "Issues" about Earth, technical puzzles drawn from sociological and biological problems on my native planet.

Before I realized that ten light-periods had passed, I had finished "Issues." Next came "Projects in Creativity." They were easy. I passed several Projects with honors—the ones aimed at solving Earth's dilemma.

One project was the design for water catchments made of local materials. Another was a foot-operated ungulate milker. The most boring project was a long list of subsidies and taxes to reduce human reproduction. Wouldn't you know? It got the highest rating.

I was preparing to tackle my last Project—chemical means to enhance the palatability of stem cell meat—when my elllonian brother Stringer was elected Ball Carrier for the Concentrate's Waterfalling Team. I couldn't resist. I tried out as a bow-rowing rock dodger and made Stringer's team.

Stringer was delighted. Our parents in this mixed family—Tandra, Orram, and Conn, even Conn's easy-going mate Lanoll—traveled to Ahl Vior for the final game against the Lake Seclusion team. I caught them cheering their lungs (or their equivalent organs) out with proud grins on their faces.

I watched as Stringer made the first and second circuit without incident, leaping up the rapids of the narrow river course as if he were born with a large ball (a basketball-sized bladder from a carnivorous plant) in his arms and another clasped between his legs. Ellls have long limbs, but even for him this was not easy.

Our team blocked a good path as Stringer fought his way through the wild water. The power of his webbed feet and hands sent him up the steep cascade as though he were flying.

At the top of the rapids, in a deep pool fed by a high, thin waterfall, I waited in the third and last canoe made from the husks of looping snarl. Our first canoe runs had made good time. I was bow rower for the final rush down a rocky stream to the eddy opposite the finish, which lies in deep water with a muddy bottom.

Some defensive hits slowed the other team, but then, on his third and last run up, Stringer, too, was hit. The Lake Seclusion team had come down the rapids in their canoes and cut too close to his shoulder.

Stringer wasn't hurt, but for a moment he lost his fore-arm ball and fell behind retrieving it. Then he somersaulted into the stern of my canoe for the final run—a fast but reckless move. He nearly upset the canoe. I righted it, pulling to the side as hard as I could, and we made our way down the treacherous stream, dodging rocks every few meters. Stringer j-stroked out of the main channel into a shortcut and we pulled alongside the Lake Seclusion team.

In the bow, I could see rocks coming at me too fast. I nearly threw the stern into a huge boulder. Stringer must have countered first one way then the other, but our timing has been good together since our childhood days canoing, and we pulled ahead.

In the stands, I could hear Conn getting hoarse from yelling. Then, suddenly, it was over. We pulled a boat length ahead of our nearest opponents. Stringer leapt out, sailing past my head. He endangered his grasp on both balls, finning so hard through deep water, but he won the goal basket first.

"Shawnooooon!" I saw Conn leap into the water, howling, along with many other ellls in the crowd, to congratulate our Concentrate team.

"You did it, elll-brother," I screamed along with the others, but Stringer would have none of it. He insisted we take all accolades together. From then on I have been known not as Stringer's human sister, but as Shawnoon, the Concentrate's bow rower, the one who threw the stern around so quickly we could take the shortcut.

After the match, we shared a meal of stuffed reeds at the Concentrate's pool with the team members' schools and our proud family.

My varokian brother Orticon surprised me by showing up in time for our spectacular finish. He works for EV Science in Ahl Vior, so I meet him occasionally for something to eat. He thinks I'm crazy to major in Earth studies—"Lost Cause Impossible" he calls it.

You won't believe the conversation we had. Brothers are brothers, even if they're ellls or varoks. And Parents are parents, wherever. Our talk went something like this:

"I hate to remind you," Lanoll said after we won Waterfalling, "but this commitment to the team has slowed your Integration, Shawne."

I knew I'd hear that, but not from Lanoll. She is the quiet one in the family, the one you go to when you're feeling bloated and grumpy. She's a beautiful blue elll, and easy to talk to. (Female ellls have blue plumes over their green tiles, if you remember from our Elll-Varok Bio-dictionary.)

"And," my human Mom said, finishing the earlier thought, "You have more problems to do."

"Projects, not more problems, Mom. I'm not going for the Professional Certificate."

"We've talked it over," Orram said. "We think you should give it a try."

I knew the certificate would give me more credibility on Earth, but I didn't say it. "Orram, you forget I'm not a varok."

He laughed. "I could never forget that, my dear human tad, not the way you tussle with Stringer. Tough nerves, you humans."

"Well, my human nerves can't take another set of Integration Issues."

"Right, Spaghetti-head," Stringer said. "You won't pass the General, unless you have me to lean on."

"Humans can't lean on algae-brains, Stringer Dear. We'd get creeping crud up our—"

"Stop it, you two," Tandra scolded. "You're ruining my appetite."

Lanoll laughed. "Mine, too."

"Munch yon *llaoon* grass, Flipper Toes," I whispered to Stringer.

"Enough, Shawne," Orram said. "You sound like Conn, calling names like that."

"I don't call names," Conn protested.

Mom stared him down, and we all laughed at the lie.

I did take the point they were all making, though. I'll look into finishing the Professional Certificate. That'll surprise them.

Enough for now. I thought you alien-fans might be interested in just what a Concentrate education is like. Okay, I know. You really wanted to know about Waterfalling. Talk to you later. This is Shawne on Varok, signing off.

THE FAMILY

Orram—at home, nearly a tenth of a Jovian year later

Unlike his biological parents, Lanoll and Conn, Stringer seems to be a normal, schooling elll—not a loner. The pressure patterns, the electro-stimulation, and the shared ultrasonic signals within a school of ells help him define himself. We always knew that; we just didn't like to dwell on it.

Our family—settled at my mother's, Orserah's, lodge and committed to the Oran Locale—was not enough for Stringer's adolescent schooling needs. During many Callisto Cycles throughout his childhood we had sent him off to the Forested Sea to school with his elllonian tutors. Now we knew he would be in no hurry to come home from schooling with the ells at the Concentrate.

Tandra's human view helped us deal with it. "Stringer is a marvel. A schooler's loner, or a loner's schooler, if you will. He's got the best of both worlds built into him."

"Do you really think so?" Lanoll's question sounded hopeful.

After the Waterfalling match, Stringer finished Integration as Generalist. Then he stayed in Ahl Vior to school with the new graduates and finish his accreditation with a Professional Certificate in Hydrology.

As time passed and Shawne didn't return home, we worried that she had found a new life in Ahl Vior, perhaps teaching at the Concentrate. Her messages were short and reassuring but not informative.

There are times when I cannot read her, only her mood, which is clear in her face, the tense quick movement of her hands, the darting intensity of her eyes. I remind myself that she is not like her adoptive mother, Tandra, a human with tamer hormones.

Could Tandra be a human exception? Or is she content with us non-humans because she has a genius for empathy? My mind-link with her is deep and warm with emotion, unquestioned in both of us. Though we are natives of different worlds in this solar system, we know each other as well as any two individuals can.

The memories I share with Tandra, the intensity of our mind-blending, the power of her love to heal—all of that overshadows my memory of our first physical joining. True, that physical closeness helped secure our mind-link, and it still has a surprising ability to keep Tandra happy.

When Shawne finally came home, she had a new look in her eye and a mind full of determination. "I have earned the Professional Certificate," she announced as we all shared a pot of stew at the hearth. "I plan to return to Earth and help them establish a secure future."

As she spoke, I got a strong impression from Tandra: *Don't tell Shawne about our invitation from Earth. We have heard nothing from Global Varok about it. We shouldn't get her hopes up.*

The thought was as clear as if she had spoken the words.

I found her eyes, a help in communicating without words. She nodded slightly as she read my agreement to stifle the announcement.

"Humans can get off their obsession with growth, Orram," Shawne declared, misreading our silence as disapproval. "They're finding a consensus."

I wanted to believe her, and to believe she could really help. But she would be taking on a task far too large for any of us—trying to convince enough people in a divided world to make a real difference in Earth's resource depletion. Somehow she would have to realize that. Perhaps Tandra and Conn were right in wanting to refuse the invitation.

After supper, Tandra and Shawne, Lanoll and Conn schooled with Stringer to welcome him home. They walked up the stones to the pond and jumped into the water feet first, holding hands. To accommodate the humans, the ellls improvised with arms, backfins and legs on the surface. When they dove, Tandra and Shawne took turns following the ellls into the deep end of the pond, where their pressure patterns impinged on Stringer from every direction.

I was happy staying out of the water. We varoks prefer not to commune or play in water unless needed. Contact of any kind can over-stimulate our superficial nerves. We find the ellls' pressure patterns and electro-probing about as soothing as sticking our fingers in a light socket.

In times of stress, I do steel myself and school with Tandra and the ellls of the family as long as I can. Then the ellls talk and listen in language common to our three species (Elllonian with some Varokian and English thrown in) until the upset is understood or resolved. The humans play it down the middle, reminding the rest of us not to overdo either the talk or the schooling.

When the water routine was over, I added my version of welcoming Stringer home—a hearty varokian spiraling hand and an Earthly high-five. The others came up to the deck or rode the water's surface so we could all talk.

"I realize how strongly you feel about Earth, Conn," Shawne said. "You had a terrible time rescuing Mom from her enemies there, but things have changed."

"What do you propose to do on Earth, Shawnoon?" the elll asked, his mood sympathetic, a touch of grief visible in the crease between his sonic melons. Water droplets glistened on his unruly head plumes. "What are you going to say that humans aren't tired of hearing?"

"I need to do whatever I can," Shawne said. "I know what Earth needs because I've read its history. I've followed what's been happening there since the horrible die offs. Most humans have moved north near fertile areas with potable water, and the situation is beginning to stabilize."

"But so much is still in transition, politically," Tandra said.

"It's a good transition, Mom. The old political divisions are recognizing ecological regions—the Coalitions. Those areas are merging both economically and culturally, like Varok's locales."

"And what about resource allocation?" It had once been my job on Varok, managing the quota auctions.

"It will happen. Once the global community knows just what is available. There will be treaties, as there have been with water."

"Sounds a bit too good to be true," Conn said.

"Orticon is already working with them and their satellite data."

The elll twisted his nasal gills. "Your varokian brother is not happy about his findings—that is, the lack of them."

Shawne took in a deep breath. "Earth's global economic system is no longer limited by the belief that it needs to grow. People understand resource depletion."

"I'll believe that when I see it," Conn said.

I gave Conn a look; it didn't help to be too negative.

Lanoll lightened the tone. "Shawne is full of information from her work at the Concentrate, Conn. I'd like to hear more about what she could do there."

"The problem is this," Shawne went on, "best I can tell. Humans need good evidence to confirm what will work best—what to cap and trade, which limits to set by vote, how to devise meaningful regulation. I can help teach steady state principles like Varok's—specific rules for equitable conservation, taxes and subsidies based on minimal use of resources. Earth will never have to suffer through a return to dictatorships. And they'll never have to go through another collapse."

Conn looked at her with new respect in his eyes. "You do care, don't you, Shawnoon." His voice echoed softly across the rocky chamber embracing the pool.

Shawne kicked thoughtfully at the water's surface, and Conn resumed catching drops flying off her toes.

"Conservation is the easy part of the story, Shawne," I said. "Now that the population is at a sustainable number, how are you going to convince humans to limit their appetite for reproduction?"

Conn leapt out of the water, sloshing some onto the deck. "The conflict between religious groups on that issue is still serious," he said.

"I know it is," Shawne agreed. "That's why a neutral alien voice might make an impression."

Shawne's comment reminded me of Ellason's history—ages ago, the conflicts that erupted when the ellls of Ellason began to outgrow their *lebensraum*. We varoks, having just discovered that outlying planet, thought the answers were obvious—tax, no subsidies, educate, guarantee equal rights. We didn't realize how much ellls loved having tads. It took time, lots of it, and too much misery to establish common values limiting reproduction on Ellason.

"It's obvious that top-down enforcement doesn't work," Shawne went on, "but we could help build a consensus among the people. That's what is needed to keep the human population stable. Europe has been a good example of that since early this century."

Tandra said nothing. I saw an ill-defined fear—or perhaps a denial—cloud her mind. It wasn't that she disagreed with Shawne; she didn't want to leave the security of Varok. The thought focused. She was happy with our simple life here. Then a memory gathered visually in her mind. After I retired as Global Varok's Governor of Living Resources, she and I enjoyed managing locale policy, as my mother Orserah had done for ten long Jovian years.

Conn caught my attention with an elliptical shape to his big black eyes that said, "Better read her, Orram. Shawne's re-inventing our future."

Shawne pulled the elll's gaze back to her own with a slow intake of breath through her teeth. "The time is right. Earth's population is low enough at two billion to be sustainable. It's fixable now. We should all go—soon."

"Sounds familiar," Conn said, clearing his gills with a snort. "We thought we had all the answers for Earth two Jovian years ago."

"I know, Conn," she said. "It must have been very disappointing. But things are different on Earth now. The disasters have ended. More people than ever are listening to your broadcasts. Meanwhile, here on Varok we've made a full recovery from Mahntik's growth spurt. We have the practical experience to know what to teach. Help me make the arrangements. Go with me, Conn. I can't do this alone."

Conn swiped his left eye thoughtfully with the elongated tip of his tongue. "The family comes first, Shawne. I won't leave your mom and Orram. I can't leave Lanoll and Stringer."

"Then perhaps we should all go."

I was amazed that the suggestion came from Lanoll. The blue elll glided over to Shawne and offered her befinned hands so the young human could pull her out of the pond. Like Conn, she adds dimensions to parenting Tandra and I cannot.

As always, Lanoll eased the disquiet we had stirred up in each other. "Tandra," she said, "perhaps you and Orram should talk to the great-fish, Oleyall. His perspective could help."

Oleyall and The Great-fish

Orram—by the hearth downstairs, at next light

Tandra sighed and turned toward Shawne after our first meal of the new light-period, her mind heavy with grief after a fitful sleep. "You know I don't like your going to Earth, Shawne, even as an expert."

"Why are you so set against it?" Shawne's frustration showed in her creased brow.

"My reason is partly based on human genetics," Tandra replied. "The human allele D4-7 gave early humans quick reactions for hunting and escaping predators. It still gives humans a dopamine high—like when 21st century hunters bag a new client or win a tennis match. That's why it's so hard for humans to do difficult fixes for long-term problems. We don't get a dopamine high from future benefits. We get it from immediate results."

"That's really cynical, Mom."

"No it's not; it's biology."

"That's it!" Conn exploded, his emotions taking full control. "I say 'No Earth' and I mean no Earth—for anyone! End of story right here and now. Period. We can't fight ancient genes." He rose from his seat at the hearth and stormed up the steps to the pool. A quiet splash punctuated his departure from the conversation.

"I'm afraid Oleyall will agree with Conn and Tandra," I said to Shawne. "They take a more holistic view of things than we varoks and ellls can, but they are also strict pragmatists. I hate to see you get your hopes up."

"Thanks, DadOrram. I appreciate your honesty. But let's wait and see what he says."

Orram—several light-periods later

Like the ellls, great-fish were immigrants to Varok from Ellason. They came ages ago as councilors to bend and flex rigid varokian ways of thinking. They viewed our varokian society, emerging out of disaster and genetic mutilation, with a holistic view that helped us grow into multi-dimensional beings capable of long-term survival. Oleyall would understand the sources of our disagreement about Earth, for I had included him in the Elll-Varok Science team focused on that disturbed planet.

Tandra and Shawne and I took the Ahlkahn to the junction for the Springs of Harinlegh, where we found daramonts to take us to the Great-fish Conference Center on the north side of the Forested Sea.

The ride across the meadows and dunes blanketing the north shore provided the enriching moments we needed. As the friendly mounts made their way across the changeable land, we were treated to a sky of brilliant peach and yellow.

We convinced the daramonts to relax their pace and to graze as they wished. It made for a smoother ride on the big spaniel-faced mounts, and the pure pleasure of moving through that wild and free land allowed us to back off from our angst over going to Earth.

On the sandy shore of that huge lake so beloved of ellls, Tahkallahn, we dismounted and promised the daramonts preserved web stalks if they would wait for us. They agreed. We entered the clear water lapping at well-worn sandstone slabs that disappeared into the waves. There, in a small bay of the Forested Sea, the great-fish often held court in what they called their communication theater.

As we walked into the gentle waves, Oleyall greeted us with a rapid approach that beached his huge cylindrical torso. He waved his left dexterous fin to me, while I adjusted to the cold in the shallows. Tandra helped him work off the sand. To Shawne's delight, he added a playful gesture with his porpoise-sized body, rising vertically for a moment in the meter-deep water beside her. He pointed seaward with the digits of his prehensile tail fin, and we joined him in a brief swim about the small inlet. It was like a token adjustment, his wide smile reflecting a receptive mood.

Back on the communication beach, he seemed to sense and appreciate Shawne's excitement as she tried to speak with great-fish sculpture language. Her ideas spilled from her mind faster than she could approximate them in sand and sea-grass, until the great-fish waved off her sculpturing efforts with a visible, bubbly laugh.

He must have read her mind more clearly than I did, even though our link was at its most sensitive. I had no idea great-fish were so capable.

Talk as if I were human, Oleyall directed Shawne and Tandra, circling around them in the shallow water. *I will understand, and answer you.*

I checked Tandra's reaction. Somehow she was receiving his thought. Shawne was not.

Tandra obeyed what she heard in her mind, and her ideas rapidly took shape as she made the case for denying a trip to Earth. She had been there and done her best to convince humans to stop overusing the Earth's resources. In return, she was pursued as an enemy of Earth's "economic health."

"When the President tricked and used me to hunt down Stabilists opposed to strip-mining the last remaining coal, I quit the game. Jesse Mendleton alerted Conn, who rescued me in time to prevent Shawne being taken from me. As you know, that was nearly one and a half Jovian years in the past."

Oleyall stopped cruising around us and erupted through the water's surface to face Tandra with one unveiled brilliant eye. His head loomed over her like a breaching whale, and the powerful thrust of his fins nearly threw me under.

I couldn't translate exactly what he communicated to her, but it was not polite—something like, "That was long ago, before the human die offs, before the migrations north and the beginning of reason on Earth. Do not let the anger of your past destroy you. Shawne deserves better. She has worked very hard to learn about Earth's dilemma."

"I told Shawne why she could never succeed," Tandra argued back. "Humans are genetically designed to fail, incorrigible, hooked on dopamine surges triggered by control and success. They will never invest themselves enough to secure a long-range future."

Ah, yes, Oleyall agreed. *Allele D4-7 is problematic but it is mutable. Humans are already selecting for corrigible offspring, and they have always been somewhat educable; they will learn from aliens with a clear mission to help find solutions.*

"I wish I could feel such optimism."

Look to your mind-partner. Orram is your answer.

"And Conn? He understood my concern about the human gene. He is strongly opposed to our going to Earth."

For how long? Ellls have neurons made of plastic. Oleyall slipped off under water and let out a great bubble from somewhere on his massive head, the great-fish equivalent of a hearty laugh. Then his long tail-fin wrapped its prehensile digits around our waists, and he led us to the conversation pools closer to shore, where he could emphasize and clarify his thoughts with mud sculptures.

"I believe that we great-fish will support your trip to Earth. Your invitation is very good news. We will urge Global Varok to supply the energy and equipment needed to make the trip."

"No. Please." I looked at Tandra. She could not understand their support.

Shawne looked at me, desperate for an explanation.

"I would do no good there," Tandra said. "My loss of faith runs too deep."

Then you should stay on the moon as a skeptical observer, Oleyall communicated in the mud. *We don't want Shawne to be unrealistic about her venture, do we?*

I saw some hope in his idea. "I will stay with Tandra at Moonbase and continue the broadcasts Conn has been sending. They can be tailored to support what Shawne teaches."

Continue to provide examples from your recovery experience here on Varok. Yes. A good idea. Now let us consult the great-fish council that will present the proposal to Global Varok.

Six elder great-fish answered Oleyall's call and joined us in the shallow water, forming a huge pulsing circle of sleek, dark forms radiating empathy for our concerns. A consensus soon became clear—they would support our plan and encourage Global Varok to support it.

I helped Shawne understand what had been communicated. Her enthusiasm exploded with an aerial somersault over one of the smaller great-fish.

There is more. Oleyall and his fellows worked hard with their symbols, their intuition, and their knowledge of elllonian Sonics to make very clear their requirements for the trip. Water sloshed over the communication steps as they consulted among themselves with an occasional slash of their lateral fins or a slap of their long tails.

For the rest of the light-period, we exchanged ideas. We agreed to a plan, after I promised Tandra that I would not leave her alone during the trip, not for a moment. She and I would monitor the situation from the Elll-Varok Science Observation Base on Earth's moon. Shawne and a team of experts on Earth data and economics would engage various peoples and teach steady state practices to all sentient beings who would listen.

"We will make it clear that we are observers with no stake in Earth's future," I confirmed.

Oleyall drifted close and draped a sympathetic fin on my shoulder. *Earth must be very different now, in healing.*

"We can only hope," Tandra replied in Varokian. "The most difficult challenge is to convince religious communities that it is unethical to bring unwanted children into an overused world."

"Or to put the rights of an insentient embryo over those of a conscious being," I added.

Oreyall nodded, baring an alarming set of sharp teeth. *A difficult issue indeed, one that has stirred human emotions to extremes.*

Oleyall turned to Shawne. I translated his message: "Now it is your turn to understand more clearly what your heart desires. Your goal in coming to Earth must be made clear to all. It is to establish a world-wide steady state economy. Policy details will then be obvious. Essential to this goal, we agree that stabilizing the human population is necessary. Humans will have a strong tendency to grow, both themselves and their economies."

Tandra reached for my hand, and I wrapped her in what assurance I could muster. Her mind was churning with a mixture of terror and hope, worry for Shawne's personal challenges and pride in the respect the great-fish gave her.

Be mindful, Oleyall continued, *do not overstay your welcome. One Earth-year should be sufficient. Finally, Conn must be an active presence on Earth.*

"And if Conn refuses to go?" Shawne exclaimed in Varokian.

The meaning of her concern rolled over the great-fish like a mental tsunami, and the prodigious mentors erupted in a visible and audible squabble over what the elll's role should be. They knew of his careless escapades—encountering a bear when first visiting Earth, risking his own exposure at a party with Tandra, "borrowing" an EV spacecraft to rescue her and baby Shawne from authoritative power brokers on Earth.

Tandra and I waited, swimming into deeper water, matching strokes, hoping the exercise would ease our anxiety.

Shawne

Shawne remained in the shallow waters, waiting. She sat down on a step far enough into the waves so the great-fish wouldn't have to beach themselves. At last Oleyall and six other great-fish reappeared, their dorsal fins cutting the waves all around her.

She remembered Orram's voice saying, "Watch great-fish eyes, listen with your intuition, feel what their sand sculptures tell you."

The great-fish leaned against the sandstone shelf where she sat. A cascade of water filled her lap, and she thought she heard a laugh.

Oleyall scooped sand into a square shape.

Shawne tried to decode the sculpture, but it meant nothing to her, so she just started talking and pushing the sandy mud into abstract forms. "I can be a voice for all people on Earth, no matter their beliefs," she said, "because I am alien to Earth. I am outside the issues that divide people. They will listen to me. I will build a consensus, promote our models for how to teach, and, when the steady state schools are established, add real input."

She felt an invisible nod of agreement from Oleyall. *The de-growth is done. What will you do if they will not listen? If they decide to grow again?*

Shawne couldn't identify the source of the comment at first. Oleyall wasn't speaking Varokian or dabbling in the muddy sand. The great-fish question rose in her mind like a bubble rising out of deep water and bursting.

"I will prove that nothing real can grow forever," she said. "I will show that the Earth can be beautiful again, that life can be lived with joy—not hunger—if it is not filled again with too many people."

Shawne reached out to grasp the prehensile tip of Oleyall's left ventral fin for reassurance, but the great-fish reaction was not what she expected. Oleyall swam away and circled back.

Do you understand what a steady state economy means?

"Just as on Varok—wastes, population, production and consumption must be minimized. All resources must be counted and quotas set according to democratically chosen standards of living. Resources that are replaceable must be replenished at the same rate as they are used. Those with finite non-replaceable quantities must see minimal use and recycling."

The great-fish modeled the figure of Conn in the wet, mud-like sand. *He should go with you. He has contacts on Earth.*

"I would like Conn to go, but he refuses. He may not be able to stand the trip, or Earth, for that matter. He is not young."

You are right, for the wrong reason. Earth's oceans are not clean.

"Perhaps just three of us should go to Earth?" she asked. "I've taken the professional exams in Earth studies, and Orticon and Stringer—"

That is not enough.

Like a warm flame filling a deep cavern with light, Shawne thought she got it. "Of course! Orram. Humans will listen to a mature alien voice, not just a re-planted human like me."

That may be true.

All the great-fish circled around the young human, pushed her into deeper water, and sent pulses of water her way with their long barrel-shaped bodies. *Think,* came their message. *You, too, have much to contribute.*

Trust, said the memory of Orram's advice. *Trust your intuition.*

Now. Oleyall seemed to speak in unmistakable Varokian. *What is known about complexity that will make your trip worthwhile, even if all your planned efforts fail?*

"Complexity?" Shawne couldn't imagine it. Then she remembered something Tandra had said. "We must balance regulation with consensus, as they do with vehicle traffic laws on Earth. Too many rules anger people. Too few trigger chaos. A good balance allows societies to self-organize safely."

Oleyall did a negative shrug with his ventral fins. *That is quite true, but there is more to my question than obvious compromise. Complexity.*

Shawne had not paid much attention to her family's philosophy. Based on a knowledge of complex systems, it seemed too academic to be relevant.

What are the indicators of complex systems, the features that make them unpredictable? Oleyall asked.

Shawne reviewed her studies in complex systems. *Chaos? Emergence? Criticality? No. Amplification. Yes. Perhaps that's what he wants.* "It is said that nothing we do is inconsequential. I think that our best chance of making a significant difference on Earth is to scatter aliens all over the planet. Some one of us, somewhere, might plant a seed that could grow and change the world. We may never know what will take root, but at least we will have tested all the soils."

"Bravo, Shawne. You will do well on Earth." The great-fish Oleyall turned slowly and wrapped his ventral fins around her, imitating a human hug. It brought tears to her eyes.

Orram

At last Oleyall called us back to the conference shoal. Before he disappeared into deeper water, he added an absolute. "The trip is endorsed. You must now present the proposal to Global Varok for approval, scheduling and financing. The plan must include the elll, Conn."

"Conn hates wearing isolation suits," Tandra said. "We have continually monitored the human germ exchange with ellls and varoks, but the mutations continue. Contact could be dangerous to any number of species on Earth, and to our family."

"Nevertheless . . ." The great-fish paused to be sure we noted his emphasis. "Conn must go with Shawne."

"Why?" Tandra asked the question more than once. I asked it in sand and mud, in English, Varokian and Elllonian. In answer, Oleyall called to his fellow great-fish, and they circled us with a reassuring massage of lapping waves. Then they disappeared into the deeps.

LIGHT HOPPERS AND THE POWER OF STORY

Shawne—a short time later

Shawne tried to contain the joy she felt. She saw that her mother looked as if she had aged two Jovian years. Tandra was staring out over the water, not seeing the dancing reflections from the blue and peach colored sky.

"We'd better go, Tandra," Orram said. "The daramonts are waiting."

Tandra took Shawne's hand. "You're sure you won't come home with us?"

"Conn said he would meet me here at the conference shoals. We'll find daramonts after we swim. We'll be home before next light."

"Will Conn listen to Oleyall?" Orram asked. "I hope so. There he is now, out about thirty *pallons*, showing off."

"We'll leave then," Tandra said. "See you both at home, Shawne."

The elll's slim arches across the surface cut the water with a silver wake, and Shawne swam out to intercept him. She soon learned he was in a terrible mood.

"We'll swim to the ruins," he said. "You can talk to the light-hoppers while I find Stringer in the deeps. He'll want to come home when he hears your wonderful news."

"What news?"

"You tell me. I met Oleyall on my way here. He said you have the full story."

She knew better than to press the topic now, so she followed him in silence along the shore and soon spotted the ruins frequented by light-hoppers.

"Wait there," the elll said, and he disappeared into the dark waves of the Forested Sea.

Shawne knew the mood wouldn't last.

On the shore, dense *laoon* grass and silver bushes covered suggestions of ancient walls the color of burnished copper. Shawne searched the narrow beach for fossil stones, then lay down and stretched out to watch Jupiter's dim portrait fade in and out behind restless white clouds.

The ruins scattered around the inland seas of Varok had left a mosaic of lime concrete foundations, old brick, and synthetic wall-boards. Shawne liked to imagine how the ancient cities must have looked, standing tall by the sea, their landing platforms shading apartments for the varoks' winged ancestors. She regretted that there were so few details left. The ruins here looked as if they had been picked clean by ahlork and overgrown with shore weeds long ago.

As she settled in for a rest, light-hoppers surrounded Shawne and set up a sideshow, the beautiful human being the main attraction. Drifting toward sleep, she heard them singing about her place in their mythology. This brown two-legs with bright, colorless hair was from the wondrous Oran family, who rescued starving humans from the ferocious, belching volcanoes of the disemboweled Earth and fed them with the healing tulips grown in their magic algae pool.

The light-hoppers looked like the tiny insects Shawne had seen in her Earth Animals book, but they had no exoskeleton and no antennae. Up close, they looked more like miniature, transparent teddy bears with twelve spider legs. Two triangles atop their heads constantly flashed with bioluminescent messages. As direct descendants of the protozooids that inhabited daramont rumens, the light-hoppers were not built with specialized cells. Each was one big, tough cell, populated with mini-organelles. They were interesting to Shawne, but annoying in that they couldn't sort out well-tested information from the exaggerated stories they loved.

Shawne's dreams shifted from speaking before a massive crowd of humans somewhere on Earth to walking on the shores of Lake Superior, attacked by the infamous mosquitoes Tandra and Jesse complained about. They were tickling her legs and arms as they landed and flew and landed again. The tickling grew intense, and she sat up, fully awake, scattering light-hoppers in all directions.

A hundred bright eye-spots gathered and stared at Shawne from the remains of the ruined rock wall that had given her shelter. "Story," the eyes demanded. "Story about Earth. Story."

"No story unless you post a watch for Conn, my elll-father," she said, knowing they understood Varokian very well. "Watch from up there, on the bricks, where you can see him coming out of the surf."

A chorus of giggles greeted the demand—irritating but too cute to ignore. "I'm serious," Shawne said, trying to sound serious. "I want to swim out and meet him so we can go quickly to our home."

More giggles.

"Promise, or you don't get a story."

"All right, human-of-Orram's family." One spoke in Varokian, with a tiny voice barely distinguishable from the hissing of waves and sand. "Now story. Story about Earth."

She thought for a moment, and decided to tell a utopian tale.

"My name is Shawne, and I don't remember much about being on Earth, because I left there when I was barely three Earth-years old."

"Story. You promise story, we promise watching for Conn."

"All right then. I'll tell you about my planet, Earth. The bright blue star, more ocean than land, more human asphalt than rain forest, more deaths from starvation and disease than births from planning.

"A human girl raised on Varok returned to her home planet, Earth, and saw her intelligent species going over the cliff like *ilara* egg-layers gone mad. Surviving humans listened to her stories of Varok's tragic history. As a result, they understood why the ruins on their coasts had been swamped. They saw the children made stupid by polluted water. They decided Earth could do better, so they learned to use less water and energy, and to keep their numbers in check. Because the girl raised on Varok returned to Earth, its green trees recovered and its skies shone blue and its water ran clean again, and people were at peace."

"Good story, Shawne," they said in their squeaky Varokian, but as they dispersed, she heard them complain about the lack of magic and illusion in the story.

"The whole story is an illusion," Shawne said. "Every bit—even the part about returning to Earth, if Conn has his way."

"But I've been denied my better judgment," Conn said, surprising Shawne from behind the crumbling wall. The light-hoppers broke into a chorus of faint whistles, as two daramonts appeared with Conn.

"Markup?"

The mount's wide shoulders lifted in a neutral shrug.

"I thought you'd like a good race on our way home, Shawne," Conn said. "I could sure use one, after taking a verbal beating from the great-fish, then from you."

He sounded serious, and his voice shook. "What do you mean?"

Shawne reached out to him. "What have I said? I understand your not wanting to go to Earth."

His eyes were glazed and clouded, as if something deep inside was broken. "I'm sure you do, and now I understand how strongly you feel. Give me a moment. I love you for caring so much."

Conn took her hand, and his eyes slowly cleared. "I'm okay now, Storyteller. Let's go home and find your mother."

"No sign of Stringer?"

"I left a message with the local school," Conn replied.

Shawne vaulted onto the neck of her favorite daramont as he ducked to scoop her up. When Markup reared high on his kangaroo-like haunches, she offered Conn and Pork Belly her challenge with an upraised arm.

Conn approached unsteadily on his webbed feet, rolled onto his daramont's lowered shoulder, and rode up to Shawne. The two daramonts backed into a racing start position, shifting until the toes of their soft fan-shaped hooves were exactly in line.

As they settled back for the starting leap, Shawne and Conn locked their feet against the beasts' shoulder blades.

"*Fan, Aloon. Aeo-o!*" Shawne shouted in Elllonian, and they were off, leaping from outcropping to outcropping as they climbed into the Vahinorral.

They crossed the mountains in silence, allowing their mounts to set the pace. When they came out of the rock-studded foothills beyond the Forested Sea, they avoided the common roads and crossed open dara-mont pastures, gaining speed, until the mounts were running eyeball to eyeball toward the web fields.

Against all the rules Orram's mother Orserah had dictated, they urged the daramonts into the maze of bushes, letting them choose their paths, knowing they would avoid the berries in their effort to hurdle toward the thick, arching mineral tree hovering protectively over the Oran family home.

"You lose, Conn." When Shawne reached the porch, she waved at Tandra, who met them with a bucket of water for the daramonts. Pork Belly nodded and drank. Shawne slid off Markup. "Mom, Conn knocked off a whole branch of web berries."

"Hey, I got here first."

"Penalty, two *hoat* candies per berry," Shawne said with a laugh.

"Since when?"

"Since an entire Jovian year ago. We made up that rule when I was nine Earth-years old."

"Daramont tails! You keep changing the rules—in too many ways."

Tandra entered the lodge, but Shawne and Conn hesitated, then sat on the porch under the mineral tree. Something was different between them, as if the pond would not help. Neither could find words they needed to say.

Nidok's Complaint

Conn

At the end of the web field under the care of the Oran Locale, the daramonts grazed. Vivid patches of white-lime broiler strands and red park lilies stretched away to the Vahinorral, where the mountains' rocky peaks flowed with a rainbow of auroral lights.

Conn broke the silence. "Nidok's flock will be here soon, Shawne. Let's go pick berries and wait for him."

The elll and the young human walked aimlessly into the fields, hoping that familiar activity would heal the wound between them.

"How old is Nidok, Conn?"

"Hard to say. Ahlork live twice as long as varoks. That's why they're twice as ornery. Nidok's nestlings are about your equivalent age—ripe, but not ready to pick."

"Conn!"

"I speak truth, human. Listen well to wise old frog."

"I've kissed you a million times, and you never turn into anything interesting."

"They'll find me plenty interesting on Earth."

"That's what I'm afraid of." With loving fingers, Shawne combed the plumes back over his sonic melons. "Maybe you shouldn't go all the way to Earth. The great-fish said it would be dangerous for you."

"They also say you're not going to Earth without me. End of story. I've been had."

"Stubborn old elll."

"I take my parenting seriously."

"We'll be fine," Shawne said. "Stringer and Orticon and I make a good team."

"Stringer is younger than you, and Orticon is a varok—they're both sorry excuses for bodyguards. Neither one of them has an aggressive gene in his body. I'll be your bodyguard. They don't know diddily about Earth."

"Orticon does. He has honors in Earth studies, once did a paper on violence in human culture. He'll have good insights into safety precautions we might need there. He's also done good work repairing the balance on Varok."

"Orticon and Stringer have not been to Earth. I have."

"I'm glad we're not walking in blind," she said. "Still, I wish Orram and Mom would go with us and not stay on the moon."

"Tandra's carrying many bad memories, Shawne. Don't ask her to go back to Earth. She was accused of treason, for preaching economic ideas similar to what you want to teach. Before the die offs, economic growth was like apple pie and motherhood."

"I still worry, Conn. Moonbase is so far," Shawne said. "What happens if we lose the shuttle and can't get back to the moon?"

Conn felt the intensity of her fear. It seemed to be surfacing with the realization of what she had taken on.

"We'll call for another shuttle when we need it. We won't lose communication, and we'll have a rescue pick-up arranged if we do, wherever we go."

Shawne picked two berries from an overhanging web branch and gave one to Conn. Together they savored the mild sourness.

"Are you sure you're ready for this, Shawnoon? There are vested interests on Earth that will reject everything we stand for—religious groups that believe all others are evil, once-rich and powerful persons fighting to regain all they once controlled, governments pretending they are still viable—"

Conn's eyes took on that deep crystal look that meant he was serious. "There will be many people you won't be able to deal with. You know that, right?"

Shawne nodded, remembering her mother's stories of Earth.

Conn continued. "What's more important is something very

different. We need to be prepared for how much time establishing a consensus will take. Once you leave Varok, you might never return, if you want to see real progress."

"I don't expect to return to Varok, Conn."

Conn's elllonian eyes grew large with emotion, and he gave Shawne a prolonged hug, then they stretched out in the shade of the web bush.

"Don't tell Mom yet, but I see this as my life's work."

"Ouch." Words were an impossible barrier. They joined hands and let their minds wander. Conn drifted asleep inventing the delusion that he would protect his daughter from anything Earth could throw at her.

He was awakened by Shawne's cry: "Ahlork alert. All ellls take cover. Nidok coming in at two o'clock."

Shawne untangled herself from Conn's sleepy embrace and ran toward the incoming ahlork, waving her arms frantically, as if to chase him away. Nidok took her seriously for a moment, banked sharply, and beat his wings to gain altitude.

It was a marvelous sight—the huge insectoid maneuvering just over their heads like a purposeful box kite with wings. Then Nidok gargled out his strange laugh, and Conn knew Shawne was in for a good contest.

Nidok unsheathed his talons, flexed his chitinous wing plates to full cock, and dove straight at Shawne as she ran further into the web bushes for cover.

"You muss Shawne's hair, and I'll make ahlork stew for lunch," Conn shouted. He ran for the bushes where the girl and the ahlork had disappeared. Nidok's screech and a piercing human scream split the auroral horizon—then all was silent.

Conn ran into the bushes toward the scream, but he couldn't find Shawne. Puzzled, then genuinely alarmed, he rechecked his position. Girl and ahlork were nowhere to be found in the rows of dense bushes. Had they had an accident?

Ahlork played rough. Nidok could have miscalculated. The aerial creature's exoskeleton was rock hard and well armed, and he was heavy, nearly half Shawne's height and weight, with an eight-foot wingspan.

Conn called their names. Starting at the edge of the field, he looked down each row of bushes. No answer. Then, all at once, ahlork wings trapped the ell, and Shawne leapt from the branch of a large bush to ride his shoulders.

"Family hug. Family hug," she sang.

"You need better eyes, friend elll," Nidok chortled. "Can't see hot ahlork, eh?"

"You don't have any decent heat waves to put out in the infrared," Conn lectured.

"Ha! You've got dimming lenses on. No wonder I blend into cool web bushes."

"Taken advantage by my best friend and my only daughter. Go eat Harrahn eggs, you foul vulture."

"You hear, Shawne? He can't see. Now has no insults. Last time I was coo-coo clock from Earth."

"Last time was far back in the distant past." Conn put one arm across Nidok's wings. "Where the hell you been, Nidok?"

"Elll's brain be empty, not remembering my rescuing ellls. Now be Celebration of Web Fruiting again, like then. No thank-you. Years we did work—"

Shawne laughed. Nidok was shameless in looking for gratitude.

"Have a good time at the festival, did you, Nidok?" Conn asked.

"The worst, elll. Clear-headed too much. Now I come for real party. This nestling, Shawne here, needs to know what drunk is. Nidok and Conn do it best. We teach this new adult. They drink alcohol at Earth. Bad as Mahntik's berry juice."

"I know that, Nidok," Shawne said. "Come on. Sit up here on my shoulders. We'll ride home in style atop Conn."

"You will not." Conn ducked out from under Shawne. She vaulted over his head to the ground as Nidok folded his wings and backed away.

"Race you, Nidok." Shawne sprinted toward the lodge.

"You go on. We come soon. Nidok needs elll-talk."

Shawne returned to the lodge, and Conn walked out of the web field to the pastures with Nidok. While the ahlork grazed on the tender parts of his favorite ground forage, Conn's mind kept hearing parts of Shawne's story to the light-hoppers.

"There," Nidok said, waddling over to Conn like a noisy mechanical toy. "That be enough to fuel this tank."

He set his torso on the ground, tucked his huge talons into the earth, and folded his chitin-plated wings into a neat package over his back. His squared-off face looked sober, and his black pinhead eyes moved restlessly over Conn's inquisitive gaze. "Sit, Conn. We talk."

"Here?" Conn was surprised. Nidok had nothing to hide from the family. Tandra and Orram had taken the scar of ahlork soon after Conn had. Their lives were bound to him, as closely as ahlork bond to anything.

"I am too angry. I dump my shame on you. Then we party by pool— get Shawne drunk on web berry wine, so she knows how."

"Angry? You mean, as in real anger, no insults?"

"Big insult. Too big. Great-fish don't name Nidok to your team."

"What team? We don't have any ahlork games scheduled."

"Your team goes to Earth, Fish Brain. Why not Nidok get invite?"

"Because great-fish know you'd be shot down as soon as you took to Earth's air. Big game aliens have no life expectancy on Earth. Don't get your scales ruffled. I'm still hoping Global Varok won't fund the trip."

"You need ahlork help. If you go, Nidok goes."

"No way, Game Bird. I don't approve of immoderate martyrdom."

"You don't go without Nidok. Old ellls be easier game than ahlork. Together we foul all nests needing it, bag the hunters, keep Shawne safe."

"You're serious."

"You don't go without me."

"We'll talk about it. There's no shame involved. Surely, you see why the great-fish thought it too risky for you. They wouldn't even consider it."

"You talk bull," the ahlork said with a gargle, "how do you say Earth slang?"

"*Bull* will do."

They laughed as they started for the lodge, but the party didn't begin until they climbed the hearthstones with Shawne and threw her into the pool.

Orram—Lake Seclusion, the next light-period

We had no luck convincing Nidok he should not go to Earth, so Tandra and I took him on a short holiday to Lake Seclusion to talk it over.

Tandra and I rode daramonts to the lake, while the ahlork circled above us.

"Nidok, come down here and . . . walk with us," I called.

"Orram means it's time you stood on my head," Tandra added.

As always, the time-tested joke between the human and the ahlork worked. With a clattering of wing plates, Nidok hovered over Tandra's wide-brim hat.

"I'll smash your crown, Cow Girl. Take off hat."

She did. He settled into her shining dark hair and set about smoothing the longer strands with the tips of his unsheathed talons.

His first head-sitting had not been so affectionate eighteen Earth-years earlier. It had been meant as an insult and a laughable threat, a test for the human newly arrived on Varok. Tandra had passed with high marks by giggling, then taunting—a bit too seriously—so the signal was established. Over the years, 'sitting on heads' meant talking honestly to deal with real issues. Insults and banter were off-limits until consensus was reached.

At times like this, I realized how much I loved her human qualities. Tandra truly enjoyed Nidok's rude attention. If I hadn't been linked to her mind, I would have gone irrational with laughter when she humored him.

When we reached the verdant park on the shore of Lake Seclusion, the ahlork hopped to the ground and opened his wings to full span. He was almost beautiful then, silhouetted against the broad expanse of rich green water. Only the crooked scar on his greater lip marred the square symmetry of his beaded face. I had to admit he was an impressive beast. The impenetrable blackness of his tiny eyes added to the frightening expanse of his armed wings and prehensile wing tips.

We sat within his wingspan, and we did not waste words. "We know you want to go to Earth with Conn," I said. "Perhaps you should, at least for Conn's sake, but it would be dangerous for you."

"You would be valuable as an extra pair of eyes for Conn," Tandra said. "You could be his bodyguard."

"Ahlork not easy to cut or smash, as ellls," he agreed.

"Yes. If Conn lives on land with Shawne, and he wishes to stay in contact with whales and dolphins, you could be his aerial messenger."

"I do that." He focused on his talons as he picked sand from small rocks. I had never seen him so self-conscious.

My patches couldn't read his ahlork thoughts, but I could feel his mood battling with the fear his imagination kept stirring up. I decided his fear could be his best defense.

After a pleasant meal by the lake we walked a short ways toward the Niorral, the foothills beneath Mount Ni. There we hoped to find daramonts to take us home, across the low passes into the wide valley of the Oran Locale. Orserah's lodge lay across the Ahlkahn's tracks, beneath the range called Vahinorral that cradled the Forested Sea on the south side.

Nidok stayed with us, soaring high to look for daramonts, or riding our heads, or trundling along between us. He chattered on and on, inventing plans for dealing with humans.

"Humans shoot at me; bullets bounce off. They throw knives; ahlork tiles break them. I spread wings, scare them off, bite their fingers."

"Listen to me for a moment, Nidok," I said. "Some humans will hate us for being different. Some will be afraid of you. Some will hunt the alien ahlork Nidok and put his head on a wooden frame, to hang as a trophy over a stone fireplace."

"Land-locked bipeds hunt ahlork?" Nidok made a laughing sound, something like the Ahlkahn derailed underwater.

"It might help if you understood how vulnerable you would be on Earth," I said.

"Humans can't hit flying ahlork target, not without electronics."

"They do it all the time, Nidok, with drones and without." I had to stretch my memory for examples. "In a few places humans still hunt birds with shotguns. They practice with flying clay disks. Your big face makes an easy target."

"They be not killing me, would they?"

"Why not?" I said. "You don't look even remotely humanoid, as Conn does. Alien hunters wouldn't hesitate. *Humanoid* means conscious communicator, thinker, and hands off to most people on Earth. *Non-humanoid* means fair game."

"Your stuffed hide would bring big money to people charging entrance fees to show it," Tandra added.

"Ahlork fly in circles, dodge bullets."

"I'll show you how wrong you are, my friend," I said. "We'll get out my grandfather's firearms. He was a good hunter, when he had to be." I didn't like being stern with Nidok, but I really feared for his life. "When we get home, we'll try some shooting."

"Yes. I learn about guns. Then Conn knows I am safe. I fly now for daramonts, over there."

Two handsome mounts followed Nidok back to us, and we were home in time to enjoy Shawne's late-day meal of eggs and *llaoon* grass.

Before I had my grandfather's "protein gatherers" cleaned and ready, the shooting demonstration for Nidok blossomed into a family expedition to the foothills of the Vahinorral.

Lanoll and Stringer packed two eager daramonts. I had found just enough workable ammunition for everyone to try two shots. Tandra improvised targets out of two old buckets.

Like a striped lizard zapping flies from the air, Stringer picked off the two ahlork-sized targets at 4 *pallons* (about 100 meters).

Nidok was so impressed he became hard up for insults. He was shocked when Conn repeated the performance, and Lanoll and I tipped over the targets by bracing our arms on a tree stump while aiming at the top rim. Tandra and Shawne hit the targets standing up.

"Humans practiced when on Earth," Nidok croaked. "Ellls be lucky."

"Yes, Sweet Target," Tandra said. "There will be toasted ahlork chitin for appetizers tonight."

Giving fair warning, he jumped on her head. "I'll be at cliffs of L'orkah—packing," he whispered in her ear, then he launched himself into the air.

"Ouch." Tandra sat down a bit hard when he pushed off. "Packing what?" she called to him.

"Leaving already, Nidok?" Conn used his name only when he had a serious concern.

Nidok circled low overhead, checking to see if Tandra was all right. "I need to tend nest, *Arl* Eye," he answered Conn in Elllonian, and then he rose high in the air.

"Wait, mighty bird," Conn called to him. "I'll be right beneath you. We need to talk. Orram, I don't think he understands."

Nidok swooped low, shouting as best his creaky voice could, "Enjoy Earth trip."

Conn hopped on a daramont grazing. He signaled to the nearby gang of mounts that Lanoll and Stringer might like a ride home, and took off after the ahlork.

Nidok's gargling laugh echoed off the hills as he disappeared into the western lights.

In the shadow of the mountains, surrounded by intricate growth patterns of looping snarl, we watched a grand display of auroral greens and yellows cross the sky. As we wandered home, we tried to agree on what to do if Nidok should make good on his promise and show up at the Interplanetary Launch Pad, ready to go.

Consensus

Conn—on the way home, minutes later

Conn was within sight of the web fields of the Oran Locale when he stopped and tried an ahlork call. Nidok turned and circled overhead, until the elll's patience wore thin. He hooted again, imitating the sound ahlork nestlings make when they are seriously hungry. It worked. Nidok landed on a tall bush, where they could talk eye to eye. Conn's race-loving daramont friend didn't like it much, until he found some ripe berries to nibble.

Conn didn't waste time. "You will not sneak on board, Nidok my dear. Global Varok does not allow ahlork on spaceships."

"Orram knows ahlork make good sky messengers."

"Nonsense. He meant you'd make a good moving target. Earth is a dangerous planet. I don't want you there."

"I know about dodging dangers. I be safe there."

"No way, Crockery Bug."

"Then conversation done, right?"

"Right."

Nidok pushed off, accidentally knocking some berries away from the daramont's mouth. Conn rode on to the family lodge, wondering what had just been decided.

Orram

Before Jupiter's moon Callisto appeared in the sky again, Shawne received a live video message on the house landcomm. "There's a call coming in." She tapped "receive" and listened to a message from Global Varok.

"This is your passport to Earth, Shawne. You have the full support of the EV Council as their ambassador. Global Varok absorbs the costs of the trip. Amplification of the nuclear electric propulsion engine by fusion pulse is approved, so the trip will take the minimal 76.6 Earth days. You and your team must train carefully to avoid physical damage, Shawne, and complete qualification for space flight at the Concentrate. The maintenance crew on the Observation Base on Earth's Moon is ready to receive you and provide housing for Orram and Tandra. Go, learn, and do what you can—while Conn can still go with you. Global Varok has recommended that your team also include Lanoll and your brothers, Stringer and Orticon—experts on Earth satellite data. Also the human Jesse Mendleton and the varok Junah. Their earlier experience with us and at EV's Earth Moonbase will be of value."

"One more thing." Oleyall had added a video message. The great-fish swept around and reached toward the camera with a prehensile fin tip. Orram translated for him as the great-fish modeled his words in the sand.

As you know, Ellason is approaching perihelion. It will make its nearest approach to Earth in a few months. Already, some astronomers on Earth have noticed a new "comet without tail" approaching Neptune. Some have already guessed its origin as an Earth-like planet in a huge eccentric orbit. You and your team will be helpful in easing fears that it might harm Earth.

Shawne moved into the gentle wrappings of Conn's softly plumed green arms. "How can I thank you for going with me?" she said. "When I first talked about the idea, you were certain I should not go."

She looked into the green lights of the huge black eyes, and he shrugged. "I've had to reboot," he admitted. "However, bottom line, we don't know what in *ahr ahnye* is going on down there on Earth, not really. So what are we doing? Just putting our lives on the line for a species that can't distinguish a fart from a wake-up call."

"Oh Conn." Conflicted, Shawne looked back to the video.

Oleyall closed with a symbol of affection. "Take all precautions, Shawne. This trip is not without its dangers."

"I think our lives have just turned a corner," I said to Shawne. "If Conn agrees to go, we're on our way."

"Apparently, I have no choice," the elll said.

Tandra's face turned ashen gray. Before I could think what to say, Shawne erupted with joy. My patches buzzed with her excitement.

She flew up the stones to tell Lanoll. Noisy splashing, then she called, "Where's Stringer? I've got to call Orticon and Jesse. Do you have Junah's contact, Dad?"

She spent the rest of that light-period at my desk.

Tandra and I retreated to the back of the house. "They see Conn as some kind of trigger," Tandra gasped. "The great-fish know he won't follow strict protocol, that he's too comfortable on Earth with all his previous visits. He'll do something to create the avalanche Earth needs in order to change."

Her words failed her, and our mind-link took over. *The great-fish know human beings need a martyr to rally around, and he's the most likely candidate.*

Orram

At first dark Shawne finally settled down to report to Tandra and me, her Moonbase overseers. "Good timing," she said. "We're in luck. Our team has found a meeting time, next light-period after this. Here, if that's okay, Orram. Mom?"

"Yes, I'll do what I can," Tandra said.

"They agreed to have ideas ready to share so we can firm up our plans. Junah was finishing a vacation at Lake Seclusion. Jesse and Orticon were in Ahl Vior, so they'll catch the same train."

The varokian woman, the human, and my son arrived at the lodge at the beginning of next light and gathered around the hearth to greet our family and eat a fragrant meal Shawne prepared.

"You have a very interesting daughter, Orram," Junah said, "and I have had the pleasure of riding the Ahlkahn from Ahl Vior with your son Orticon and this fascinating human confidant of yours."

"My pleasure, Ma'am," Jesse Mendleton said.

I was delighted to see how comfortable Junah was, despite our history.

She smiled. "This adventure to Earth is just what I need to cap off my career. I would like to hear what you have learned in your studies, Shawne. What should we know about Earth in its year 2068 C.E.?"

Shawne sat forward on the hearth stones and activated her personal recorder. "Earth has had nearly a decade to recover from the massive die offs. However, the overall picture is as complex as the human species. I promised Oleyall that we would focus on one goal—and I think we had better discuss that goal to be sure we are all in agreement.

"Our charter is to teach steady state economics and ethics: an economy scaled low enough to be sustainable for all time. We're to explore reasons and practical ways for humans to stabilize their population and limit the use of resources democratically, in order to sustain an equitable, global standard of living, as we do here.

"Strategies to emphasize include tax incentives, sharing infrastructure and work hours, education, minimum wages and income limits, trade rules to protect the environment, basic rights to food, water and shelter for all—"

Conn interrupted. "Do we have to memorize that entire laundry list?"

"Yes, absolutely," Shawne said. "Do we all agree this encompasses the focus of our courses and broadcasts? Did I leave anything out?"

"Sounds like a good start," Junah said.

Orticon looked at me, and I encouraged him in mind to air his concerns. "The list is too ambitious, Shawne. Humans aren't ready for such direct implementation of steady state ideals."

"No doubt the list will grow and evolve," I added. I sensed that the others agreed.

Shawne turned to our source on current human affairs. "Jesse? How about our reception on Earth?"

"Scare headlines have stirred up a lot of people. There are die-hard para-military groups watching with antique radar equipment for invasion by 'the alien menace broadcasting from the moon.' The good news is that we have also been getting electronic mail from some equally creative supporters."

"Sounds like business as usual," said Conn. "Next it will be splinter groups splintering into more splinter groups."

"Human tribal instincts make it impossible to enact broad cooperation on economic questions," Orticon said.

A quick scan confirmed my impression. My son still wrestled with strong discomfort at human predilections. He picked up my diffuse awareness and nodded. The others turned to us, awaiting explanation.

"I have concerns," Orticon said, "that make me skeptical about our mission. It's not just the dopamine high linked to immediate gratification that Tandra has identified. It's conflicting world views. And worse—how should I say this? Humans are addicted to violence. They enjoy it, use it as entertainment. It worries me, as does the lack of concern for other life and the health of their planet. Can we make any difference with such a blindly destructive species?"

"Their entertainment might not be a good indicator." I tried to defuse his angst. "Human psychologists suggest that fiction, like ancient fairy tales and modern dystopias, gives the human brain a place to bottle up its tendencies toward violence or fear of the unknown."

Orticon wasn't convinced. "And that is supposed to counter the effects of imprinting and imitation? Or ignorance and fear of science?"

"Education is on our to-do list," Conn said. "But I share your lack of optimism. We're taking on too much. The human population is too apt to honor prejudice above hard facts."

"Indeed, scientific illiteracy has been a problem for some time," Tandra agreed, "but I worry more about your anger, Orticon, as I do mine. We must work away from it, focus on the good people on Earth who are trying to help."

"Of course, you're right, Tandra. The great-fish must have their reasons for supporting this trip. However, defining my frustration—"

"Helps all of us, Orticon," I said.

"Still, I don't think I can relate effectively with anyone on Earth."

"I understand," said Shawne. "We will need to approach people with empathy."

There was no light in Conn's eyes as he stared into Shawne's. "And we need to be just a bit realistic about what we're dealing with."

"Indeed. And above all, we can't be seen as favoring one group over another," I said. "We have to start from where different groups of humans are, emotionally and ethically, as well as socially and culturally."

Orticon's temper started to flare. "That's not realistic, father."

"Humans can be very creative, letting their imagination drive their thinking," Lanoll said, trying to keep Orticon rational.

"That's what we'll have to count on in Shawne's School for Economic Longevity," I said, trying to add some optimism. "We have a good start with Shawne's proposed courses of study, but as we get feedback from the students, our ideas may change."

"We'll need to stay close in touch with what's happening in the global economy," Jesse said. "Already, many humans have been talking about re-growth, using up scarce resources in the name of big profits for the short term."

"They need to be stopped." I could see Orticon's frustration spiking through his calm veneer, which was thinning dangerously.

"And how do we do that?" Conn asked. "Varok's millennia of experience have done nothing to discourage the human belief that growth is essential."

"This is not just a question of economic theory," Orticon said. "Economic restraint runs against human nature. We can't change that."

"Maybe we would be most effective using hit and run tactics," Conn said, facing Orticon. "Now that we've captured attention, let's get the remaining national governments together to dictate quotas on resource mining and pass out replacement certificates to limit reproduction to one child per person, then organize watchdog institutions and go home. If it doesn't stick, it's their problem."

Tandra turned to Conn. "Sarcasm does not help."

"But that's exactly what we should do," Stringer said. "We've been broadcasting those ideas for years, but it hasn't influenced a thing."

"You're right," Tandra agreed. "Our broadcasts haven't helped much. We should ask why."

Lanoll wrapped a webbed hand around Tandra's. "Probably because we did more talking than listening."

"That's only a small part of it." Orticon's voice crackled with tension. "We're being naive if we think anyone will ever act on what we teach."

"We have to try," Shawne countered. "We must show how the steady state could work, then specific plans will come from local regions with common economic and cultural bases."

I tried to defuse the conversation. "Let's focus on the specifics."

For the moment it helped. Tandra and I would continue the Elll-Varok Science broadcasts from Moonbase and keep everyone updated with the latest developments from world news sources.

Orticon would concentrate on making ties with Earth's sustainability movement.

Shawne's team at the school would reference the excellent work done by human theorists in the 1800's, like John Stuart Mill, and the substantive books written in the early 21st century. We would approach from the differing human perspectives, as well as we could.

Shawne closed the discussion with a pointed statement. "Above all, we must encourage faith in human potential."

I won't try to describe the look on Orticon's face as she said this, and I'm thankful that Shawne couldn't read the thoughts that went through his mind.

Junah and Nidok

Orram—moments later

After the others had gone, Junah lingered to help Shawne clean the food bowls and store the leftovers.

There was only room for two in the wash area by the hearth, so Tandra and I decided to retire. She said her farewell and disappeared to the back of the lodge.

"We'll say goodbye for now, Junah," I ventured. "You're welcome to stay in the office lounge during dark, if you like."

"Thank you, Orram. I've made reservations at the locale's guest lodge. I was so taken by Shawne's faith in human potential, I wanted a few moments to talk more with her."

"Thanks for your compliment, Junah," Shawne said, putting away the last bowl. "I need all the feedback I can get."

Junah held out a hand to give me pause. "Do stay and talk with us if you like, Orram. I see that Shawne has questions about our early years."

"Of course I'll stay, though I'm not sure I have anything to add."

Shawne opened with a direct question. "Am I right, Junah? You were once in love with Orram?"

Junah put a smile on her handsome face and sent me a quick patch check. *Are you okay with my answering?*

Yes. My personal history is as open to my family as I can manage, but your perspective might not match mine.

"I thought humans were shy about mating issues," Junah told

Shawne. "Thanks for your question. Have you been reading Earth romance novels since Integration?"

Shawne's glance wandered to me in fun. "I would never admit that in front of my father."

"Of course not," Junah laughed. "None of his business. But you should know that *in love* is a human phrase that doesn't translate well in Varokian. I would guess that the word *obsessed* is more accurate. I admired Orram's careful thinking. He was so kind—"

"And we enjoyed a pleasant mating," I said, not wanting to skirt the issue, "a rare privilege of friendship among varoks—not the hormonal imperative so easily triggered in Earth's species."

"I understand that now," Shawne said. "It's probably the most significant characteristic that makes you truly alien to humans."

"My problem, Shawne, was that I couldn't accept Orram as just a friend. I tried to force the mind-link between us, felt that I needed it with Orram, had to share his every thought, his every living moment. No one else would do. What I didn't want to know was that—like human love—the mind-link is a gift between varoks that cannot be forced. I learned all about that when I saw how naturally your mother found Orram's mind. That's a story you know very well, I'm sure."

For a moment, she and I silently exchanged a smile. "That's all, Shawne," she said. "I just wanted to share my experience with you, now that you are a mature woman and will soon meet attractive men your age. Your human boy friends will teach you things you didn't know you didn't know, even about yourself."

"You're confirming everything Mom has been trying to tell me."

"And thanks for the help cleaning up, Junah," I said. "Now, please stay."

I gestured toward Conn's favorite lounge in the office, and she gave in. "I am too tired, and your invitation is too kind. I will cancel my reservation in locale center. Do wake me at first light and put me to work, both of you."

Shawne and I retreated toward our beds.

"Any questions?" I asked as I left her.

"Too many," she said with a smile.

Conn—two light-periods later

"We've got a message from the maintenance crew on Moonbase," "Conn announced at Shawne's next team meeting. "Amateur comet spotters on Earth have calculated Ellason's trajectory. They're saying it's a new object in the sky. Its estimated size is terrifying them."

"Congratulations," Conn radioed to Earth in his next scheduled broadcast. "I'm delighted you found my home planet, Ellason. I left it as a young tad, but we are always in touch with the Ellasonians. It's still a gorgeous deep sea planet, self-heated from its core, but the price for traveling there is far too high for casual visits, even now, when it is near perihelion."

"Big mistake," Moonbase told Conn hours later. "Your message has set off a storm of angst."

Conn and I got busy calling our human astronomy colleagues. "Ellason's trajectory will take it to perihelion in the vicinity of Neptune's orbit," I confirmed. "Surely you can convince people that it is a safe distance from Earth. Ellason gets no closer to the sun than Neptune."

Elll-Varok Science agreed to add information about Ellason and its eccentric orbit to their broadcasts. "To help assure people on Earth that Ellason can't harm them, get in touch with the World Astronomical Society. They will quickly verify your calculations." We did, and they did.

In spite of all this, word grew among the paranoid on Earth's Worldnet that Ellason would bring within striking distance a population of alien invaders. The news made Conn laugh, until he tuned into the nightly news. The Defenders of Earth—dedicated to the eradication of any alien influence that might contaminate Earth—were celebrating their ten-thousandth member.

Orram—at launch time, at the spaceport in Ahl Vior

Nidok showed up and boarded the *Lurlial* as if he owned it. Fearing his exo-skeleton might crack, he had padded himself against the extra g's of launch with an odd assortment of scraps no doubt gleaned from the ruins near his home cave.

Conn's eyes dropped open to fill his face when Nidok approached him in the flight deck. His mind was an unreadable mix—thoroughly surprised, angry and delighted. "Orram," he croaked, "who let this disposable insect into the ship? What does he think he is—the first ahlork in space?"

"Right, *Kaehl* Lips," Nidok said. His gargling reverberations shook the edible moss lining on the ship's inner walls. "I am *Aen Naran* (Specialist) Nidok, First Space Ahlork."

"Go sit down and strap in every tile," Conn said. "We've got to lose Varok and keep out of Jupiter's grasp or its magnetosphere will make purple toast of us all."

I was co-pilot to Conn, who expertly shot us out of Varok's orbit with one fusion amplifier burst to the ionic propulsion engines. We rode blindly through Varok's dense atmosphere, which kept the planet's albedo low enough to act as an invisibility cloak.

"Kick it right," Conn directed. "Three, two, one, now." With his expert maneuver, we veered away from Jupiter's huge magnetotail, avoiding the deadly radioactive particles that traveled in a giant stretched pear-shape all the way to Saturn's orbit.

I caught a glimpse of the moon Io far below, its bright yellow and orange volcanic surface nicely accented by the darker side of Jupiter.

"Sorry, the Red Spot is not visible right now," I said into the ship's intercom. "But look back at Varok, Nidok. There are some nice auroral lights visible over the north."

"Where? Where? Where?" Nidok croaked.

"You have to look out the starboard port," Conn said. "But don't get up and move. Tandra, keep that square-headed *ara* beast tied in."

"Mind your driving," Nidok said. "We be floating in space, not deep water. Use lungs elll, quick, before brain quits."

"He's fine, Conn," Tandra said, and from then on, while we were safely on a trajectory toward Earth's moon, and throughout the entire three-month trip, the fun between them continued. Tandra and I hoped we had made the right decision, inviting Nidok along.

II. Commitments

"It's not communism, socialism, capitalism or whatever-ism the steady stater seeks, but rather environmental protection, economic sustainability, national security and international stability."

—*Supply Shock: Economic Growth At the Crossroads and the Steady State Solution by Brian Czech. Canada: New Society Publishers, 2013, p. 278.*

THE TEAM

Tandra has seemed depressed, so I told her to try and think of her passage back to Earth as a rebirth. "You can't expect to be one of them now," I said. "You're consummated to a varok, and are half the being of an ell. You are no longer human, Tan. You are a universal creature. Your eyes no longer see as human beings see. You see with Orram's eyes, even with mine when we snuggle up in water. The heat of a summer day will never be the same to you now, for you know how it blinds me. Black and white are no longer simply dark and light, for you know what they are to me, cold and hot, absorbing and reflecting the infrared, the heat, in my eyes.

"We are one mind, one body sharing life with everything we sense, everything we learn. Promise. Earth won't tear us apart again."

Our shared sense of beauty shouts volumes about the meaning of consciousness. Our relationship tells us love is integral to creation, that our search for truth launches us into leaps of faith that integrate us with creation.

Since a family of three species is a bit unusual, I had better get something into this record for posterity to worry about. Like what's a family? It's a commitment for lifetime support, that's what. Ells and varoks don't equate it with mating and procreation. Neither do human beings, really.

Different as we are, we are all the same at the most basic levels. We are made of enormous numbers of nested complex systems that seek out the most efficient use of bio-chemicals. From that emerges our awareness, and our shared sense of beauty, wonder, and love. We are family—everyone in the whole weird universe.

We're traveling on the *Lurlial*, an interplanetary space cruiser, built by the varoks with some badly needed elllonian help to maximize enjoyment and comfort. We ells don't mind doing a little engineering when it's meaningful. That's why the *uuyvanoonl* are moss-lined, and the recreation room and food center comprise the largest areas on the ship, except for the heat shield and propulsion systems.

Now—about Shawne's team: On board the ship are three varoks (Orram, Junah and Orticon), three ells (myself, Stringer, and Lanoll), three humans (Tandra, Shawne and Jesse Mendleton), and an ahlork (Nidok).

You readers of this diary have already met Orram, my life-partner in family. He is a beautiful, exceptional being, and I am utterly prejudiced in his favor, so I cannot give you an objective view of him.

Next, Junah. Before Tandra became Orram's *alyakah* and they consummated mentally, Junah was Orram's casual mate at base. Junah is a beautiful woman, I'm told, with the typical varokian bright streaks in her hair. She was Chief Geologist at Earth's Moonbase when I was there.

Orticon, Orram's son, is a serious young varok with some significant political accomplishments in his résumé. It's hard to believe he was once a rebel, caught up in Mahntik's web. He believed her rhetoric about human plans to invade Varok, with good reason. He understands neither the conflicts nor the greed nor the mindless imprinting called entertainment that drives human violence and their irrational failure to compromise. I worry about how he will manage on Earth.

It took a growth disaster generated by Mahntik's treason to prove to Orticon that a few firm guidelines and consensus on resource preservation and population stability were necessary to maintain Varokian well-being indefinitely. Now he's an expert on ecological economics. He recognizes all too well the problems Earth will have in trying to move to a vibrant steady state.

I should note that Junah is not Orticon's mother. Orticon was born when Orram was young. The birthing mother did not wish to maintain a lasting relationship, which is an acceptable option on Varok as long as there is a stable family to raise the child with love.

The ahlork, Nidok, is our four-foot high, flying insectoid with an exoskeleton like a de-railed boxcar, a face like an overbaked *arl* cake, and a brain as if filled with Mahntik's berry wine uncorked.

The ellls on board the *Lurlial* are myself, Lanoll—my life's mate—and our son Stringer. Lanoll is beautiful and round, a blue elll, an accomplished environmental *hoat* counter who worked for Orram when he was Governor of Living Resources on Varok. A loner like me, she is devoted to the family, and a bit overprotective of our sometime-schooling son. While she is the plum, we are the string beans on the elll side of the family.

Stringer and Shawne play and fight like any siblings. Lanoll wants Stringer to be a Concentrate professor, but he specialized in hydrology because he likes water. I worry that he might want to go out to Ellason, whether he decides to teach or not. Life on Ellason is life in deep water.

The humans include Tandra and her daughter, Shawne, Superhuman. She speaks Varokian quite well and clicks off Elllonian clearly enough to get along with strange ellls. I often forget she is human.

Tandra adopted her at birth, two years before we came to Earth looking for a microbiologist to check out germ exchange dangers. Smart happy little mammal, twenty-one Earth years old now, with brighter hair and skin than Tandra. She has learned to swim at peak performance for an adult human. I dubbed her *Shawnoon* at age three, when she swam the length of the pool underwater at Moonbase. Not bad. Humans don't have gills, you know. Now she prefers the name Shawnoon. (The Elllonian suffix *-oon* implies water or moisture.)

Then there is Jesse Mendleton. On Earth long ago, he selected Tandra as our token human microbiologist to study first contact problems on Moonbase. You know the rest. I like him. He keeps his mouth shut most of the time.

Jesse has been good for Varok and will be great backup on Earth now. Pragmatic and taciturn, we thought we knew him—a simple human devoted to keeping economic growth contained in Varokian society. Then, one night on this trip, we learned he is also a talented musician.

Suddenly, after sharing music, we are now more friends

than business associates, no longer alien to one another. He's been tinkering with our electronic stuff ever since. These 76.6 Earth-days will pass quickly enough with him on board.

Too many light-periods later

A-a-a-e-o-o, I'm tired. We've been shooting the *Lurlial* toward Earth more than twenty days now, 56.6 to go, and already I need a good swim. Maybe I can get Lanoll to give me a pounding tonight, but what I really need is a ten-mile race at twelve fathoms. I need to stir up the sediment that's clogging my filters and get some of it back into my gut where it belongs. I think it's all settled in my brain—all this talk about Earth's water problems.

I proposed to the team and the Southwest Coalition that if we can convince people in the Southwest U.S. to do something about the Colorado River problem and the population surge on the southern California coast, we could set a powerful example that might help the whole world find a sustainable track.

I think the team bought the idea, and we'll look for a sponsor there. I could use a warm climate. Even the Pacific Ocean has warmed a bit. I can't believe Stringer is so focused on the Arctic.

PLAN OF ATTACK

Orram—on the space flight to Earth, day 64

While Conn, Tandra and Jesse composed melodies to make time pass, Shawne's steady state teaching team met every simulated light-period to organize their thoughts about what to teach and how to deal with Earth.

"Okay," Conn told Shawne, "I'll come to every meeting, if you gather in the sleeping area so I can soak during all the dry talk." And so they did, the ellls floating in *uuyvanoonl* while the others gathered nearby on chairs or lounged on bed pads to discuss strategy.

"Let's start from the positives today," Shawne began during one mid-cycle gathering. "As you know, Earth is now much like Varok has always been. Nearly all fossil fuels are gone."

"Great," Conn said. "I've always wanted to ride in a horse and buggy."

"Seriously, now," Shawne gave Conn a warning nod and continued. "Gas production collapsed in North America before 2030. Cheap oil was gone by 2035, and the remaining coal could be gone by 2110."

"It is still being burned," Orticon said, his eyes intense with frustration. "Now the methane hydrides are being mined from deep under the ocean. It's an insane experiment, continuing to gamble on Earth's tolerance of CO_2."

"Amen," Conn snorted. "And you'd think someone would have sense enough to save some of that energetic slop for the future."

Lanoll pushed the blue plumes from her eyes. "Ellls and varoks were lucky to evolve on planets without fossil fuels. They were too plentiful on Earth and uniquely efficient. No wonder it's been a difficult transition."

"Transition? A lot of blather about energy efficiency and no 'do,'" Conn said. "Orticon's right. They're burning even more coal per person now than before the dieoffs."

"We should not forget to focus on the good signs," Shawne said. "Energy efficiency is up overall. Wealth has been invested in rail service—at least a thousand times more efficient than automobile transport. We won't need to focus on transportation or communication issues."

"They'll come up, one way or another," Orticon said.

"And as they do, we'll deal with them," Jesse said. "We've got several other positives on our side, like the strong movement toward sharing infrastructure and jobs."

"You really think anyone on Earth is going to share work hours?" Conn asked. "Maybe the older elephants."

Jesse continued, unruffled. "We're also seeing big increases in repair work now that manufacturers nearly everywhere are responsible for the full life cycles of their products."

"*Nearly* everywhere," Conn said, rising from his *uuyvanoon*, "excluding three out of seven continents."

Shawne gave her elll dad a look. He sat back down.

I didn't like Orticon's silence.

Stringer broke the tension. "The United Nations Convention on the Law of the Sea has been an amazing success, a real boon for northern countries, now that the Arctic Ocean is free of sea ice in September."

"Except they're still battling over the location of their continental shelves." This time it was Orticon making the counter-point.

"Humans have done quite well coming to terms with reality in regard to sea level rise," Junah said. Her steady gaze invited Orticon to read her impression of humans. "Millions of people have pulled back from coastal cities and deltas and other areas prone to flooding from severe storms."

"Insurance rates drove that home," Conn said.

"Whatever works," Jesse said.

Orticon turned away from the others and released his pessimism again. "And how many worthless levies are being built? As if the sea rise is going to be temporary?"

"They'll learn the hard way." Tandra was looking gloomy. "And it's too late for the 28 percent of species in the south that couldn't move north, like the polar bear."

"I'm sorry, Mom," Shawne said. "At least polar bear genes still reside in hybrids with the grizzlies. All we can do is save a decent future for what is left."

Tandra nodded. "Of course we should focus on the present and the future. One of the key aspects of the increasing temperatures has been the large migration north."

"The largest cities now include Stockholm, Toronto and Anchorage," I reviewed. "Crop yields have increased in Canada, the northern United States, Scandinavia, United Kingdom, and Russia."

"The good news is that now only a billion people go hungry every day," Conn said.

"Which reminds me," Shawne said with a level gaze at Conn. "We should keep watch on the health of Earth's satellite data collection capability. It's critical if Earth is to develop a global resource policy."

Jesse motioned to Shawne. "As a basis for resource modeling, we might start by studying the cultural and economic development of the eco-regions. Cascadia in the northwest of North America, and Atlantia in the northeast have been doing very well across borders."

"But there are border skirmishes over water in other regions," Orticon added. "It's so ridiculously obvious, all the tension—don't humans know what drives the lemmings into the sea?"

"Ease it down, Orticon," I said.

"So let's go back home," Conn erupted. "They're doing just fine down there without us, when they aren't killing each other."

Orticon erupted. "That's hasn't stopped since the 1900's. What are we thinking? What can we possibly—"

I leapt to my feet, hoping to shut off his loss of control.

Shawne's frustration set off another alarm in my patch organs. "That does it," she said. "Conn, you and Orticon be my bodyguards, whatever, but stay away from my school."

Orram—several artificial light-periods later

In time, when our frustrations simmered down, the team members' personal preferences for interacting with Earth became clear.

Stringer and Lanoll were most interested in contacting cetaceans to evaluate their biological and social health. They also expressed the desire to work together.

"I can't replace an entire school," Lanoll said, "but perhaps I can meet some of your need for contact, Stringer. We could look for pods of dolphins that might accept us."

Junah jumped in with enthusiasm. "I'd like to understand what has happened in the Arctic. What do you think, Jesse? We could be surface backup for Lanoll and Stringer."

"That sounds like a great idea," Shawne said. "You can provide us with input on conditions in the Arctic while the rest of us stay and organize the school."

Orticon shook his head. "Of course you have my technical support, Shawne, but I need to focus on something else first, or I could endanger this entire effort. I respect Oleyall too much to fail—" He couldn't continue.

I checked his mind as he retired to his space. He would recover.

By the third month of our trip, the spaceship was approaching

Earth's moon. Applications for hosting us were coming into our website, but we had little patience for all the deliberations. Seattle was too cold for ellls. Denver was too high for varoks. Small cities and large cities in recovery would be hard-pressed to provide facilities for and protection from a public fascinated with aliens, especially for the full year Global Varok had specified.

"And where are we going to be?" Conn asked. "Where do I land this space eggplant of ours? Or are we going to be orbiting Earth until our ions fizzle out?"

"How about San Diego?" Shawne asked. "We could focus on the Colorado River problem there, as you proposed, Conn."

"I love the idea of palm trees and ocean waves," Lanoll said. "That will be a welcome change after our time in the north."

My receiver pulsed. "We have our call. Oran Ramahlak here."

"Orram?" Carliano's amplified voice came through the radio after the 1.28 second delay.

"We like the idea of working in the San Diego region," I told him. I tried to remember what I had read. "I think some water is piped from northern California, but most of it goes to the Los Angeles area. Bob?"

"San Diego hasn't applied to host you," he replied.

"Could we ask them?" Tandra said. "San Diego has been a wealthy town, so they've done some serious thinking about changing their ways."

"However," Conn said, "they have also started shipping water from Alaska, instead of cutting back in response to the Colorado River dryup."

Shawne set her shoulders. "We feel we could make an impact there."

"Let me check my notes," Carliano said. "I realize it was on your list. Yes, here it is. One canal supplies Southern California through the Mojave Desert. A second canal is pumped uphill 300 miles to Arizona and California. The situation was manageable until surviving migrants moved toward the coast instead of relocating in the north."

"I like the idea of teaching in San Diego," Jesse said. "And the *Haemophilus* epidemic there has pretty much run its course."

I was surprised at the enthusiasm in Tandra's voice. "What do you think, Bob?"

"It's a mixed bag there—all kinds of people. All I can do is ask," he replied.

After we signed off, the team disbursed. We waited with impatience and some anxiety for Carliano's answer. The delay was longer than usual, and his voice stumbled with embarrassment when he called in again three light-periods later.

"San Diego doesn't want to provide hospitality for the public you would attract."

Conn laughed. "We can't blame them."

"San Diego would be an ideal location," Shawne argued. "It's on the Pacific Ocean, so the eills can contact the whales. See if you can talk them into applying, Bob."

The pause was very long this time. "I'll try," Carliano said. "Meanwhile, chose some alternatives."

Over the next two light-periods, the team watched Earth's cloud-decorated blue orb grow in their monitors. The vision of such living beauty, growing steadily out of the intense dark sprinkled with far-away stars, gave us an overwhelming sense of how miraculous and precious life was there. We called it the sapphire of human souls.

When at last Carliano radioed, his voice rang with enthusiasm.

"You'll be hearing soon. An invitation will come from a place near San Diego. I don't know why I didn't think of it earlier. SCBA has invited you to stay at their campus."

"What's an essceebeeay?" Conn asked.

"The Southern California Benthic Associates. They have a long pier, several research ships, conference rooms, labs set up for ocean studies of all kinds. They will also supply rooms for Shawne's school. They support ocean bottom research, and they have watched your broadcasts from the moon for eighteen years."

"Sounds good," Shawne said.

I didn't like the idea of being responsible to a private organization. Their requirements could conflict with those of Global Varok, which had to have priority. "Do they receive money from sources who may not agree with what we teach?" I asked.

"I don't think so," Carliano said. "The money they have now is from hard-core reformers. Most public funds have dried up. The invitation comes from the staff, with full knowledge of their supporters. They just want to look over your syllabus. Most likely they'll put out a disclaimer, saying your opinions are not necessarily shared by the Associates. Look at their web site. If I were you, I wouldn't hesitate. It's perfect."

"We'll call you right back, Bob," I said.

We recessed until everyone had looked at the website and reviewed SCBA's invitation. It took less than an hour, and our next gathering was more or less like a celebration.

The dark trip through a sea of bright and dim stars to our blue sapphire was coming to an exciting end. Earth loomed large and welcoming through the view ports.

Conn had one minor objection. "Rotten *kaehl* eggs," he swore, "the view of the Pacific Ocean from SCBA makes it too hard to refuse, but the place is built on a steep hill. That's hard on ellls."

"Wait. Wait." Nidok said. "Aren't sharks be in California coast, Conn? Big ones. Great white?"

Conn looked thoughtful for a moment, his eyes narrowing slowly. "Do I look like a seal? Am I torpedo shaped? They'll think I'm sea weed."

"There have been pollution problems on the Pacific coast," Tandra said. "You'll need to stick to the pool SCBA provides, until we get an analysis done."

Conn tilted his left melon.

As the meeting ended, the *Lurlial* ducked around Earth and found the moon. We radioed Carliano to tell him we would accept SCBA's invitation. He was delighted. Orticon was silent.

I looked at Nidok, and he raised his head to peer sideways down at me from his perch on Tandra's head.

MOONBASE

Orram—on the Lurlial approaching Earth's moon, day 76

When we achieved lunar orbit, Nidok sat by a viewing monitor watching the craters go by. He was awestruck, and so silent we thought he was sick, or scared witless.

I had finished my tour of the *Lurlial* in preparation for landing. In a few minutes the d'Alembert Mountains would appear on the horizon. Conn was in the pilot's seat, and I was relaxing next to him, watching the moon's familiar craters pass by, when Nidok joined us.

He clutched the arm of my couch with a wing-tip turned white with tension. I was tempted to try reading him.

"We land at Moonbase now?"

"Yes, we'll see the mountains behind the base very soon. We'll all stay there until it is safe for the team to go to Earth," I said.

"Is never safe for Nidok?"

"I'm not sure you and Orticon are ready to deal with humans." I hoped the implied threat would trigger a response I could interpret.

"I help him. We make plans," Nidok said mysteriously. He acted confident, but I worried that he did not respond with an insult. "I go to Orticon. I fix it."

He vaulted off, and I felt sorry that the ahlork species had been underestimated for most of Varok's history. Only since Mahntik's treason, when the ahlork helped stop her, were they allowed to sit on Varok's Councils.

In minutes, Nidok returned to the flight deck, quite recovered and looking as cocky as ever as he hopped onto Conn's head.

"Get off, Nidok," Conn said. "Please. It's time to land this thing."

"I will land it," the ahlork jibed, reaching for the control bank. "Nature taught ahlork flying, not ellls."

"Out. Out. Out, or we'll have ahlork lips for lunch."

"*Alye* elll." Nidok touched Conn's upper lip and left the deck.

"What's got into him?" Conn asked me.

"He is working with Orticon. On something serious, Conn."

The landing was uneventful, except for Shawne's excitement and Nidok's nervous moments. Conn guided the *Lurlial* over the craters and headed straight for the hidden hangar beneath the d'Alembert Mountains. I knew Nidok hated being strapped in for landing, so I went back to the cabin to check on him as soon as we touched down.

Tandra said that when the hangar entrance had finally yawned open at the end of the long landing strip, the ahlork had buried his big face in his plated wings and curled into a box-shape, awaiting impact.

"Come on, Nidok, silly bird," Shawne said, tugging at an exposed wing tip after *Lurlial* had settled to a gentle stop. "We're here, inside

Moonbase. Let's go bouncing. I'll race you to the food center."

"Do you remember where it is?" Tandra asked. "You were not yet three when we came here and prepared to emigrate to Varok."

"It's like I never left," Shawne sang out, and she skipped away, laughing and holding Nidok's wing-tip so he wouldn't fly off.

As Tandra and Conn and I left the space cruiser and entered the long central hall of the base, old memories poured over us like warm air sweetened with new grass.

We knew exactly where we wanted to go first.

"I'd like to see Earth from the observation deck, Mom." Shawne came back to us, breathless. "Orram, please come. It's where you first made love, isn't it?"

"No," Tandra said, while I said, "Yes."

"Give us a break, Orram, old boy," Conn said. "Falling asleep in a human's arms is not making love."

"It is to us touch-sensitive varoks. I couldn't have stood such close contact, unless we were in mental synch."

"Tsk tsk. Mental synch, when you'd only just met," Shawne said. "I remember that wild party to celebrate our being out of quarantine. I remember moth cakes and Conn taking me into red water. And you two going off together."

Tandra and I had spent time in the observation deck after our first contact and the raucous party of welcome at the base pool. *Was it really only eighteen Earth years ago?* In many ways it seemed forever. Together we had talked long hours, then slept on the couch facing the window that overlooked a crescent Earth. Tandra had nestled against me as she grew tired, and I found the contact tolerable, for our minds had already met.

She didn't understand then that she read my mood and knew my thoughts, that we had found a common consciousness during that first encounter, as if our minds had been poured from the same mold.

Now, as the landscape of craters turned away from the sun, we stared out across the deepening shadows of the terminator.

"Full circle, Tan," Conn said, as he sprawled next to us on the soft couch.

"It's been a very long way around, hasn't it, Conn?" Tandra said. "But we've done it together. It's been a good ride." She smiled up into my eyes and nestled into the elll's body plumes.

When Lanoll joined us, Conn cupped a wide be-finned hand to hold her lovely blue-plumed head, and we five sat there together in silence watching the bright Earth.

"There it is, Shawnoon," Conn said. "Behold your home planet."

"It's very beautiful way out there," she said in wonder, "so far from everything, so alone."

"Like a perfect fruit," Tandra said, "being eaten too fast, before it can ripen."

"Hey, hey, let's not get maudlin," Conn said. "Humans may change things, but life will find a way to go on, in spite of them."

"For as long as the sun behaves," Tandra said.

"So perhaps we will help others enjoy the now," I said. "We'll have to remember that when we go down there, right Shawne? We may have to deal with some mind sets that have forgotten how fragile life is."

An hour must have passed before we got up and moved to the pool for the adjustment with Stringer and the ells of the Moonbase crew.

We found them on the pool deck, watching a telecast from Earth. "Will you listen to that?" a med-tech said. "They're saying Ellason is coming in close to Earth. Since when is Neptune's orbit *close*?"

"Turn it off," Conn said. "They're into hype, not accuracy."

He jumped into the pool. More crew members appeared, and we humans and varoks waited until the ells had finished their deep water greeting. As they appeared on the surface we dove in and coasted around them, circling five times until they broke the pattern and invited us to the deck for the last meal of their work day.

For many light-periods—synchronized to Earth-days—we rested and exercised, trying to rebuild bone and muscle lost on the trip from Varok. Then we continued studying and planning for the practical problems the landing team would face on the blue planet.

As the spring sun warmed Earth's northern hemisphere, Carliano called to say that the Eco-Region government of San Diego had offered support for the Southern California Benthic Associates to host us.

"A new group calling themselves the Friends of Varok and Ellason have offered housing near SCBA, overlooking the Pacific Ocean. It's within walking distance of SCBA's marine laboratory. The San Diego Eco-Region will host a brief arrival celebration, and SCBA will provide us with security."

Carliano failed to mention the other group, called the Defenders of

Earth, people certain that Ellason posed a threat. They had staged two protests against our visit so far. I decided it wasn't worth mentioning.

"The arrangements are complete to land at the old Naval Air Station on North Island, near San Diego," I announced that evening at dinner. Only then did Orticon allude to his discussions with Nidok.

"Our plan," Orticon said, as we ate, "Nidok's and mine, will work in very well with your cautious approach."

"What plan?" Shawne asked. "You're helping me teach, aren't you?"

"If and when I'm ready, Shawnoon."

Splitting Pains

Orram—on Moonbase, just before the landing team departs to Earth

"We've got a problem, Father." Orticon came to me well into our dark cycle at Moonbase. Everyone else was asleep. "We need to share heads. It's Shawne. I hate to leave while she's setting up the school, but I feel I must."

I followed Orticon to the observation deck. As we watched the barren miles of craters, we talked. I cherished the moment. Such talks had been all too rare after he became a consulting expert helping to maintain the steady state on Varok. Too often we had conferred with short, business-like mind scans, especially after he began work with Earth's resource data.

Orticon tuned in to my mind and together we explored Shawne's history, my memories of her stubborn streak, her convictions and passion, her tension with Conn's protectiveness and irritation with human society.

You will be caught in the middle. A good role for you—the mediator between human and elllonian passion.

Orticon had to suppress a huge surge of emotion. *Good Harrahn, help me!*

Yes. You will need all the faith you can muster. In dealing with humans and ellls, you will learn what trust means, as I did.

I hope Shawne can trust her students. I wonder if she realizes how difficult it is to simplify one's lifestyle.

At least she recognizes the steady state as an ethical mind-set. She's focused on helping people put long-term well-being above immediate profit.

Orticon spoke in Varokian. "But I'm not ready, Father. Nidok and I need to start slowly. Humanity is more volatile than Conn, and less predictable. We need to learn about Earth from the inside out. We'll tell everyone about our plans when we know Shawne's timeline."

Orram—later that light-period

We were all gathered on the moss decks of the Moonbase pool, reviewing plans for the alien mini-invasion of Earth—Tandra's favorite phrase—when Shawne announced that the school should begin recruiting teachers immediately upon their arrival.

Her televised broadcasts were attracting listeners, all quite welcoming and eager to hear about her youth on an alien planet. "I'm getting a little better at talking to the public, and I haven't heard one negative word," she said. "There is no reason to wait."

I have never seen Conn so firm with Shawne. "You're not going public right away, not until we are sure the coast is clear. End of story. End of story."

"You're repeating yourself, *Aloon*," she said calmly. "It's not the end of story. It's the beginning. I've made my plans. You can help me set up the Longevity School or not. Your choice."

They had always been very close. As Shawne was growing up, Conn was the one she ran to for sympathy when Tandra and I stood firm with discipline. Ellls love children of all kinds. Conn and Lanoll could relate to a childish viewpoint when Tandra's temper flared or I grew emotionally steely. With Conn's fatherly hugs and Lanoll's understanding, they would bring Shawne around—yet they always supported Tandra and me. We four adults made a good parenting team, but I couldn't remember if the ellls had ever experienced Shawne's outright defiance. This was a new experience for Conn.

"All right. All right. Anything," Conn said. "You and Orticon can begin classes in North America on one condition. I stay with you. I

stick to you like glue, Shawne, and Nidok sits on your head every minute you're in public."

"Orticon and me, we not be long in San D'ego," Nidok announced.

"What do you mean?" Shawne said. "Orticon, I can't set up the
school without you."

"Of course you can," Orticon said. "It needs to be done . . . with a
human touch."

Angst. Or was it depression I sensed from my son? *I am failing*
Shawne, and I hate the failure humans will press on her. He moved close to
his young human sister and spoke directly to her, searching her eyes
and her mood.

"Nidok and I have considered this very carefully, Shawne. We will
not be useful, unless we can understand more about Earth and fear
humans less."

Agreement. Orticon and I both sensed it in Shawne.

"We need to know the source of so much xenophobia among humans," he continued. "It must be related to the violence we see in so
many cultures."

Agreement.

He took a deep breath before he went on. "You see why I think that
your school will fail?"

She shook her head. *No. Confusion.*

"It's the tragedy of human imagination . . . or is it the human talent
for double-think?"

Confusion. "Oh. Orwell. 'Nineteen Eighty-four.'"

"Yes. Also, the refusal to credit time and space for Earth's isolation,
the belief humans can escape to someplace else. We're not sympathetic.
Nidok and I have decided to retreat to Australia and explore the Great
Barrier Reef."

"Why the Barrier Reef, Orticon?"

"We should study what is happening there. People have moved
away from the equator to escape the heat."

Agreed. Fewer people.

"Nidok can forage safely there. It is most like his native shores."

"Be sure to guard against exposure," Shawne said.

"All tests are negative. The biochemistry is too different, but we will
stay in isolation suits."

Appreciation.

"We'll get people talking, explore options for that part of the world. We can keep watch on news from the Southern Hemisphere."

"And just how do you plan to travel so far, without causing a huge ruckus?" Conn asked.

"There is an expedition going south from SCBA, on their research ship *Shearwater*. We have been in touch with the captain. They will be doing bottom profiling and mapping of currents around the Great Barrier Reef. If I agree to bunk with Nidok and take responsibility for him, they may agree to take us."

"What a wonderful opportunity for you." Tandra was ready to sign on with them.

"How will you keep Nidok safe?" Conn said. "We should stick together."

"We be hidden," Nidok assured him. "Only captain, crew know of us on Earth. You take attention and cameras, flashy green elll."

"They have a point," I agreed. "This will give us a chance to understand the southern hemisphere of Earth better, firsthand."

So it was settled. The team firmed up their arrival plans: After the welcoming ceremonies in San Diego, Conn would follow Shawne's every move and play the roll of token friendly alien. From Moonbase, Tandra and I would relieve the varokian crew currently running the Elll-Varok lunar broadcasts to Earth. We would embellish the presentations with periodic news about the activities of Shawne and Conn, the "first aliens on Earth."

If accepted by the SCBA research team, Orticon and Nidok would sail on the *Shearwater* to the southern hemisphere. Meanwhile, guided by Jesse Mendleton and Junah from a long-distance survival dinghy, Stringer and Lanoll would contact cetaceans and get a first-hand look at the situation in the North Pacific.

We radioed the plans to SCBA along with the identity of personnel attached to each assignment. Our first objective: assessing the quality of life in different ecosystems on Earth and gathering input for Shawne's school. We added the public portion of our plans—Shawne and Conn's landing and the school's launch—to our regular broadcasts.

Of one thing we were certain—our lives would be forever changed once we set feet and fins on Earth. As a precaution, we asked Moonbase engineers to reinforce the *Ranat*'s land rover, in case xenophobic crazies decided they could take no chances with us.

Orram—just before launch to Earth

"Conn! Connconn, you look wonderful!" During the final fittings for our trip from moon to Earth, Shawne's excitement took the edge off our fears.

Conn's helmeted figure, tall and trim in the sleek silver of his protective isolation suit, looked anything but threatening. His red and yellow forehead plumes framed huge soft doe-eyes blinking behind the face plate.

"Of all the sacrifices I have made for this tad of ours," he said, "to go back into an isolation suit for you, Shawne, is the utmost in parental martyrdom."

Tandra drew a quick breath. "We hope and pray that will be the extent of it," she said.

"Stop moving around, Conn" I said. "I haven't finished checking your seals. Stringer, you're next. Excess salt may be no better for elllonian skin than the excess acid in the ocean."

"Ellason's oceans have a wide range of salt concentrations." Stringer was the calmest one of all. "We'll adapt quickly."

"Perhaps," Conn said, "but Ellason's water is warmer than Earth's. We may need the insulation."

"How are we supposed to school?" Stringer asked. "This isolation suit damps out most hexline signals, as well as tile-pressure."

"Go slowly," I said. "Adapt gradually. Do not swim without the suit. If you must rely on pressure, electrical, or chemical signals, do not expose yourselves to ocean water for more than one hour a day for the first week, then two hours a day. No more. Be sure you and Lanoll check each other continually—"

Tandra's frown shut off my compromising. "I don't like the ellls being exposed to Earth's sea water at all, Orram. Gradual adaptation won't help if it's polluted. There have been too many oil spills. Islands of waste still gather. Promise us—Conn, Stringer, Lanoll—minimize your risks. Stay completely suited."

"We'll be fine, Tandra," Lanoll said. "We know what we're getting into."

The Glass Bubble

Conn—a short time later

"We have the Alaska Peninsula in sight. Nice clouds." High above the North Pacific, Conn spoke to Tandra and Orram from the pilot's couch of the reliable old space bus *Ranat*.

Launch from Moonbase had gone well, but Conn knew that Tandra and Orram would not be able to relax, watching from their office, until both the *Ranat* and the Arctic team landed safely.

"Seals locked," Stringer said. He and Lanoll, Jesse and the varok Junah had strapped themselves inside the *Ranat*'s landing pod awaiting ejection into the North Pacific Ocean near Unimak Island. "We're ready for the drop. Parachutes armed."

"All-systems check complete," Shawne confirmed.

"Bombs away," Conn said through the radio. "Bon voyage, you all. See you in San Diego in two months. Three, two, one, land ho."

Orticon fired the landing pod. Shortly after, the drogue chutes deployed.

Shawne gasped. "I don't like being split up like this," she murmured, as the chutes disappeared into a solid bank of clouds far below.

"Jesse knows Earth very well," Orticon said. "He grew up here, and Junah has done her homework. Stringer knows as much about dolphins and whales as Lanoll does. They'll do fine."

Conn looked closely at Shawne sitting at the navigator's desk, next to Orticon. "Can you see all right, Shawne?" he asked. "I don't want you to miss anything as we come in through the clouds."

"It's been very beautiful, Conn, watching Earth grow larger and bluer and greener."

"You may be a child of the universe, Shawne, but your human nest is Earth," Orticon said. "You're bound to have some kind of genetic pull—"

Shawne gave the young varok a look, then joined him in staring out the view port. "The clouds have swirled all around. They look like great gobs of Orserah's whipped *llaoon* sap over the ocean."

Exclaiming in awe at snowcaps perched high on the Rocky Mountains, she fell silent when they crossed hours of deserted cornfields, desolate flatlands, then came out of orbit over a quiet New York City. Many of its high-rise buildings were deserted, stained and broken from too much salt water. "Like the Ruins of Tahkin on Varok," Shawne said.

Orticon shook his head in sympathy. "Not quite. It's still a viable city—struggling with food supplies and hard hit with New Plague, but still busy making music and clothes."

"Let's cover as much of North America as we can," Shawne suggested. "Let's fly over what's left of Florida, then back over the Great Lakes across the new development in Canada and down the west coast. I'd like to see the redwood forests."

Conn's eyes widened a bit. "No problem," he said, considering it, and enjoying the challenge. "Be my co-pilot. Orticon, navigate. We'll have to re-program part of the flight plan and adjust the San Diego approach."

The trip was too short. They all hated to see it end, for it left them with the impression of a planet in transition, "a wounded planet not yet healing," Orticon said.

As their glide path took them over San Diego, they noticed the city's grand old houses sprinkled over the hills, away from the shore and into the nearby mountains. Shawne was entranced. "Are those palm trees? The hills are green. They must have had rain, real rain, Conn, from clouds. Will we see lots of clouds? And sunsets?"

"Right up close," Conn said. "The clouds sit on the coast a lot. It's called fog."

"Mom?" Shawne tuned in to the frequency of Moonbase and described what she was seeing.

"I wish I could be with you, Love," Tandra said. "Enjoy it for me—"

—*while you can,* she left unsaid, and Conn imagined what she might say to him. *We made the right decision. Shawne needs to be on Earth without my garbage spoiling her dreams. She is so excited, and so hopeful.*

As the braking engines quieted and the *Ranat* glided silently toward the city, Shawne seemed to grow tense.

"We're holding true, Shawnoon. Confirm your clearance," Conn said, making a small adjustment in their glide path. "No wind to worry about. Visibility is good. No fog down there now."

Shawne switched the radio to the control tower frequency. "This is the EV cruiser *Ranat,*" she said, "requesting permission to land, North Field from EV Moonbase."

A cheer went up, heard distinctly over the ship's receivers.

"Is that good sound?" Nidok asked. He had switched on the intercom from his self-designed padded passenger harness at the stern.

"Very good sound," Conn was grinning ear plaque to ear plaque. His ultrasonic melons tilted forward in reflex, to catch every nuance through the radio noise coming in the isolation suit headgear.

"Permission to land granted. North-south runway two," the voice from the control tower enunciated carefully. "Repeat two. Lighted. No other traffic. Confirm."

"Roger," Shawne said. "Runway two, lighted. Length noted."

"Warn them about the settling rockets," Conn said. "They won't expect them."

"Settling rockets at five thousand meters. Expect short glide path."

"Is runway width adequate? Is runway adequate?"

"More than adequate, San Diego."

"Welcome home, Shawne." The new radio voice was Bob Carliano's.

"Hey there, good buddy," Conn broke in. "Get out the champagne."

Another cheer flooded their isolation helmet coms.

"Conn—" The former astronaut's voice broke with emotion. "Will you hurry that crate? Get your green butt down here."

Conn flipped the *Ranat* out of auto-drive. As soon as they were over the runway, he fired the settling rockets and warmed up the vertical blades. Setting the craft down in a near vertical emergency landing would be good theater, he thought.

He was right. The crowd lining the far end of the runway went wild as Conn pulled the front hatch open and stood up, waving like the star he was, his mind filling with a mixture of pride and fear. Seventeen years of broadcasts from Varok relayed by our Moonbase had made a celebrity of the elll, a commentator of Orram and, recently, a heroine of Shawne.

"Show off." Carliano laughed into the radio.

Nidok huddled in his braces, and Orticon sat frozen in his seat, fighting to control the strange emotion generated by the crowd's cheering. He seemed both excited and terrified.

In spite of the majority's enthusiasm, however, Conn decided the human audience gathered for the family's arrival was not entirely friendly. He thought he spotted several factions, represented by various signs and banners scattered throughout the crowd: hopeful people entranced with the idea of neighborly aliens, with signs like "Welcome Conn!" and "Come on Down, Orram"; students of steady state economics, with "Nothing Real Can Grow Forever," "Enough Is Enough"; staunch supporters of growth economics, with "Growth Means Jobs," "No Growth Means Stagnation"; and finally, xenophobes, with "Aliens Go Home," "Stop the Ellason Threat."

The team took heart from the cheer that sounded across the enormous crowd. Conn realized that if it had not been for the armored exit tube sent to meet the *Ranat*'s egress, Nidok would have bolted deep into the ship.

When the tube was in place, Orticon, Shawne, Conn and Nidok moved quickly down its length and onto the back of a welcoming platform. Shawne's enthusiasm drained from her face when she caught a glimpse of the mass of people. Her question surprised Conn. It had nothing to do with the signs they waved.

"Why do they gather in such a large crowd?" she asked. "Surely no one can see us beyond thirty pallons. Are we humans some kind of swarming mammal?" She was serious.

Conn moved close and put a comforting arm around her shoulders. "Remember the tapes you've seen of the year 2000 celebrations all over the world? This First-Alien-on-Earth thing is another great reason to party. It's perfectly harmless."

"But how did they all get here? I thought transportation was still hard to come by."

As she spoke, they were joined on the platform by three officious-looking greeters and three well-armed guards.

"Many people walked, many rode bicycles. Some hydrogen trains are running for the occasion," one greeter answered Shawne's question. The officials extended welcoming hands and Shawne took hold of Nidok's wingtip before he could fly back toward the ship.

Without further incident, the aliens were escorted forward onto a small stage enclosed in a transparent protective bubble. Conn squinted into the bright lights, glad for the dimming lenses he wore under his isolation suit.

"Our differences don't really sink in until you see them amplified," Orticon said. "This is not Ahl Vior. These are not varoks, Shawne. These are creatures with . . . eruptive emotions."

"Amen," said Conn, thankful Orticon hadn't said *violent emotions*. "You're the prodigal human, Shawne. It's time for you to introduce Nidok and me. Are you okay?"

"A little shaky."

"Listen." Orticon now seemed confused by the emotional crowd and its party mood.

People were shouting louder than ever, and a chant had begun, "We want Conn. We want Conn . . ."

A tall human approached and introduced himself as the newly elected Southwest Coalition Overseer. "This way please, Miss Shawne," he said.

After giving Conn a hug and Nidok a touch on the lower lip, she followed the tall man and a lovely older woman to the front of the platform. She took a deep breath and looked out over the massive crowd through the bullet-proof bubble around her.

It reminded Conn of the Theater of Great-fish, but here the audience was outside the bubble, not within it.

When she appeared, the crowd roared. Shawne waved and opened her arms and threw kisses.

"Omigosh, she's plugged in," Conn whispered to Orticon.

The chant began again, "We want Conn. We want Conn." Then, as if she had been appearing before mass gatherings all her life, Shawne raised one hand for silence and approached the microphone.

Conn snapped his gills tight.

"I can't tell you what it means to me, to us, to be welcomed back to Earth, to my home, this way, with so much love." She choked with emotion and looked up.

What is Shawne doing, surely not playing up her feelings? Conn looked up at the moon shining white in the darkening blue sky, wishing Orram and Tandra were not so far away.

The crowd roared its approval. Shawne took the mike from its stand and began again, tears running unchecked down her cheeks.

Okay. It must be real. Interesting, Conn thought to himself.

"Earth is more beautiful than I imagined. It is good to be home." She stifled a sob, and the crowd roared.

Minutes later they quieted so she could continue.

"Thank you for your warm welcome. Thank you for inviting us to San Diego, for providing us with a beautiful home." Shawne paced the stage. "Special thanks to the staff of the Southern California Benthic Associates who have so generously invited us into their research program. We will make sure San Diego will be forever proud to be the winners of our hosting contest."

More cheers.

"I don't want to waste any time before we start our work here. Our mission is to remind you of Varokian history and the system that has guaranteed its prosperity, its equity and its security for so many ages. We want nothing but the best for Earth. If you are familiar with our broadcasts, you know how much we worry about Earth's future. Therefore, before I introduce my family from Varok and Ellason, I want to announce the establishment of the Elll-Varok-Human School for Economic Longevity. You are all invited to join, in person or online. I invite those experts in ecological economics and steady state theory to apply for . . . a variety of positions with its faculty. We thank the Friends of Varok and Ellason for helping San Diego and SCBA with the funding."

She looked at Conn for some sign that there would be funding for such positions, and he shrugged. Go for it, Sweetie. *You're the blistering show here tonight.*

Part of the crowd cheered, but they were soon drowned out by a renewed chant for Conn.

Shawne laughed into the mike, and set about—*what is the phrase?* Conn asked himself—*pumping up the crowd?*

"Ellls are wonderful, aren't they?" More cheering. "But so are varoks. They are not as decorative as ellls, they look too much like us, and they are a bit fragile emotionally, so be nice to them, too. Give welcome to my older varokian brother, Orticon, an expert in Earth Studies and a trouble-shooter when economies and debt grow wild."

Orticon stepped into the glare and nodded to a mixed reaction—polite applause and a few shouted comments, "He doesn't look very alien to me," and "Where's the mind-reading patches?"

The cameras focused in on Orticon's patch organs, just visible behind his face plate at the side of his head. A murmur spread through the crowd.

"You want alien?" Shawne teased the crowd. "Meet Nidok the ahlork, a flying insectoid, native to Varok's steep shoreline cliffs, the ultimate of recyclers, miner of precious metals from the ancient ruins on Varok. Nidok is bonded to our family."

Shawne motioned for Nidok to enter, and he waddled to the front, and then jumped on her head. The crowd loved it.

"What is this? Swarming humanity?" He croaked into the microphone the questionable English Conn had taught him.

The crowd laughed politely, not sure how to react.

"You are looking like swarming locusts, so many. 'Now we be eating San Diego. Next we eat Los Angeles.'"

People roared their approval, and Nidok was off and running at the mouth. Insult after insult in Varokian—some aimed at Shawne, some at Orticon—flew from his clacking lips, until Conn could stand it no longer.

The elll made his appearance in his trim isolation suit, clasped a hand over Nidok's lips and pretended he had been bit. The crowd erupted with laugher.

"Nidok is too square and too sharp to be related to ET," he said into the microphone, and he slowly wiped one eye with his long tongue. "But wait until I get this suit off. We ellls are gorgeous, brilliant and sensitive, with soft, wavy plumes and mossy skin tiles. Very sexy."

For twenty-two minutes the din continued.

Nidok was disgusted. "They treat you like weird hero," he shouted in Conn's ear. "Tell me how you deserve stupid hollerings?"

Conn shrugged. "Charisma, Bug Lips. Charisma. Watch this." He gave Shawne a hug, then a huge, fatherly stage kiss through his helmet. The crowd roared even louder, and shouts of "Conn! Conn!" rocked the platform.

Conn later admitted they would never know if Nidok was upset at being upstaged or whether, as he claimed, the smallness of the shell enclosing the platform got to him, but he started flapping his wings.

It was all Shawne, Conn, Orticon and the human officials could do to duck out of his flight path. As the microphone toppled, he discovered the vent in the top of the bubble. Out he went, flying high over the crowd, then swooping low, "looking for a way back to Conn," he said later.

Conn wondered if Orram was going irrational back at Moonbase. From his 1.28 second-delayed perspective, it must have been a terrifying spectacle. Good thing he had Tandra nearby to keep him focused. "Human crowds love this kind of thing," she would say—but then the pandemonium began.

A House on the Cliffs

Conn—at San Diego, moments later

The crowd panicked at the escape of the wild alien, "Conn's pet." A dangerous exodus began. People took action to protect themselves. Conn, Orticon, and Shawne were forcibly hustled through the tube back to the *Ranat*'s hold and into the ship's land rover. They disappeared from Moonbase's sight.

At first, Shawne and Conn were terrified that Nidok was lost to them, soon to be shot down by security conscious police, if not bounty hunters, but Orticon said he had heard a thump and faint scratches on the top of the *Ranat*'s rover as they left North Island. Driving the Varokian land vehicle, Conn laughed and followed the police escort away from the crowd.

A half-hour later, their security caravan moved into the walled compound surrounding a large old house nestled beneath Torrey pines. It stood on steep cliffs near the town of La Jolla, a secure haven prepared for them by the Southern California Benthic Associates.

Nidok hopped off his perch on the rover's roof, and greeted Conn with a maddening, "Welcome. This be Lodge for Aliens, Brother Elll. What keep you so much long?"

"I couldn't have put it better myself." A burly older man, nearly as tall as Conn, got out of the lead car and offered the elll a warm, two-handed shake, then a hug.

"Carliano, old buddy," Conn said, feeling a huge wave of relief. It took him only a second, clutching his human friend, to calm his tumbled emotions. "Will you join us for dinner? We're having roasted ahlork."

"No one was hurt," Carliano said with a laugh, "but you'll have to keep your ahlork on a leash until the excitement dies down."

Nidok stood looking up at them, saying nothing, *probably wondering what he had done wrong*, Conn thought to himself.

Carliano and the welcoming officials showed their guests around the lodge. Conn found the two-story stucco house spacious and pleasant, with a view of the ocean, a well-stocked kitchen, a deep algae pool, and the annoying presence of a security guard at every corner of the walled yard.

"Escort," the officials graciously explained, "will be provided to Shawne and Orticon as they set up the School for Economic Longevity. SCBA will happily provide whatever you need. Your colleague, Tandra Grey, has recommended the food we supplied. Do tell your entire entourage to stick close to campus for the time being."

For more than an hour, Orticon, Nidok, and Shawne did nothing but stay close together in the living room, talking with Bob Carliano until their nerves simmered down. Conn took himself all around the house and noted carefully the contents of every shelf in the refrigerator.

At last the elll admitted he was exhausted.

"I'll see you later, my friends," Carliano said. "I'm sure you could all use a good soaking in the hot tub. I've left some topo maps for you, including one of the ocean floor, out a few hundred kilometers. There's also a road map of the San Diego Region."

"Thank you so much, Mr. Carliano," Shawne said, "for being here to greet us. I'd better call Mom and Orram. Who knows what they might have seen on the newscasts."

"They've been contacted, but I'm sure that's a good idea, Shawne. We'll be in touch shortly. Good night, Nidok. Orticon, it's a real pleasure to see you again."

Conn escorted Carliano to the door, saw him off, and then walked again around the beautiful house, checking the air and testing the strain his legs felt in Earth's gravity.

"Go slow, Nidok," he said, "go easy on your wings. You'll tire easily here. You getting enough oxygen?"

The ahlork answered by landing on a deck chair. Shawne and Orticon joined him and Conn on the deck overlooking Alligator Head. Like a snaggled tooth, a small point of land curved back on itself in the Pacific Ocean. Conn loved the broad vista over the Pacific Ocean, bejeweled on the periphery with the scattered lights of the city in the turquoise evening glow.

Shawne stood watching the waves whacking against large rocks below the hillside covered with ice plants and dotted with palm trees.

"The city lights in the distance remind me of the deeps of Ellason," Conn said.

"You hardly remember Ellason," Shawne chided. "You left there when your legs were still wobbly."

Later, Conn remembered the remark he had made and found it odd. He almost never referred to Ellason. Was its near approach weighing on his mind? He had never imagined he might want to return for a visit.

More likely, he decided, he was feeling orphaned on this alien planet, Earth, without most of his dry land school—Orram and Tandra, Stringer and Lanoll—his family. He already missed them all. He reached and took Shawne's hand as she stood beside him, and she moved into his arms, trembling as she watched the waves far below. Beside them Nidok squatted on the deck railing, and Orticon stood near him.

We understand one another, Conn thought. *Our family is secure, but Shawne is on a strange cliff here, not really belonging. We brought her to Varok where she learned nothing of normal human society. What have we done to her, raising her there as if she were a varok? How will she handle the hormones that define what it means to be human?*

Conn looked down at Shawne and gathered the waves of light hair in his hands so they wouldn't blow across her delicate face. *Now that she is a grown woman, how is she to live on Varok, unable to mate and bear a child of her own? Is that why she really wanted to come here, back to Earth?*

During the next few days on Earth, Conn busied himself with

"taming" Nidok, while Shawne and Orticon worked out details with SCBA on how to interview candidates for teaching positions at the school. Applications to teach came in by computer link. Many volunteered, and a group of citizens called No-Growth Advocates offered to pay for some salaries.

Most people saw the school as non-threatening, even helpful. Shawne, a human being raised on Varok, drew little attention wherever she went. It was her return to Earth with the famous Conn and his pet cockroach, Nidok, and a varok (someone related to the mixed family) that drew a deluge of responses from all over North America and overseas.

The reponse was more than Conn expected. Most human survivors of the mid twenty-first century spent their daily lives growing and bartering for food, filtering and boiling potable water, and protecting sustenance and shelter from the dominant scavengers: looters, coyotes, crows, and cockroaches. Not many had the means to travel to California to study alien economics. Few understood why aliens should concern themselves with Earth, unless they had ulterior motives.

Cold Pete Dawson

On an island east of Cairns near the Great Barrier Reef, an amateur astronomer spent many hours at his telescope. He had learned there was a new light in the sky, so he watched, night after night.

He realized it was the planet Ellason, expected to reach perihelion near Neptune's orbit. He didn't like the idea, nor that of aliens arriving on Earth about the same time. Were the two related?

He had kept watch for the alien space ship, found it as it orbited, and again when it then changed course over North America. He startled when a small object split off from the ship and moved toward Earth's North Pole.

He mapped its position and concluded it was an alien space pod, approaching unannounced, ready to strike while Earth was in a weakened state and distracted by the official alien visitors.

He used his implanted landcom to call a friend in the North Pacific. Cold Pete Dawson answered.

"Dawson here . . . Yeah, we know they've got a planet coming in. Supposed to turn around near Neptune. No worries, Mate."

The astronomer couldn't get Dawson excited about Ellason's approach.

"That'll wait, I tell you . . . What d'you mean, we've got more immediate problems here? An unidentified falling object, U.F.O. sited near Alaska? Got it . . . Yeah? You say it splashed down just before the aliens landed in San Diego?

"We're outfitted for killer whales," Dawson continued, "but sounds like we've got more interesting fish to fry. You could be right. That nonsense in San Diego was a smoke screen for the real alien invasion."

Dawson listened to the astronomer for a minute. "Well, so what if their plans listed an expedition to Arctic waters. They didn't ask my permission to fish out here." The fisherman's face started to go red. "Don't tell me they won't eat fish and dump alien pollutes while they're—what? Talking to cetaceans? What the hell are *cetaceans*?"

III. LEARNING

"[Listing] ways to contain or overcome . . . the world's 21st-century threats[:] eradicating poverty, conserving resources, reforming the world's food system, raising energy efficiency, and developing renewable energy."

—*World on the Edge: How to Prevent Environmental and Economic Collapse, by Lester R. Brown. New York, London: W. W. Norton & Company, 2011.*

Gimp

Splashdown. In heavy rain, Stringer, Lanoll, Junah, and Jesse Mendleton retrieved the ocean survival dinghy from the *Ranat*'s escape pod, then rode out the storm while munching dried *llaoon* grass.

"What fun," Stringer hollered to Jesse and Junah. "Varok never stirs up good waves like this."

Jesse grumbled something incoherent.

"Dropping the pod into this storm was a good cover tactic," Stringer exulted. "Apprehensive humans couldn't have spotted our entry."

"The pod will wash up on the nearest shore," Lanoll added. "We can track its homing signal later. Are you all right, Junah?"

"I'm staring at the shoreline. Tandra said it would help if—" and she lost her *llaoon* grass snack over the side of the dinghy. "There. That's better. I'll be all right now."

When they had rested, and the winds had calmed to a pleasant gale, Stringer and Lanoll set out in isolation suits to make contact with conversant sea life. They tried cetacean Sonics, Ultrasonics and Elllonian, which was a system of throat sounds in the varoks' audible range. No response. They repeated a simple message of introduction, composed from their limited vocabulary of dolphin signals, then tried whale song.

Junah and Jesse followed their radio signal from the enclosed dinghy. They kept Tandra and Orram, the fretful watchers on the moon, informed with live reports, as best they could.

As the storm moved away, the sea revealed the distant hint of the Aleutian Islands under a clear moonlit sky. Days passed. Stringer recorded the events of their trip, encoding and sending his reports whenever he had a chance to radio Orram and Tandra:

We've had three days of cold swimming, dodging the damnedest stuff floating around here. Yesterday it was cushions from a sitting couch made of some bright, durable synthetic. Often it is oil-soaked bits of past horror from petroleum spills.

The seas are silent, except for the distant hum of shipping vessels. There's a lot of human activity up here.

We have received no answer to our whistles or clicks. I even tried some Ultrasonic probes. This time of year the whales should be up here. And why no dolphins?

Today we are in the dinghy taking a break from our fish diet, which is hardly worth the chase, since the fish are so small. Jesse and Junah are catching more fish with lines than we eells are with speed.

Water is no problem. The photonic water splitter is OK using seawater, so the hydrogen supply will keep us going. Don't worry about us. The isolation suits are tolerable, and we're staying close to the dinghy. Our suits' landcoms are working well, at least good enough for emergencies.

We're checking our Ultrasonics against our tapes of whale and dolphin sounds. We'll add more Sonics to the repeating patterns. Our match is good. We don't think language is the problem. Something else is wrong.

Orram—hours later, on Moonbase

Eight long hours passed before Tandra and I received another encoded message from Stringer.

We've been cruising east along the shores of the Aleutian Islands on the North Pacific Ocean side," he reported. "We've seen a few pods of killer whales, the big black and white dolphins called orcas. They have a crazy beat we can feel through the isolation suits. It has no rhythm, very different from the feel of waves crashing on rocks. So far other pressure signals are too faint to identify. No whales yet. The orcas run whenever they pick up our signal. Smart animals, they seem to know we're strangers—or perhaps they've been hunted.

Stringer—a day later

"Junah, we're picking up a distress call." Stringer hung onto the side of the dinghy as it rode a three-foot swell ten kilometers south of Sanak Island near the end of the Alaska Peninsula. "It's dolphin, high sonar, a whistle. Hold your position."

"Better take the emergency kit. Wait."

Junah disappeared into the dinghy and came back with a small watertight case fitted on a waist belt. Stringer strapped it over his isolation suit and slipped back under the cold waves. With Lanoll nearby at twenty meters, they bounced locator Sonics off the dolphin.

"It's a wounded dolphin all right." Lanoll spoke quietly into her suit's radio, using Varokian. "It's sinking. It will need air. Let's bring it up."

They dove, staying close enough to each other for visual contact. Their combined probe tracked the dolphin's silhouette, and they easily overtook it. The large fluke of the big gray animal was trailing behind, motionless. It was dragging a long metal rod.

Signaling reassurance in their limited dolphin vocabulary, Lanoll and Stringer swam under the wounded animal and nudged it toward the surface. It seemed to understand that the strangers were trying to help. How many times had some dolphins of his pod done the same for their own kind, and for wounded humans?

At the surface, the problem became doubly clear. The dolphin had taken a harpoon. The barbed head was stuck fast, deep in the thickest part of the muscles driving the fluke.

"We can do nothing in this water." Lanoll had reviewed what they knew about Dolphinese, but could only imitate poorly the intricate whistle patterns. "We'll have to beach you, to get the harpoon out."

The dolphin whistled, "Yes. Help," and quit struggling. Stringer scanned the sloping shore and soon found a low shelf of tundra occasionally washed with large waves.

"We can shove you up there on the soft turf," Stringer told the dolphin. "I'll check it out first."

Lanoll stayed in contact with the ailing mammal. "Stringer, the dolphin is too relaxed. I've lost eye contact with him."

"Give him something to eat."

Lanoll offered the dolphin a biscuit from the emergency pocket in her isolation suit, and he opened his eyes in acknowledgement. "I've got contact, Stringer. Let's get him beached."

Stringer rode the waves, waiting for one that would wash him high enough, then he somersaulted onto the shelf to clear away the rocks that lay hidden in the thick growth of sedge and cottongrass. As his dimming lenses adjusted to the sun, he spotted a signal light from the survival dinghy. Junah and Jesse were heading in. Far out, another vessel appeared as a speck riding the waves. Stringer dismissed it as a fishing boat.

Back in the water, beaching the dolphin looked more difficult. "Use your flippers," Stringer urged. "You've got to help." The dolphin either ignored him or couldn't understand. At last a large surge washed onto the shelf, and the ellls managed to brace themselves against the dolphin's flippers and slide him beyond the ocean's reach.

"Anesthetic first," Lanoll advised, as Stringer opened the medical kit, "then warmth. He's in shock. And we'll have to keep him wet. In dry air, dolphins are more sensitive than we are."

"Our wet-sweaters are in the dinghy. I'll swim out and get them."

"Be careful, Stringer. The surf is wild right here. Don't dive. It's too shallow."

"Wild and beautiful," he sang in Elllonian, and entered the water as a wave pulled him under with a noisy splash.

Lanoll shook her head. Though a schooling elll, he was still his father's son. A quieter elll than Conn, but a lover of adventure, Stringer relished every new experience. Earth was not disappointing him.

Soon he came back with the wet-sweaters to cover the dolphin. They were made of a sterilized, tough Varokian moss material, thick and absorbent, designed to provide good insulation when wet. Soon the dolphin breathed easier.

The ellls helped Jesse and Junah pull the dinghy up onto a sandy niche in a stand of crowberries. Toward the horizon, the fishing boat seemed much closer.

Jesse said he didn't like it. "Let's move the dolphin into the drainage over there, where he's not so exposed. Roll him onto a survival blanket. Four of us can carry him. I'll camouflage the dinghy and be right back."

When Jesse returned, the dolphin was made comfortable out of sight and away from the blast of cold wind. "I don't want to alarm you," the human said, "but I'm convinced that our dinghy has been spotted. That fishing vessel may be patrolling the shoreline. Control of the fishing grounds is a sensitive issue here. We know that poachers are ruthlessly hunted."

"We'll be cautious," Stringer said. "I'm glad you said something. I'm not Conn, you know."

Jesse smiled, a rare event. "Indeed, your cannon is not near so loose."

Junah looked puzzled, until Lanoll told her what a loose cannon meant. "A human term reflecting the culture of violence Orticon's so worrried about?"

"Not really," Jesse said. "It implies that someone has an unpredictable nature, like Conn's."

As they talked, the dolphin became more alert, for the local anesthetic had numbed his pain.

"We're going to cut out the harpoon," Stringer tried to explain to him. "Then we'll stay with you for a few days—here—until you heal. I'll bring you fish."

At least Stringer's clicking "fish" got through. The dolphin's eyes shone with a glimmer of hope.

With deft hands and a sharp knife, Lanoll soon had the barbs of the harpoon extracted without tearing more muscle. Sixteen staples closed the wound, and the healing began.

Stringer looked forward to the days, perhaps weeks, of waiting as a restful time. He planned to soak up the cold Arctic air, school with Lanoll and try hunting unfamiliar fish. They would enjoy sunsets over the featureless land, while practicing their cetacean languages.

Though he had never visited Ellason, Stringer surmised that this North Pacific Ocean was like his ancestral planet, with all the moons and bioluminescent lights turned down and more stars turned on.

As planned, he explored the sea floor and rocky shoals with Lanoll, enjoying the richness of the marine life—barnacles and sponges, crimson anemones and moon-snails boring into mussels. They caught polar cod and soon learned to find dark blue-green herring and their sticky eggs on the rocks.

Often Stringer called for any sentient life in the sea. The only response came from three cold-water cuttlefish who raised their antennae in curiosity. Or was it a threat? He answered with a gloved finger, and they darted away.

Orram—meanwhile, on EV Moonbase

Tandra and I heard from Stringer more often while he and the others waited for the dolphin to heal. The same fishing vessel had appeared in the distance every few days. Then, we lost hope for a peaceful time when we received Stringer's last transmission.

Dark Harrahn. That fishing vessel has come in close this time. It's beginning to move along the shore. Jesse did a good job camouflaging our camp. It couldn't have spotted us yet. Signing off.

"Signing off?" I hollered back at the radio.

Tandra put a cool hand on mine. "Stringer's got to do what he's got to do, Orram. He'll radio again when he can."

We went back to work. Tandra expanded our knowledge of conditions in Australia so Orticon would know what to expect. I was trying to understand how the local communities in California were managing water distribution.

I couldn't concentrate. "Why did we let them go off alone?" I demanded of Tandra. She met my mind and shared the angst.

I could see she was torn, wishing we had not stayed on the moon. "I am ready to consider contacting SCBA, Orram. There is room for us in the house they provided."

"Let's give it more time. So far our work is better done from up here."

We continued transmitting information and analysis from Moonbase, coordinated by the Elll-Varok Directorate there. The week that passed on Earth while we waited to hear from Stringer's team strained Tandra's ability to keep me rational.

At last a live radio call came from the North Pacific. "The dolphin is doing much better," Lanoll reported. Trust an elll to worry about her patient above all other considerations.

"What about the fishing boat Jesse didn't like?" I asked.

"Jesse didn't want to take any chances," Lanoll said. "Since it had reappeared so often at first, we stayed radio silent. We're going to stay here a few more days to be safe."

Stringer—days later

The days stretched into eternities, as Jesse and Junah lay hidden, hoping they had not been spotted. Lanoll and Stringer spent a lot of time underwater.

Jesse suggested they avoid using the radio again until they could decipher the odd behavior of the fishing boat, still patrolling the shorlines day after day. "I don't like it. I don't think he's just looking for poachers—or poaching, either one."

One evening, after another week had passed, the fishing boat disappeared around the peninsula to the south. Junah crawled into the beached dinghy to send a short radio message to Moonbase, "All is well."

She realized Tandra and Orram on the moon—as well as Conn, Orticon, Nidok, and Shawne at SCBA—were frantic for news, but she dared not send a longer message. Conn would realize that direct contact was out of the question.

The next morning, the fishing boat reappeared, its crew on deck, scouring the coast with binoculars.

"We're being hunted," said Jesse. "I'm sure now. They've picked up the radio transmission. Take no chances and stay out of sight."

ORCAS

Stringer—days later, a small island in the North Pacific

With his wound nearly healed, the dolphin grew restless. He threw off his blanket of soaked wet-sweaters when he could work his fluke back and forth without pain, and his whistles started in earnest.

"Wait, wait," Lanoll clicked to him, "just a few more hours, until the men in the large boat have disappeared from view for the day." Stringer enjoyed her ingenuity, as she tried every sound she knew to convey the meaning. During his two weeks' recovery, they had improved at communicating.

The four far-north observers waited until they had the cover of dark and a restless sea before they repacked and launched the dinghy. They managed to slide the dolphin onto a survival blanket and pull him down the drainage into the surf. Lanoll and Stringer followed him into the water, while Jesse and Junah headed straight out to sea in the dinghy.

The dolphin agreed to wear a radio tag so Jesse or Junah could stay in contact with him. As non-threatening aquatic creatures, the ellls had no trouble convincing him to school, stay with them under water, and lead them to his pod.

They set off at high speed, the ellls barely able to keep up with the dolphin. He moved his head back and forth, sweeping the ocean ahead, sending out trains of clicks.

Lanoll called the dolphin back, and Stringer broke the surface beside the dinghy. "We've had no luck contacting the dolphin's pod, Junah, so we're going hunting," he said. "We can learn a lot from the dolphin about the local fishery. We'll bring you back a fresh protein dinner."

"Two hours. No more," Junah called, but Stringer was already gone, chasing the fleeting dark shadows of Lanoll and the dolphin beneath the waves.

As natives of the warm ocean planet Ellason, the ellls were well equipped for deep diving. They expected no problems in the shallow North Pacific. However, in the deeper water they soon encountered orcas hunting cuttlefish.

Stringer felt the beat of their presence on his hexlines. It felt different than the single thrust of the large squid they had seen earlier. It was a small pod of ten killer whales, led by one huge male nearly thirty feet long. Lanoll whistled a warning to their dolphin friend, whom they now called Gimp, for the twitch he gave his wounded fluke when he accelerated.

Lanoll's alien whistle caught the attention of the lead orca male, and he left the cuttlefish hunt to go for a larger meal of ellls or dolphin.

"We're leaving. We're leaving," Stringer whistled, but the orca was focused on a dolphin snack. Stringer sprinted for Gimp and stationed himself upright between the orca and the dolphin, looking as human as he could. Lanoll joined him when she realized what was happening.

Relying on the orca's intelligence and good nature, Lanoll whistled, "Friend, friend," with as many nuances as she knew. Stringer drew his long knife from his waist belt and pointed it to meet the orca's throat if he charged.

The killer whale circled them, confused by their conflicting communications, but curious. He watched Stringer lower his knife and return it to his belt. Whistling to his pod, he began circling again, and before Stringer could decide what to do next, the entire group of ten orcas had formed a fence around all three of them, pushing them to the surface.

Lanoll swam with Gimp to calm him. "Act like a human. Reach out to stroke them, Stringer, while I tell them who we are." She began a whistling commentary, explaining that they were visitors, trying to define the ocean's worst problems, when the whine of the dinghy's engine brought Junah and Jesse to the scene.

The family of orcas disappeared. Stringer and Lanoll whistled and shouted Ultrasonic pleas after them, but they could not be persuaded to return.

Lanoll and Stringer surfaced with Gimp. Unperturbed by the engine noise, the dolphin seemed delighted at the prospect of having a small boat to chase. He circled the dinghy faster and faster, trying to stir up some fun.

"Apparently, the orcas were badly spooked by the engine noise," Junah said, helping the ellls into the dinghy. "It's curious that our dolphin was not."

"He's played with Zodiacs before," Jesse said.

Lanoll clutched the side of the dinghy as Gimp raced too close.

"I'll talk to him." Stringer went back in the water, found the dolphin with sonics, and finally convinced him that the dinghy wouldn't play. Gimp's sounds then came in trains of clicks faster than the elll could decipher.

"Try whistles," he urged, and the dolphin complied. Lanoll and Stringer decided on a translation. He had wanted to play earlier, but now did not like being in the water alone.

"Let's find a pod for Gimp," she called to Jesse. "Any pod may do. Dolphins are good at caring for one another."

The ellls swam on both sides of Gimp, slowing him down so they could stay close to the dinghy.

Stringer was trying to convince him to call for his pod again, when Jesse pointed back toward land. "We've got uninvited company again," he said.

The familiar silhouette of the fishing boat was leaving the restless horizon and heading straight for them.

"Don't flinch," Stringer signaled quietly to Lanoll, "but we've got company below, too. The orcas are tracking us."

THE TEACHERS AND ORTICON

Shawne—in California at SCBA

Shawne opened the School for Economic Longevity with a teachers' conference, scheduled to meet at SCBA the week before Orticon and Nidok were to leave for Australia.

She was delighted with the faculty, which included Full Earth and ecological economists, SCBA's representatives, Bob Carliano, satellite data specialists, and two university professors of steady state theory.

The morning shone bright with a blue sky pushing back the morning sea mist. Shawne, Orticon and Conn walked the winding mile along the cliff road between their house and SCBA's Presentation Hall.

"Are you ready for this, baby sister?" Orticon teased.

"You wouldn't believe how ready," she replied. "As long as Conn keeps a lid on his sarcasm. We have twenty teachers on board who are seasoned experts in long-term sustainability. They have been involved in recovery successes in every corner of the world. Some were instrumental in the universal adoption of the Earth Charter. Some have worked on ecoregion directives or modeled balance-of-power concepts—"

"So why did we bother to come here?" Orticon was serious. "What can we add?"

Conn didn't laugh, as Shawne expected.

"The great-fish believed outsiders on Earth could be the catalyst that would trigger some serious listening by those who believe in business-as-usual, those pushing for re-growth."

"You mean humans haven't solved all their problems?" Conn jibed.

Shawne wondered if her family would ever take her seriously. "Stop it, you two. That's why we're having this conference. We'll party first, meet and greet, then focus on the difficult issues."

"The intransigent split in religion and politics?" Orticon asked, "or the imprinting of youth with violent movies."

Shawne's voice took on a confident tone. "Humans know better than to be simplistic about their differences."

At the SCBA campus, the bevy of scholars who would offer courses in steady state topics greeted them. Many knew each other by name or reputation, and conversation flowed freely among them all.

Shawne was inspired by the questions she was asked. When she called the conference to order, she knew exactly how to address the crowd.

"Welcome to a secure future for Earth."

The teachers applauded and a few cheered.

"I'm honored to share this endeavor with you. You have already achieved remarkable progress, with so much of the world reorganizing into ecological regions. Many areas are once again connected by efficient rail service and electronic communication. Its encouraging to see that the Worldnet is still alive with cooperative ventures.

"You in America were the first to build too rich a life. Now you must do better. You know how to become the example to the world you used to be—an example of a much simpler, time-rich life that will preserve and enhance Earth's beauty and diversity for all its natural time.

"Please allow me to introduce our team. My father, Oran Ramahlak, called Orram, is broadcasting from EV Science's Moonbase with my mother Tandra Grey. They are consulting with those hoping to organize the Resources Institute on Earth. Orram was once Governor of Living Resources on Varok. My brother Orticon, who is here with us today, is using satellite data to monitor total resources with Earth's experts. My elll family members, Stringer and Lanoll, the varok Junah and our first human contact Jesse Mendleton are taking data and exploring options with cetaceans in the Arctic. My elll dad Conn—seated in the back with my varokian brother Orticon—will focus on the southern oceans."

Applause. Then Shawne continued.

"This school will focus on the more difficult issues in Earth's recovery—those that require a consensus among citizens, agreement on some basic values, so that regulation can be minimal. In order to further define that focus, I suggest we start by introducing ourselves and presenting in one sentence—"

Congenial laughter erupted in the crowd.

"Actually, two sentences—"

More laughter.

"One: what you feel is most needed in certifying steady state economists. Two: what you feel is most urgent for the public to understand."

Friendly chatter broke out as the teachers greeted each other and shifted their chairs.

"Dr. Chopatia, would you please begin by introducing yourself and your concerns."

A tall bearded man in turban and jeans stood up. "I am Sufar Chopatia, former Relocation Advisor to the Bangladesh flood plains region. Our public continues to believe that technology will find substitutes for what the natural world can no longer provide. They need to understand that technology's only advantage is to improve the efficiency of end resource use."

"Thank you, Dr. Chopatia. On Varok we call it selective technology."

As each teacher got up in turn, Shawne took notes, while Orticon took count. The overwhelming concern focused on population stabilization. Ideas flowed freely: Regulation, all agreed, would never work. It had been tried and failed, both under practical and humane conditions. Enforcement was out of the question. Education and women's rights were known to help. A debit tax on excess children was possible. Tax credits for more children above replacement numbers should no longer be given.

Orticon sat in the back of the room, listening. He sent Shawne a look that said he was amazed at the congenial exchange of ideas. She nodded in agreement.

"Within any economic system we prescribe, we must guarantee our right to privacy in personal family affairs," said the expert in human rights.

"Which includes the right to life of all conceived children, of course," said an older woman.

"What?" Conn reacted. Shawne stared him quiet.

"The government has no interest or right to govern our bedrooms," another person argued, "or our bodies. The suffering of forced child—"

"I agree. The less government the better," said someone from Texas.

"Except where human need dictates," another countered. "We are all in this together, I assume."

"Yes, of course, as responsible individuals."

"According to the ancient dictates we all respect. The Bible instructs us to be stewards of the Earth."

"As does the Q'uran."

"As does the concept of *ahimsa*."

"However, we must use our God-given brains, and accept the fact that much excellent ancient wisdom was written 2100 years ago, by people who had no information about how extraordinary this universe really is."

"Or how complex and unpredictable."

"But the Bible—"

"I'm afraid we're out of time." Shawne was relieved that the scheduled two hours had passed. She had not expected their first discussion to take such sharp turns toward seriously divisive opinions.

She took a deep breath and spoke quietly. "Thank you all for sharing your diverse viewpoints so respectfully. Our awareness of that diversity will serve us well as we develop the orientation and focus of this school."

Everyone rose to their feet, and soon the room was filled with small groups continuing the conversation. Shawne and the team were engaged for the next two hours.

While walking home from the conference, Orticon drew a deep breath. "Whoa. Your faculty will get along fine if they ignore religion—and steady state economics."

"It was all over the map, wasn't it?" Shawne said.

"You realize," Conn said, taking her hands and wrapping them in his digital fins, "that your teachers represent the two basic ideological splits that threaten this world. *Numero uno*—the choice of science or religion as a source of credibility. And two—the sociological split between those who believe in the need for nurturing and those who insist on the need for authority. You've got your work cut out, Sweetie, herding these cats."

"Right, Elll-dad." Shawne answered. "That's why the great-fish endorsed this trip. Ellls and varoks are outside those arguments. You have no vested interest. They believed humans would listen to you aliens."

Orticon disagreed. "But they won't listen, Shawne. Everyone here today had their own agenda. Those who don't want to listen will tune us out. Others, I suspect, will have a lot to teach you about human nature."

"I think you're in for a difficult meeting of minds, if any," Conn said.

"I think I had better stay out of your faculty discussions, Shawne," Orticon said. "These people are still recovering from hundreds of years of war and disaster. I don't want to snuff out any hope you might give them."

Shawne—the next day

Shawne's next challenge erupted during the second day of the conference, in her review of resource management.

"When a consensus is reached on acceptable standards of living in a given area," she said during discussion, "then the parameters begin to fall into place, like the sustainable rate of using nonrenewable resources."

"Then the parameters you mention will all be thrown out of court because of so-called 'inadequate science.'" The interruption came from one of her older teachers, a man well into his forties who had once worked for the United States Environmental Protection Agency.

"Court?" Shawne was confused. "You mean a court of law?"

"You think any of your parameters are going to stand unchallenged?" The sturdy-built man put a broad hand under his red beard. His tone was kindly.

"Why should they be challenged?" Shawne asked. "We are assuming the standard of living has been chosen by consensus."

"Highly unlikely, but we'll let that go for now. The problem is numbers, 'inadequate science' they called it, when the courts threw out the old EPA standards for fine particles in the air."

"I don't understand why such standards were challenged in court," Shawne said. "Surely no one wanted to cause health problems."

"Right. But, you see, Shawne, the court ruled that scientific studies had not proven the precise 'safe' levels for pollutants. For example, it could not be proven that exactly 0.41 but not 0.40 micrograms per cubic meter of a particulate in air caused disease. Therefore, they threw out the EPA standard of less than 0.41 for reasons of 'inadequate science.'"

"That's nonsensical. Causes of disease are a matter of probabilities, not tenths of a microgram. Surely there were data relating chemical exposure with harm, regardless of exact amounts?"

"Yes, naturally." The man nodded.

"And beyond that, we should be talking the Precautionary Principle here—assume harm when in doubt, until you can prove safety. Europe wrote that into law in the last century."

"But we're in the U.S. Because harm has to be proven, the U.S. industry for coal-fired electricity makes higher profits by not bothering to clean up their smoke."

"I don't see the connection," Shawne said. "Please remind me, Mr. . . ."

"My name is Charley, Shawne. Charley Hazard. You see, when specific numbers are cited in law here, the regulations using those numbers can be challenged in court, the same way the air standards were challenged, then thrown out for not being precise."

Shawne felt as if she were drowning. "I had no idea such vicious manipulation was possible in the U.S. courts. Are you ready to propose The Precautionary Principle for adoption here now?"

"Of course. I'm on your side. The right to safety—the need to reduce the risk of damage to the environment or to health—should trump the interests of business."

A handsome woman of fifty spoke. "Government was mistrusted and business interests ruled supreme in this country at one time. It was always cheaper to pollute than to clean up, Shawne, cheaper to dump than to recycle. The new coalitions, the powerful eco-regions, will no longer allow that to happen. The price paid has been too great."

"So we're back to our basic premise," Shawne said, relieved. "We must find the reasonable balance between regulation and consensus. Everyone wants a healthy Earth."

Early that evening Shawne and Orticon sat together on a picnic bench in the small lawn next to the original SCBA building. Not far below, the ocean spread a blanket of water over the Earth, its edges decorated with a thin, restless fringe of white.

They had been to the welcoming party for the *Survivor II*, SCBA's largest research ship. It had just returned from its first survey trip since the *Haemophilus* epidemic that had devastated the California coast in 2062.

"Please do join into the conversation more next session," Shawne asked Orticon, "help me flush out some of these differences among the faculty."

"I can't help you yet, Shawne. Nidok and I need to explore Earth, talk to more types of people. I wish they were all like you, but clearly they're not. We'll do our walk-about on the reefs of Australia, then perhaps I can get involved with your school."

"You're not going to find human nature on the Great Barrier Reef, Orticon."

"Well, give us a break. We'll find someone to talk to."

"Please, don't leave yet. Just one session first, Orticon. Please."

He smiled and a surge of love for his human sister sent him out of control for a moment. "Stubborn human. All right. One session, only one. Two hours. After we know our departure date."

LITTLE KONIUJI

Stringer—in the North Pacific Ocean

"How far to the Shumagin Islands?" Jesse asked Lanoll, as the human gave the blue elll a hand up the last step of the sea ladder. Quickly he moved aside as Stringer shook his plumes dry. Their dolphin friend, Gimp, circled the dinghy, waiting for the ellls to return to the water. Junah stood watch in the broad craft, hoping the dark clouds on the horizon would move south.

"Two hours, three with a head wind. Lanoll and I got a good scan of Sand Point," Stringer said.

"Let's go for it," Jesse said. "If this storm develops, we can lose the fishing rig in the islands. They won't be able to maneuver their big tub in the narrow channels. Love this dinghy."

Stringer whistled to the anxious dolphin. "Follow our boat. You can easily keep up. Keep scanning for your pod. We won't leave you alone."

The dolphin didn't like it. "Killers below. Killers below," it whistled.

Stringer dove back into the water.

Lanoll's temper flared. "That tad is just like Conn. Do first. Answer questions only when necessary."

Junah peered into the water. "He's reminding the dolphin about our laser pens. The orcas won't risk coming too close while the light knives are flashing about."

"The lasers won't do any damage," Lanoll countered. "If they decide to attack and butcher the dolphin, we're as helpless as a clump of *llaoon* grass."

Junah couldn't argue with that.

"Let's get going, Stringer," Jesse called over the side.

The young elll surfaced, shouted in Sonics to Lanoll, and took off due north just beneath the surface, leaping in shallow arcs as he gained speed.

"He'll ride on the dolphin's dorsal fin," Lanoll translated. "Let's go, Jesse."

The varokian survival dinghy took off with a grumble, then settled into its powerful hum, taking the mixed crew toward the Alaska Peninsula and what they thought was the relative safety of the Shumagin Islands.

They made good time, and were soon out of sight of the fishing rig that followed far behind. Occasionally, signs of human habitation appeared on the low-lying shorelines. As they worked north past Simeonof Island into the tortured coastlines of Big and Little Koniuji, Stringer reported that the orcas had not followed them.

Gimp's calls attracted a pod of common dolphins fishing in the warmer waters between islands. They seemed delighted to find human-like creatures that could swim with some speed and execute a decent running leap. There was no problem getting them to accept the ellls' wounded friend.

Stringer made himself understood with the dolphin signals he had learned from Gimp. "We need to rest, out of sight of human boats."

Lanoll joined them in water, and the ellls' rough clicks and whistles attracted the entire pod. They gathered around, chattering translations and correcting the ellls' attempts at their language. Every success brought a leap of delight from the dolphins. Stringer grew alarmed at the commotion and repeated his message about the human boats with a danger warning.

"No problem," came the answer, and the dolphins led the dinghy into the sizable bay called Little Koniuji. Its narrows faced north toward the other Shumagin Islands. There Lanoll and Stringer challenged the dolphins to race. The ellls lost by some lengths. They were busily inventing games when Jesse and Junah sent out an ultrasonic alert: "Fishing vessels have appeared at the western jaw of Little Koniuji. We are trapped in this bay."

"What are they doing?" Stringer surfaced, while Lanoll cautioned the dolphins to stay deep and quiet.

Jesse pointed to the two fishing boats at the mouth of the bay. The boats were moving apart as if to cover the width of the bay where the narrows spilled into the ocean. One was the boat that had followed them all the way from the Sanak Islands.

"Oh my God! Junah, take a look." Jesse handed her the binoculars.

Stringer climbed onto the dinghy and cleared his dimming lenses. "They're laying a net across the mouth of the bay."

"I've got to get the dolphins out of here." Stringer dove back into the water.

"We'll make a run for it," Jesse shouted after him.

Somehow Stringer made the dolphins understand that nets used by such boats were huge. They would be hard to detect with a normal sonar sweep.

"Stay close to the southwestern shore," he whistled to the dolphins. "Run. We'll follow. We can pick pressure patterns off the net better than you can. It will close off at the bottom first. Watch it."

At ten knots, Lanoll was the slowest. While leaping and swimming on the surface, she could do twelve knots for short sprints. There was hope she could just clear the fishing line before it closed off the bay. By that time the dolphins would be well into the open sea.

The ellls had just relaxed into a swift pace, when they sensed a confused schooling pattern in the dolphins. They had stopped running, and the reason was clear. A sonar scan showed the looming figures of the orca pod, the killer whales, hovering deep, blocking their escape.

"Keep running. Keep together. We'll distract them." Stringer's frantic ultrasonic message helped. It needed repeating to keep the dolphins moving out the narrows toward the killer whales.

Lanoll dove and tried a call in orcan Sonics. "Help us, friends. Hunter boats. It's a trap for you, too. Lead us out of here."

The dolphins stopped short of the nets. When the ellls caught up to them, the small dolphins were beginning to turn back to avoid moving toward five huge orcas. Lanoll and Stringer circled them, trying to convince them the orcas would not side with human hunters. Suddenly, the huge killer whales turned and converged on the boats.

"The orcas are ramming the boats. Run." The dolphins heard Lanoll's call and cleared the nets. Gimp was among them.

"Llll-ooo," Stringer sang out, as they all swam free past the rocky jaws of the bay. Turning sharply southwest along the coast of Little

Koniuji, they were soon in open water south of the Shumagin Islands, believing Jesse and Junah has also escaped in the dinghy.

Orticon and Nidok

Orticon—days later, at SCBA, another faculty session

At first Orticon felt encouraged during the teachers' session he led for Shawne. Perhaps he had misjudged the antipathy in the faculty members' opposite world views. As agreed earlier, they spent some time reviewing the advantages of no-growth economics and condensing the list of advantages in such a steady state. All agreed.

ADVANTAGES OF A STEADY STATE ECONOMY

1-An end to overcrowding and its stress.

2-More time for family and personal development.

3-A strong sense of place with handy local business.

4-Needs met with responsible consumption that doesn't damage the biosphere.

5-Democratic workplaces that provide valuable services with more creative jobs, shared so that all who wish can work, while shrinking income gaps.

6-Cities made more livable and efficient with a smaller ecological footprint.

7-Decentralized agriculture that is more efficient, smaller and healthier, less dependent on expensive machinery.

8-Decentralized government, local problem solving, and global government focused on monitoring living populations and material resources.

9-Natural areas and wildlife diversity providing recreation, food and medicines, pure water, and climate regulation.

10-Energy conservation.

11-Investments to improve infrastructure and ecosystems.

After a noon break, Orticon introduced the second topic for the day.

"I am most concerned about the question of water," he said. "One of the reasons we came here was our hope to find a sustainable solution for San Diego. Since the snows have gone—"

A noisy clatter of wings interrupted him as Nidok flew into the room through an open window. Several people jumped from their seats before Orticon could react.

"What is that? Someone get it out."

"That's the halhork. It's got sharp plates under that isolation wrap—don't grab it."

"Nidok, I'm teaching."

"You need packing. We go soon."

"Out, Nidok," Shawne demanded. "It's not time. Tomorrow is the day you leave. Thank goodness," she added quietly.

"Right. Don't be forgetting." The ahlork flew out the window.

"I'm so sorry for the fright," Shawne said. "He won't bother us again."

Orticon continued as if nothing had happened. "Since the snows have gone north, the Colorado River is no longer reliable. Shipping Arctic water will become too expensive as the last of the cheap fossil fuels are consumed. Cooperation is needed to monitor available water and allocate its use."

A handsome older woman shifted in her seat, and Shawne saw her glance at the man, Charley, with a faint grimace. "Many will not appreciate interference in the water trade. Water import is a growing business in this area."

Shawne and Orticon exchanged a worried look. *Just as you predicted, big brother.*

Charley Hazard misunderstood their silence. "There is a long tradition here of rights to water as a commodity to be bought and sold, a kind of wealth," he explained.

Shawne nodded. "By that model, if I am dying of thirst, and you own the water rights, my life is dependent on your generosity, not on my right to live?"

The others murmured in agreement.

"On Varok," Orticon said, "water is seen as a precious silver liquid, to be treasured and conserved with great care for all life. The same principle also applies to the land."

"Are you advocating community ownership?" someone asked.

Charley shook his head no.

"No one owns the land on Varok," Orticon said, "not even the governments. Its use is simply recorded, and exchanged for its care."

"As a faculty," Shawne asked, "are we ready to take such a position on these critical resources?" She looked to the elders, and they nodded, as if to encourage her.

Charley looked grim. "Basic needs for living should trump market interests. Should."

"Indeed, life should trump both fiscal and other selfish interests."

Charley and the elders looked at the woman who spoke out. "Together with water and land, life itself requires protection. The church is firm in this, and we should make our stand clear as well. Abortion must be outlawed from the moment of conception."

"And no morning-after pill?" Charley asked.

"New life is God's business."

"Not at all," others responded. "God gave us brains. He's shouting at us, 'The world is too full!'"

"You should no longer have so many children. You know how. You're in control of your bodies—"

"And your destiny," another person added.

"That's blasphemy. The Bible says be fruitful and multiply."

Orticon locked eyes with Shawne and stood silent.

Shawne knew he would stay quiet now. "It said many different things 2000 years ago," she said, "before the Earth was overpopulated, and babies were born to starve."

"I'm sorry, Shawne, but if population control is part of your solution, we can't be a part of it."

The blood drained from Shawne's face. "It's not control. We can't advocate forced population limits—or forced pregnancies, either. Population limits must come from personal or consensus values—"

The elder woman packed up her papers. Three others left the room with her. The meeting broke apart into scattered conversations. Shawne didn't even try to bring order, and others began to leave.

Charley Hazard stayed to talk with her. "You've got a wide spectrum of viewpoints to deal with," he said. "I wish I could be more involved."

Shawne was visibly shaken. "I wish you could, too."

"I've got a fishing trip to run. Why don't you come along? Clear your neurons."

"I can't, Mr. Hazard. We've just begun, and there's so much to do."

"You'd love it. We go out to a fishery south of Baja. It's known for huge fish, especially manta rays, and many species."

"Maybe after we're established. You're always welcome to come back to the school."

"I plan to. Good luck, Ms. Shawne. Don't let all these arguments get you down."

He waved as he turned and exited the building. Shawne admired the red sheen of his hair as it caught the sun. *Why couldn't they all be more like that?*

Walking home, Shawne turned to Orticon. "I can't believe those people walked out. Could the paradigm changes required by the steady state be such a huge challenge? How did varokians re-define themselves? I never understood that. They had no trouble adopting the replacement-only ethic."

"Shawne?"

"Don't tease me, Orticon."

"Why do you think Orram and your mom are bonded?"

"They share thoughts somehow, read moods almost like two varoks. I don't know."

"Wake up, my adult sister. Varoks are not human. Varokian men are driven . . . not by their hormones. They're driven by their need to establish a mind-link partnership."

"You're saying humans are driven only by sex hormones?"

"That's the theme of every story written on this planet. Look at the elk in the fall rutting season, the boom and bust population cycles of rabbits—"

"Okay. Okay. I'm not in denial. I know I'm human. I grew up with varokian kids, and learned all too soon that I was different. But I need to understand how we humans manage with all that . . . biological pressure. Help me, Orticon."

"You've got to be patient with me, Shawne. I'm not sure I can understand it either."

Orram—meanwhile, at Moonbase

In spite of their disagreements, Shawne's remaining faculty set a date for opening registration and beginning classes. Orticon and Nidok called Tandra and me at Moonbase to tell us their plans. "We will travel quietly," Orticon said, "without public notice."

"Don't be afraid to engage people," I suggested. "There are areas in the Southern Hemisphere that might welcome your input. They have a long history of asking questions on our broadcasts."

"So has the ship's crew." Orticon sounded as eager as I've ever heard him. "We're on our way with Dr. Mark Panhiro and his SCBA research team. He plans to take the *Shearwater*, their oldest and largest ship, on an extended voyage to the southern oceans before the rainy season. We'll help survey the coral reefs."

Tandra was not happy. "Orticon, do you have to leave Shawne? It does seem like a good opportunity for you, but—I guess I worry too much."

Orticon agreed. "It must be difficult for you, sitting up there on the moon, watching us scatter all over Earth."

I could hear Nidok clacking his wing plates. "Who thinks ahlork like water?" he croaked excitedly. "Orram, tame your son."

"You'll do just fine on the reefs, Nidok," I said. "You'll float like a cork in sea water."

"We haven't heard from Shawne today, or from Stringer in several days," Tandra said.

"Shawne's fine, working too hard, but she'll be comfortable with the teaching staff now. The first meeting went well, but she lost a few faculty opposed to birth control. Today we toured the rooms she will be using at SCBA. Everything looks ready to open on schedule."

"How will she begin?" I asked.

"The school will review Varokian history first, with examples of steady state advantages. Specific classes will all emphasize two themes: minimal throughput and ethical commitment. Later they'll look at local carrying capacities."

"Good," Tandra said. "But the school should not avoid the ongoing controversy over the role of government."

Orticon's voice shook. "Her school is a long way from going into those issues, or any that involve religious belief."

"Shawne knows that consensus will be a long time in coming on those issues, Orticon."

"Seems overwhelming, or maybe I'm just tired."

"You need time away to confront your doubts," I said. "Don't hesitate. The Australian reefs are waiting. Shawne and Conn have made a good beginning. We'll be here to back them up."

"So I be fish bait for giant clams, Orram," Nidok complained. "We leave tomorrow."

Shawne—the next day, at the SCBA house

From a local thrift shop, Shawne collected a pile of clothes to disguise Orticon on the trip. She chose a few shirts, jeans, a knit cap to cover his patch organs and a rainproof jacket, hoping he could pass for human.

"If anyone asks," Shawne said, "your family grays early. Some humans do, you know. And remember, you're in your early thirties. You couldn't pass for your real age."

"We don't need passing anyone," Nidok gargled anxiously. "We don't socialize, right, Orticon?"

"Not much. We'll stick to the ship and keep our distance from strangers. We'll be on the ocean, exploring reef life." Orticon looked through the pile and found a pair of shorts. "These would be cool, but my knees would give me away."

"All walking straightups have weird knees," Nidok observed. "Even *ilara*. Even horses."

"You saw a horse?" Shawne threw a light sweater into Orticon's pack.

"I saw horses in hills. People sit in middle, not like daramonts."

"You shouldn't fly so far from SCBA, Nidok. It's not safe."

"I fly high. No one notices."

"Well, in Australia, you stay close to Orticon. Don't take any chances." She pushed Nidok aside to look in the drawer he had pulled out. "Oh oh. We forgot. You'll have to wear these, too, under your trousers."

"Trousers?"

"Pants. Jeans, slacks." She held up a pair of men's underwear, a Jockey style with elastic waist and legs.

"What are they for?" Orticon asked.

"I don't know, but Mom says everyone wears them. Better take two."

"Put them on your head," Nidok said. "Cover warty patches behind your ears."

Orticon gave Shawne a widening of the eyes then turned to Nidok. "And how will I disguise you, friend ahlork?"

"Nidok stays on ship?"

"We're taking the rover. SCBA also has some uses for it on the voyage. But I feel bad, Shawne, leaving you and Conn without it."

"We have bicycles the Friends loaned us, and a boat is always on call. There are some public buses. We'll be fine."

"Just be safe, Shawnoon. Don't take any chances with too much public exposure."

"Speak for yourself, brother varok," she said.

"My patches tell me you are eager to be on your own."

"Not really." Shawne rolled the clothes and stuffed them into Orticon's pack. Then they walked to the rover parked outside. Shawne stuffed the pack beside Nidok, who had hunched down in the second seat behind the operator's couch and navigation panel.

"Keep the rover sealed, especially over water," Shawne said. "The sun here is too hot for both of you, and it will be worse as you cross the equator. No flying free, Nidok. Promise."

His beady eyes looked back at her blankly.

"Promise."

"No Promises," he croaked with a grumpy twitch of his long neck, and Orticon started the power pack. With a nod to Shawne and a signal to Moonbase, they were off down the hill toward the SCBA pier.

Shawne suddenly felt the alienness of them both, as if for the first time. There were no hugs, no good-byes, just the silent assumption of emotion too strong to express.

OLD FRIENDS

Shawne—a few days later, at the SCBA house

With Orticon gone, Shawne and Conn found themselves busier than Conn liked. The public demanded live presentations from the elll so they could ask him questions.

"What the hell for?" he complained. "They've heard it all before."

Reluctantly, Conn agreed to hold public lectures at the school, about water conservation—only. "You're so smart, Shawne, you convince them twentieth-century Western Earth economics is bull."

"Everyone here knows that now," Shawne said. "Their new economic theory includes resource limits."

Conn spoke about perceived water needs and ways to redefine them to be more in line with local reality. His sessions were popular at first, but people interested only in alien-gawking soon drifted away, irritated by the elll's hard-line approach. One day after the lecture, Shawne passed the complaint on to Conn.

"Forget it, Boss-lady," he told Shawne. "I'm ignoring their fuss about lawns and prize flower beds. I told them to get busy and squelch human habits that waste too much water. Roses, smoses," he grumbled. "The San Diego area is semi-arid steppe, not rain forest."

"Their usage is too small to matter. It's the big operations that need to get more efficient."

Conn couldn't argue with that, but didn't let it go. "The cumulative effects of smaller uses could also be very powerful, you know. Let's go for a swim before dinner."

Shawne smirked at his deliberate self-contradiction.

Moments alone playing sound dodge in the lodge pool preserved

Shawne and Conn's close relationship. As time filled with school work, those moments became too short, and visits with their few friends on Earth too rare.

"I'd sure like to see more of you," Conn told Bob Carliano one morning. The elll had called the former astronaut on a whim. "I hope you're not waiting for invitations. They say it's Saturday, whatever that is. You're not teaching or preaching today, are you?"

"Nothing I can't cancel, Conn. I'll be right over."

When Carliano arrived, the morning fog had burned off the shore, clearing the view across Mission Bay to La Jolla Cove. They sat out on the lodge's small deck watching the shallow waves march up to the shore with broad, tiered fringes of white foam.

Shawne came out onto the deck and collapsed into a chair. She looked tired.

"Be good to yourself, Shawne," Carliano said, looking worried. "Earth will take some time to heal, I suspect."

She said nothing.

"You've got quite a view from this deck," Carliano said. "We call that little snag of land out there Alligator Head. La Jolla Bay spreads to the south and curves back on a rocky point topped with Torrey pines. There used to be a lot of large, flat gold fish out there."

"And now I suppose they're gone," Shawne said.

"You sound discouraged."

"I have my rotten moments, all right. I guess it's harder than I expected, getting even our supporters on the same page. We've lost more faculty. It's the Q'uran now. Two people started arguing about what it says about stewardship of the Earth. Then they got into what tribal custom dictates versus what individual integrity means and where Allah is in all this."

"There's an old English saying—you probably know it, Conn, as a student of English slang. Perhaps, 'the honeymoon is over.'"

Carliano offered Conn a cigar and thoughtfully sipped at his beer.

Shawne snatched the cigar from Conn's gloved hand as he pulled off the helmet of his isolation suit to sniff the tobacco. "Cigar smoke will clog your gills, Mr. Elll."

"Hey, young lady, give that back." The elll's eyes narrowed. "It's rude to refuse a gift from an old friend."

She hesitated, and he took it back.

"Put your helmet on. Mom would be furious if she knew you were breathing this air."

"Sorry, Conn, Shawne. I didn't think." Carliano put his cigar back in his shirt pocket.

"Give me a light, old buddy. I've always wanted to try one of these." Conn studied the cigar and put the correct end in his mouth. "I won't pull smoke through my gills, Shawnoon. Promise. Goodbye now." He gave her an affectionate pat on the back that added an unmistakable push.

She resisted and sunk into her deck chair. "Sorry, Mr. Carliano. I need to know what you mean by 'the honeymoon is over.'"

"Well, let's see. You probably realize the size of the task you've taken on. A bit overwhelming I suspect. Right? Call me Bob, Shawne. I've wanted to talk to you. I've heard that your students love you."

"Several have quit, even though we've had a good start in some ways. Most understand steady state theory as it was first published on Earth nearly one hundred years ago. We're building on that."

"And on your image—a human raised on Varok by an elll. I don't see why you turned out so beautiful."

"So what'd you expect?" Conn mumbled, as he wrapped his tongue twice around his cigar. "Light this thing, Bob, my boy."

Carliano found a lighter in his pocket and fired the end of Conn's cigar.

"I don't want you to breathe this side-stream smoke, Shawnoon. Go away, inside somewhere." Conn pulled at the cigar, setting it glowing, and came up coughing.

"Easy. Draw easy, old pal, or I'll be sorry I came."

Shawne smiled. "Ha!" She passed Conn the large bottle of oxygenated water he kept on the side table. "Coat your gills with soot, if that's what you want. I've got some mascara you can add to the edge of your slits to top it off. Should look great."

Conn dunked his face and drew a nose full of water past his gills.

"Sassy, human. Ellls can take anything Earth has to dish out. Bring on the whiskey, Bobby dear."

Carliano's visit was putting an old glint back in Conn's eye, so Shawne went along for the ride, acting the outraged guardian. It was good to see the elll laughing and swapping jokes again. With Nidok and Orticon sailing south, and Tandra and Orram on the moon, Conn had taken on Orram's role as the supposedly responsible supervisor of the family's venture.

Shawne didn't know how to deal with him like that. She was eager to encourage the old Conn to kick up his heels. Maybe cigars wouldn't hurt him. He wasn't that fragile, she thought.

Carliano trapped the emerald gleam in Conn's eyes with a frown. "Seriously, you two, the novelty of aliens on Earth has worn off. You have some real opposition. There are huge profits to be made as population growth regains momentum."

"That's the key, of course, money and overuse—but, in the end, too many humans. You can't sustain anything when the population continues to grow." Conn drew gently on the cigar and closed off his nasal gills. The smoke warmed his throat for a moment and he blew it out his mouth. "Not a bad taste. What's all the fuss about?"

"Cancer, Elll Head," Shawne said.

"Better not smoke the whole thing, Conn. Might make you sick. Just thought I'd satisfy your curiosity."

"Nicotine and oral gratification." Conn put out the cigar with a reluctant groan. "On Ellason there's a weed you would love, Bob. Grows in the shallows near the Viortahk. My friends and I would sneak in there, close to the old Varokian Observation Base, and load up. You could chew it, smoke it, stuff it up your gills—"

"Wasn't that dangerous?" Shawne asked. "There were *eefl* in those waters, and it was cold."

"All the more fun." Conn stroked the dead cigar with his long tongue. "We carried knives and schooled close. We called ourselves the Lethal Wet Knots. I remember one time—"

Shawne touched the cigar and dove into Conn's eyes, until she got his attention. "Anything new in the astronaut business, Bob?"

"You mean manned space shots? No. Not even tourist rides. Serious research will take a while to recoup. Decades, I expect."

"Any new sightings? Theories?"

Carliano glanced sideways at Conn with a smirk. "Some people thought we had a new comet coming in from beyond Pluto. Got the amateurs excited it was so big. Too faint to be icy."

"Such a fuss over home sweet home—Ellason."

"Some think that calling it Ellason is a cover-up, that it's really an asteroid about to ram Earth. Some think it's just a dirty lens. When are you going to do another news release?"

"Not now. Ellason will reach perihelion in Neptune's neighborhood in a couple years. End of story."

"C'mon, Conn. You've got to say something about it publicly again now that it's getting some attention."

"Okay, I'll do another broadcast."

"Are you going out there some day?"

"I'd like to."

"What?" Shawne wanted to believe it.

"It won't be this close again for a very long time, you know," Conn said, "but we'd never get the funding."

"Twelve thousand year orbit, right?"

Conn gave his friend a turn of the lip, his version of a grin. They looked out over the bay and watched the seagulls soar over a sparkling sea.

Carliano turned to Shawne. "What's up, sweetheart? It's not all about cigar smoke, is it?"

"Not exactly. Have you finished modeling Nuevo San Diego and the Imperial Desert, Bob? How many people can this region support—max?"

Carliano hesitated. "The limiting resource here is fresh water, always has been. Without shipping it in from Alaska or going to desalinization, I'd say seven hundred and fifty thousand people, max, with no high-use industry, no wasteful habits. Agricultural exports have to be limited."

"Only seven hundred and fifty thousand?" Shawne paled. "Bob, the population in this water basin is already that high."

"When the World Federation gets tough on population control, we're going to see trouble." Carliano blew a mouthful of smoke away from Conn, but the breeze off the ocean carried it back to the elll. He doused the cigar.

"What do you mean, trouble?"

"Think about it, Shawne," Carliano said. "North America had its share of plagues when the population density was high—COVID, Hemolytic TB, Resistant Strep, Killer Bee Malaria, Cholera—but it never experienced extensive famine like the rest of the world."

"That's because North America could afford the fuel to ship water to its southwest," Shawne said.

"Lifestyles have not changed much here," Carliano mused. "Ethics related to preserving the future haven't kicked in."

"What can trigger a basic shift in outlook, in people who have never seen their own children starving?" Shawne felt she understood at last why Elll-Varok Science had given up and gone home years before.

Conn stood up and shook his plumes. "Enough talk. Time to play."

The lodge overlooking SCBA north of La Jolla Bay was well protected from public view and uninvited access. From there, local authorities decided, Conn would have access to the ocean for daily schooling or whatever ellls did in oceans. In these first months, however, he had chosen to soak in the algae pool designed by the La Jolla Water Garden Club. Until now, he had not entered the surf.

"Let's take that swim you wanted, Bob," Shawne said. "The tide is up, and we could use some exercise."

"You're on," Carliano agreed. "Swimming with Conn at your Moonbase pool was an experience I'll never forget. I would love to see what ellls can do in open water."

"Okay Buddy, you're in for the best water show south of Jupiter," Conn said, and, before Carliano could get his wet suit out of his bag, the elll was off down the path through the ice plants to the beach.

"Conn," Shawne called. "You've forgotten your helmet."

TROUBLE

Nidok—weeks later, with Orticon near Australia

The trip from San Diego to Australia had been uneventful, except for Nidok's complaints about the contamination prevention procedures. The ahlork was very restless, however, so the crew of the *Shearwater* agreed to let him fly most of the way, if he would stay close above the ship. He didn't, so he was ordered to stay aboard.

The ahlork shifted on his talons. Too much sitting on flat boards made his toes ache. When no one was looking he spent some time perched on the ship's railing. Flying was not much fun in his isolation wrap anyway, flexible as it was.

The crew talked with Orticon a lot about Shawne and the school, and Orticon did some laughing, even smiling. Best Nidok could tell, Panhiro said nice things about Orticon's ideas, agreed with saving energy and all that.

The crew used precautions when they caught live critters from the sea. They caught and threw back some ugly ones, after lots of measuring and scraping. Some cuttlefish got a pretty metal tag. Only special fish went to the cook below.

At last, they slowed down. Nidok flew high and saw land in the distance. The sea was shallow here and there, showing reefs that looked like coral, but not quite like the photos Nidok had studied. The color was gone, sometimes too white beneath the water.

At the Great Barrier Reef near Michaelmas Cay, the ship went off on its mapping job, leaving Orticon and Nidok in the Elll-Varok Science rover. They skimmed it like a small hovercraft over the calm seas, stopping now and then to search for healthy coral.

When a storm drove them closer to the coast, they found some shallow waters near island reefs, rich with colorful fish and weird sea life. Nidok floated along with the varok as he catalogued marine creatures.

"Watch your feet. Watch dangling feet," Nidok croaked.

The tip of Orticon's right swimming fin had touched a clam's flesh, and the shell, nearly four feet in diameter, was slowly closing. With one stroke, Orticon coasted away from the clam and secured his mask for a closer look at the bivalve.

"Now sticking head close. It grabs you. Watch." Nidok floated back and forth, staying well out of the clam's reach. He had learned to use the chitinous plates of his wings as effective paddles and the full wings as oars.

"Settle down, Nidok. I'm not suicidal. I'm trying to get a better view inside the clam."

"Well, not so close." Nidok rowed himself away. "There goes green turtle, big as ahlork."

"I'm coming. Hang on."

Orticon glided smoothly after the turtle. "Don't startle him," he called, but it soon outpaced him.

Nidok flapped into the air and circled back. Skimming along the surface in flight, he was blown about by every turning of the warm sea breezes, until he settled onto the clear water and ventured a look under the surface. His isolation suit kept the salt water from his eyes. "Another bommy," he shouted. "Fish there."

Orticon stayed on the surface, stroking toward a small island of blue coral standing alone on the sea floor of white sand. The water was warm and clear, its six-foot depth shallow enough to catch the bright morning sunlight. A huge school of small fish shone like a silver tapestry floating brilliantly in an aquamarine sky. Clown fish nuzzled among the waving fingers of their colorful anemone hosts. A parade of parrotfish in rainbow colors circled the bommy and paused to crunch the coral with chisel-like jaws. A bright fish dressed in blue and yellow rushed straight at Orticon's nose.

"Away. Go away." Orticon tried to wave the fish off, but it was no use. It defended its territory with repeated attacks, until the varok gave ground and swam away from the bommy.

"Ha! Never thought varoks so polite." Nidok had a good laugh.

In their entire trip, the ahlork had never called Orticon names. His insults were gentle prods compared to the free-for-all he enjoyed with Conn.

"Shark! Shark! Orticon, no. Come back."

"He's shy, Nidok. I won't push him too far."

A leopard shark moved around the bommy as Orticon passed above. Its behavior put out an unmistakable message, "Leave me alone." Orticon followed it to get another look.

"No. No, Orticon. No sharks. Go to shallow reefs. Watch blue star fish."

"The sea snakes in the shallows are far more dangerous than any small shark. See? He's gone under a ledge. You need to calm down, Nidok. It's beautiful, all this sea life. If you were to invent the craziest assortment of animals you could imagine, planet Earth would show you six even more crazy and ten more beautiful and 200 more inventive."

Nidok jumped as a passing fish took a nibble at the trailing edge of his isolation suit just behind his left wing tip.

"What's got you so spooked? You were having a good time in Palau and the eastern reefs before we came down here."

"Everything be poisonous here."

"Nonsense. You're well protected from the jellyfish in these waters. Just keep your big lips to yourself and you won't get stung."

"And you? What about raw varok? Good meat for sharks, under isolation suits."

"Nice of you to worry about me, Nidok, but I'm not their kind of food. Let's go back to the boat and relax. I want to start writing up our prognosis for these waters. They're looking better than I expected."

On their way to the far side of the island where the SCBA research vessel was anchored, a black tip reef shark surfed past Nidok, nearly knocking him over with its wake. Before his invectives stopped, another sailed past, then another. Orticon held onto the ahlork as best he could, trying to calm him. Then they saw the attractant for the sharks—the previous day's wet garbage from the resort, dumped from the pier.

"Look, Nidok. Look. Feast your eyes on that collection of fish eating the food waste." Orticon towed the ahlork around the school of hungry fish. "There must be four kinds of shark cruising the edge of the feeding frenzy. What a great opportunity. We'd have to travel miles to see so many different fish. Look. There's an electric eel."

Orticon went on and on, exclaiming over the display, until the food was consumed and the congregation of fish dispersed.

Once back on the boat, the worried ahlork and seasoned, headstrong young varok rapidly agreed on two conclusions: (1) The recuperative powers of Earth's biological systems would prevail. Some form of life would survive the eons. The inventive potential of Earth's DNA pool was healthy. (2) Life on Earth was nothing short of awe-inspiring in its beauty and miraculous in its variety. They were so eager for Conn and Shawne to see the huge clams and brilliant fish of the Great Barrier Reef that they decided to try and bring them back for a visit before the rainy season came to Australia in late November.

Nidok didn't say so, but he realized he and Orticon were gathering impressions of the Southern Hemisphere but doing nothing to adjust to humans. The SCBA crew didn't count, for those humans thoroughly accepted the aliens for who they were, and agreed with everything Orticon said about Shawne's school.

"We better not be meeting humans," Nidok decided. "We love clams better, I am thinking."

Jesse Mendleton—moments later, in the Varokian dinghy

Meanwhile, in the North Pacific, Jesse and Junah's luck began to run out. "We're okay," Jesse called, as he and the varok escaped from Little Koniuji, riding the waves in the dinghy.

With a flash of black and white, great mounds of angry orcan flesh rose from the ocean and rammed the nearest fishing boat. The orcas disappeared and rose again, causing the boat to rock and roll away, unharmed. It was too large for them, so they concentrated on the humans' net, with well-aimed, coordinated pulling and slashing.

The Alcut fishermen hollered and shot at the orcas, knowing the killer whales could easily rip their net to shreds.

Jesse prayed that no bullets found flesh, and was relieved when the huge dolphins disappeared. He knew there was no cooperation between human and orcan hunters in these waters. Humans ate orcas.

With the orcas gone, the fishing boats concentrated again on trapping the alien dinghy. The fishermen held their rifles ready. Jesse saw a huge automatic weapon on the deck of one fishing vessel, and the boat that had pursued them for so long very rapidly came alongside.

"Hold up there, mates," Cold Pete Dawson called from the deck of his ship. "We don't want to hurt any visitors from outer space. That wouldn't be friendly. Come on board now, you two, and you won't get hurt. Where are the others?"

CONN IN THE PACIFIC

Conn—an hour later, swimming the Pacific Ocean near San Diego

While Shawne and Bob Carliano swam at a leisurely pace, Conn cruised ten meters down, near Mission Beach, along a reef made of old construction waste concrete. The elll was delighted with the sea life that had taken refuge there. Barnacles stood sentry against the waves, like tiny volcanoes mimicking their big brothers far up the western coast of North America. Sea urchins threatened Conn's delicate interdigital webs with long spines, and anenomes tucked themselves away from his teasing fingers. He decided to explore the artificial reefs more thoroughly later, alone.

At Point Loma, the land quit where the red and white buildings of a tall lighthouse graced the shore. The three friends turned there and swam back north past the ruins of an old surveillance equipment yard, still marked with a Naval Research sign. There they found a small beach framed with miniature cliffs of sandstone cut by wind and wave. Two families with small children played in the sand. Others explored nearby tide pools. Three hundred feet above, on the top of a rounded hill covered with coastal sage scrub, stood the old lighthouse. Beneath it crouched a small whale-observation shelter.

Conn couldn't resist the chance to show off his elllonian skills. He parked Carliano and Shawne on the beach and went searching for a pod of dolphins. He didn't find any, but his sonic scans located two large gray whales and their calves.

He whistled to the whales and soon got their attention. "Let's have some fun," he said. Apparently they understood him.

Shawne—a moment later

Shawne was the first to see the whales approach, but she did not expect to see Conn with them. When a lithe green figure suddenly broke the surface with a series of leaps over the cruising grays, someone in the small crowd of people visiting Point Loma looked up from exploring the tide pools. "That's no dolphin out there! It must be the elll!"

"It's Conn, being a total jerk," Shawne said. "He's taken off his isolation suit."

"What?"

Shawne ignored the question and jumped down from the sandstone rocks to enter the water from the sand, leaving Carliano to worry about the surf tearing at the point.

"I hope she's a strong swimmer," someone remarked. "Look. Conn has those baby whales playing games."

With a high speed somersault, Conn landed feet first on one whale's rough back and rode him to within fifty yards of shore.

"Get Shawne out of there," Carliano shouted. "Rip currents."

Carliano

Conn swam in on the surf to see why Carliano was gesturing and shouting. Eager hands in the gathering crowd reached out to touch the elll as he stood up in the sand. It was some minutes before Carliano's message got through: Shawne was in the water looking for him.

"She'll be back for supper, I expect," the elll said, and seated himself in the sand.

"There she is now." Those with binoculars shouted. The two female grays were circling around her.

Carliano knelt beside Conn and spoke quietly. "Look, old buddy, I think you should go back out and get Shawne. The whales that pass by here are not as curious and friendly as they once were. They seem to have some sort of group memory."

"Of course they do. Why wouldn't they? They're not dumb, you know."

The human wondered why he wasn't getting through to the elll. "Too many have been pestered by tourists and hunted for meat. They're dangerous, Conn."

"I'm sorry to hear that, but Shawne's in no danger. She knows as much Cetacean as I do, and they'll catch my scent on her. She's got the lungs of a Varokian blow-fish."

"I'm worried," Carliano said. "For me then—go and get her."

"She needs to learn she's not my mother," Conn laughed.

Carliano heard no mirth in the laugh and began to feel desperate. "This is not the time to get stubborn, Conn. She could be in real trouble. She can't fight the current and the whales. You're not on Varok. Think Ellason. Think *eefl*, the predator. Some whales are more like *eefl*, only smarter. They could have you fooled."

"They were glad to see me. We're planning to meet again and make a deal to farm tuna."

"Not now, Conn. Go find Shawne before it's too late." All he could think was that Conn was too alien to understand. He wasn't able to communicate danger to the elll.

"I don't think—"

"What's the matter?"

Conn gathered himself slowly, not sure what to answer.

"Are you sick?"

"I'm okay," he said, slowly rising onto his webbed feet. "I'll go swim with Shawne." He didn't look at Carliano, but shuffled backward through the surf, turned, and disappeared into the first sizable wave.

Conn

As soon as he was under water, Conn sent an ultrasonic ID to the gray whales, and he introduced his calf, Shawne. The whales responded immediately to his call. Their pressure patterns were calm, and their whistling showed some understanding with no hint of threat.

Conn was right. Shawne had never been in danger. She was keeping the whales busy considering ideas for the farming venture.

Conn made his way out to where they circled and joined the conversation. "The humans can help you farm the tuna in exchange for a share of the harvest." The concept of cooperation with humans seemed to take a lot more convoluted signaling and translation, but, when they grasped the idea, the whales signaled their enthusiasm with a coordinated fountain display.

After setting their next meeting time with the whales, Conn and Shawne headed for shore. They had gone less than a hundred meters when the elll fell behind.

"I hate to be an interstellar sad ass," he called, "but I'm in trouble. Not sure what's wrong. I'm losing pressure sense."

Shawne—a second later

Shawne swam to him and echoed the alarm in cetacean Sonics. As she surfaced for a breath, an older female gray whale appeared and offered her dorsal fin, as if she understood the problem.

Conn's unfocused demeanor grew more and more alarming. Shawne had never seen him so obtuse. His temper, like an antidote to trouble, might explode, but it rarely fizzled. Never like this.

The whale refused to take them closer than fifty meters from shore. "Too much smelly stuff in close," she clicked.

Conn waved the whale off. Shawne headed toward shore, expecting the elll to pass her, but she soon missed him and turned back—too late. A strong current had pulled her to the north, away from Conn. She called to the whales, but they were gone.

THE ALIEN EFFECT, SEPTEMBER 12, 2068 C.E. The first wave of nausea came without warning, and Conn lost everything he had eaten. It disappeared into the voracious sea. He swam hard, trying to escape the gnawing in his gut, then he could no longer swim. He drifted in a curled position, as if he were an embryo back in the egg. No pain he had ever experienced came close to this awful feeling. The ache surged, and surged again, and he hoped to die, anything to stop the pain. With explosive force, his waste voided and a sharp pain seared his cloaca. He saw the yellowish tinge of blood in the white excreta, then the worst of the pain was over. Feebly the elll worked his fins, trying to get to shore, then he lost consciousness.

Shawne

Shawne let the current take her, then edged south to escape its pull. They had been swimming south along the coast and were approching Point Loma, some miles along the shore from the SCBA house cliffs. When she returned to the spot where she thought she had left Conn, he was nowhere in sight.

Cursing her lack of sonar, she began to swim back and forth on her way to shore, whistling her ID, calling for Conn. Many times, in the Forested Sea on Varok, she had called him with that whistle, and he had always responded within seconds, bellowing in Sonics so she could hear his approach. Now she heard nothing. She saw no sign of him in the murky water or the foaming surf.

Too much time had passed since the whales left. She knew she was tiring, and she was feeling the cold. One last zigzagging pass with the surf, dodging rocks, and she let the waves beach her.

Strong arms supported her as she stood up. Carliano was crying with relief. A crowd had gathered on the small beach.

"It's okay," she said. "I grew up with ellls. Early on I had to learn my limits. Where's Conn? He must be laughing his head off."

"We thought you were together. Last we knew you were both riding toward shore with a gray whale. But that was more than a few minutes ago." Carliano forced a smile as he wrapped Shawne in a borrowed towel. "It's good for Conn to have some time in water. It's been a dry six months for him, hasn't it?"

Shawne's imagination began to stir. "No, not really. He spends a lot of time in the pool at the house." She remembered the silence following her calls to Conn. "Bob, Conn wasn't feeling well. He always answers me in water. He would not disappear this long without telling me."

"You look pretty cold. Better wear a wet suit next time."

"Conn should have kept his isolation suit on. It left him without an emergency radio." Angry at his stubbornness, mad at herself for giving in to his yearning for open water, she found strength to act. "Let's find a dory and make him come in."

"It's a long walk to the next pier," one of the onlookers volunteered. "There's only Sunset Cliffs to the north."

"I'd better go for help," said Carliano, and he set off, hoping to find a boat of some kind.

"Does anyone here have a car?" Shawne asked. "I don't think we should try to swim back home. Conn isn't feeling well."

No one had a land vehicle, but they knew the bus schedule. It was past time for the peak gray whale migration, so there would be infrequent pickups at the visitor center on top of the hill, beyond the old lighthouse.

"Is there a path up the hill?" Shawne asked.

"Over here, Miss."

She followed a young boy past the sandstone shelves, up the hill, and a short way into the sagebrush. She found the bus schedule tacked to the door of the visitor center.

As she made her way back to the beach, Shawne saw several people working in the surf, trying to keep something away from the sharp rise of sandstone rock that caught the waves and tossed them into breakers. Two men lifted a body and pulled it away from the rocks, then carried it from the water. It was long and limp and gray-green.

"Conn!" Shawne screamed and ran, joining them just as they lay the elll gently on the small sand beach beyond the reach of the restless water.

Carliano came running back and bent over Conn's limp body. It had turned a nasty shade of grayed chartreuse. "I don't know what to do, Shawne." Carliano's anxiety distorted his face. "CPR? What? What do we do for an elll? He's unconscious. He's not breathing."

IV. Unexpected Wrinkles

"We humans are hard- and soft-wired with genetic and psychological programming that can make it very difficult for us to undertake costly short-term behavioral change in order to avert future catastrophe. . . . On the primordial savanna, we got a hit of dopamine every time we discovered a tasty root or bagged a prey animal; today, stock trading lights up the same brain circuitry."

—*The End of Growth: Adapting to Our New Economic Reality by Richard Heinberg. Canada: New Society Publishers, 2011, p. 261-2.*

More Trouble

Orticon—at the Great Barrier Reef

"I am curious about the resort on Green Island," Orticon said. "Before we begin to work our way north, I want to spend a night there. Could I pass for human?"

"Not without a new hairdo," the SCBA Institute captain, Panhiro, said with a smile. "I like the silver streak-job, but you know—"

Orticon appreciated his gentle humor and the low-key manner in which he ran the expedition. The aliens were a bonus, as far as the captain was concerned, worth any inconvenience. Their observations had already been helpful to the ship's oceanographic studies.

"I can cover my patch organs with a hat."

Nidok flexed his wing plates in anger.

"What?" Panhiro offered Nidok his chair back to perch on. "Why do you care if Orticon covers his mind-readers?"

"Funny, funny, salt-water human! I don't like Orticon alone on nasty island."

Orticon's face broke with a chuckle. "You're well protected by the crew running this boat, Nidok."

"I don't like fish, eating garbage. Sharks there."

"Don't be angry. I won't jump in with the garbage. And you, don't go ashore. You've made lots of friends on this ship."

"True. Not true," Nidok said, flapping his wings as if to shake them clean. "I don't like poison brown snakes. I don't like boats that follow."

"Understandable." Orticon caught the thought.

"Someone follows us."

"I don't think so. No one knows we're here."

"They follow this boat." Nidok raised a wing and waggled its prehensile tip to the north.

"Okay. I'll give you that," Panhiro promised. "I'll check out your suspicious boat."

After the captain called in a reservation for a room at the Green Island Resort, Orticon spent a restless night, unable to sleep. In the morning he practiced speaking in English and agonized over how to present himself. Maybe he could be a student. No, a recent graduate.

Late the next afternoon he disembarked at the Green Island pier and checked in at the resort's front desk. His room in an aging shack was one among many, set back from the pier and separated from a large common restaurant by chipped flagstones and palm trees. He felt odd in borrowed tourist clothes, a stocking cap pulled down over his patch organs, but he enjoyed imitating Carliano's relaxed saunter. Though still feeling nervous, he did enjoy hiking the trails that wound through the trees and around the island following the shore.

When he entered the restaurant, no one turned to look at him. Good. So far no one suspected he was not human.

His table sat against a window facing the pier. The SCBA research yacht lay at anchor well away from exposed reef that extended far to the north and west. As the sun set, it sent a pleasant glow through the simple, square room. One by one the elderly couples at the other tables finished eating. Some of them stopped to chat with the newcomer on their way out.

"So you're a student, from . . . where?"

"From Uzbekistan. I'm sorry. My English is not clear, I know."

"Our son was at Harvard. The medical school. A doctor like my husband here. Of course, we're retired now. Have a pleasant stay."

"Good day."

"G'day, they say here." A pleasant laugh. No aggressions, not even any suspicion.

Then pleasantries from another couple and the next, each mentioning what their children were doing, then where their next tour package would take them. No one responded when he said he was studying nudibranchs for the SCBA Institute.

Orticon's patches told him the tourists were tuned closely to their families, to their health, to their need for confirmation. In spite of the recent disasters and loss of life, there were still people who could travel half way around the world for pleasure, openly assuming their right to an unequal share of global wealth. He saw their great capacity for seeing what they needed to see, for hearing what they needed to hear. And he recognized, with a flush of shame, that his judgment was harsh.

As he finished eating, Orticon saw a small fishing rig approach SCBA's research ship. The fishing boat ran alongside, then cut across the bow and disappeared on the other side.

When it did not reappear, Orticon grew alarmed. He hurried to his cabin and called the SCBA yacht. "Tell Nidok to stay out of sight,. He may have been sighted. Watch out for the small boat on your port side."

Panhiro sounded concerned. "We see it, Orticon. It's heading east to the outer reef. Is everything okay there?"

"Yes. I'm a nonentity here. I'll stay the night and do some more sociology tomorrow morning. Can you pick me up at ten a.m.?"

"Enjoy the morning garbage feeding frenzy. I'll keep Nidok below."

In the morning the sun shone bright on the quiet sea. The air was heavy and warm. Orticon sat beneath the palms with a banker from New Zealand and his wife. He had problems staying silent when they began talking about the huge comet about to pass by Earth. It had something to do with the aliens in San Diego.

They were so pleasantly interested in him, he found himself blathering something about a crewmate's drive into the country above Cairns, how he had mistaken black parrots for ravens perched in trees beside the road. Some bird watchers he met later had been looking for them for two weeks, but he didn't dare tell them.

"He must have been in the outback west of Cairns, young man," the wife said. "There's marble out there, and turquoise."

"Now's your chance," the banker agreed. "With the population down and everyone scrabbling for a living, the market is wide open for the taking. In a few years, you'll be a wealthy man, if you can put a few dollars into good land now."

Orticon didn't know what to say. The concept was alien to him, but not unfamiliar. He had studied Earth's marketing system, the so-called "bottom line"—immediate profit or payback within three years, with little thought for resource depletion. In spite of all his hours studying human economics, he was shocked to experience such unethical greed so blatantly encouraged.

"I can't . . . take advantage . . . I don't have extra money," he said, "but I'll keep your suggestion in mind. Excuse me now. I see the research boat has come for me."

"Good luck then, son."

As Orticon moved toward the pier, he heard the banker's wife ask her husband about "that peculiar young man."

"I think he must have had a childhood disease," the banker said in a whisper that carried to Orticon in the still air, "or one of those genetic abnormalities."

Orticon pulled his cap down and hurried on to the docks to meet the *Shearwater*.

Nidok called to him from somewhere on deck. Orticon found him folded into a compact square underneath the survival dinghy wild with fear. "Boat is back. Boat is back."

"Have they seen you, Nidok? Have you stayed out of sight?"

"Out of sight. Out of sight."

"Then we're okay. Just ignore them. On Green Island no one guessed I was not human. Panhiro plans to work north to the Melanesian reefs, then head east to San Diego. We can go straight back to SCBA then if you like."

"While boat hangs here, all ahlork flights cancelled."

"I'm afraid so."

"My wings will rot. Plates fall off."

"Life is rough." For the first time, Orticon was tempted to throw out an insult, Conn style. But he decided not to start the exchange. He didn't want to alter his relationship with Nidok while it was working so well. "I will call Tandra and Orram now. They will want to hear about my visit to Green Island."

They did, but then they started asking questions about Conn. Had Orticon heard from him or Shawne? They hadn't heard from either one. It had been almost an entire day.

Conn—on the beach near Point Loma

Conn opened one eye when he heard Shawne cry his name.

"Watch out," he groaned, and he rolled onto his side and coughed out onto the sand all the seawater in his lungs. "Better. That's better. Get me home, Shawnoon. Call Tandra." With that, he collapsed again.

"Oxygen. He needs oxygen." Shawne looked to the crowd of humans.

"There's a first aid station at the lighthouse," someone said. "Be careful cutting through the sage. Watch out for prickly pear cactus."

Carliano was off at a run, followed by two young men.

They had to break into the lighthouse, but the young men, experienced in diving these waters, knew where to find a portable oxygen tank. Within an hour, Conn was breathing oxygen and enjoying a stretcher ride to the bus stop.

Shawne was adamant. "No hospital. They wouldn't know what to do. He needs to be home in his bathtub, with clean water."

Carliano didn't like the way Conn looked. What if Shawne didn't know how to fix the elll?

Lanoll—meanwhile, after she and Stringer escaped

The orca's message was clear: "Fishing boats won't come out this far." The big black and white dolphins dove to feed, and Stringer and Lanoll were left alone in water too cold for long exposure without swimming. They had no idea what had happened to the dolphins. Their dinghy was simply gone, along with Junah and Jesse and the long-range radio they needed to call Orram at Moonbase. They swam to the nearby shore and wrapped themselves in wet-sweaters, then nestled into the deep grass out of the wind.

Stringer was full of ideas Lanoll did not want to hear. "Let's go back to the fishing boat. We could climb on board and introduce ourselves as cute, fuzzy aliens—then wait our chance to get away in the dinghy with Jesse and Junah. That must be where they are."

Lanoll shook her head. "I think it was guns we heard firing as we swam past the nets. Loud guns." She hated the knot she felt behind her gills. Stringer's imagination was not helping.

"Sure, they would lock us up, but they wouldn't shoot us. They couldn't keep us long."

Lanoll was tiring of the argument. "That's no option, Stringer. Someone went to a lot of work to follow us and gather more boats to set that trap at Koniuji. They're not friendly. They probably saw the pod come in and are bent on capturing aliens."

"I do remember the old human movies I've seen. Many of them are about alien invaders as bloody horrors from outer space. Even cute, friendly aliens are captured and threatened, but that can't be real."

"There's a reason for it, Stringer. Those plots are credible to humans, or they wouldn't have been re-broadcast all these years."

"You think those fishermen are really afraid of an alien invasion?"

"Either that, or they want to capture us for some money-making scheme. Think of Ellasonian history. Remember how many ellls were captured when the varoks first came to Ellason? It took hundreds of years—Varokian years—"

"I don't need a history lecture, Lanoll." Stringer vented his frustration with a blowout of his nasal gills, then his good faith in life surfaced again. "Look, we can convince them we're the good guys— friendly aliens here at last, here to save humans from their path to oblivion. We've been broadcasting from Moonbase for years."

"They might believe that. But of this I'm sure—getting captured will help nothing."

"So what in hell do we do now, Mom?"

Lanoll smiled. Stringer didn't often use the mammalian word, *mom*. He had picked it up from Shawne. Lanoll loved it.

"For one thing, you quit using your father's language," she said, quickly putting down her rush of emotion. "The word *hell* might offend someone. I think we had better convince the orcas to take us full speed south to San Diego. You need their school, and we both need warmer water—soon. Alone, there's nothing we can do for Jesse and Junah, even if we could find them."

Heading North

Orticon—a day later, on the ship Shearwater sailing northwest

Orticon turned away from the radio receiver. The news tore his emotional control to its limit. What could he do? They had to get back to Conn and Shawne, but they were far out at sea again, scheduled to travel even farther from San Diego.

Otherwise, the trip had been thoroughly enjoyable. Panhiro and his crew had expressed attitudes toward the future that surprised him—they were as concerned for Earth and the impact of human society as he was. They were also concerned with the news of Ellason coming so close. Reports were exaggerated in the press.

"We must go back to San Diego now," Orticon told Panhiro. Our rover is able to make the trip. It was made for long-distance excursions."

Captain Panhiro no longer sounded mild and accommodating. "I am not going to let you go north alone in that hovermobile of yours. I understand your eagerness to tell your friends about the Great Barrier Reef. Perhaps you would like to go on the next SCBA expedition. It's scheduled for our sister ship the *SeaDuckII* within the month."

"I'm not being clear. We have no choice, Captain. We've just had a message from SCBA. Conn is ill."

"I'm awfully sorry. Still, I tell you it's not safe to travel that far across the ocean in a small craft."

"We can head for the small islands south of Baja. A fishing guide to that area was in one of Shawne's early meetings."

"Oh yes, Charley Hazard. He's done some counts of Baja ocean life for SCBA. He's interested in what the school is trying to do, but has expeditions to lead. Soon, I believe."

"There's more. No message has been received from our team in the North Pacific. We must get back to San Diego."

Panhiro finally agreed that Orticon and Nidok could leave the *Shearwater* if they headed northeast to the islands in Charley Hazard's fishing waters, before they tried to go on to San Diego.

The seas were calm when the *Shearwater* made its way east, leaving Orticon and Nidok to head northeast. They skimmed along rapidly for several days before the sea grew rough, then rougher. Storms

marched past, one after the other, until the small hovercraft was reduced to pitching helplessly for days, making little progress across the
ocean surface.

Nidok—in the Varokian hovercraft

On the tenth day, the rover sputtered and settled onto the churning
sea, dead in the water. Orticon's caramel complexion turned the color
of birch bark, but he maintained control.

"Here. Here. Lie down. Head down," Nidok gargled excitedly.
"Varoks can't faint. Too dangerous. Your brain dead or we wouldn't
lose all fuel."

"You got that right, Nidok. We need another drive pack. The seas
of Varok are nothing like this. The storms ate up our power. I never
expected . . . this."

"Stop talking. You lose blood from face again." Nidok took off from
the rover's bow and circled high overhead to settle his nerves. His eagle
eyes raked the waves in every direction, as the Pacific Ocean heaved
and broke into white caps far below. He circled once more, and then
flew off to investigate a line of breakers to the north. Tall white clouds
were boiling high and growing darker. The wind caught him, tossing
him off course, but he headed into the gale long enough to see that the
sea was broken by a small island, sitting as if alone in the immense
ocean, just north of the rover.

Orticon

Hours had passed by the time Nidok found the rover again. Orticon
was nearly irrational with fear for the ahlork's life. When the irritating
beast landed with a loud thump, Orticon cried with joy and let himself
indulge the emotion for a moment. He tried to set the ahlork upright,
but Nidok's wings got in the way and Oticon cut himself on one of the
ahlork's chitinous plates.

"Sorry. So sorry," Nidok whistled. "Ahlork lips dry."

Orticon collected a cup of water from the keel reservoir and poured
it toward Nidok's lips. Most of it flooded his air intake, and he snorted.

"That's all. Okay. Enough. Turn your brain on, Orticon. There is
small island one long flight north. There someone can find us. I pull

rotten machine to safety. You fix rope, eh? Wing tips not so good for tying knots."

"Don't you realize? I thought you were dead."

"Not dead, just blown around like empty bottle, empty plastic bottle. Strong nasty winds. There better now. We go to island."

"You stay here with me. I'll row. We have plenty of navigation gear. See? Here, on the chart. The island you saw must have been one of the Mexican Islas Revillogigedo, probably Clarion. We're right on course."

"San Diego too far. We go to island I see first."

"Right." Orticon secured a rope over Nidok's frame and around the base of his wings, and they were off.

"Lower," Orticon called. "Fly lower. You're tipping me out of the rover. I can't keep the oars in the water."

Nidok croaked with laughter, but he flew lower as requested. More than once Orticon had to argue him into changing course, for the winds were blowing them well to the west of the islands. The Mexican coast was too far to the east to be helpful.

Before the small island came into view, Nidok grew exhausted fighting the increasing winds. One wing cramped, and Orticon saw him tilt and swoop dangerously close to the water. Pulling on Nidok's rope with all his strength, the varok managed to bring him overhead until the ahlork dropped into the rover. "Can't. Can't," he croaked.

Orticon rearranged himself so Nidok could rest. The rover heaved and rolled. Both wind and current worked against them. The oars Orticon had used to temper the craft's thrashing about felt useless in the young varok's hands. He berated himself again for the lack of a spare power pack or backup radio. Orticon wanted news of Conn. No use. The storm was closing in. Tandra and Orram would begin to worry, up on the moon, without word from him. So would his family in San Diego.

He had no idea how long Nidok slept while they sat anchored, but at last the waves settled down. When Nidok awoke, he insisted on taking the harness again, but he was not laughing as he pulled the rover over the last half mile to the island.

"Nice ride, Nidok, thank you," said Orticon. "This is a good place. Pull here onto the south side of the island."

Together they beached the rover, then engaged the wheels and pulled it well above the high tide lines.

Nidok perched on the rover's bow and looked around. "What is that mess?" he asked, his polished beady eyes aimed at an abandoned wreck on the shore nearby.

"Hard to tell," Orticon said. "I suspect it's an old tuna fishing boat."

"Why isn't wood mined?" the ahlork asked, thinking of the ahlorks' recycling profession on Varok. "And that?" Beyond the wreck, a few small buildings nestled in thick vegetation against a hill the shape of a large watermelon.

"That is hope," Orticon said.

"Hope does not fill stomachs. I look for dinner. I be tired of dry crackers."

Nidok sailed over the island and disappeared behind the tallest hill, while Orticon hiked up the gentle slope toward the buildings. A light rain blew in the varok's face, and the strong smell of salt air whetted his appetite as he dropped off the hill onto the north side of the island. *Even a crunchy salt beetle from the Forested Sea would be most welcome right now,* he thought. *I have never been this hungry before.*

"Hola," a voice cried out.

Spanish. Of course. These islands belonged to Mexico. Orticon felt helpless. It had been some time since he had used Spanish at the Concentrate during his Impression of Human Languages.

"Hola," he answered. Two men were heading toward the beach. They wore earth-colored uniforms, and Orticon sensed they were not interested in him.

Help, Orticon thought, *What is the Spanish word for help? Yes.* He remembered, as the two men reached a small rowboat and began to push it into the surf. "Socorro," he yelled. "Socorro, por favor."

The men waved and pushed off into the surf.

"Si. Socorro. Si. Adios, Yank."

They rowed hard against the noisy wind, pulling their skiff to a small navy vessel tied at anchor in the northern bay.

"Oh no." Too late Orticon realized his mistake. These were the Socorro Islands, sometimes called the Mexican Little Galapagos. The man thought he was a fisherman pausing here before he went on to the largest island, also called Socorro, which lay several hundred miles to the east.

Orticon walked along a path through the dense scrub, until he came to the group of small buildings he had seen earlier. It was a weather station. No one was about. The buildings were locked. He and Nidok were alone on this tiny island, and their help was already out of sight.

Coming Clean

Orram—a day later

When Tandra and I pried the news of Conn's "accident" from Shawne and Conn, we knew immediately what had happened. He had been thoroughly contaminated, his hexagonal tiles, gills, and sensing lines—like lateral lines in fish—thoroughly clogged.

There was no way we would stay on the moon with Conn facing such a long, dangerous recovery. We left Moonbase within the hour.

During our trip to Earth, Bob Carliano sent a brief message. "The radio call announcing your arrival has been intercepted. Expect a welcoming crowd. We'll have security waiting for you."

Our crew of two varoks landed the *Lurlial* at North Field in San Diego, and parked it next to the EV spaceship *Ranat*. As Tandra and I drove the ship's land rover *Nalkah* out of its docking bay, we found ourselves surrounded by a sea of people. They didn't look friendly. Many were armed.

I made a good guess. These were the people who feared Ellason's approach, feared an invasion. We had been amused; now we were alarmed. Human reporters and TV news had played up Ellason's size and the eccentricity of its orbit.

Tandra opened the rover's top and stood up. "It's only us, Conn's family," she shouted.

A shot sounded, and she ducked back inside the rover. We turned on our sound system and stayed inside our reinforced vehicle.

"Conn is very ill," Tandra continued through the *Nalkah*'s external speakers. "We've brought an elllonian cleanser for him from Moonbase."

Sympathizers in the crowd converged on the reactionaries. "It's

Tandra and Orram, you fools. Don't you watch the Moonbase broad-casts? Out of the way." There were other cries of support, and no more shots were fired. We were able, slowly, to move the rover toward the highway.

"We're okay. Get ready for launch," I radioed to the *Lurlial's* crew, who were already preparing to return to the moon. I left the outside mike on to confirm our good faith. "The spaceship's leaving will de-fuse the people who are worrying about invasion. No sightseeing this trip. We've got to get to Conn."

As we watched the *Lurlial* move from the landing strip to the launch pad, I felt Tandra's mood shift from concern about Conn to fear of hu-man intransigence. We moved on to the highway, only to be stopped by a police roadblock. Tandra's fear was like a tidal wave washing every-thing else from my mind.

"Stay in your . . . car. Identification please." The voice came from a bullhorn.

"What does he want?" I asked Tandra.

"Your driver's license." She choked, then settled into my mind for support. In spite of our frustration and the eruption of her histori-cal fears, our mental bond worked to calm us both. "Show him your Varokian Maintenance Share Tag," she said.

I held my arm out of the *Nalkah's* front window, and a policeman approached slowly. He looked at the small plate I held in my fingers, checked my face with the holographic image in the center of the plate, and backed away with a queer look on his face.

"We have a medical emergency," Tandra pleaded. "Conn, the elll, is our . . . responsibility. He is critically ill, and we have medicine for him. We are Tandra and Orram from Moonbase. You've seen our broadcasts, sponsored by the Elll-Varok Directorate there, I'm sure."

"I recognize them, sir," another policeman said.

"Please," Tandra added, "we need a police escort to get to Conn, ASAP."

We heard the *Lurlial* start its launch engines. The anti-alien crowd running toward the spacecraft stopped in their tracks to watch.

"Follow my car." A huge bulk of a man in uniform approached and leaned over to peer into the rover. "We'll get you there."

"Thank you, sir," I said, taking Tandra's cue.

My alert patches sensed Tandra's thoughts flash back to an early

21st Century movie car chase, as we followed the police car to the lodge overlooking Alligator Head—sirens screaming, lights flashing around us all the way. At the door, we got out of the vehicles. The two officers seemed reluctant to leave.

"You would be most welcome to visit the elll later," Tandra said, "when he can thank you in person."

They followed us into the house. "Thank you, ma'am, but we'd better stay now . . . for security reasons," the big one said.

Before Tandra came apart with her overload of worry and distrust, Carliano came to the door and diplomatically ushered them out, then sent them on their way with a firm "thank you."

We found Shawne pouring dish soap into the bathtub. Water overflowed into the safety drain. Only Conn's tunic plumes showed on the surface, streaming toward the drain like strands of golden kelp. Carliano sat down on the toilet, obviously feeling helpless—blaming himself.

Shawne's tears poured down her face as she ran into our arms.

"Mom, he's got to take another load of detergent into his lungs," Shawne said. "No more excuses, Conn. Orram, he's still got oil down there."

"Tandra." Conn sat up and reached for her. His voice was reduced to a bubbly croak. "Orram, you traitor, you shouldn't have brought her down here."

"I couldn't stop her," I said. "She would have stolen the *Lurlial* to get here."

"Come here. Give us a hug, Lady."

"Wait a minute." She drained the tub and refilled it with clear water. "We've brought some solvent from the medical supplies at Moonbase."

As I poured the cleanser into the water, Tandra stripped off her flight suit and slid into the tub next to Conn. "Hand me your head pillow, Shawne. There." She gave Conn a soapy nudge under the chin. "Now, do as you're told. Flush your lungs out again."

Conn smiled weakly, the first smile Shawne had seen since his accident, she told us later.

Our beloved elll sank into the powerful solution. I couldn't contain a gasp as he erupted from the bath, voiding gray liquid from every orifice and sloshing it all over the floor. Tandra braced his head while he leaned over the bidet to expel more.

Carliano was ready with the mop.

"How long has he been in the soap bath?" I asked.

"Too long," Shawne said. "It's not clearing out of his moss tiles as we hoped it would. Your stronger solvent had better work."

"I think it's similar to what humans used for oil spills early this century. It's been used for years on Varok, for ellls who get into bad water in the sunken ruins."

"It's my fault, Orram," Shawne said, her mind tortured with self-blame. "I never should have let him swim the ocean without his isolation suit. Even the gray whales have sense enough to stay off shore."

"I'm not sure we could have stopped him," Carliano said, "once I gave him the excuse. He was eager to explore the concrete reefs and swim with the whales. Damn! I thought these coastal waters had been cleaned up better than that."

Shawne looked Carliano straight in the eyes. "Conn's poisoning was my fault. You had nothing to do with it. We should have analyzed the waters here before Conn swam. Ellls are like Earth's amphibians—very open to the environment. You couldn't know that."

During recovery Conn didn't spend much time out of his solvent bath. Occasionally he would get under a shower of clear water and let Tandra fluff up his moss tiles with a soft plastic brush.

"Tandra, I think I lost some live flora out there." Conn knew, from studying Earth's human history, how deadly small pox had been to non-immunized people.

"Most of your germs don't have a chance in Earth's polluted shores. You're right that some could be dangerous to Earthlings, however."

"Sorry I dumped on your planet, Love," he said.

"You nearly die from human waste in the ocean—and you apologize?"

"You tried to tell me. You're the biologist. I shouldn't have gone out there without the isolation suit."

"There have been good efforts to clean up these shores, Conn. I didn't anticipate this."

"No worries. I like breathing soap."

"Conn, be serious for just one long minute. We really should find out what happened to you. Did the severe cramping happen more than once?"

"Twice."

"And you've never experienced anything like it before?"

"No."

"It sounds like an attack of food poisoning."

"Well . . . I couldn't resist munching a few sand bass. They're easy to catch."

"You ate raw fish out there? Good grief, Conn." Tandra stopped brushing him and stepped out of the tub. "So this reaction may not be entirely due to poisons you took in through your skin?"

"Guess so. One bass was a beauty. Took me for quite a ride before I bit through his neck."

"You ate the whole thing?"

"Tan, it's been a long time since I've had fresh fish."

"Raw, not fresh!"

"I didn't eat the heads. You don't get much there. Eyeballs. Small brains. Too much work."

"You haven't hunted fish since I've known you."

"Not since I sprouted legs on Ellason," he admitted.

"Right." Tandra handed Conn a towel. "Don't you dare shake your plumes dry until I'm out of here . . . you . . . wild animal. Shawne has gone to get samples of ocean water. We'd better get some sand bass, too. We'll zero in on the most likely toxins and decide if we should do anything else to get them out of your system."

"I don't think there's much left of my gut."

"What do you mean?"

"I keep losing strings of yellow in the John. I must have lost some blood in the ocean, too. Sorry to gross you out, Tan, but I'm tired of going around with soap in my hole when it feels like red ants are having a feast down there."

"Ouch. I'm really sorry."

"At least I've got hope in my soul. "

"Stop it, Conn. This isn't funny." Tandra finished dressing in a hurry. "I'm calling the med techs at Moonbase. We need to get you on antibiotics. Then we'll re-populate your gut with some decent elllonian microorganisms. I think you've been poisoned with Salmonella."

THE ALIEN EFFECT, 2068–2070 C.E. As a precaution, Tandra had made sure that all alien waste was sterilized in the composting toilet of their temporary home. Like human waste, Conn's elllonian excreta contained useful microorganisms—useful to ellls, that is.

Within the blood cells of ellls, there lives a tiny creature somewhat smaller than Earth's bacteria, but more complex. It was free-living eons ago. Then it became an elllonian symbiont for a while. Now, it was as essential to the ellls' cellular metabolism as mitochondria are to human cells. When Conn voided into the Pacific Ocean, huge numbers of the tiny creature—we'll call them Conn's Org—rode off in the blood cells from his poisoned stomach lining. Before a new sun rose over San Diego, voracious sea mites nibbled away Conn's protective cells. Thus set loose, Conn's Org struggled to find food and shelter. Many perished, but some found refuge in rotting debris caught in warm pockets of waste concrete on the ocean floor. There they reverted to their independent state.

CHARLEY

Orticon—a few hours later, 250 miles south of Cabo San Lucas

As the sun set, Orticon finished a rapid tour of the two-by-five–mile island in the middle of the South Pacific. He found the west side quite rugged, with volcanic rocks rising in sharp pinnacles just offshore. Nidok met him at the rover, looking a little strange.

"Your lips are sagging, my friend," Orticon said, trying to boost his mood with a friendly insult.

"I am hungry. I caught this. I think is good eating." This trip had taught Nidok that the young varok preferred a vegetarian diet.

"What have you got there?" Orticon looked under the rover, where Nidok had pushed his catch. Two giant lobsters stared back at him from the rear axle, their claws bound with the rover's towrope. "They look like your great grandmother, Nidok. Okay if I throw them in boiling water? We will have a feast."

Nidok couldn't decide if Orticon was serious or wanted to exchange insults. "What is this thing 'great grandmother?' You speak riddles."

"Lobsters are considered quite a delicacy here. Good hunting. I'll make a fire and we'll use the rover's bucket to boil water."

That night, as the wind swept the clouds away, and the stars filled the sky with other suns too numerous to count, they had a fine meal on the beach. Nidok didn't watch the lobsters' demise, but he demolished his share afterward. Orticon had to crack the lobster's chitin and harvest the meat, for Nidok was uncharacteristically too squeamish to do the job. Orticon decided it really was because the lobster resembled an ageing ahlork.

When first light hit the beach, Orticon awoke to find Nidok roasting pieces of an enormous fish he had caught in his talons.

"I wish I'd seen that wrestling match," Orticon said, meaning it as a compliment.

"It was no struggle. No struggle for ahlork." Water dripped from Nidok's wing plates, good evidence that he'd had a dunking.

When they had eaten, they sat looking at each other for a moment.

"I will fly—" Nidok began uneasily.

"No," Orticon said. "It is too dangerous for you."

"No way to radio at Conn?"

A shadow passed over Orticon's face as he remembered Conn's illness. "No power, no radio."

Nidok shifted on his big feet. "Conn will laugh."

Orticon smiled. "He'll laugh from now to the end of time. We ran out of gas, to use his twentieth century Earth jargon. He'll love it."

"I will catch more lobster. I will catch another fish. Everyday, until men return here."

"It's a weather station, Nidok. They may not be back for many days."

"I like eating lobster. Like eating nasty cousin Margar."

Orticon laughed until he lost control.

"Now I be stuck on nowhere with varok gone la-la," Nidok said. "I go to stretch wings. Pulling at boats not good for ahlork."

"Have a fine adventure," Orticon said, struggling to regain control. He stretched out in the shadow of the rover, determined to enjoy the warm breeze off the ocean.

Two hours later he was awakened by an ahlork sound close to his right ear. "We better go," Nidok said. "No fishing boats here. We better find them."

"All right," Orticon said. "Will you tow the rover?"

"Why not?"

Orticon re-tied Nidok's harness and they set off toward the other Socorro Island, San Benedicto, about 50 miles north. Before long, a pod of bottlenose dolphins was playing along beside them.

"If you be elll, you get dolphins to pull," Nidok called down. "Useless varok."

It was a fine day for a float, ruined only by the gnawing worry for Conn. The sky shone like blue marble, and the water reflected its beauty. Hours passed, and Nidok grew very tired.

"You'd better come sit," Orticon called. "I'll row for a while."

After an hour struggling with the craft, which was designed more for land than for sea, Orticon began to watch the locator closely. He was losing the battle with the westerly currents. "It's no good, Nidok. We're not going anywhere. We should go back. Someone will return to tend the weather station."

"I tow from air while you push from water," Nidok said. His tone held no room for argument. "I saw boats far away. They will help us. I will hide up in air when they come."

Obediently, Orticon stripped off his shirt, vaulted over the side, caught hold of the boarding ladder, and kicked.

"Much easier," Nidok shouted down to him. "Good varoks have ellls for fathers."

"I never thought of Conn as a father," Orticon called back. "He eats Lanoll's eggs for breakfast, you know."

"Ellls have no manners." Nidok flew on, and Orticon had to make a quick dive as the ahlork relieved himself.

"Watch it, Bird Hips," Orticon shouted. "The wind's shifted."

Nidok looked down with an ahlork's excuse for a smile, then he suddenly dropped the towrope and flew high into the air.

"Why did I agree to travel half this planet with an ahlork?" Orticon shouted, but Nidok was well beyond hearing. He climbed into the drifting rover and looked around to see what had startled the ahlork. A large boat had appeared in the west and was bearing down on the rover at high speed.

It was a handsome fishing rig with two decks and big game tackle in the stern. Ten men and a boy leaned on the deck rails. As they came alongside, one man threw a rope to Orticon. Another shouted into a bullhorn, "Better stay out of the water. Lots of sharks about."

"Could you give us a tow?" Orticon said in his best English accent. "We've lost power."

"I'd say you'd lost your tow." A young man in white shorts kneeled to help Orticon up the side ladder onto the deck of the large boat, then he fished up the towrope and secured it to the stern. The deck was slippery with blood, and Orticon went down hard, losing his knit cap into the water.

His wet hair stuck to his head like bleached seaweed, revealing the warty patch organs behind his ears. He decided he must look very alien, but he had to take his chances with these men. There was no arguing with sharks.

"Here now. Sorry about that. You all right?" A huge man took his arm to help him up. His skin was like leather, tanned to a deep gold that reflected his dark red-brown hair. He looked familiar. Orticon stared at the wide hairy chest, and the man stared at Orticon's left patch organ.

"You shouldn't be out here alone," he said. "Where are you bound?"

"He wasn't alone, Charley," a boy in white shorts said. "Where's your friend? He was real short, like a midget."

"Have you been following us?" Orticon's fears threatened to close in on him.

"We came around the north side of Socorro and spotted you. Couldn't figure out what you were up to, tying some ropes on your friend."

The ruddy-haired giant didn't sound angry, but his mood was cautious. He was determined to take no stories. "Where do you think he's gone? Is he in a storage hold?" He turned to the boy in white shorts. "Get down there and take a look, Tim."

The boy climbed onto the rover. He took a long time looking into every hatch. When he came back on board the big fishing rig, he was very pale, and he whispered something to Charley that made him laugh.

"Of course, Tim, hadn't you noticed? I believe this is a varok, one of the alien team teaching steady state economics in San Diego. Welcome aboard, Orcon . . . is it?"

"Orticon. I'm Shawne's family-brother." There would be no pretending to be human on this ship. The problem was Nidok.

"Charley Hazard." The man offered his hand. "I remember you from Shawne's school."

The other six men and two women had moved closer to surround

Orticon. He was feeling trapped and exposed, wanting to run, when Charley lowered his hand and dismissed everyone.

"Let's not be rude to our visitor, folks. He's had a right frightening accident. Give him some room there, now. Tim, you get everyone set up for the run. The Revillagigedos Achipelago has provided more world records than any fishery in the world. Olive Groupers at nearly fifty pounds, Black Jack, KawaKawa, Rainbow Runners at 37 pounds. Catch your big ones now. We can't make these trips very often any more. I'll give our friend here a nice cup 'a tea. We'll keep you informed."

Charley took Orticon's arm to guide him to the ship's galley, and the varok endured the touch, for his patches sensed that the man was feeling compassion for him as a defenseless alien. After Charley ushered Orticon to a long dining table, he busied himself making tea. When at last he sat down at the table across from the varok, he consciously invited him to read his thoughts.

"Do you see inside my head? They say varoks can do that. You see I mean you no harm, son. But I can't read your mind, and we can't have any rough stuff out here. Gives the fishery a bad reputation, it does, and we're hurting for clients these days. Not many people have time or money for the big fish now. Sip your tea. Have you eaten?"

"Yes, thank you," Orticon said. "I see you are very kind."

"Then tell me what you're up to, lad. I thought you folks were in San Diego."

"We were heading there. Shawne had mentioned that you guided fishing trips to these islands, so we came this way on our way back north from Australia."

"We?"

Orticon knew he had lost the battle of words. Subterfuge, secrets of any kind were impossible on Varok, a planet of thought-scanners. He didn't know how to protect Nidok. Words came hard. Fighting to read the man while he spoke, Orticon said, "I have . . . lost my companion."

"Lost." Charley sat looking at the varok. "We don't understand why you didn't radio for help. Your water-car is very well equipped."

"Our radio depended on the rover's power," Orticon said. "We made a stupid mistake, coming this far without a backup power unit."

"And why should I believe you? I put my passengers at risk taking you on board."

"I am not armed. Please let me call Shawne."

"First, I need to know about your companion."

Orticon couldn't answer. Ahlork could be deadly, but, as slow-flying boxes, they were also quite vulnerable. These expert fishermen were known to take fish as trophies, to stuff them and nail them on boards to hang in their lodges.

Charley sipped at his tea and studied Orticon's frozen face. "You do read minds, you varoks, or is that a myth?"

"We don't intrude uninvited, and we see only mood or the flow of immediate thoughts and renewed memory."

Charley smiled. "I read faces, you see, and yours is good for poker, except that your eyes dart about with fear—for your companion?"

"He could fly back to San Diego, but he won't leave me."

"And he thinks he's in danger. From us?"

"He fears humans for good reason."

"You should see no reason for him to fear me."

Orticon focused his patch organs on the man's mood. He found curiosity, as he expected, but he also found compassion, and no pugnacity. Imaginative thoughts flew past, and they all had to do with hiding the short, flying alien and keeping him safe.

"Can you guarantee us safe passage to San Diego?" Orticon asked.

"No, I can't. I have been hired to take seven people fishing for eight days. I don't know who they are or what they care about. I have two crew members who will back me up, but the others may hate aliens."

"That's why we have taken this trip, away from the spotlight, you might say. We don't understand human violence." Orticon kept his patches tuned to Charley, and what he found gave him hope.

"If you want my advice, son, I'd get up top and join in the fun. Let the folks satisfy their curiosity. Most people are decent sorts, not what gets hyped in TV shows or news stories. You'll soon have them on your side. You seem a decent sort yourself."

"Nidok won't do well with curiosity."

"That's the ahlork? The person they call Conn's pet beetle?"

"I suppose. He shouldn't stay up in the sky all night."

"We'll signal him down after the folks retire, if you'd like."

"We can try. He has good night vision."

"Say your name again, varok. Ordacan?"

"Orticon."

"Let's go make your call. Then I'll introduce you to the passengers

and crew. We will have four more days of fishing before we head back
to Cabo San Lucas. Then I'll take you up to San Diego. We need some
work done up there. Might as well be now. The season doesn't run
much longer, and business is slow."

Orticon followed Charley to the upper deck. "Are the
fisheries recovering?"

"They're okay here. Big game fishing is expensive. Always has been."

After they checked in with the family in San Diego and learned that
Conn was recovering under Tandra's care, Charley led Orticon out on
deck. They passed several large tunas hanging by hooks at the stern.
Four people were seated and belted in, fishing with enormous poles.
Three more looked on. Two crew members joined Charley when they
saw him emerge from below with Orticon.

"It's slow today, Charley," Tim said. "I say we give it up and move
west, maybe to Roca Partida."

"Sounds fine. It'll give us some time to meet our visitor from Varok,"
Charley said, ushering Orticon into the gathering. "We'll check out the
big rays then give him a tow to Cabo. This is Orticon from Jupiter's
stepchild, Varok, an embarrassed tourist with a bad power pack. We've
got a nice opportunity here to get to know a varok first hand."

"Welcome aboard, Orticon," Tim said, stepping up and offering a
hand. "Sorry about the misunderstanding."

"Conn's pet beetle is with him," Charley said, "flying free right now.
He's very shy. Best ignore him when he comes on board."

Orticon shook Tim's hand and the other passengers followed suit.
An awkward silence fell over the group.

"Miller time," Charley announced. "Get out the beer and we'll
down a few while Orticon tells us about life on Varok."

Orticon's brain sopped up the alcohol in the beer like a dry sponge,
and he was soon embellishing stories of his childhood with vivid
descriptions of daramonts that raced across the mountains called
Vahinorral, leaping from boulder to boulder, the ellls atop their shoulders whooping with powerful lungs, their nasal gills flapping and
making rude noises. He told of looping snarl that grew larger than tree
trunks, of auroral light that filled the skies with creamy pale colors,
of the rapid silence of the Ahlkahn's sleek cars on steel rails carrying
varoks and ellls across the land.

The questions and answers couldn't come fast enough, and Orticon was disappointed when Charley hustled everyone off to bed. "Early morning we pull anchor," he threatened, but Orticon could see that he was worried about Nidok.

When everyone was settled in for the night, Charley took Orticon to a large spotlight on the bow. "Let's sweep the sky for a few minutes, then I'll fix the light on you. Get up on the bow. Point and wave your friend down."

"That should work," Orticon said.

"Unless he's gone back to San Diego."

"He wouldn't."

The spotlight worked, and soon Orticon saw Nidok sail past the fishing boat. He wouldn't land, however, and Orticon wondered how long the ahlork could stay in the air, concerned about the seven species of sharks and other large animals that made these islands famous.

Cabo

Orram—meanwhile, at the SCBA house

Gradually, the solvent Conn voided ran clear. Tandra and I drained the tub and helped him to the pool. He was still very weak. We didn't know if he would ever fully recover.

"At least. . ." I hesitated. It would be a lame comment, considering Conn's near escape from death by clogging and food poisoning. "At least now we see firsthand why ocean farming has failed—because of problems with shoreline contamination."

Conn eased into the water. "Didn't I tell you, Orram? The gray whales have agreed to help farm tuna—away from shore." He coughed and lay back on the surface.

Conn's voice sounded like he was blowing bubbles through a straw, but he went on. "It can be done, Orram. Orcas know tuna behavior better than whales, but farming plans will have to wait until we get their list of requirements for successful breeding. I wish Stringer and Lanoll were here. What do you hear from them?"

"All we can do is hope they're in touch with dolphins or whales in the North Pacific," I said, feeling great relief at his show of concern. "Now quit talking and let us help you get to the kitchen for some good varokian soup."

Orticon—the same night, in the Pacific south of the Baja Peninsula

Very late that night, Charley went below, leaving Orticon to worry about Nidok. A large thump on the deck startled him awake an hour later.

"You don't trust me and my human friends?" Orticon asked. "It's time to relax, Nidok. We have a ride to San Diego guaranteed, and a chance to examine human specimens up close. You'll like them, especially the hairy captain, Charley."

In the morning, the big man came up the ladder from below and waved at Nidok, but he had the sense to disappear again. "Good fish for breakfast down here," he shouted up to them.

"Thank you," Orticon hollered. "We'll be there, all both of us." He stretched and turned over on the canvas hammock Charley had hung for him. "Where are you, Nidok? It's breakfast time. We're going below. No arguments."

There was no answer, not even an irritated croak. Orticon searched the deck, the sky, the rigging. No ahlork.

"Nidok!" he shouted to the sky. He walked to the bow, then back to the stern. The sea was calm, the air pleasantly cool. Humming along at a good clip, the boat left a wide wake in the quiet sea. "Nidok!"

"Rude varok."

It was Nidok's voice, muted.

"Where are you?"

"Man said breakfast. I save you breakfast." The ahlork's boxy face appeared at the top of the ladder.

"Come back down here Nidok," Charley called. "Give us the last verse of that song you've been croaking."

The ahlork scrambled down the ladder, and Orticon followed. As he descended to the mess hall, he heard Nidok's rasping tones punctuated with human laughter and clapping.

There once was varok Mahntik,
Whose mind was sort of freak,
Cause she lied through teeth
And made out like thief,
Until Nidok took her off in his beak.

Loud cheering covered Charley's voice kidding the ahlork about his loss of rhythm.

Nidok harumphed with the gargle characteristic of his species. He was not one to ignore a captive audience. "Is Shawne's fault. She made up English words."

Late in the eighth day of the fishing trip, Charley's ship eased into its berth at Cabo San Lucas on the end of the Baja Peninsula. A heavy rain was soaking Nidok. He sat on the deck hunched up under his wings, wishing he were on Varok, where water stayed put in the seas.

One by one, Charley's passengers and crew found the ahlork and wished him well. It had been a good trip. The humans were entranced with his sense of fun and peculiar command of English. Their emotion embarrassed Nidok, however, and he wasn't sure that farewell insults would be welcome, as they would be with Conn, so he restrained himself. It was exhausting for him.

As the last of the passengers left the ship, Nidok followed them to the end of the docks. Orticon found him perched on a tall mast, looking down over the lines of white boats birthed near rows of orange and yellow terra cotta hotels and restaurants lining the shore, not yet filled with their winter visitors. A yellow gravel beach framed the resort and set off a golden sunset.

"We don't have time to explore the beach," Orticon called up to him. "Charley is leaving for San Diego after we get something to eat. Here he comes."

Charley had dressed in a clean shirt. "Let's go folks," he said.

Nidok sailed off the mast onto the dock and opened his wings in an instinctive move to look larger to people passing by. It worked. They gave him wide birth. Some giggled. Others hurried on.

"We'll wait for you here," Orticon said.

"No, no, Orti," Charley laughed, "that won't do. I've made reservations for three." He pointed to a palatial restaurant. Its deck looked over the beach, already crowded with people in glittering dress.

"We can't take—" Orticon looked at Nidok, still grandly pacing the dock. "We can't go to a public place."

"Nidok will sweep all the glassware off the tables, if he struts around like that." Charley laughed. "But I can't take no for an answer, Orti. No sir. It's my payback for hauling you to San Diego. Show off to my friends, you know. Give an old sailor his one big moment, eh Nidok? Hey there, big fella. We're goin' to dinner now. Keep your wings folded tight and walk straight and dignified. That'll show 'em. Play the human game. Know what I mean? You're my guests in that fine restaurant there."

"We be guests?" Nidok snapped his beak twice. "This is human's insult? There? Is bad idea, sailor."

"I heard ahlork were cowards. Oh well, I'll bring you soup from the kitchen garbage cans." Charley started to walk off, but the insult did the trick.

"I'm with you, Hair Chest," Nidok said, folding his wings and preening his rear. "I sweep glasses to floor if I feel like it."

"Good idea, Nidok, Old Box. Show these humans your good side." Charley laughed heartily and strode off toward the restaurant with Nidok and a very nervous Orticon following close behind.

"Here we are. To the patio," Charley said. "Come on now, Nidok. Walk in through the front door like my honored guest—which you are."

Orticon and Nidok followed Charley into the carpeted restaurant, Nidok tiptoeing by the tables as best he could. On their way to the patio, people nodded and clapped, then went about eating, minding their own lives.

"Lobster all around?" Charley asked, as he helped Nidok onto an upholstered chair.

"I roast tourist, if lady's eyes don't quit me," Nidok said.

"Sorry, no roast tourist on the menu. She's just curious, Nidok."

Nidok perched on his chair with talons carefully draped over the front edge, away from the upholstery. Charley pushed him up to the table, and his head was on a level with the big man when seated, so their table presence was reasonable, if a bit unusual.

Charley read a few selections out loud. "I'll have fish. How about bouillabaisse? You can try all different kinds of sea food in one bowl."

Their waiters were obviously agog, and Orticon delighted them with a few words of mangled Castilian Spanish. During the meal they attracted only a few glances. Nidok managed his fish soup with a delicate wing tip and understood in time how to use the finger bowl. Fortunately, the table full of glassware had inspired him to sit on his wing tips when he didn't need their prehensile dexterity.

When they were finished eating—enjoying lattés after a delicious flan, which Nidok managed with clever, if not silent, lips—a group of children cautiously approached their table.

Orticon had seen the children climb the stairs that led from the beach to the deck. Their hair was ratted from lack of combing, and their clothes were not clean, but their eyes were wide and beautiful, like ellls' without the green glint. They approached slowly, nodding, as if asking permission.

"*Por favor*, Meester Alien, can we have autograph?" the eldest asked, holding out the stub of a pencil and a scrap of paper.

"*Certainment, Señor*," Charley boomed. "Meet my friends from Varok, *chickitos*. This is Orticon and his friend Nidok the ahlork. But you must use my pen, Orticon, so your mark will not fade."

The children crowded around Nidok's chair, scaring the insults out of him for a moment. Soon their friendly chatter and curious touches had him teasing them in pantomime. Slowly a crowd gathered around the table, and, before the evening was over, Orticon was able to get past the pleasantries and learn something about the human tragedy as it had played out in Mexico.

Mexico City had learned about water problems the hard way, for their sinking aquifer had taken valued buildings with it. As heat and disease gradually reduced the population, the people enjoyed cleaner air and better housing. With gasoline expensive, life was less frantic, and they began to like it that way. Some grieved for their conflict with church teachings that still prohibited the use of birth control, knowing future children would face hunger and water shortages.

Looking into such tortured minds moved Orticon deeply, until Charley decided to call the party to an end.

"Is sensitive human, I am thinking," Nidok said to his new friend.

"Thanks, Charley," Ortican whispered.

"It is midnight," Charley called out over the crowd. "We have a long boat trip back to San Diego. You can continue the conversation with Orticon and his family on the Worldnet. They are here to help us preserve the future."

Orticon then spent another half hour giving out information about the EV Science broadcasts from the moon, the computer links and Shawne's School for Economic Longevity.

On the way back to the boat, Orticon noticed that Charley was now very quiet.

"You have been very kind," Orticon said to him, "but we have one more favor to ask. The news of ocean health here is not good. On our way north we would like to visit a few reefs, if they are not too far off course."

"Sure," Charley said. He looked at Orticon with serious concern in his eyes. "But what about you two? How are you feeling about humans now?"

Orticon was moved by his insightful question. "I see my mistake. It does no good to blame all humans for their bad history. I understand better your terrible dilemmas. The people on the boat and the people here are kind beings, eager to make us feel comfortable—*welcome* is the word. But the young have seen too much violence in entertainment and now in real life. I grieve for them; such imprinting is hard to overcome. It cannot be healthy. If we are lucky, the lessons that we teach will not be lost. Either way, given a chance, life will recover here, but it will be changed."

"And you, Nidok? You had a good time signing autographs, eh?"

Nidok aimed both prehensile wing tips into the air.

"But I must warn you." Charley sat on the dock and focused on Nidok's tiny black eyes until they focused back. "Stay vigilant. Almost all humans are decent folk in real life. Almost. Some are not, and they can be deadly."

Dr. and Mrs. Mitchell

Jesse Mendleton—captive with Junah on the fishing boat

"Now we know what you're talking about." Traveling east through the Aleutian Islands, Jesse faced their captor on the deck of a well-used fishing boat sporting a faded chartreuse hull. He put on a good act. "We saw something come down out of the sky when we were trolling for halibut out near the Sanaks. Looked like a powered capsule at first, then a parachute opened. We assumed it came from Shemya Air Force Station."

Pete Dawson rubbed his nose, sniffed, and drew himself up to his full five feet ten inches. "Go on. You met the pod, beached it on Sanak for several days." His lip was set in a permanent curl, tilting his tawny beard at a strange angle.

"You must have seen our research boat here," Junah said, putting on her best English accent. Her hair was tucked into a knit cap that covered the varokian patch organs behind her ears. "We found a wounded dolphin. It was a good chance to study his behavior, while he . . . it recovered. We saw no one else, no aliens. I thought the aliens came in at San Diego. Didn't they?"

"How many more will be coming in to San Diego, Missus?"

"More aliens came in?" Jesse looked at Junah and shrugged.

"Could be. We've been out of touch." Jesse held out his hand. "Say, we'd better introduce ourselves. I'm Doctor Harold Mitchell and this is the missus, Jean."

"I heard the aliens' planet will soon be closer to Earth than it's been in 12,000 years," Junah said. "Wouldn't it be exciting if they invited some humans to visit? How about it, Sweetheart? Shall we sign up to go?"

"I don't know, Love. What do you think, Mister . . . Mister?"

"Dawson's the name," he said. His eyes shifted between the two, looked them over, as if their wet suits were wrong, too fancy, baggy in odd places or something.

"Say, could you give us a tow into Anchorage?" Jesse said. "We've got a testy motor."

"That's a mighty fancy little boat. Where'd you get it?"

"Designed it myself. Sea life is a hobby of mine." Jesse knew Conn would be proud of his cool lie. "I'll pay you well for the tow."

"We'll tow you into Anchorage, all right. Then we'll see about payment."

During the trip along the Shelikof Strait into Cook Inlet, Junah feigned sickness, but "recovered" in time for the landing in Anchorage. It was then that she and Jesse realized they were not free to go.

"We'll have the authorities check you out," Dawson explained, setting a six-pack of beer and a box of stale Fruit Loops on the dresser in the crew quarters. He closed the door and locked it from the outside.

If Jesse had been a varok, he would have gone irrational for weeks he was so angry.

Junah had to laugh. "So much for your acting career," she said. "I guess we don't have to worry about avoiding radio signals now." She called SCBA on the communicator in her survival pack.

Tandra answered.

"Where are you?" Jesse asked. "We've got lousy contact."

"Orram and I are in San Diego. Conn needed some . . . medication. He's okay now."

"That explains a lot. The xenophobes are gunning for aliens."

"What do you mean, Jesse?" I asked.

"Some fishermen up here are afraid of Ellason coming in close enough for contact. They've got us locked up, Orram. I'm worried about Junah. They think she's English, at least for now. I'll kill the bastards if they touch her."

It didn't help defuse Jesse's anger when he thought he heard Conn chuckle. "They thought Junah was English? Good show, my deah. I didn't think varoks could act."

It took Jesse a while to appreciate the elll's humor, but he settled down when Conn took over the radio conversation.

"Look, Bubba," the elll said to Jesse, "this Dawson character can't be all bad if he left you with a box of Fruit Loops. He'll be back. Your passports are good until 2075. Did Stringer and Lanoll get away with the orcas?"

"We don't know, Conn. We didn't want to use the radio and risk Dawson catching their signal."

"Then there's no way to contact them, unless we get help from the dolphins or whales out here." Conn's voice rose in frustration.

"If Dawson has captured Stringer and Lanoll, that dumb shit could have dried them out and never realized why they shriveled up and blew away."

"Dumb what?" Junah asked. "That's a new one, Conn. "What—?"

"You don't want to know," Orram interrupted. "Conn is a little obsessed with waste products these days. Be sure to stay calm, Junah. Better come here as soon as you can, so we can regroup. Do not try to find Lanoll and Stringer with those fishermen watching you. We will make contact or find them somehow. We'll try the cetaceans. The pod of killers you encountered might like the farming idea. The orcas and gray whales here do. They may help us."

"The two pods may be in communication already," Conn added. "They've got quite a network."

"Conn sounds funny, Orram. What's wrong with him?"

"He got into some bad water, Jesse, but we've got him flushed out. We hope Stringer and Lanoll stay well away from shore and keep their suits on. The orcas know all about polluted ocean water, so they may help keep them safe."

"Elll tiles are like sponges," Jesse mumbled.

"Or worse," Orram said. "They have never evolved the defenses they need here. Ellls have always lived in relatively pure water. I'm not sure how long any of them should stay—"

"Don't listen to Orram," Conn cut in. "Let's shut down before your fishy friends trace this signal."

Jesse looked at Junah with a nod. "Conn's probably right. We're okay for now. Roger and out."

Jesse and Junah waited several hours, trying to sleep and failing, until at last they heard footsteps on the deck above. Heavy steps sounded on the ladder, a key rattled in their door, and a young man stepped in front of Dawson to enter the stateroom.

"So! Caught in the snare of old sea dogs out hunting aliens!" He laughed and held out a friendly hand. His grip was firm. Half a head taller than Jesse, he seemed all legs and fur in shorts, boots and a parka. "Jeff Passage here. You'll have a hard time living this one down, Dr. Mitchell." The young man looked directly at Jesse, then Junah. "Mrs. Mitchell, nice to meet you at last. I've been eager to see this new research vessel you two have designed."

"Call me Harold," Jesse said. "It was a simple misunderstanding.

No blame to Dawson here. We were well treated, considering his worry about the aliens." Jesse gave Dawson an even look. "Jeannie had a touch of flu coming in. We couldn't have done much this week anyway. Any news of that pod Dawson saw?"

"It was probably an experimental survival capsule. They're shooting off a new design from the base at Umnak Island. The ellls and varoks are somewhere near San Diego—all accounted for. No aliens loose on Earth, I'm afraid. Too bad. We could use some excitement up here."

The genial conversation continued as they proceeded to the "research vessel," ignoring Dawson.

"I'd sure like to take a ride in this thing," the young man said. "How about it, Dr. Mitchell?"

"Sure thing, Jeff. Come aboard. But do call me Harold. I've known your dad a long time. How is he these days?"

"Lost him to cancer last year."

"Sorry. So sorry to hear that," Jesse said. "Cast us off there, would you, Dawson? Thanks for the tow. Wait. Let me write a check first. How about a thousand? That should cover it." Jesse found a transaction box in his pack and keyed in the electronic transfer. The transaction was good; it wouldn't bounce. Jesse liked the look on Dawson's face. The check would get him off their backs.

When the varokian survival dinghy had cleared the Kenai Peninsula with no sign of pursuit, the young rescuer calling himself Jeff Passage turned to Junah and slowly pulled the knit cap from her head. With a smile and a tentative finger, he combed her long, silver-laced hair behind her right ear plaque.

"Welcome to Earth, Ms. Varok," he said.

Universal, Adolescent, Infectious Humor

Orram—hours later, at the SCBA house

Tandra and I were in the SCBA swimming pool treating Conn when Orticon appeared on the deck. Prolonged exposure to the sun had painted his skin the deep golden tan of those living on the acid plains of Varok. His face was alive with relief and anticipation, until he saw Conn.

I climbed out of the water and greeted him, my mood cautionary. With a quick scan of my memory, he saw the details of Conn's poisoning.

He stripped off jeans and T-shirt and dove in the water to greet Conn with gentle schooling before helping him onto the deck.

"When Shawne gets back, I want to hear all about your trip," Conn said. "Where is that flying boxcar, Nidok? Is the Great Barrier Reef healthy? The concrete reefs here are doing well, in spite of the pollution, but the more delicate critters have been weeded out. When we get the shore cleaned up, I bet we can re-introduce all kinds of sea life here. Maybe even release some star fish."

"Conn, stop jabbering," Orticon said. "How are you?"

"As in really?"

"In words. Your mind is a worse than usual jumble of confusing phrases. I can't read a thing."

At that moment Nidok lumbered into the room with Charley Hazard close behind. Conn moved toward the ahlork and they touched wing-tips to handfins. I saw that the elll was both relieved and delighted to see Nidok.

"Sorry to disappoint you, Nidok, but I'm still alive," Conn said. Welcome home, world traveler."

Nidok gargled, a noise difficult to interpret, then said, "It was not easy. Varoks can't swim. Varoks can't fly. What good is he?"

"Thanks anyway, big bird, for bringing my dryland son home in one piece."

Conn knew what he was doing to help the ahlork's mood. He had thrown out the worst insult, calling Nidok *bird*. For the first time since we bound our lives to the huge Varokian insectoid (by taking his scar), Nidok was silent. I think he would have cried if he had tear ducts, for

Conn's poor condition must have brought back painful memories.

Long ago on Varok, Nidok had saved the elll from imprisonment and dehydration at the hands of the traitor, Mahntik—but just in time. This looked worse. Conn's plumes were scattered and broken, his hexlines gray as if smeared with ilara droppings, and his tiles drooped like tired shale worms.

After a moment Nidok recovered and gave a rude snort. "So what do I eat here? I pick elll bones?"

"You'll have to pick through the garbage can, you pleated vulture. It's out back, in the alley. Just follow the crows."

"I bring you moldy bread to go with Orram's foul soup," Nidok retorted.

Charley laughed, and Orticon introduced him as an expert fisherman and naturalist. When Tandra approached, he drew back and stared, then he restrained himself politely, but Conn and I could see that he was intensely interested in her.

Nidok broke the tension. "This human deserves big eats, Orram. When is lunch?"

"How did you know I was doing all the cooking here?" I said.

"This skinny female on two legs. She knows better."

Tandra gave Nidok an affectionate touch on the huge lip that dominated his square face. "While Orram cooks, I do communication to earn my soup. You told me you enjoyed playing tourist in the tropics. What else did you do besides tow rovers?"

"I feed young varoks old grandmothers." Nidok lunged at her, trying to sweep her back into the pool, but she dodged and bumped against Charley.

Charley caught Tandra's arm. She smiled warmly up at him. "I understand you run fishing trips to the Socorros. It's famous for its large sea life. How is it going?"

"We are surviving, as are the huge rays, but the tuna are not doing so well."

He was about to go on, but she turned to Orticon. "Go to Conn again—alone in water," she whispered. "He could use a good elllonian breakdown. Recovery has been frustrating. Too slow."

Orticon nodded, and he and Conn disappeared into the far end of the pool, where the Elodea, Hornwort and Willow Moss chosen by Bob Carliano grew thick, oxygenating the water.

"This way to the kitchen, Charley," Tandra said. "We'll fix some lunch while we tell Nidok everything we know about Conn's problem. Nidok has some history taking care of ellls."

"Short of dunking him in kerosene," I said, "I don't know how we're going to get the residual oil out of his tiles. It's congealed at the base of every plume clump and has moved into the moss follicles."

"Ahlork spit," Nidok said, as he hopped behind us into the kitchen. He sounded as if he thought it was obvious.

"What?"

"Give me acid fruit," Nidok said. "I make strong spit, work into rotten ell skin, right? Ancient Nidok preening juice gets Conn clean."

"Yes." Tandra understood. "Ahlork carry an enzyme that breaks down petroleum residuals. They must have run into a lot of waste chemicals diving for fish long ago, when Varok was polluted. Good idea, Nidok."

"Get me big glass. Cabernet, Napa Valley, 2043," he said, shuffling back to the pool, "so I make spit."

Entering the kitchen, Orticon heard the comment. "Your turn," he said, and he pulled the ahlork toward the pool with a practiced grab at his wing tips. "Go school with Conn, Uncle Nidok."

We brought sandwiches out to the pool deck and found Nidok bobbing on the surface of the water. He disappeared with a "ploop" as Conn pulled him under. The rough play gave Nidok a chance to show off his new Pacific Ocean skills. He rowed along the surface, using his wing plates as canoe paddles and his rear plates as a rudder. His natural fishing dive involved pulling his wings forward then back, kicking with talons pressed together and thrust back.

When Bob Carliano walked into the poolroom for his daily visit, I introduced Charley, and the ahlork repeated his demonstration. He enjoyed showing off, especially for humans who had rarely seen a talking insectoid. Carliano was greeted with an exhibition dive, tail end up, accented by an unmistakable release of intestinal gas.

"I would say . . . that's a Fazz," Charley said.

"That's a what?" Conn's head perked up out of the water garden, his eyes wide, hoping for mischief.

"That ahlork sound could be rated as a Fazz." Charley's face took on the sober, thoughtful countenance of a maverick professor.

"Rated?" I watched the fun rising in Charley's eyes.

"There's the Fizz, the Fazz, the Fizzfazz, the Rip Snort, the Tear Ass, and the kind that goes 'Pooh,'" Charley explained. "I'd say that was a Fazz."

"No way, Charley," Tandra said. "You've left out a few, like the Zuup."

"Mother!" Shawne's entrance couldn't have been better timed.

Her reprimand set us off.

Belly-clenching laughter erupted. We varoks totally lost control for minutes. All that day, the slightest suggestion set off a cascade of giggles.

"Just proves it," Tandra said. "There's no such thing as an alien, a living being we couldn't possibly understand."

Nidok, Charley, and Carliano quickly became fast friends, for the humans were almost as good as Conn at trading insults with the ahlork. Together they worked out a system for Nidok's licking (to put it politely) Conn clean, and we shall never know what triggered his rapid recovery—the ahlork saliva or all that laughter. Probably both.

"Now," Shawne insisted some days later, when Conn felt well enough to think about going back to work, "first things first. Tuna farming."

Conn agreed. "Yes, let's get a more detailed proposal to the gray whales. Contact Charley. He will be in San Diego for a while. He certainly knows more than we do about tuna."

"I know where Charley fixes boat," Nidok said. "I fly out, ask him, ask whales. Bring back whale ideas."

"All right," Conn said. "You do a good job imitating sonic codes. You can make all kinds of noises."

Shawne gave a disapproving look as Conn's remark set off another round of laughter.

Jeff Passage

Junah—minutes later, in Anchorage

Junah took back her knit cap from their rescuer, pulling away, not sure how to react but failing to stifle her natural reaction to touch. The young man, Jeff passage, had recognized her as a varok, even while calling her Mrs. Mitchell. The subterfuge confused her, for varoks do not tell lies; their mood and thought sensing make it nonsensical.

While Passage sprawled comfortably on the rear bench of the Varokian survival dinghy, Junah stayed close to Jesse. Dawson, still sulking, had motored off with his one-thousand dollars for towing the "Mitchell's" dinghy to Anchorage.

"Go ahead, search my mind, Ms. Varok, if that's what you do," Passage said, "so you'll know just who I am."

Junah relaxed enough to see that the so-called "varokian mind-reading patch organs" were a curiosity to this person. It would also be a chance for her to learn just how precisely and how deeply she could read another human mind. Passage didn't seem to realize that varokian patches sensed little beyond the flow of current thought or mood.

"All right," she agreed, and she moved closer to him. For Jesse's benefit, Junah summarized what her patch organs read from the youth. He was older than she thought. "You are in your early thirties, but that is just a guess. You work the ocean." Junah shook her head. "I'm sorry I can't get much more than that."

"Hmmm. Okay," he said. "My name is Jeff Passage. I am Captain of a fleet of refurbished single-hull tankers commissioned to haul fresh water from Alaska to San Diego."

"Nice coincidence that you found us here," Jesse said.

"This meeting is no coincidence," Junah said, as she picked up Passage's fleeting memory. "You grew suspicious when Pete Dawson's call went out for a fleet of fishing rigs. You had learned that a falling object had been sighted. A few beers with the right people in Anchorage told you Pete was after alien invaders. Supposedly we were dropped from the Varokian spacecraft before it landed in San Diego. You decided to intervene when Dawson sprung his trap, regardless of the catch."

"Nice job." Passage was impressed with Junah's reading.

"We're looking for a ride to San Diego to join the rest of our crew," said Jesse.

"We've got a loaded tanker preparing to steam south. We can meet it at Sitka and take you and your . . . impressive . . . boat along, courtesy of Freshwater Enterprises."

"Of course, we need to talk about that." Junah looked pointedly at Jesse, who immediately thought of Stringer and Lanoll. *They must be found.* "We have survey work to do before we leave these waters."

"Survey work?"

"For Shawne," Junah said. "The human daughter of the Oran-ElConn-Grey Family. Perhaps you've heard of her School for Economic Longevity. It is based in San Diego. She's interested in long-term survival tactics. She needs to know how Arctic sealife is faring, problems with salmon fisheries, that kind of thing."

"Perhaps I could help."

"How do you think you can help?" Jesse was growing suspicious. Perhaps they had been rescued only to become pawns in some larger game.

Junah probed Passage deeper. What was driving this man? She sensed nothing but curiosity. "Speed," she said. "Right now, speed would help. We've been delayed too long by—what's his name?"

"They call him Cold Pete Dawson. He's a well-known character up here."

"I see. Dawson has set our schedule behind. Do you have any broad-beam infrared scanners on your tanker?"

"Afraid not, Ms. Varok. We're just hauling fresh water. Our tankers are fitted with radar, but it's fairly simple, primitive really, barely enough to keep us out of trouble. The tankers were originally built to haul oil cheaply."

"I don't understand what *cheaply* implies," Junah said.

"When too many spills occurred, double hulls were required for oil. Have you heard of the infamous Valdez accident? That spill killed a lot of wildlife. The area has never fully recovered. Damn shame. Not long after that the single-hull ships were phased out. Now they've been converted to carry water."

He was sincere. Junah was encouraged. Perhaps Passage could be trusted, at least until they knew Stringer and Lanoll were safe.

"I've got a week before I'm supposed to be in Sitka. Let me help you do your survey. Looks like you've got some interesting equipment right here on this dinghy."

"All right." Junah nodded to Jesse, but he did not nod back. She sensed a negative reaction in him. Apparently he did not trust this man. He didn't like Passage's interest in their little boat. "You know, I need to apologize. We haven't introduced ourselves properly."

"Not Jeannie and Harold Mitchell?" Junah felt Passage's laugh erupt from a deep well of good humor.

"Well, we could be. Maybe we varoks invaded Earth long ago, and are just now getting serious about integrating."

"I see," Passage said, "and I am Superman, here to rescue this human man from life with a lovely, evil alien."

Junah laughed. "This is Jesse Mendleton, a long-time friend, our first human contact on Earth. He's been a great help on Varok for the last eighteen Earth-years. He helped us ease back to Varok's steady state—sort out what we needed to do to stop the illegal profiteering that was triggering growth."

"Sounds familiar. We're all greedy, I suppose, in one way or another." Passage looked to Jesse, expecting some polite agreement. He got only a stony silence, so he went on. "Greed makes the world go around, they say."

"Who's 'they'?" Jesse was not in a mood to be polite.

"The ones like Dawson, who would take advantage of your being alien. Stay clear of him. Wear your cap, Junah. You're here for a good purpose. I have friends at the new School for Longevity—"

"Economic Longevity," Jesse corrected. "We appreciate your help in freeing us. We will continue to be cautious."

Junah broke in to introduce herself. "I am called Junah. The varokian custom is to derive the familiar name by contracting part of the first formal name and the family name. I am of the family Nah."

"Junah. I'm ready to be more help, if you'll allow me." He looked at Jesse, who nodded compliance.

"Tell me what to do. I'm good with gadgets—my specialty as an engineering student."

"We were using the infrared scanner to track a small pod of orcas when Dawson blocked our exit from the bay at Little Koniuji."

"The orcas stay well away from shore. Odd that they would be in so close."

"They were curious, I suspect," Jesse said. "They were heading south when the . . . when we tried our dolphin codes on them."

Junah spread out Conn's sea floor maps of the North Pacific. "They said they planned to hunt squid off the continental shelf near Tall Sea Mountain. We interpreted that to mean the Pratt Seamount. Nearby, the sea floor drops to 2300 feet. It's part of a mountain range off the continental shelf."

The details were not lost on Jeff Passage. "Nice work! How did you keep track of the dolphins and the sea floor?"

"Nothing very mysterious," Junah said. "We've broken some of the dolphin codes—enough to make correlation with data from some refurbished North American satellites."

"You've been busy."

"Perhaps you don't realize we've been watching *Homo sapiens* since before your ancestors left their caves. Our permanent Moonbase was set up during World War II. That's more than a century ago. Our broadcasts have been transmitted to Earth for nearly two decades now."

Passage's mood turned sober. "I've been too preoccupied to pay attention . . . with oil reserves and clean water so scarce."

"If you really mean to help us, we'll put the infrared scanners on full width and run south," Jesse said. "The Pratt Seamount is west of Sitka. We can go there and still get to your tanker in plenty of time for a ride to San Diego."

"Sounds like a workable plan," said Passage. "I'd love to see what this watercar can do."

Junah turned on the infrared scanners as well as the intercom, hoping Stringer and Lanoll would be calling in from somewhere within their helmet coms' range.

Nothing. Junah had messages from San Diego waiting for pickup. In spite of Conn's illness, Orram had put out search calls every hour.

"Good to talk to you, at last, Orram," Junah said. "Sorry for the interruption in reports. We were detained by a rather dangerous character, a man called Pete Dawson, then rescued by someone from Freshwater Enterprises. He's hauling water to San Diego from Alaska. He will help Jesse and me complete the infrared scan of the Gulf of Alaska, then we'll come by tanker to San Diego with him, if . . . all checks out here."

"Sounds good." Junah was relieved when Orram assumed he should not say too much. Her reference to an infrared scan was meant to tell him that she and Jesse would search for Lanoll and Stringer.

"No worries. We have progress here, with news of a pod of orcas heading south," Orram said. "You might contact them. They are interested in the cooperative sea-farming venture Conn has initiated with whales here. Try the Pratt Seamount, then run south. Stay well off the shelf." As a hopeful precaution, Orram gave her Stringer's last coordinates in Varokian.

Junah pretended it was Varokian for a fond farewell. "Greetings to all there, Orram. Expect to see us before ten days pass."

Much relieved, Junah distracted Passage. "Now, what else would you like to see? Our navigation system, no doubt."

Jesse noted the coordinates Orram gave Junah, and plotted a course south. If Stringer and Lanoll were with the orcas Orram mentioned, they were a full day ahead of them, moving faster than ellls swim.

Jeff Passage was no fool. Junah saw with her patch sense that he was trying hard to keep all questions and suspicions about ellls out of his conscious thought. He must have guessed that we had more interest in orcas than in sea farming. More than anything, he wanted contact with ellls, Junah read, and Ellason was very much on his mind.

The Alien Effect, circa 2070 C.E. In rooting for food on the concrete reef, the large, flat gold fish of the San Diego coast 'inhaled' Conn's Org, and a few were trapped in their gills.

Feeling very much at home in fish gills, the little organelle/microorganism from Conn's blood cells sought out a source of food and found easy prey in *Haemophilus* germs, which were giving the gold fish an irritating gill cold.

Conn's Org, full of nutritious *Haemophilus* bacteria, rode the fishes' coughs into the ocean, where it quickly found other fish gills in which to live. In those gills Conn's Org found other viruses and bacteria to eat, and the microscopic alien opportunist further developed the habit of gill hopping. The niche was wide open.

Due to decades of human dumping in the oceans, the fish of Earth suffered from a large variety of disorders. Conn's org feasted and spread.

V. Family

"As soon as the costs catch up to the benefits, growth becomes uneconomic. . . . Each additional dollar of growth actually makes us poorer . . . Uneconomic growth continues . . . because the benefits accrue to a few rich and powerful people, while the larger costs fall increasingly on the poor and disempowered."

—*Enough Is Enough: Building A Sustainable Economy In A World Of Finite Resources by Rob Dietz and Dan O'Neill. San Francisco: Berrett-Koehler Publishers, Inc., 2013, p. 46.*

Larger Traps

Stringer—meanwhile, heading south with Lanoll and the orcas

Stringer preferred to ride the lead orca male just behind the big dolphin's dorsal fin. There the elll could stretch out full length, with his arms linked around the six-foot fin. The elll extended his backfin for balance and added a little velocity with his befinned feet.

At first, breathing was a problem, for the transition from gills to lungs came too often for the elll's comfort. Apparently, the orca had assumed the elll needed to breathe air like a human, when in fact it was the orca who needed air.

During their first hunt, a successful partnership in trapping cod, Stringer gave the orcas a short lesson in comparative anatomy. The gills of the cod were similar to those lining the nose-like gill structure on his elllonian face, but he could shut them down and inflate his lungs out of water—something he preferred not to do too frequently in cold air. He suggested the orcas stick to their habit of catching quick breaths as they arched over the water's surface. He and Lanoll would keep to their gills as they rode.

The Bering Glacier dipped into the sea to their left, but they caught only a glimpse of it when the orcas surfaced.

"Hey ho, *Ahl Ara*," he called to Lanoll in Ellonian, as they sped past Kayak Island under water, "*Naran lu?*"

"Translate. Translate." The lead male did a side breech that threw Stringer free, and the pod came to a halt. The big white and black hunting dolphin was eager to learn as much Elllonian as he could, Stringer guessed, so he would have an advantage in the farming venture. He'd need it, with the gray whales already working with Conn. The big males, accustomed to leading their separate pods, would tussle for command as their first order of business.

"I asked Lanoll if she was comfortable, '*Naran lu*' in our speech," Stringer translated for the orca male. "'*Okay*' is the human sound. It's quick and easy for asking 'good or not tired.' We are ready for the fast trip past the Juneau area."

"Sound for sound. Translate," the male clicked.

Stringer tried, but concept for concept was as close as he could come.

The orca's huge convoluted brain eagerly soaked up every expression and repeated it in Orcan, so Stringer could add it to his vocabulary.

"Could we move on?" Stringer asked. "The water here is a bit cool for us if we're not swimming."

The alpha male urged Stringer to climb on his back. They would race past Juneau, then feed and rest below the Pratt Seamount. "Good squid, deep off the shelf there," the orca whistled.

Lanoll preferred to ride on her orca mount in front of the dorsal fin, letting the pressure of the water push her feet or legs firmly against the broad edge of the fin. Their trip to the Pratt Seamount passed quickly, and they were soon on their way south along a range of steep sea mountains.

Stringer and Lanoll's isolation suits kept them warm enough—barely—but as soon as they passed Sitka and found warm currents surging north past the Queen Charlotte Islands, they packed the suits away and enjoyed the freedom and pleasure of their pressure sense, which was especially useful when schooling free with the orcas during their hunting forays.

In diving for squid, the ellls discovered they had the advantage. Their prehensile hands and maneuverability sped up the gathering process, and they could dive deeper than the orcas. Evolved on the larger planet Ellason, with gravity nearly 1.4 times Earth's, their built-in high-pressure tolerance allowed them to follow the squid beyond the orcas' range. The huge hunters were delighted with the cooperative effort. The leisure gave them precious time to recoup and learn more of each other's languages.

The lead male, whom Stringer named Orcam in Orram's honor, became very curious about the elll's trips to the surface to report with the short-range radio in the isolation suits. When he had learned enough Elllonian, he understood that Stringer was giving Orram their position. (He didn't use English, considering it too risky.) Immediately, Orcam insisted on whistling into the mike.

Stringer stifled his laughter as Conn and Orram translated for the others in San Diego. It was the orcan male challenge for leadership of Stringer's 'pod.'

How do you translate 'not necessary' to a person so strongly driven by genetic programming and cultural imprinting? Orram couldn't get the idea across.

"Information only," Stringer said.

"Orram and Conn are father to Stringer, and Conn is mate to me," Lanoll tried.

It was no good. The killer whale was convinced Stringer and Lanoll were tied by obligation to call Orram every two hours. He must be their alpha male.

In many ways Orcam had the right idea. A cross-species decision-making routine would be necessary for a successful farming partnership. Stringer realized that we would have to draw on Varok's rich history with cross-species negotiation. The Varokian Pact Between Species of 1982 *ir* (24,554.5 BCE, Earth) would be our model.

Orram whistled the orcan code into his transmitter. "In the ocean, you are the pod leader. I do not live in water. I am called varok, more like humans."

Orcam seemed satisfied.

"Harrahn's good luck," Orram whistled, hoping the general idea would be understood. "Over and out."

THE ALIEN EFFECT, 2070–2120 C.E. While the first human-orcan mariculture became established, the fish of the mid-Pacific grew healthier. Conn's Org was busy cleaning up *Haemophilus* in fish gills. The org had spread into deep waters where the sea bass and tuna enjoyed its benefits. The human population, recovering rapidly on a steady diet of healthy sea bass and tuna, didn't realize they were eating Conn's Org. Hearty opportunists that they were, a few of Conn's Orgs found the human gut and lungs fine places to live. There were *Haemophilus* germs to eat there, too.

Orram—a moment later, at the SCBA house

Shawne was at home and overheard the radio conversation with the alpha male. She laughed when I put down the transmitter. "Dad," she said, "I think you told that orca he was king of the sea, that you were a shore crab."

"I did not. He understood . . . well enough."

"Good thing Stringer could interpret. You're hopeless."

"Varokian lips don't whistle well," Tandra said.

"Another thing, Orram." Shawne was serious. "I see hope in the cetacean effort, but serious problems for my school." Her forehead wrinkled and I felt a surge of grief lift the tears welling in her eyes. "Some feel our school should support the water import business. They're ignoring realistic resource cost accounting. Eventually the population will have to limit itself to what the locality can support. Imported water is dependent on very scarce shipping fuel. It can't continue."

"Do your students agree?" I asked. "The people I've talked to would rather not support any more regulation than necessary."

"The students . . . that are left . . . are not the problem." Shawne paused, thinking. "It's the business community that hates regulation. It's been overdone in the past, dictating numbers or attacking symptoms, not revising basic rules that drive the economy as a complex system."

"Perhaps we should expand our community workshops in practical complexity economics," I said.

"All right, Dad. But be prepared for old Earth mentality. Business people are talking about economic growth as a panacea. They just can't shake their early-life imprinting."

Shawne sank into the soft couch I had added to our office for Conn's recovery, and he joined us there. "There's so much to do . . . and so little understanding of what danger they're in or what a stable future can mean for their grandchildren."

"So don't you feel you're teaching the right topics?" I asked. "It sounds like your syllabus is right on target."

"It is. It's not that. We've got two more divides in the faculty to resolve. After some students and faculty quit for religious reasons, others complained that we were just talking to each other, feeling good about agreeing and not getting anything done."

I couldn't think of anything to say except to stress the importance of their programs to educate the larger community. "Too many in government ignore the impact of resource limits, and most legislators are still illiterate in science."

Tandra agreed. "We hear echoes of old postmodern ideas that science is just another belief system, a product of sociology rather than a system for testing and re-testing what's real."

Shawne nodded. I could sense she was hesitant to speak her main concern, but she did. "There are not enough positive visions driving the faculty or the students. They'd rather argue than do the hard work of envisioning what a steady state could be and how to get there."

As we puzzled over what to say next, a call came in from Stringer. His voice was breathless and hurried. "We're in trouble, Orram. The orca pod is caught in a huge seine net. The bottom of the net was closed off before we could get out."

"We?"

"We were dozing on our orcan mounts. Our sonar can't spot the large mesh of seine nets any better than the orcas' sonar. They spotted tuna and gave chase."

Conn took the mike from me. "Cut your way out, Stringer."

"Lanoll is working on it with her laser pen. It's steel, Conn. Have you heard from Junah and Jesse?"

"They're fine, but too far away to help."

"Where are Junah and Jesse?" Conn asked me.

"On a water tanker south of Sitka, hours away."

"Stringer, get yourself and Lanoll out of there. Give me your coordinates, and then get off the surface. You don't want to be seen. We'll get help to you . . . somehow. Dive. Now."

Junah

Junah called in to San Diego as soon as Stringer signed off. "We picked up Stringer's call but couldn't get the coordinates, Conn."

When Conn gave them to her, she repeated them back. "We'll try to get help to them. There may not be time to save the orcas, though. They have to surface to breathe, within fifteen minutes, tops."

"Thank God eIIls don't need to surface," Shawne said.

"How far away are you?" Conn asked.

"I'm not sure," Junah glanced to Jesse. "Most of our instruments have been shut down since we brought the dinghy onboard this tanker. There's no easy access to them."

Jeff Passage took Junah's mike from her.

"San Diego, this is Jeff Passage, tanker captain. We'll pick up your friends—thirty minutes at the outside."

"Conn here, Passage. Explain. We thought you were near Vancouver."

"Farther out. We decided to escort your friends—"

"Our family, Passage. Family. And valuable orcas, if you can help them."

"We'll try. Our helicopter is on the way. I'll go along to supervise. I'm handing you back to Junah now."

Passage left the cabin, with Jesse close behind.

"That tanker has been tracking Stringer and Lanoll?" Conn asked.

"Yes. I didn't know until now, Conn," Junah said. "I suppose Passage has been monitoring all our transmissions, probably following Stringer's coordinates."

"We can be thankful for that," I said. There was an inflection in Junah's voice I didn't like. I continued in Varokian. "You sound like you don't trust him, Junah."

"I don't. Not entirely," she said. "He let us know he recognized me as a varok, and he invited my mind scan, but he keeps his mental distance. He tries not to think about ellls. When he offered us a ride south, I invited him to meet you, Conn, but we've never mentioned Lanoll and Stringer. Until he overheard my last transmission, he didn't know they were ellls. Now he's sure. I suspect that's why he's so eager to join the rescue effort."

"You mean capture them," Conn said.

"I hope not, Conn. He's been very kind to us." She looked up from speaking into the transmitter, surprised to see Jesse. He had not been allowed to board Jeff's helicopter.

SHORT-RANGE CREATURES

Orram—moments later

Conn looked to Tandra for help. "Should we call the Coast Guard?"

"It's worth a try."

"I'll call them," I said. Then Tandra surprised us both.

"Not unless Charley is still in San Diego. He said his boat would be ready by now. He could be more help."

I had forgotten she was in contact with the fisherman, but I thought no more about it just then. Conn was miserable with worry. Feeling helpless was terrible for him. With both Lanoll and Stringer in trouble, he needed to join the rescue effort.

"This Passage character," Conn said. "Who is this guy?"

"We'll soon see," Tandra said. "Jesse is no fool. He'll be sure Passage does all he can to save Lanoll and Stringer and the orcas."

"Orcas? Who is more valuable? Ellls or orcas?" It was not like Conn to put relative values on life. The questions were a measure of the extreme anxiety he felt.

"Ellls, of course, Conn," Tandra said with a ring of sarcasm. "Ellls are especially valuable to Passage, if Junah has read him right."

"I don't like it. He could run off with them."

"That's why the Coast guard will agree to find them," I said. "They were eager to help us whenever they could. They will keep us informed."

"We should go with them." Conn was desperate, but Tandra shut down his emotional fires with a firm voice.

"Not in the shape you're in," she said. "You can help us all by getting back to full strength as soon as you can. Half your plumes need to grow back. Orram, while you call the Coast Guard, I'm off to see Charley. If he can help, I'm sure he will."

As Tandra departed, I contacted the Coast Guard. They responded as we'd hoped, promising to send the nearest vessel to help. They would contact the fishing ships that had trapped our family.

I signed off and found myself alone in the front room of the SCBA house. I wished I was on the yacht with Tandra and Charley, joining them in their evolving relationship and working out a plan to bring the ellls home safely.

Though it seemed a Jovian age, Tandra was gone less than a half hour. She came into the house out of breath, with a hopeful look that painted her face with vibrant beauty. She saw the questions in my face before I realized they filled my mind.

"It's going to be alright, Orram. Charley knows Passage by reputation, but he is keeping tabs on the situation for us. He says we have nothing to fear from Passage. And you have nothing to fear from Charley, Orram."

She met my eyes and put her hand to my patch, then went to the pool to check on Conn.

I didn't see it coming, Tandra's attraction to Charley. She and I had been of one mind for so long, for eighteen Earth years, I suppose I thought it beyond possibility. Had I forgotten her needs as a human female? Had I neglected her uniqueness? The questions rose like poisoned darts in my mind as I stared out the window and toward the SCBA pier where Charley had docked the bulky white fishing boat he called home.

I am the alien here, I reminded myself. *Tandra has every right to find a human mate. It needn't disrupt the family any more than Conn's finding Lanoll.*

The lie rang out with deafening discord when I found Orticon watching me. He knew very well that Tandra's withdrawal in favor of a human mate could destroy me.

She shares your mind, Father, Orticon reminded me in thought. *Share hers.*

Orram—moments later

"Gad, I hate being stuck here." Conn stirred the pool until the water lilies lay limp and bedraggled on the surface, shredded by his frustrated thrashing. Forty-five minutes had passed since Passage left in his helicopter to search for Stringer and Lanoll and the orcas. "We can't tell what's happening out there. Lanoll and Stringer could be dead. The orcas could all be drowned."

Tandra stayed close in water with him, and it helped ease his frustration. The Coast Guard was on the scene. There was nothing we could do for Stringer and Lanoll but wait.

"We must stay in contact with the gray whales," I told Conn when he joined me in the kitchen. "Didn't you talk to them during your ocean swim? When you got sick? Whales? Tuna farming?"

"Orram, I can't go back in that ocean any time soon."

I ladled some stew into his bowl. "Send Nidok," I said. "Until the oceans are clean and you are well, Nidok can be your liaison."

"Get real, old pal. Nidok would piss off the whales and get himself whalloped before they figured out why he was bothering them."

"So teach him what we know about cetacean Sonics. Better yet, work with Orticon. He's found that the National Marine Fisheries Service is using nonlinear time series analyses to set fishing quotas. You would love it."

"All right. All right. If they're actually putting complex realities to work." He downed his meal and retreated to the pool. "Call me the minute you get word of Stringer and Lanoll."

Shawne came in, happy with some success with her classes. Her face fell as we told her about the ellls and orcas.

"We don't know when we'll get news," I told her. "It could be hours. Conn is grieving for moments lost. Tell me some good news. What is going on at school that put a smile on your face when you came in?"

"It is good news for a change. Most students have chosen to go to their regional offices and encourage them to publish population limits based on naturally available water. One group is also working on a list of 'necessities' that could be imported from other areas."

"That can't be easy," I said. "I'm sure everyone has a different definition of necessity."

"We have to start somewhere, Orram."

"Exactly. But please remember—that's all you can do—start. And keep your sponsors informed. They may allow you to try and change initial conditions here and there, as best you can, but the long term will play out as it will. You're dealing with extremely complex interlaced systems, Shawne. Don't expect things to fall into place in your lifetime." I hated to say it. Perhaps I had said it too often. She smiled indulgently at me, and we finished eating.

Tandra came in, looking frustrated. "Charley has tried contacting Passage's tanker again. He can get nothing but their recorded message saying they are still 'executing emergency procedures.'"

"Have we heard from the coast guard?" Shawne asked.

"They have no details yet," I said.

Tandra went off to check on Conn and found him asleep on the bottom of the pool, so she and Shawne and I retreated to the outside deck with the radio. We watched the sunset, awaiting word of our lost family members.

Shawne sat quietly in the warm light of a pink and gold sky, her light hair glistening.

"Tell us more about your classes, Shawne," I said. "You seem more hopeful now."

"It's so changeable, Orram. Just when I'm sure we can't make a dent, there are signs of hope."

"What are the students like?"

"Most are quite young, and ready to learn. They're full of ideas. One of my students is participating in a project to oversee hearings for environmental regulations. Another is campaigning for replacement ethics in the San Diego eco-region. Some have already begun work on population distribution. Others want to work on local projects, like water conservation, but every time a good discussion gets going, questions about Ellason's approach interrupt. I just don't have the patience for the endless second-guessing that goes on. Their worries are groundless. I keep telling them that human astronomers have confirmed the reports from Moonbase. Bob Carliano seems to be our only credible spokesman. I don't understand why people insist on worrying about space invaders, when they're facing real problems, like continued warming."

Tandra and I kept our silence. Only rarely did we break down into what Tandra called our "ain't-it-awful" mode. Self-fulfilling, defeatist attitudes had been tried—and proven to fail. We didn't talk about it much, but we elders saw all the signs in human nature driving toward long-range cycles of boom and bust.

The hardiest species had already adapted to the human-dominated environment. Cockroaches, crows, coywolves, and raccoons flourished during the human die offs. They would continue to evolve. We weren't so sure about humans.

"We grieved together," Shawne continued, "for the loss of Earth's more exotic species. They listened when I said there was nothing on Varok to compare to the colorful quetzal bird, to the speed and accuracy of the eagle, nothing on Ellason to match the peculiar elephants and the creatures of what remain of Earth's coral reefs."

The planet's conditions were so varied, yet so perfectly set within viable ranges, that nature's wildest experiments had thrived time and time again, recovering and soaring to new heights of conscious existence after every wave of extinction. I longed for a time-lapse movie of all that had moved and grown on Earth since atoms of carbon and nitrogen had found their sources of energy in sulfur or oxygen and learned to dance to life's beat. I would use time-lapse to record what was happening now—another major shift in that beat.

Tandra and I were in the same mood. She guessed correctly why I was staring at the geometric center of a lovely purple and white hellebore, planted by the La Jolla Garden Defenders next to our lodge.

"Is it drought tolerant?" Conn , still dripping from the pool, had joined us on the porch. He touched the large flat petals with a shaking webbed finger.

"Not really," I said, "but some of the Defenders were apologetic that xeriscaping was not yet enforced in the southwest."

"What are you doing out of water, Conn?" Shawne said.

"It's too empty," he said. "You're doing good work, Shawnoon. You're really making waves. I just wish I could be more help. All I've done is cause trouble."

"Nonsense."

"Seriously. The great-fish thought I should come here, but I can't fathom why, unless they knew I'd get poisoned sooner or later and make the case for ocean cleanup."

I had had a similar thought, but dismissed it.

Conn went on, his depression lasting longer than usual. "Maybe I should go back to Moonbase and wait for you all there. I can't even provide you any protection, Shawnoon. The San Diego police have a constant watch on the lodge, and you have an escort everywhere you go. I'm only good for attracting attention. As soon as Lanoll and Stringer get back, we eills better get off this planet."

Shawne expressed what we all felt. "They should have been out of the net hours ago."

The Alien Effect, 2120–2220 C.E. As Conn's Org found comfy places to live in the gills of fish and the intestines of humans, chaotic change of another sort began. During the twenty-second century humans bred freely. Once again their populations reached stress levels. Hydrogen and hydro-electricity powered a mobile society similar to that of the twentieth century. Sewage and waste continued to find its way into the Pacific Ocean.

Before a hundred years had passed, San Diego Bay and the North American shorelines became unsafe for swimming once again. The coral reefs went into another decline. In the re-polluted ocean, one strain of Conn's Org found a new source of food in the weakened cold-water coral.

A Game of Tennis?

Orram—late that evening, at the SCBA house

At last we received the radio signal we wanted; it came from Passage's tanker. The radio operator put Stringer on. He was breathless with excitement.

"Conn, *dara vahn*, everything's okay, finally. You'll like this guy Passage. He bought the whole orcan pod, right out from under those *kaehl-din* pirates—"

"Bought?" Conn was incensed.

"It worked, Conn. The orcas are free—on their way to consult with the gray whales—the ones working with you. Passage can see the benefits."

"Why didn't you contact us sooner? We've been sick with worry for hours."

"We had a terrible time getting the orcas out of the net. Lanoll and

I had to work together to help orcas up for breaths of air. Passage and Charley were working with Jesse and Junah on the surface. We haven't had time to get something to eat. I'm sorry."

"We're so glad you're okay," I said.

"Thanks, Orram. Orram? Are you with Conn?"

"There are problems, Stringer. Tandra and I came down to the surface from Moonbase. Nidok is finding trash and foul water everywhere. Stay out of the water near shore, unless you've got a sealed suit on."

"We found that out."

"Are you sick?"

"A little."

"There's oil everywhere. Don't eat shore fish."

"Did you get into it, Conn? Are you all right?"

"I am now. Don't risk it. It's not fun."

"But we can't feel a thing with the suits—"

"Don't risk it. Let me talk to Lanoll."

Conn's mate knew how to defuse his temper. "If you say anything to worry Shawne," she said, "I'll have your toe-fins for lunch."

"Is that a promise?"

"We're fine, Conn. We just picked up a little oil—"

"Swimming without your isolation suits," he said.

"Look who's talking, *Aloon*. Stringer needs to school, remember? He's surviving, but how are you?"

"Lonely," Conn said. "What I need is a good elllonian—"

Lanoll laughed, relieved.

And so was I. Conn sounded like himself again. It would be hard to get anything serious out of him.

"Let me talk to Tandra," Lanoll said. "I need some reliable information."

Tandra took the receiver. "Tandra here, Lanoll. I don't like what I'm hearing. Are you all right? Conn got into some oil, and bad fish, but he's nearly clean now. How is Stringer doing out of water?"

"We're okay, Tan, but I'll be glad when we're all together again. Stringer and I have each other and a large ship's hull full of fresh water. That will be enough for now. We'll all climb in the pool and do a good adjustment when we get back. Schooling in the isolation suits just doesn't work."

"The neuromasts in your pressure line meshwork don't pick up anything through the suits?" Tandra asked.

"Only huge disturbances in the water, like a propeller at three *pallons*. Not enough to school by. The oil clogs our pores, too."

"Conn is getting restless, and I'm a walking prune these days. With you gone, he wants me in his water whenever we're not working. I've got to find some outlet for his temper, or we'll have to ship him back to Varok."

Lanoll did not laugh. She probably knew Tandra was serious. "How about one of your land sports? I've always thought we ellls would be good at tennis. It's like *llaoon* grass sky ball with a net instead of rocks to leap."

"Sky ball is similar, Lanoll. Tennis might be worth a try. I'll find a way to pad his feet."

"Wrap the fins up out of the way so he can run."

"Really? Up? I'd better review my elllonian anatomy."

"Yes, up. I'll sign off now. We'll see you in five days."

"Do you have something you can use to clean out your lungs and gills?"

"Yes. The ship's dish soap seems to be working."

Tandra hesitated. "We have a new friend. He suggests a solvent called PES-51R. Get it, if you can. Please be careful. Over and out."

I looked at Tandra. The new friend was Charley. He filled her thoughts, and I could feel an emotional tug strike home.

Orram

Six days can be an eternity—especially for an ell waiting on land for his mate. Since Conn was steady on his flippers, Tandra remembered Lanoll's suggestion and took him in the land rover to a little-used tennis court east of the city.

"You need the exercise," she insisted, "and you're not going back in the ocean."

I went along for the ride and soon found myself, along with our ubiquitous guards, busy picking up stray balls, then making line calls. I doubt if elllonian vision in air is as accurate as human vision, but as the balls warmed up, Conn's infrared vision gave him an advantage.

"I saw where that ball landed very clearly, Landlubber," he hollered at Tandra. "It was on the line."

"Sorry. It's my call when the ball bounces on my side. I saw red concrete between the ball and the line. The play area is green. You call the balls on your side."

"Orram?"

"Don't ask me," I said. "I was retrieving the ball you hit out of the fence."

Conn's hand-eye coordination gave him a quick, accurate forehand, but his swimming musculature sent his backhand attempts all over San Diego. The next ball flew over the fence and bounced off the roof of an electric car as it pulled into the parking lot.

"Hey," Charley called, as he got out of the car, "does that mean I should drive on?"

"Not at all," I called.

"Hi, Charley," Tandra said. "Come referee. We need all the help we can get. Conn is out of control. He can't see in dry air."

Conn ignored Tandra. He walked to the car and went into a huddle with Charley.

With an explosion of laughter, Charley walked onto the court and parked himself near the net. "I'll call the lines," he said. "Play ball."

"That's not what you're supposed to say," Conn objected.

"The umpire rules." Tandra laughed.

The noise of our shouting attracted some people, and they began to gather in the parking lot. Somehow the word spread that the elll, Conn, was on the court. More people came running from a nearby baseball field.

"Better stay outside the fence," Charley called to them. "We've got a wild elll in here." The crowd laughed, and Charley took up office as referee on the sidelines. I called the back lines.

"Conn, it's time you played a real game," Tandra said, loud enough to get a cheer from the crowd.

"I can't count by fifteens," he smirked.

"Up or down? Call for serve."

"Up what?"

"Up yours, my dear elll. Your racket. Spin it. P is up."

"Up."

"You always say up when we flip things. It's down."

"It's always down when you flip."

"Then why didn't you call down?"

"Down!"

"Sorry. Too late. My serve."

Tandra's serve was flat but swift. Conn easily slammed it down the line for a winner.

"My mistake," she said. "No more serves to your forehand, elll."

The crowd cheered. The next serve was hard to Conn's backhand, and the ball sailed into the surrounding desert. Some boys in the crowd retrieved it, but wouldn't return it.

"Sign it. Sign it, Conn," they insisted, and that was the end of that game. Conn signed the ball, then chatted with the crowd about his problems getting around the court.

His long legs gave him the advantage of good mobility, but his webbed feet soon tired and got in his way when he tried making quick turns.

"Tell us about Ellason," someone asked. "Why are we seeing it for the first time?"

"How close will it come?"

"Will we have killer tides?"

"Do you want killer tides?" Conn asked. "I don't understand why you humans are always hoping for disasters, or alien invasions. Sorry, we're no good at invasions. We don't even have a decent backhand."

The crowd laughed.

"Seriously, Ellason's perihelion will be somewhere around Neptune's orbit, no closer. There will be no killer tides, and no invasions. Personally, I'm delighted Ellason is coming in for a visit. A few of our ships may go out from Varok soon. I'd love to go out with them. I haven't been home since I left as a tad."

"Why did you go to Varok so young?"

"To study Earth's wonderful languages and kidnap this here fair maiden." Conn pulled Tandra into his arms and wrapped his tongue around her neck.

The crowd loved it, but Conn was drying out, so we had to say goodbye to the audience. Our security escort soon had us all back at the lodge.

"You picked a good one that time, Tandra," Charley said. "Aliens playing tennis is good public relations."

"This aquatic scoundrel would have made life miserable for all of us at home," Tandra said.

"'Aquatic scoundrel?' Give me the proverbial break, Tan," Conn said.

"You know," Charley broke the tension before it blossomed, "Conn's antics and his great exchanges with the crowd reassured a lot of people worried about Ellason. Alien invaders don't play tennis." He scrolled through the screen on his pocket computer. "Someone's been taking videos. It's gone viral."

"Thanks, Charley, I guess," Tandra said.

"And now I better go," he said. "I forgot that I have to see the dentist. Bad tooth kicked up on me the other day."

"We'll see you soon I hope," Tandra said, and she walked him to the door.

When she returned, Conn and I were eating, silently. "Did you leave me any soup, you two?" Tandra said. "What's the matter?"

"Read your life partner, Tan. What do you see? I see pain and worry in Orram, and I'm just an elll."

"It's okay, Conn," I said.

"So I'm not supposed to have male human friends?" Tandra asked. She wasn't kidding. "Who's jealous here, Conn? You or Orram?"

Pool Time

Orram—at the SCBA house, two days later

Jeff Passage's tanker lumbered into San Diego Bay and anchored at the water transport docks on North Island. Passage kept his word. There was no public notice of our family's reunion. Flying the helicopter, he brought Junah, Jesse, Lanoll, and Stringer from the tanker directly to our home overlooking Alligator Head.

Passage was amazed when everyone headed straight for the pool.

There we gave Stringer a rousing adjustment, then we left Lanoll, Stringer and Conn in water to reconnect. Shawne had not yet come home from teaching. Orticon and Nidok were connecting with some gray whales and a sperm whale passing along the California coast.

Stringer was hungry. Passage showed no sign of leaving, so I asked him to join Tandra and me in the kitchen. While I cooked up Chihuahuan posole garnished with lemon and lettuce, Tandra told him about our customs on Varok.

My mother's pot on the hearth had always been ready with warm stew for family and friends, so I had tried to carry on her varokian tradition when Tandra and I came down from Moonbase to nurse Conn back to health. Our diet was not too different from humans on Earth. We ate some eggs and fowl, but our staple was a protein-rich combination of beans, rice and vegetables, with fruit for dessert. No chocolate. It gave Conn headaches. Sour spices were a favorite on Varok. They were difficult to duplicate on Earth, so I used a lot of lemon, fennel, and curry.

Passage soaked up everything we said, until Shawne came home from her day of teaching. When she came in the door, she headed directly to the pool, leaving a string of clothes behind her. She was eager to welcome the ellls home and add to their adjustment.

Our conversation with Passage came to an abrupt end as he watched Shawne pass by the kitchen.

"*Aeo-oo* Stringer," she shouted. "*Bayon. Bayon* Lanoll. Junah, Jesse, welcome home." She somersaulted into the water, and stayed under, soaking up her family's schooling embrace.

"Our daughter," Tandra said pointedly. "We'll introduce you later. She will spend some time with the ellls. She has missed them."

Jesse entered the kitchen, looking grim, as usual. He had told us that he didn't trust Passage.

Junah followed him. "Orram, your stew smells wonderful, almost as good as your mother's."

"Lemon and English white pepper," I said, "a gift from the Ambassador. The pork and garbanzos soak it up. If we had some red potatoes and ilara meat we'd have a good imitation of Orserah's root soup."

"The only thing missing would be dried snarl loops," Tandra added.

Passage could not hide his curiosity any longer. "Would the ellls mind if I watch the adjustment?"

"Let's go see if they're ready to eat," I said to Tandra, proud of my diplomatic answer.

"This way Jeff." Tandra led him to the pool and cautioned him to be quiet. "We'll wait until they surface."

"Where is Shawne?"

Tandra saw her nose reach up for a deep breath. Then, without a ripple, she sank quietly to rejoin the ellls without disturbing the pressure patterns of their adjustment.

Passage did not see Shawne take the breath in the midst of the pool lilies, and Tandra wasn't about to tell him. "She can stay under quite a while, having grown up with ellls. It's a wonder she hasn't sprouted gills."

"And you're a biologist?" Passage laughed.

I could see that Tandra was beginning to like this direct young man, and she began to look him over more carefully.

Suddenly the water boiled with the underwater wake of racing. Shawne's smooth brownness arched across the surface and was soon followed by the three green figures of Conn, Stringer and Lanoll.

When he saw Tandra sitting on the deck, Conn raced close by, and, with his backfin, threw a wash of water over her and Passage. On the next pass, he slid onto the deck. "Why are you sitting up here, Tan? You're missing a good one."

"I'm entertaining our guest, if you'd care to notice." Tandra disappeared with a yelp of protest as Conn pulled her in, and the water fell quiet.

It was more than Passage could handle. "Wait for me," he hollered, and he jumped into the pool. Less than a minute passed before Shawne surfaced, rolled onto the deck, and ran for her robe hanging on the wall. "Why didn't someone tell me we had company?" she demanded.

I laughed, and Jesse answered. "You didn't ask."

"I hope Conn remembers most people have to breathe," she said, joining us at the pool's edge. "It's good to see you, Jesse. I'm so glad you're back. I need all the help I can get, keeping the students on track."

Jesse didn't have time to answer her, for Passage surfaced, sputtering, threw his shoes, jeans and shirt onto the deck, and dove again to rejoin the ellls.

Tandra was the next to surface. "You know, Baby Girl," she said, "we should sit on Conn until he agrees to some decent pool rules. He's embarrassed you and ruined my new sweater."

"You do look a bit soggy, Mom."

"I'll impose some varokian order to this menagerie," I said, "as soon as Conn agrees to wear clothes in public."

It was an old family joke. It went back to the days on Varok when, at age six, Shawne suddenly realized that varoks and humans wore clothes. Hers got in the way in water. Ellls don't need them, Tandra would say, for their body plumes look like tunics, and they provide insulation and modesty. For a few years, until Shawne started to mature, we had a hard time convincing her she was not an elll and would need to dress. To this day she prefers to go nude at home.

"Who let this human in the pool?" she asked. "He doesn't know an elll from a lizard, best I can tell. Who let him in here?"

"We couldn't refuse, Shawne. Not after he saved Stringer and Lanoll from fish netting and brought them all back here. He paid some fishermen a lot of money to release the orcas."

"Bought himself an elll show, did he?"

Tandra and I looked at each other.

"Don't you two start reading each other," she said. "Use words. That guy is a jerk. I don't want him around here. We've got serious problems."

"What's up, Shawne?" Jesse was always a good one for cutting through family dynamics.

"It's Nidok," Shawne said, changing the subject. "Orticon called in before I left school today. The orcas won't deal with him."

"Why am I not surprised?" Tandra said, checking my mood.

"We'd better go out and see them," I said. "Maybe we can persuade the gray whales to connect with the pod of orcas that brought Stringer and Lanoll down from Alaska."

"No need, Orram. Nidok is flying in, and Orticon won't be far behind him with a full report. I wish this crazy family would stay out of trouble." Shawne left the pool and disappeared for the rest of the evening.

Conn and I stayed up late, waiting for Nidok. Time passed quickly for Conn while he tried to satisfy Passage's curiosity about ellls.

Then Orticon came home, without Nidok. "I thought I was catching up to him, then I lost sight of him. He should have been home by now."

Shawne and I sat down with Orticon in the living room to sort out what to do about finding Nidok.

"Orram, that clatter-plated bird has no manners," Shawne complained. "He stole fish right out of the orca's bubble-net."

"The orcas were incensed," Orticon confirmed. "Stringer had promised not to take advantage of their routine harvests. They saw Nidok's piracy as a breach of trust."

"How angry were they?" I wasn't sure how Nidok regarded the orcas. If he treated them with real contempt, they might lure him in and pull him down. "Were they circling? Leaping to attack, or just breaching as a warning?"

"Circling. If they caught him, he'd be crushed and swallowed without a second thought." Orticon fell quiet when Conn and Jeff Passage entered the room. Tandra followed.

Conn's eyes narrowed. "Spill it," he said.

Passage startled. Conn's mood change was sudden and unmistakably angry.

"Nidok's missing," I said. There was no way we three could keep anything from Conn. He knew by our faces that something was wrong.

"For how long?"

"He should have been here long before you arrived, Orticon," I said, "unless he stopped along the way. Were there any other distractions, any other pods or fishing boats?"

"There are always fishing boats along the coast. He's never shown any interest in them."

"Not even to tease?"

"No. He knows better than to tease humans he doesn't know."

"I'll put in a call to my launches to keep a watch out," Passage volunteered. "I'll need a better description. Was the name Nidok?"

"Yes, that's right." With his offer of help, Shawne dropped her guard a little.

"Nidok what?" Passage took a note pad from his pocket.

"Just Nidok. Describe him as a forty-pound alien with an eight-foot wingspread, wings with prehensile tips, covered with chitinous plates, small black eyes, large fleshy lips, squared-off head."

"How large?" Passage had stopped writing. "I don't mean the lips." His laugh was infectious, and the snowballing tension began to melt.

"About two feet square." Shawne answered with a friendly tone in her voice that surprised us all.

Conn's voice turned serious. "Nidok is family to us. We've taken his scar." The raised wound on Conn's wrist told Passage this was not an elllonian joke.

"He's risked his life to help us. We'll do the same for him." Shawne spoke as if the commitment should be obvious, and Passage responded as she hoped.

"Of course," he said.

"Better make that a quiet search," I told Passage. "We don't want any alien trophy hunters alerted."

"I hear you," Passage said. "Shawne, please come with me to radio the missing-person call. I don't want to say something that would broadcast a lost-alien message to the wrong people. And I'd like you to see the tanker. I understand you have some questions about shipping water—"

They went off, talking, without a goodbye or a backward glance.

Tandra and I looked at each other. She was too far away to read clearly, but I'm sure we shared the same thought.

"What? What?" Conn caught the look and threw it back in our faces.

"You don't want to know what we're thinking," Tandra said.

"I always want to know what you're thinking." Conn's eyes narrowed in a mock threat, and we knew there would be no escape. We would be in the pool again with him before he was satisfied.

"Lead the way," I said, dreading another dose of intense tactile stimulation.

THE ALIEN EFFECT, 2220–2416 C.E. As Conn's Org searched for sources of nourishment, it came upon the coral that had once overrun the concrete reefs of Conn's Marine Park. The weakened coral was vulnerable and tasty, while healthy reef coral adapted to warmer waters gave shelter to Conn's Org. Those corals that escaped being eaten found the waste products of Conn's Org quite nutritious. Eventually, both the coral cells and Conn's Org prospered in the warming ocean, and a symbiotic relationship was established between them. The human population was suffering another major die-off, so few people had time, health, or fuel to visit the reefs.

NIDOK GONE

Orram—at the SCBA house

Days passed with no word of Nidok. Every few hours, when Shawne was at home, Passage called, telling us where his employees were looking and what authorities had been notified. Late on the afternoon of the third day, the tanker captain arrived at the lodge with four tennis rackets. Conn met him at the door, eager for news of Nidok.

"Get on your white shorts, Conn," he said, "we've got a foursome. Shawne will meet us at the courts. You need a diversion while we wait for news. I hear you have done some good PR on the courts. Where is Tandra?"

"She's at the Sea Food Kitchen," I said, "working on a use for sea urchins, maybe something humans will find palatable."

"Well, then, Orram, I expect she'll be back very soon." Passage laughed heartily, failing to notice we didn't join in. Sea urchins were a serious problem.

"There's too many, you know," Conn snarled.

Tandra saved the moment by arriving home just then. "Tennis, Jeff? Good idea. We are all going crazy, wishing we could do something to find Nidok."

"I guarantee we'll know something very soon."

"Guarantee? That's wonderful news, Jeff. Charley is not so optimistic. I assume you'll tell me more than you're saying. Are you ready to go, Conn? Shawne will beat us there, if we don't leave soon."

"I need to borrow your white shorts, Orram." Conn made a move for the dressing room.

"Go. Leave. Play tennis," I said. "You're driving me into overload, hanging around here. Bob and I have work to do. He should be here soon."

Tandra—at the La Jolla tennis courts

Tandra produced a pair of large tennis shoes with the toes cut out and some large rubber bands. "Put these on, Conn," she said. "You nearly ruined your feet last time."

"Sorry I'm late, Mom. Hello Jeff," Shawne called. She had jogged to the courts from the bus station. "Conn, where did you get those shoes? They're hilarious. All you need is some white shorts."

"Very funny. Very funny, young woman. Orram wouldn't loan me his."

That set the mood, and for a precious two hours, worry over Nidok was nearly forgotten. Passage and Shawne teamed up against Tandra and Conn, for Tandra was the more experienced player, and Conn was wild.

Tandra could see that Shawne was watching Passage's response to the play.

Jeff hit well in the next few games and the score became 4 to 5, with Jeff and Shawne one behind Tandra and Conn. Then Shawne went tense, trying too hard, and they lost the set.

"This is the most frustrating game," Shawne stormed. "I shouldn't even bother. Look at Conn. He's only been playing a few weeks, and he hits much better than I do."

"Didn't he play with you on Varok?" Jeff asked.

"Only in water," Tandra said.

"Look, Sweets, it's only a game," Jeff said, "a very psychological one, I admit. It's easy to get down on yourself when you miss a few, then it's a self-fulfilling prophecy. You feel you're no good, so you play no good. I do it all the time."

"That's a tiny bit hard to believe," Shawne said.

"You just tensed up a bit there in the end. I bet if we counted all our bad shots, I'd get the prize for the most. You must have played with your mom a lot. She's a good teacher. You've got some good strokes. You put your body weight behind your serve. Most people don't do that."

"She told me to throw the racket like a baseball when serving."

They talked on and on as Tandra and Conn packed up. Jeff had managed to turn Shawne's mood one hundred and eighty degrees.

"It would be a much better game," Conn said, "if the server only had one ball, and if, on the return, the ball could be hit twice, like a volleyball set-up. Two bounces for aliens over fifty Earth years."

Shawne laughed. "Let's do it next time."

"You're on," Jeff said. "Sounds like fun."

When they pulled into the SCBA compound, he took his leave gently. "I'm going to skip dinner here, if you'll excuse me. I think my last lead on Nidok should have something for us by now."

He drove off in a hurry, and Shawne stood outside, watching his car disappear.

"Not such a jerk now?" Conn said.

"What do you think of him, Conn?"

"I think tennis is great for revealing basic personality quirks and qualities."

They went inside, and Shawne was quiet that evening. She kept to herself, at a noticeable distance, so Orram wouldn't be tempted to read her.

Orram—the next day

"Shawne has gone off with Passage again," Conn announced at the next evening meal. "He'd better have something this time."

"Or what?" I asked. "We've alerted everyone we can name. Going after Nidok ourselves won't help. We need to be here to coordinate."

"Well, her going off with Passage all the time is driving me crazy," Stringer said, putting down his bowl. "I don't trust him. I've warned her to keep her distance."

"Big brother strikes again," Lanoll said. "You worry too much, Stringer."

"Maybe no one worries enough about Shawne," I said. "She's been so self-assured, starting her school, finding competent economists to translate Varokian law into human possibilities—but Tandra and I have realized how young and inexperienced she is socially."

"She thinks she's the universe's *femme fatale*, being raised by ellls," Stringer quipped. "Lanoll, please. Conn? I'm too worried about Nidok." In such emergencies, elllonian mood-swinging was not helpful. He needed to school, so we all moved to the pool.

Stringer and Conn dove into the crystal water, and Lanoll sat with Tandra and me on the deck. Her toe webs fanned out and closed and fanned out again in the water.

Conn surfaced and said nothing. He dove back in with Lanoll for a time. When they emerged, we four huddled together on the deck and talked. Stringer stayed underwater.

"So you think Shawne went off to mate with this guy Passage?" Conn asked Tandra.

"No, of course not. She's too worried about Nidok," Tandra said. "But she's interested in Passage."

"Interested."

"Humans take their time, Conn," Lanoll said.

"Some don't." Conn looked at Tandra, remembering the evening they met. He had been fully disguised in an isolation suit, and she had assumed he was human.

"Guilty as charged," Tandra said. "There's something subtle about Jeff Passage that has fired Shawne's romantic imagination. "I'd hate to have her go through a painful disillusionment."

"Like Tandra did with me." Conn knew better, but still, after a volatile and complicated twenty years together, he enjoyed teasing her.

"Not really," I said.

"Exactly," Tandra countered, and we laughed at the contradiction. "I went through a difficult transition from fantasy through horror to reality, learning to know and love you, Conn. I would rather not see Shawne repeat my mistakes."

"Spoken like a true parent," Jesse said from the entrance to the pool room. "Sorry to interrupt, but we've had a radio call from Shawne. Passage has some new information from friend Charley. He thinks he knows where Nidok could be. Passage wants to follow through before they lose any more time. Shawne asked if Orticon could take over her classes until she gets back. She won't be home tonight. She's going with Passage to get Nidok."

Conn turned ashen lime-green.

"She's not spending one more hour with that human tanker jockey," he said, and he was out the door.

Shawne—the same evening, on Passage's water tanker

Jeff Passage commanded his fleet of tankers from the wheelhouse of the *Sounder*, the smallest and oldest of the single-hulled oil tankers that had been converted in order to haul potable water from Alaska to Southern California.

Soon after the turn of the century, when the southwest water disputes were still being fought in the courts, creative entrepreneurs and city water commissions set in motion trial studies to sandblast and recoat the hulls of single-hulled oil tankers, which were to be phased out in 2013 for carrying oil. The tankers, thus saved from mothballing, were put to use hauling water from Alaska to San Diego.

The Colorado River no longer supplied water to anyone beyond Arizona, and the Imperial Valley conservation water promised to San Diego did little to ease their natural desert conditions. With the new supply of Alaskan water, people continued to immigrate from valleys and low deserts to enjoy the milder coast climate. To our astonishment, many refused to accept purified sewage water or to enforce the use of composting toilets.

Shawne stared out over San Diego Bay from Passage's dining table, listening with irritation as Jeff took command of more than the search for Nidok.

He talked into the radio at a rapid clip. "We think Cold Pete Dawson has the Oran-ElConn-Grey family pet. It was Dawson's seine net that trapped the two ellls up north. They got out and we picked them up with the 'copter. . . . The tanker is slow. He beat us south. Okay—he or one of his buddies. We had to buy the whole damn pod of orcas from those pirates. . . . Because the ellls insisted. The killers had given them a free ride down from Alaska. They're interested in farming tuna. Nidok and one of the varoks were taking them out to meet the gray whales Conn and Nidok were working with. There were a number of fishing boats in the area. Now we know one of them was Cold Pete Dawson's— can't miss that ugly green color. The varok had sent Nidok back to the SCBA house, and that's the last he was seen. Until we locate Nidok, the farming effort will be on hold."

"Is that right?" Shawne gave Passage a look. "Just talk on," she said. "No one is paying attention to you, anyway."

It set him back on his haunches. "I didn't mean to intrude on your family's venture—"

"Then don't," she said with a pleasant grin. "Let's go out and see what the orcas have to say about Nidok."

"Well, sure."

"It's only a few miles. It shouldn't take more than three hours. They'll come in as far as they can, once they hear my ID."

"You want to swim out to the killer whales? Seriously, Shawne, you can't do that. They're not in the best mood. When that fishing boat netted them, they were trying to adjust to the idea of partnering with grays. It wasn't going well."

"No problem. Human skin is nowhere near as sensitive as elll tiles."

"Why don't we take a launch? It would be much faster."

"Wastes fuel."

"Shawne, time means everything when someone is missing. If this Pete Dawson character took Nidok, we have to track him down sooner than later. He kidnapped Junah and—what's his name? The grim, rough character."

"Jesse Mendleton."

"Dawson was dead serious. He spent a lot of money putting that net across Little Koniuji to trap the ellls. He could be out for revenge now. Men like that are dangerous, especially with big money at stake."

"All right," Shawne said. "We'll take your launch."

They headed straight west, chasing a red-orange sun into the horizon. Shawne had little fear for Nidok. He was well armed and shielded, with not one serious natural enemy on Varok. If anyone tried to capture him, they would have their hands full of slashing chitin. She suspected he had taken the chance to help calm the two cetacean pods.

Meanwhile, she had a good excuse for spending time with this exciting person, Jeff Passage. No one's fool, this one. And a great sport. Tennis courts tell all. Every hormone in her body raced when she looked up and down his lean body. She loved the feeling.

He caught her hand as she reached out to touch the powerful muscles of his upper arm.

"I'm no elll," he said.

"Not at all."

"Nor a varok."

"You're very human, very male."

"And you are very young." He pressed her fingertips to his lips. "And very desirable—and far too lovely to throw yourself away on the first pirate who comes along. Take your time, Shawne, You will have your choice among the princes of Earth."

"Yes." We never taught Shawne to mince words, and there was nothing shy in her vibrant temperament. "But right now, I want to kiss you, prince or no. I have seen it done."

"In the movies or in your family?"

"That is none of your business."

He laughed and kissed her, passionately, and she did not want it to end.

"You're wonderful," he said, one hand minding the wheel. "You're exquisite. There is no one on this planet anything like you. Let's go talk to the whales before we get in trouble with your family."

The launch cut straight to Point Loma then headed west, until Shawne asked Jeff to cut the engines.

"There. To port. Orcas."

"I don't see anything." Passage leaned on the rail and scanned the seas, but he could see nothing but dark swells and reflections of moonlight on the water.

"I'll be right back," Shawne said, and she dove overboard, slicing the black water with a quiet plunch.

"Shawne, are you crazy? Stay with the boat."

"Keep the motors off," she called, and then she was gone.

"Put a searchlight on her. Find her, off to port," Passage called to his crew at the back of the launch.

The light cut the night air, and a faint command coming from the sea was heard by everyone on Passage's launch. "Shut that damn thing off. You'll spook the orcas."

Shawne put out a string of vocalizations and whistles. Her orcan code was not as polished as Stringer's, but her trouble-call was adequate to bring the orcas to her.

"Nidok the ahlork did not come home," she signaled. "Did you see him with the varok Orticon?"

A cascade of sound answered her, and she asked the approaching orcas to repeat their message slowly. After several tries, she pieced it together: "Orticon was here with the big insect. The rude one left by air over the small boat. A larger fishing boat followed them. It sported the color of a sick sea turtle. There were loud noises. Some of us saw killer sticks, and we ran. We breached to see what was happening. The insect was falling from the sky."

The blood drained from Shawne's face, and the nearest orca rolled gently against her in sympathy.

"You're sure? You saw Nidok fall, hit by gunfire? Where did he land? In water?"

"We didn't see that." One orca repeated his message. Quickly then, the pod escorted Shawne back to the launch, for she was clearly distressed by the news and would soon be in trouble in the cold ocean.

THE TROUBLE WITH PASSAGE

Orram—a little earlier, at La Jolla Cove

At a comfortable distance, Tandra and I followed Conn along the shoreline path to the beach at La Jolla Cove. The elll needed time alone to digest the fact that Shawne was a grown woman, capable of handling her emotions—and the powerful pull that human hormones exert.

Before Conn entered the surf, however, we stopped him. I will never forget the look on his face when he turned to acknowledge our call. It said many things we three had felt on returning to Earth. The elllonian eyes—so huge, designed to take in all the light they could get on bioluminescent, moonlit Ellason—searched for escape from the chaotic signals of his conflicting emotions.

Shawne was too young, too vulnerable to the ravages of her hormones, and we were young no longer. The silver in my hair outshone the bronze. A touch of gray graced Tandra's temples. Conn's head plumes were fringed with gold. Our children were grown. We saw that our lives were winding down, and the future was slipping from our grasp.

"Let's take a shore train down to Passage's tanker," I said. "We'll see that Shawne's okay, and by the time we get there, Jeff should have some news of Nidok."

"There's nothing else we can do, Orram. Conn?" Tandra dove into the elll's eyes and stayed there, until all the arguments in Conn's brain quit boiling to the surface. "Some things can only be learned by direct experience. You taught Shawne that yourself. Let her go, Conn, so she can come to you for help when she really needs it."

When Passage's crew ushered us into his quarters, Shawne ran to Conn and broke down in his arms. "Nidok's been killed."

"What makes you think that?" he asked, when he heard the orcas' story. "He's covered with disgusting, thick chitin plates. A shotgun would knock him out of the sky, but it wouldn't do him any harm."

"Are you sure, Conn?"

"No, but it's better than assuming he's dead. His body would float. Has it washed up anywhere? Have you read the morning news?"

"This is no time to joke, Conn. We've got to find him. From the description we've heard, Nidok was seen on an ugly tub like the fishing boat that captured Junah and Jesse near Alaska."

"Who's joking? What do you think, Passage? Can we run down this Dawson character and search his boat?"

"We can give it a good try. Are you willing to be the bait?"

Tandra was never one for inviting trouble. "I don't like it. What's an alternative?"

"I think Nidok will get home as soon as he can," I said. I knew the ahlork's mind very well, for he and I had spent hours trying all kinds of patch reading. The problem with our varokian patch organs is that they are only good for catching well-organized thoughts. Ahlork thought is so jumbled, it poses an interesting puzzle that defies most mood reading and renders normal thought sensing useless.

"Hold on a minute," Passage said. "We've got a message coming in."

His answers on the radio were short and not informative. "I see. Go ahead then. Don't delay the next run to Alaska. We'll probably take the *Sea Wind* south." He shut down the receiver and looked around at all of us, as if to gauge how best to tell us bad news.

I summarized for him the thoughts running through his head. "Dawson's ship is heading south southwest toward Australia at full speed. You think he has captured Nidok and intends to hold him for profit?"

"It's very likely."

Passage was a bit surprised that I could sense his thought so accurately. He felt naked, exposed. He didn't understand how limited our patch sense was, how it depended on the voltages generated by the flow of thoughts. We varoks can't pry old thoughts and memories out of the neuronal net, it's far too complex. I apologized and explained our limits, for I wanted to befriend this person Shawne so obviously admired.

"Orticon wanted you to see the Great Barrier Reef, Conn," Shawne said. "Maybe this is your chance. I'll call Orticon. He said he would do some teaching when he got back. He'll have Jesse and Junah, as well as Bob Carliano, to help him out while we're gone."

"We'll wait. Make your call," I said.

While Shawne was talking to Orticon, I confronted Passage. "This could be a very long trip, Jeff. Can you afford to do this?"

His wry smile said more than I wanted to know, as if he could afford anything. He had already made a huge conquest in the water trade.

"Is your ship fast enough to intercept him?"

Passage's smile broadened. "I'll take you down there, fast," he said. "It could be the best hope for your ahlork, but when we catch Dawson, I don't know what kind of trouble he'll make for us."

"The offer is accepted, with our deepest gratitude," I said, looking to Tandra and Conn for confirmation. "We have no other choice."

"Then we'll start as soon as you can get ready," Passage said. We'll take two boats. Charley can run backup."

"We're ready," Conn said. Of course he had no changes of clothes to worry him. For an elll, food could always be found where there was water. Without money or passports, we would be dependent on Passage, but Orticon, Jesse and Junah were within a few hours' call. Our interplanetary bus, the *Ranat* was always ready for emergency evacuation.

"The *Sea Wind* is kept ready to support a crew of ten for two months." Passage was eager to begin the trip. "She's docked nearby. If you don't mind using borrowed clothes, we could leave now. That would give us a fair start on catching up to Dawson."

Shawne reappeared with a message from Orticon. "He says we should not miss this chance. He'll get Jesse and Junah to help teach, maybe even Bob. No problem, but I won't be surprised if he makes his own additions to the curriculum."

"Okay," Tandra said. "We can manage somehow. I prefer to travel light."

Passage took a bag and a set of keys from a bank of lockers along the wall. He motioned for them to follow, and exited the cabin.

"I didn't want to get you into this, Mother." Shawne looked relieved that we were along for the ride, and she smiled at me, inviting me to know it directly from her mind. "Thanks, DadOrram."

I gave her the hug she needed as we walked, and Tandra gave her the real story. "You didn't get us into this, Shawnoon. Conn did. He used Nidok as an excuse to be the over-protective father, worried about your going off with Jeff."

Conn pretended to ignore the conversation, as did Jeff. Once Passage was preoccupied with setting a course for Australia, Shawne confronted Conn in her usual direct way.

"I'll mate when I want, with whomever I choose, Elll-daddy, and you had better not follow me again." I could hear her as an eight-year-old, scolding him for following her to the Vahinorral when she took off alone, riding her favorite daramont. "You're being overprotective."

"So what else is new, Shawne?"

"If you hover, you'll ruin my chances to be happy."

"You really think so?"

"I know so."

"Then I won't—but I won't keep my opinions to myself. Don't sell yourself cheap, Shawnoon. You deserve full measure. Don't settle for less than Tandra and I have—"

"And you and Lanoll. And Orram and Mom. I can't measure up to all that. You've solved the impossible four-body problem."

"Yeah." He wrapped a long green arm around her and laughed. "Just promise me this. Answer two questions before you choose a mate: Do you two share identities? Do you see a lifetime of growth with this person? You're too precious to waste in brain-dead struggles and untried potential."

"I've got to try it out for myself, Conn."

"All right. I'll be good. I know you humans have to play all kinds of psycho-babble games before you get to it."

"Get to what?" Jeff Passage turned to call back at them from the dock. Behind him, an enormous white luxury yacht sported the name in sweeping letters: *Sea Wind*.

"Nothing important," Shawne smiled, hiding her surprise at the massive floating show of wealth. "Give me a tour of the ship, Jeff."

"See what I mean?" Conn called after her. "'Nothing important!' Good grief, Shawnoon. I thought we'd raised you free and honest."

One by one Passage helped them step from the dock to the ship's spacious rear platform. They mounted a long, textured white stair to the main deck.

"See you later, PapaConn."

She went up to the helm with Passage, and he maneuvered the *Sea Wind* past the concrete reefs of San Diego Bay. From then on, as we slowly caught up to Dawson's fishing boat, she rarely left his side.

THE ALIEN EFFECT, CIRCA 2416–2525 C.E. Conn's Org made itself at home in living coral cells, devouring the weaker ones, silencing some genes and releasing others, thus enabling the corals to thrive in northern waters.

As the decades passed, Conn's Org protected itself with intracellular membranes, until it became a resident organelle within the coral cells. The organelle gave the corals a huge reproductive advantage, and they colonized the entire west coast of North America. Fish found comfortable places to hide in the expanding reefs, and their numbers increased.

FRUSTRATION

Orticon—meanwhile, teaching at SCBA

Orticon was not happy. The oxymoron "sustainable growth" was still in use by politicians and business people for their imagined advantage at the polls—and real advantage in their pocketbooks. Orticon talked over his concerns with Carliano, who agreed with him.

"Your school's teachings are losing out to old paradigms, Orticon," Carliano said, "religion, old growth economics, and now inequities. The wealthy, like Jeff Passage, are calling the shots and giving themselves advantages again."

"Themselves and those who interest them—like us. Passage's wealth is enabling the hunt for Nidok."

"True enough," Carliano said. "No one's all bad."

Orticon appreciated Bob's attempt to calm his growing sense of futility. "We're caught in the same trap the students are beginning to understand. How do we save for the future when the present needs loom so large? Still, I do not understand how knowledgeable people can disregard the long-term impact of their short-term profits. Furthermore, the divide between those who are science-tech savvy and those who are not is making reasonable choices for a truly selective technology nearly impossible."

"You're right. We can't even get funding to maintain the satellites that are essential to monitor the planet's health and resources. Too little is known about world resource totals."

"We've got to face it, Bob." Orticon saw that the lack of focus in human environmental efforts loomed too large for the school's influence. "The most difficult requirements—population stability and consensus on equitable consumption levels—are the first conditions required for indefinitely sustaining anything, and they just are not going to happen."

In frustration, Orticon called the entire school—Jesse, Junah, Bob Carliano, teachers and students alike—to a weeklong retreat to discuss fundamental problems and approaches.

Orticon opened the conference with a direct challenge. "We need to restart our stalled discussions about the school's position on limiting human reproduction to replacement levels. All your efforts are wasted, if human populations don't remain at a sustainable level."

"We understand that. The problem is enforcement," a student countered.

"Exactly," Orticon agreed. "There is no acceptable enforcement. Without a shared morality, there will be no consensus, hence no stable population."

Most students agreed to put out a policy statement: "Replacement only—we can do it. Anything is better than the suffering we've seen."

The students who didn't understand Orticon's "shared morality" or objected on religious grounds abstained or simply walked out. Those who agreed felt satisfied and focused next on growth as a false panacea for economic health. Only the wealthy gained by it.

They liked Varok's solution, running a free market based on a resource quota system instead of a debt economy.

"Humans have been hearing that since before 1970," Orticon said. "You students realize change requires a major shift of focus from the individual and the present to the entire world and its future. That will take time, continuous education and persistence."

"We know that, Mr. Orticon," a young woman said. "That's why we're here, and why we won't ever give up. We refuse to be part of just letting it happen."

The student's remark reminded Orticon that new thoughts could pay off somewhere, sometime, in ways no one could predict. The school wasn't dead yet.

Orticon

After the conference, as if to deny his pessimism, the handsome alien Orticon drew large classes. People came from as far as they could, when they could find transportation, and more and more were tuning into Orticon's lecture livecasts on the Worldnet.

Others chose Jesse's seminars on changing the monetary system. The taciturn human found himself leading crowded sessions in local currencies, fee-for-service banks, and a debt-free society. Again, many students, having been imprinted with credit cards, and ignorant of historical practices, didn't believe that saving up to buy something would ever work.

Junah covered equity considerations—capping gross income, including rent, profits and interest. She explored how a maximum difference in incomes could be set, say at 15 percent.

"No one would go along with that," someone said, and apparently the class agreed. Junah explained that a real "trickle-down effect" would occur if excesses went to public purposes and safety nets for the poor and disabled.

Orticon soon found that other issues—limiting transportation and food to locally available produce—were nearly as difficult as population leveling.

"Some of you grew up," he lectured, "during a time when many fruits were available all year long. If you grew up with bananas all year, you assumed you should have bananas all year, shipping fuel or no shipping fuel. Still—apples, peaches and tomatoes bred to survive shipping tasted like unsalted cardboard.

"A case in point is Jeff Passage's company, shipping water from Alaska. The San Diego area could support only seven hundred and fifty thousand people, if it were limited to local water resources. By shipping fresh water into the area, Passage is making it possible for new people to move in. Once again, the area's population will be dependent on a water supply that cannot be sustained without a great expenditure of energy."

Silence.

"People are going to live where they want to," one of the more outspoken students said. "We have the technology and the energy supply to make the desert an oasis again."

"For how long?" Orticon challenged him. "And at what cost to the Earth?"

"Until future technology gives us new ways to sustain it."

Orticon paused and spoke quietly. "Technology is costly, unless its resulting end use is more efficient. I'm afraid you are forgetting that there are limits to the number of humans Earth can support."

Silence.

"Difficult shifts in life style, like reducing water and energy usage, may take generations to achieve. You must start where you are and institute gradual change."

The silence in the room was like the silence at the eye of a hurricane. More students walked away and never returned.

THE ALIEN EFFECT, 2525–2575 C.E. Along the northwest coast of North and South America, coral reefs were healthy again. Giant staghorn forests covered the ocean floor for miles. Brain corals flourished under their protection, and tiny crystal corals decorated with every color of the spectrum lay down carpets over the skeletons of older growth. The old growth provided small crevices for fish eggs to hatch, tiny caves in which the young could thrive, and large tunnels for safe refuge. As the fisheries recovered, so too did the human population, again—especially those immunized to *Haemophilus* courtesy of Conn's Org.

Orram—in the North Pacific, heading south in Passage's cruiser

"Dawson must be keeping Nidok down below, probably in the hold," Conn said. We stared out to the horizon where Dawson's boat cut a ragged silhouette in the golden sunset. "He would trash everything of value, given half a chance, once he realized he was captured."

"How long can Nidok survive in captivity?" Passage asked.

"Too long." Conn and Shawne answered together, then laughed, remembering his appetite. "He'll eat anything that once grew cells," Shawne continued, "and he can sleep anywhere, doing anything, even flying."

"But can he stand boredom?" Passage asked.

"Good question," I said.

"He can't." Shawne looked worried. "He could do himself harm.

He'd do anything to get free. We'd better move as fast as we can. If you can get ahead of Dawson and keep him busy with a direct approach, Conn and I can swim to his boat and sneak on board."

I nearly went irrational. "For the sake of Harrahn—Conn shouldn't go anywhere near Dawson. That pirate would love to take another alien captive."

"He'd be taking a big risk, trapping the most popular alien," Tandra said.

"We'll carry laser pens," Shawne said.

That was supposed to reassure us. Tandra and I knew we couldn't stop her or Conn.

It did not reassure Passage. "I'll go with you, Shawne. Orram can take over. My crew knows how to create a diversion. Tandra, you should stay out of sight and act as backup. The procedure to call for help is noted here by the radio. Charley's crew can get to us in ten minutes."

I was impressed. Passage took command easily. "You're very thorough," I said. "I wish we had been. Conn's isolation suit is hanging in our bedroom closet. You shouldn't risk swimming without it again, *Aloon.*"

My comment gave Conn pause, but not much. "The crud is pretty dilute out here. There's probably enough ahlork spit in my plumes to take care of a few hours' swim."

Passage was thinking. "We have wet suits on board, but I doubt they would help."

"They might," Conn said. "How cold is the water? You better wear one, Shawne."

"I will, if you will."

"Let's go then."

The sun was leaving its last track of orange light as Conn, Shawne and Passage entered the water. Tandra and I stood on the deck watching their smooth wakes move away in the quiet sea.

"Conn, we love you," Tandra called. The silence swallowed her call, but, a moment later, Conn did a high flip. As he arched back into the water, the elll's hand passed by his chin and the interdigital webs spread into a wide fan that threw us a loving elllonian farewell.

I looked into Tandra's tear-drenched face and took her in my arms, holding tight against the fear that we might never see our life-partner again.

THE ALIEN EFFECT, 2575–3575 C.E. As the fourth millennium C.E. reached its mid-point, competition between elllonian-coral variants became fierce. The most vulnerable corals continued their age-old, haphazard method of spewing sperm and eggs willy-nilly into the ocean currents. But one particular mutant of Conn's coral hybrid found itself with a great advantage when it became free-living. The females sprouted a bright green receptacle with a yellow biolumi-nescent edge, and the males developed a primitive eye, thus en-abling a more deliberate method of delivering sperm to egg.

VI. CHOICES

"We depend on the natural world for our survival, and this fact needs to be reflected in our economic decisions."

—Enough Is Enough: Building A Sustainable Economy In A World Of Finite Resources by Rob Dietz and Dan O'Neill. San Francisco: Berrett-Koehler Publishers, Inc., 2013, p. 196.

ANOTHER TRAP

Shawne—moments later, swimming from Passage's ship to Dawson's

"Conn, for our sake if not your own, will you please swim underwater?" Shawne clicked off a scolding in Elllonian. He answered by swimming just underneath her.

Dawson's fishing boat was still hundreds of *pallons* away when Conn stopped. "Listen. Orcas. I'll be right back."

Shawne swam back to Passage. She could see he was beginning to tire. "Let's wait for Conn," she said. "He's calling to the pod of orcas tracking Dawson's boat."

"Beggars looking for an easy tuna."

"We'll see."

"Shawne." She looked at him expectantly, waiting for him to say something significant. "How far can you swim?"

"As far as I need to. I don't know. Two light-periods. Six or eight hours without sleep I suppose. Why? I can always catch a nap or a fish, and swim on."

"You're not part elll, are you?"

She took the question seriously. "Only by being raised by ellls, with ellls. Conn is a loner, but he still needs to be in water. He taught me to swim, using what body equipment I had. We experimented a lot. Then he and Lanoll chose an egg and raised Stringer, who turned out to be a schooling elll. I used to go along. Here comes Conn with the orcas."

THE ALIEN EFFECT, 3575–3625 C.E. Late in the thirty-sixth century, the Great Barrier Reef and the reefs of the South Pacific started their slow-moving dance across the ocean floors. Ever-changing, seeking out safer havens or richer waters, the reefs were dominated by the new elllonian free-living hybrid coral. Sea charts showing dangerous reefs were no longer valid for more than six months.

More slowly, the humans who had been infected with Conn's Org, hence resistant to the dangerous *Haemophilus* germ, began to outnumber those unprotected.

Shawne

"How do you know Conn is coming with orcas?" Jeff asked, as they waited, treading water together in the sea and trying to keep a low profile.

"I heard Conn's whistle," Shawne explained. "He felt their distinctive beat in water. You'll have to learn sonic code, Jeff, if you want to be involved in the orcas' farming venture."

Conn surfaced, sitting on the alpha bull's back. The big orca tossed him off, took a good look at us, then circled back to the pod and dove.

"That's the pod that rescued Jesse and Junah," Conn said. "When they spotted Dawson's boat in the waters around San Diego, they kept watch on it. Then when Nidok disappeared, they left the farming pod and followed Dawson at a distance. Suspicious lot they are."

"Have they seen any sign of Nidok?"

"Nothing, not a trace—but they wouldn't see him, unless Dawson hung him up as a trophy."

"Conn."

"That would be a noble end—to be stuffed. For a Smithsonian exhibit, I think. First living box-kite on Earth." Conn swam along the surface, then dove again.

"Is he always so abrupt?"

"You've got to realize, Jeff, he's in constant communication with the orcas or dolphins or whatever is underwater one hundred meters in all directions. He gets all kinds of input from his lateral lines and pressure-sensitive moss tiles, as well as from his nasal gills, his eyes, and his melons. It's all one continuum of clicks and whistles, pressure patterns and more, if he can get them through the wet suit. Scent trails, our English, ultrasonic echo scans—"

"The orcas," Conn said, surfacing quietly. "They'll cover for us while we go to the far side of the ship, Jeff. Signal your crew with Shawne's laser pen. They can start their performance, and then we'll take off. I'll surface every twenty seconds so you can catch a breath."

"Where do we hang on to you?" Passage wasn't expecting an underwater ride.

"I can tell you where not to hang on. Show him, Shawnoon."

"Do this," she said. By grasping one wrist with her other hand, she locked her arms around Conn's hip. "Help by kicking with a straight, flexible leg. Stay away from his legs and backfin. Hurry up, Jeff. Breathe in. Okay, Conn. Go."

Orram—meanwhile, on Jeff Passage's ship, Sea Wind

Though they probably had no great love for Nidok, the orcas were loyal to the ells, and couldn't resist the chance to join the fracas. As Jeff's crew sent his ship *Sea Wind* toward Dawson's rig, we could see the orcas bumping it from below and breaching nearby, simulating a feeding frenzy.

Shawne—moments later, on Dawson's ship

From the *Sea Wind*, Tandra and Orram had distracted the crew, calling and shouting from their starboard side, so it was no problem for Conn, Jeff and Shawne to surface near the hull of Dawson's ship portside, find a ladder, and climb on board.

"I'll stay hidden on deck," Conn said, "and search up here."

As Jeff and Shawne descended into the hold to look for Nidok, they heard someone moving in their direction.

"Hey there. Pete Dawson on board?" Passage called out, moving back up the ladder.

"I'm right here, Mr. Passage."

Jeff acknowledged the gun Dawson pointed up at them. "Sorry for the intrusion. You got any fish to sell? We're a little short on supplies."

"You're a little short on manners, my boy. Get back on deck." As Passage and Shawne moved out onto the deck, Dawson pulled Shawne's hair behind her ears looking for patch organs. "They're both human. Throw them overboard," he said, tossing her aside.

Orram—meanwhile, on Passage's ship

Dawson's crew hauled Passage and Shawne to the deck rail, pushed them off the ship, then hurried them on their way by shooting into the water behind them. It gave us a good scare aboard the *Sea Wind*.

"Hey there, Dawson. What's all the shooting about? You got some sharks after your catch?" It was Charley, calling through a megaphone from his yacht on the port side of Dawson's boat.

"Who the hell are you? What are you doing here?" Dawson cried.

"Thinking of expanding my operations," Charley answered. "I run trips over at the Socorros. Cabo's not doing too well." He pulled alongside. "Throw me a rope. Let's have a beer."

We were thankful for the distraction Charley provided as he climbed aboard and engaged a suspicious Dawson. When Shawne and Passage got back to us on Passage's ship, she was as near hysteria as she had ever been in her life.

"What kind of monsters are these people? Why did we come here? To save this scum? We left Conn on Dawson's ship. We've got to get him off there."

Passage folded her in his arms. "We'll find him, Shawne. Conn is very clever. A hack like Dawson is no match for him." Passage got through to her. She settled into the same mood of fierce determination that had brought her to Earth.

"We can't tip them off," Passage said. "Dawson is determined to snare an alien. He mustn't suspect that an elll is still on board with him. We've got to move away, fast."

Tandra and I gathered around the large table in the central cabin with Passage, going over our options. We decided to head away, south southwest, as if we wanted to put distance between the *Sea Wind* and the Dawson's *Fish Hook* as quickly as possible.

THE ALIEN EFFECT, 3625–3827 C.E. Sixteen hundred years after Conn visited Earth, his free-living coral symbiont successfully rebuilt and extended the coral reefs all over Earth's oceans, providing rich environments for new fish populations. As food availability spread, the population of human beings, strengthened by Conn's Org, once again began to dominate their environment. These new people were unlike *Homo sapiens sapiens*.

Marine farming ventures were reestablished with orcas and with smaller dolphins. Whales declined to participate, so a dedicated group of people, with a long history of fighting for cetacean survival, set off into the oceans to find out why.

WORST FEARS

Conn—moments later, on Dawson's ship

From the holding tank of the *Fish Hook*, Conn heard everything Dawson said to Shawne and Passage. When the alien hunter threw them overboard, Conn exploded with rage—silently—and tore an interdigital web smashing fish. He wished he were wearing an isolation suit instead of Passage's heavy wet suit. He'd have to be careful, get out of the holding tank and carry only enough of the foul water to keep himself from drying out.

At first he thought Charley might still be on board, but that hope dimmed when at last Dawson's motors fired.

Hour after hour the *Fish Hook* ran without stopping, day and night. Conn explored on quiet webbed feet. It wasn't long before he knew the boat very well, all but Pete Dawson's quarters. The rough man locked it whenever he left the room, and when he slept at night. Conn was sure Nidok or Nidok's remains were in there.

More than once each day, Conn thought about jumping ship. He wasn't sure where on Earth Dawson was going, but he knew the oceans well enough to believe he could catch a meal and avoid sharks long enough to call for protection from a pod of dolphins or whales.

Conn's idea of leaving the ship quickly left him. The beer, chips, and fish on board were tolerable, and Nidok had once risked life, limb, family, and flock to rescue Conn from captivity. There was no way the elll would leave the ahlork to a similar fate. He had to get Nidok out of the captain's quarters.

Conn thought of stealing a gun and shooting the door open, but he had handled only my grandfather's hunting arms. He knew Nidok would never give up trying to escape, so he had nightmares of the ahlork working on the lock just as he was blowing it away.

At last the engines slowed. Conn could hear shouting alongside the boat, and it bumped a mooring. He had to get Nidok now.

He hid under a tarp near the captain's door and made his move when Dawson placed the key in the lock and opened the door to enter. Being taller and stronger than Dawson, Conn easily subdued him. He shoved him onto the bunk and sat on him. He looked around for Nidok.

Nothing. Not one chitinous plate. Nidok was not in Dawson's quarters and never had been.

THE ALIEN EFFECT, 3827–3950 C.E. Someone among the whale preservationists was able to reconstruct the cetacean language Conn had taught humans eighteen hundred years before. Using that ancient language, three divers approached the whales with a plan for them to cooperate with humans in order to enhance the fisheries. They learned that the humpback whales had done some reconstructive history themselves. Laid bare was the long historical horror of slaughter by humans for the sake of whale oil. The whales could understand predation for food, but not for oil, with the food wasted. They were not about to deal with humans on any level. The gray whales—who had been cheated out of their fair share of tuna in their early history of partnering with humans—heard the story and agreed to the boycott.

In human society, the long-dead fossil oil economy was replaced by ubiquitous solar, tide and wind energy sources, supplemented with carefully rationed hydrogen. With the elllonian coral hybrid flourishing and the clean oceans filled with fish, the dominant humanoid population once again took off into a period of nonlinear growth, marked by an accelerated mutation rate.

Shawne—days later, on Passage's ship

If our team hadn't been on a desperate mission to save Conn and Nidok, the trip to the Great Barrier Reef could have been, for Shawne, something out of a romantic movie. In spite of their differences, she and Jeff enjoyed being together. The evenings were gems of light and silence, with quiet seas reflecting the changing color of spectacular sunsets.

Then Orticon called. His report was not good. Active resistance to practical ideas, even innocuous ones, like using flat rooftop space for solar collectors, was building among Shawne's students. As always, immediate costs, not long-term benefits, dictated decisions.

Under Orticon's proactive direction, more students joined the school to debate the advantages of no-growth economics, but then more and more left, attacking its practice. Discussions were empty of critical thinking.

Shawne grew more and more depressed. Though the Earth seemed immense, she saw the human imprint overwhelming everything it touched. Worse, since their arrival, her family's efforts had been concentrated on saving themselves from disaster, not saving the planet. Her increasing sense of failure became intensely personal.

"Shawne," Orram said after dinner one evening, "two hundred years in. Two hundred years out to attain *ahlnat*, with luck. A sustainable culture takes a long time, an unwavering ethical commitment, to self-organize."

"Do they have that much time, Orran?" Shawne excused herself and walked out to the deck. Passage followed.

"Why do you struggle against the inevitable?" Passage asked.

"It's a simple choice, Jeff," Shawne said. "I have to believe that humans are smarter than lemmings."

Passage leaned on the railing, watching the wake form under the bow. "Your limits will never work, Shawne. People want what they want—now. They're not going to quit moving to San Diego."

"They would if the water was limited to what was locally available, and all the housing was taken, and the local food supply was already allocated. It's the only rational way to go—now—as you rebuild."

"And we would have no profit to keep helicopters running and to sail to Australia to save your family," Passage said.

"Yes. Why do you think I've been so depressed? We have taken advantage of your wealth, and I've enjoyed it. I've been thinking of little else."

"And your dreams are a lost cause."

"Maybe not. Not if people like you set the example. You could phase out your shipping business and concentrate on San Diego's local sources of water—rebuild the sewage treatment so there is no waste water, so it can provide clean drinking water. Sell gray water kits and composting toilets. Find a good way to market sea urchins as pleasant food. There's so much you could do, Jeff. It could make a huge difference. You're big enough to grab markets and watch them snowball."

"I'll think about it, Star Eyes, if you will tell me a secret." He took her chin in his hand and lifted her face to his. "Have you ever been loved, by someone old enough to love you for who you are?"

"I've met forearms with two others, two varoks."

"Like this?" He laced his fingers in hers and drew her close.

"No." Her laugh was like a child's, but taunting, and a little wild. "Like this, no hands."

Their forearms met, varokian style, bringing their bodies into gentle contact. The experience surprised Passage with its intimacy. "Maybe a human kiss, as icing on the cake?" he said.

Starting from the forearms, the kiss soon enveloped them both in a passion they did not deny, and they disappeared into his cabin.

Orram—days later, at Cairns, Australia

Jeff Passage and Charley Hazard didn't skimp in their efforts to track Dawson's boat. Their network of friends, paid or proven, followed Dawson's progress from Alaskan waters south to the Barrier Reef with impressive accuracy. Charley was never far behind him. As soon as the pirate anchored at Green Island on the Great Barrier Reef, we knew it.

"We'll dock at Cairns," Passage radioed Charley. "Set us up with a tourist rental, like a small sailbot. My crew will take the *Sea Wind* out of here before Dawson sees it."

Passage turned away from the *Sea Wind*'s radio and announced the news to us. "Dawson's fishing boat is anchored at Green Island. We'll cruise the area in a sailing yacht, a touristy tub he won't recognize. I'm having the rest of your crew flown into Cairns tomorrow, so we'll look more like a party. Could you please call them, Orram?"

"Of course."

Within hours we learned that Jesse, Stringer, Bob Carliano, and Lanoll would arrive in Cairns early on the second day by Navy jet. The U.S. government was eager to do anything they could to help find the popular aliens Conn and Nidok.

"Now we go hunting," Passage announced.

At Cairns Port, Tandra, Shawne, Passage and I disembarked from the *Sea Wind*, and Passage's crew took it north to Cape Tribulation.

We motored into Cairns Port with Passage eager to host the ells. Stringer and Lanoll couldn't get off their Navy jet fast enough. Jesse Mendleton and Bob Carliano were also dry and tense with worry for Conn. No one had been able to enjoy the long flight, but all were grateful to be part of the hunt.

Shawne—moments later in Cairns, Australia

Shawne made a call to Orticon, still teaching at SCBA. "I didn't realize Jesse and Bob were coming down here, too. Are you all right with the classes? Are we losing ground chasing all over the planet like this?"

Orticon hesitated. "No worries, Shawne. This old world keeps turning with or without us. Settle yourself. Jesse and Bob did a great job with their seminars, but Junah and I can carry on with the teachers we have left. Go and find Conn and Nidok. I won't expect to hear from you for a while. Love you all."

Not satisfied, but determined to get a report from Jesse and Bob later, Shawne boarded the old sailing yacht Charley and Jeff had rented. It had worked out of Cairns for decades.

Passage made sure the ellls Stringer and Lanoll were willing to go on the small sailing yacht with him. Jesse and Bob Carliano went with them to help keep track of Dawson, to deal with him if need be.

Tandra seemed delighted when Charley appeared on the dock and invited her and Orram on board his fishing boat. "I've got your parents here, Shawne," he called to her.

"We still have a bead on Dawson," he reported to Passage. "Followed him all the way down here. He left Green Island, but he couldn't have gone far yet. We'll keep a watch out for him, while we run backup for you."

"We'll stay in close touch," Shawne promised.

Passage ran the sailing yacht with an expert hand, while Shawne plotted the search route on a sea chart of the northeastern coast of Australia. They were covering a wide swath south of Green Island, when the yacht attracted a pod of bottlenose dolphins.

"Slow it to five knots, Jeff." Shawne stood on the fore deck and threw her robe off. "I'll see if I can learn something from them."

Before any of them could object, Shawne dove over the side and soon had a dolphin towing her alongside. As she braced one hand in front of the dolphin's dorsal fin, she whistled questions into his ear hole. He didn't understand her, until she tried a few orcan signals, which startled him into realizing this human was able to communicate.

Shawne described Conn and Nidok as best she could, and the dolphin quizzed the others, but none had seen or heard of any such creatures.

Dawson's boat, *Fish Hook,* was another matter. The dolphins knew immediately what boat Shawne meant and who ran it. A seasonal visitor to the Barrier Reef, it was infamous for a killing stick pointed at unsuspecting dolphins riding the boat's wake. During some afternoons it was seen anchored to the north at a long cay, a spit of sand on the outer reef, where many birds roosted and small bushes grew in a line.

Shawne got the dolphins' latest estimate of the *Fish Hook's* position and size, asked them to keep watch out for Conn and Nidok. She hollered for Passage to slow and climbed the rope ladder on to the sailing yacht to report.

"There are a lot of long sandy cays out farther," Passage said. "Let's hope your elll friends find something here near Green Island."

DAWSON

Conn—meanwhile, on board Dawson's Fish Hook

"Where's Nidok, Dawson?" Conn got up from sitting on the xenophobe, picked him up by one arm and stood him on his feet, pulling his arm hard against his back.

"Your friend from Varok? The halork, I believe."

"Ahlork. He's more than a friend. He's family. Does that tell you anything, Broom Face?"

"No problem. No problem. We'll take you right to him, won't we, Cisco?"

Conn looked up into the barrel of a handgun. A large figure of a man filled the doorway to Dawson's cabin.

"We wondered when you would come up for air, alien. You stink of dead fish. The hold of a fisher must be just like home. Couldn't resist it, eh?"

"Actually, I rather preferred your dark lager and fresh chips," Conn said, releasing Dawson and brushing himself off. "Blueberry muffins and halibut for breakfast weren't too bad, either. I'll tell Passage to hire on your cook."

"Passage ran like the headless chicken he is," Dawson said. "Take him alive, Jake. Cisco, watch it."

Conn whirled, caught the big man with the flat of his broad hand, then ducked. The gun went flying. Conn ran up to the deck, where four more men from Dawson's crew caught hold of his limbs. They hoisted him off the boat, carried him across the white sand of Michaelmas Cay, and threw him into an underground storage pit.

He landed hard but unhurt on damp sand. A wooden hatch slammed shut, and a lock snapped in place. His eyes picked up a vision of something moving before they adjusted to the dark. The place was empty, except for a heap of crumpled beer cans. On top of the heap sat Nidok.

"Welcome at Michael's Messy Cay, Brother Elll," he croaked. "Have a beer."

THE ALIEN EFFECT, 3950–4052 C.E. With energy sources limited to the sun and wind, various human populations learned to get along with local sources of food, water, and shelter. As a result, when a population reached stress levels, it tended to be self-limiting. There was no place to go and no more to eat. This time the die offs were spotty, due mostly to drought and epidemics from local water pollution. The fisheries survived.

Conn's Org flourished in most humans, and its DNA had a heyday recombining with the rapidly mutating human bacterial flora. No one noticed when the recombinants took over the bulk of bacteria in the human gut and started digesting the tough plant fiber, cellulose.

Stringer—meanwhile, near Green Island, Australia

Following the tip from the dolphins, Stringer and Lanoll searched the coral reefs and Green Island for any sign of Conn.

"Watch out for the big clams, Lanoll," Stringer said. "The tide's going out. They'll be just under the surface."

"I'm not about to stick a fin in their mouths. Look over here, Stringer."

The ellls hovered just off the bottom, watching a parade of parrot-fish swim by. Suddenly a tiny fish darted at Lanoll's face.

"Look at the colored patterns on that little fighter. It's a young yellowface trigger fish," Stringer said. "It's the one Orticon told us about. Watch it. He's going for your nasal gills again, protecting its territory. Have you ever seen such bright patterns on a fish? This place is a wonderland. We've got to bring Conn here when we find him."

"You don't suppose the dolphins were wrong, do you, Stringer? What would Dawson's ship be doing near this tourist island? There's no elll-sign here. I thought I lost Conn once soon after we met, when he was kidnapped by Mahntik. I'm not going to lose him again."

"We'll find him, Mom. Just not here."

The name helped. "We'd better get back to Passage's sailboat. It's getting dark, and we can't afford to lose any more time."

They swam out to deep water. Clear enough to see one hundred feet ahead, it shone with a deep blue light, cool to the ellls' infrared vision. Like liquid crystal, it enclosed the remains of the Barrier Reef. The ellls had never seen such a variety of weird creatures. A multitude of brilliant forms hid in the coral, much of it bleached.

As the ellls drifted toward the surface and started back to the sailboat, a pod of dolphins raced at them and circled, making sounds Stringer had difficulty understanding. It translated as "go to narrow sand, birds, some distance toward open water, bad boat."

Orram—meanwhile, near Green Island

Passage's crew had been keeping the sailboat at anchor, waiting for Lanoll and Stringer to return, when we approached in Charley's fishing boat and tied on. Before long we spotted Stringer and Lanoll swimming back.

"No worries, mates," Stringer announced in Australian. "Dolphins have given us a new clue—something about long white sand and birds farther out."

"We couldn't understand all they said," Lanoll added, "but I thought I heard a pattern that meant humans or lots of tall-legs."

"They could have meant Michaelmas Cay," Passage said. "It's a popular tourist spot, but it's not much more than a spit of sand."

"I think we should go out there," I said. "The dolphins would not make such a point of telling Stringer and Lanoll to search there, if it didn't mean something."

"It's worth a try," Passage agreed. "We can approach both sides of the cay with this sailboat and Charley's fisher."

Tandra agreed but was puzzled. "Are you sure you saw nothing odd near Green Island, Stringer? Why did the dolphins send you there?"

"Maybe the dolphins think we're fishing, and they wanted to lure us away," Lanoll said.

"I'll ask them." Stringer dove back in and was gone.

Passage watched him go and shook his head. The abrupt directness of ellls frequently caught him off guard.

It was Carliano who insisted on caution. "Let's be sure our radar scan locates Dawson before we anchor at the Cay to do a quick search."

MICHAELMAS CAY

Conn—meanwhile, with Nidok

"Still alive, are you, Clacker? How come?"

"Ahlork eat brass bullets for lunch. Spit them back in human faces. But now we drink beer, celebrate your capture."

"You're drunk, you nincompoop. Why haven't you dug your way out of here?"

"I wait for you. Why else?"

"I know why else. Free beer, that's why."

"It's good for ahlork. Builds sharp chitin."

Conn had to laugh. Nidok always had his world by the tail. The ell looked around, but he couldn't see where all the beer had come from. "What's in here?" He crawled through a small opening leading to a chamber filled with cases of beer. "Good grief, Ahlork Dear, there are no potato chips in here. We'll have to do without. What are you drinking? Lager or watered-down horse piss?"

"Get me lager. I give you bath in horse piss." The ahlork scooped out a deep hole in the sand, and, while Conn downed a dark brew, he ceremoniously emptied two cases of light beer into the hole.

Conn sat down in the puddle of beer, and Nidok sloshed the golden liquid over the elll until all his tiles were thoroughly soaked.

"Improves your scent," Nidok snorted. "You stink like dar'mont gone fishing."

Within minutes, Conn's tiles had soaked up enough alcohol to make him as drunk as Nidok. Before nightfall they had emptied twenty cases of light beer into the hole and jammed the entrance to their prison with crushed aluminum.

"Once again, my dear Nidok, ugliest alien on Earth, you have saved me from a drought worse than death." Conn rolled out of the beer. "But the time has come for you to save me again. No seaweed ropes this time. No sharp plates to cut beer cans. I enlist your kind assistance in digging a tunnel out the back, while I stack the lager cases against our aluminum sculpture."

They tried to work at their tasks, but the effort was more than either could sustain. Conn fell asleep draped over a case of lager, and Nidok dozed in the tunnel he had started.

Hours passed before they woke, found themselves reasonably sober, and continued the project. It didn't take Conn long to move all the lager cases. He tucked two cans in his hip pack, then tried to help Nidok move wet sand.

"Hey, watch that right wing, Nidok my love. You nearly sliced off my head," Conn hollered.

"Move away, Green Bones. Not helping. I do beetle act, so we be out sooner."

"Go for it, Sand Flea. I bow to your ancient genes."

Nidok disappeared in a flurry of sand, and soon reappeared, pushing the last of the loose sand into the lager cases stacked against the aluminized entrance. "After you, Tough Elll. You stick head into open first and get blown off. I escape later."

Before the ahlork finished his slowly pronounced nonsense, Conn was out of the tunnel, crouching in the sparse vegetation. "It's still dark out here. Let's go."

"You go swim. I fly low and stay close. When I float and rest, you bring fish."

"Good plan. Look for reefs, waves breaking, good food sources. I'll put out an alert when I echolocate a pod of dolphins. There's a good chance Orram and Passage have a ship looking for us."

They crossed Michaelmas Cay on the side away from where Dawson's *Fish Hook* lay at anchor. Conn entered the surf, and soon they left the tiny island of sand far behind. Shortly before dawn, a sailing yacht passed them, cruising slowly toward the cay.

Orram—meanwhile

"I've always been entirely honest with you, Shawne," I said. "I've told you all thoughts, as if you could read them yourself. I can't fib to you. You must know that." We stood on the lower deck of the rented sailboat, watching the sun rise over a sea busy with small waves. Shawne had taken a morning swim and joined us for breakfast on Charley's fishing boat.

None of us had slept well, anticipating the fake picnic on Michaelmas Cay, hoping to search it quickly and move on before Dawson saw us. But that was not all that bothered us. Shawne's attachment to Passage was no secret, and it was no secret we didn't like it.

"We can't bless your union with Passage, Shawne. We think you're headed for disaster."

"I'm not asking you to bless any union, Orram. That's something you picked up out of Mom's ancient history. I don't even know what it means. I just want you to be happy for me. I've found a mate."

"Is it really that simple? You're not an elll, Shawne. When humans mate, their emotions get hot-wired at every level. It's as if the 'in-love' hormone ties your nervous system into one big knot dripping with neurotransmitter juice."

"That's Conn talking."

"We concur. It's unanimous. He would hate to see you like this—irrationally in love with a man who is working against everything you believe. Jeff Passage would see San Diego grow on and on, along with his water business. He would find some other way to cash in on the regrowth of this area and make it happen faster. Have you talked to him about all this?"

"He understands my concerns."

"But he won't use his profits to help your efforts for stability."

"I don't know. Maybe he will—eventually. We are using him, Orram, to find Conn and Nidok. We owe him more than we can ever repay."

"Is he that kind of friend, Shawne, one that we have to repay?"

"No. I'm sure not."

"Good. And you realize that if Dawson didn't have similar resources—profits that were made on the heels of the die-off—he couldn't have caused the kind of trouble that only a Jeff Passage can fix by chasing all over the world like this."

"He understands that resource limits need to be global."

"I feel better, knowing you can talk about your differences."

"Let Mom know."

"Of course." She nestled against my shoulder.

"Let's talk every evening, Orram, like we did on Varok."

"I thought you'd never ask," I said. "We parents don't want to impose, you know."

She laughed and kissed my cheek. "Have I ever let you impose?"

"Not since we adopted you at age three. You made it quite clear I was not to read your mood without your permission."

"And did you sneak a reading now and then?"

"Only once—when you were nearly five and too upset to talk."

"Really? Only once?"

"Really."

"I love you for trying to lie to me, Orram."

"I love you, too, Shawne. Don't ever forget it."

She dove over the side and climbed aboard Passage's rented sailboat.

The sun grew hot, and the minutes stretched unbearably as both boats dawdled along toward Michaelmas Cay. Passage had loaded two large coolers with soda and beer, and while the sailboat passed within sight of Dawson's ship, the passengers made laughing noises and turned on loud music as they played with hoses on deck—all except Shawne and Passage, who hid below.

At a respectful distance from the alien hunter's ship, Passage set anchor and loaded a rubber raft with a cooler, a large ground cloth, and a credible lunch. Tandra and I left Charley's boat on the other side of the cay. She swam toward the white beach while I boarded Passage's sailboat.

Still laughing and talking loudly, Passage, Shawne, Jesse, Carliano, and I left the sailboat and set out on a raft to land on the cay's wide beach. Hundreds of gulls rose into the air at our approach. Tandra had planted herself on the white sand above the tide line. From the far side of Passage's yacht, Lanoll and Stringer slipped into deeper water. They planned to stay submerged and keep watch, as best they could, as backup.

We couldn't have been on the beach more than half an hour, when a small dory moved away from Dawson's ship. A peculiar hump of sand at one end of the cay had us desperate with curiosity, but we dared not go near it.

"Here they come," Passage said. "Shawne and I will go beach-combing and give the dory a friendly wave while they're still far out. Then we'll disappear to the other side of the cay in shallow water."

The three men in the dory ignored the young couple chasing each other in the surf. They headed right toward us on the beach. I stretched out with a hat over my head. "G'day, mates," Tandra called, waving from the shallows. "Catchin' good stuff ar' ye?"

"How long you planning to be here?" The question was rude, its tone threatening.

Jesse put one hand in his pocket.

"Just long enough to get a bite, Love," Tandra said. "You got problems, have ye?"

"Yeah, we do, missus. We need someone to run a catch over to Green Island for us."

"What's for us then, disturbin' our holiday?" Carliano grumbled.

"There's a crisp fifty quid in it for you."

"Crisp, eh? Seventy, and we're on our way." Tandra stood defiantly, her hands on her hips.

I nearly choked, trying to keep my laughter bottled up. Tandra's Australo-cockney accent was terrible, but it was working.

Two of the men hoisted a box out of the dory and set it on our raft.

Tandra walked up to them, her hand out. "That'll be seventy quid in advance, pleez yer self."

"Give 'er seventy, Marty."

Disgusted, the black bearded Marty counted out seventy Australian dollars. "Now get that box to Green Island—to the cook at O'Dunnigan's Fish Lodge. Off you go."

Tandra gave me a good shove with her foot. "Come on, then. Wake up, ya' big blighter. We got us some important work to do." She called to Shawne and Passage, "We're taking a little boat ride."

I rolled over and took my time getting up, using patch sensitivity to check Tandra's view of Dawson's dory as it pulled off the beach and returned to the *Fish Hook*.

Shawne and Passage heeded Tandra's call by running straight across the cay, over the peculiar hump near the dune grass at the far end. It was enough to tell them the area was hollow. In hurrying them along, Jesse got a glimpse of a trap door made of weathered boards.

"Come on, ya two," Tandra called. "We haven't got all day ye know."

When we were well on our way to Green Island, we called Stringer and Lanoll to the boat with a sonar horn I had rigged. They boarded the ship, and we agreed they should check out the underground vault that night, after we made the run to Green Island. We were a third of the way to the island, when, as if from nowhere, Nidok appeared over the deck and landed on Tandra's head.

"How fast you think ahlork fly? How fast? Slow down, rude bipeds."

THE ALIEN EFFECT, 4052–4086 C.E. Since the local die offs did little to relieve the again overpopulated state of human society, there was no relief from the ever-changing epidemics and the scarcity of potable water. Only one segment of human society seemed to thrive: the segment that relished alfalfa salad.

Dawson—meanwhile, near Michaelmas Cay

"Any more tourists on that radar contraption, Cisco?" Dawson was eager to get started. He stood on the deck of the *Fish Hook*, admiring the new additions to the foredeck. Two transparent enclosures of bulletproof polyphase metal occupied the entire deck just below the captain's wheel lodge. The two aliens would be displayed in full view from three sides of the ship. Access for providing food and water was built into a double entrance lock on the roof. A waste tube in the back emptied directly into the sea. A simple pump continually re-circulated ocean water from the bow of the ship across the enclosed deck. A narrow walkway encircled the enclosures and met at steps leading down the middle to the main deck. From those steps, Dawson planned to present the aliens and provoke them to the kind of anger he knew Nidok could exhibit.

Conn wouldn't be so flashy, but he was green enough to display as a mysterious aquatic man from outer space. Converting the fishing rig to an alien show vessel had cost Dawson everything he had. Unlike Passage, who kept his prices for water in line with people's needs, Dawson sold fish at inflated prices, which were forced up by scarcity and the growing demands of recovery.

Australians would love seeing the dangerous alien invaders safely subdued. Wealthy tourists, the nouveau riche, recovery scab-pickers, would appreciate the irony of exhibiting the know-it-all intruders in a growing human business. Dawson would soon be wealthy again, with a political advantage when governments of North America reclaimed effective power and interrogated his captives in preparation to defend Earth from the alien hordes.

"No more small craft in sight, Captain Pete, sir. Transport cages are loaded. We're ready to pick up the buggers."

Orram

Later, we got this story from one of Pete Dawson's employees who had defected. He was one of the few in Dawson's gang who had seen our broadcasts from the moon and had heard Shawne, the beautiful elll-woman, and Orticon, the alien, lecturing on survival economics from San Diego.

Dawson was eager to retrieve the aliens from their underground pen on Michaelmas Cay. After Passage's sailboat was out of sight, he led his crew off his ship's lifeboat and ran over the white sand to the wooden trap door. With a mighty blow from the butt of his shotgun, he tore the lock from its moorings, threw open the door, and plunged into a giant heap of mangled aluminum.

Shreiking with rage, he tore into the sharp debris and tried to scatter it, but succeeded only in bloodying himself. Someone ran for a boat oar, and Dawson pounded at the aluminum until it was cleared away, revealing a blockade of lager cases jammed tight from floor to ceiling.

Frustrated beyond reason, Dawson shot into the cases again and again, punching holes in the remaining stash of lager. Rage consumed the pirate, and he tore the shelter apart with his bare hands, revealing for all to see the undeniable evidence of his captives' beer bash and simple escape.

His crew made a strategic retreat to Charley's ship, which had been keeping watch close at hand. Dawson was left alone, standing ankle deep in lager and crumpled beer cans.

ONE KIND OF FUTURE

Orram—moments later, on Passage's rented sailing yacht

"Be quicker," Nidok hollered down at Conn. The elll was following the sailboat's wake at high speed, trying to catch it. "What is matter, Conn? Can't swim fast as sails?"

"Conn?" Tandra waved Nidok off her head and scanned the water. Conn's long green body arched over the wake and skimmed alongside before it began to fall behind again.

"Conn!" Carliano bellowed. "Passage, stop the boat. Orram, tell Jeff to roll in the jib."

Lanoll and Stringer dove in to greet Conn. Minutes later they climbed aboard, and Conn fell into Tandra's impatient arms.

Shawne came to him with a sob of relief—and just a little hesitation. "We thought we might never see you again, Conn. Don't ever leave us. Don't ever."

"Right." He clung to our human daughter as if she were the core of existence, then slowly he took her face in his webbed fingers and planted his wide lippy kiss on her cheek. "You're your own woman now, Shawnoon." He smiled, and his eyes grew wide with emotion. "Be happy, Baby. Be true to yourself."

Shawne knew that his finely tuned senses could tell she was mated to Jeff Passage.

Making memories fit for eternity, we soaked up every moment of that reunion. Charley met us at the Green Island Pier. He was a good companion to all of us. Knowledgeable about sea life, he identified many of the fish we saw, and he knew where to look for eels.

Conn had noticed how Charley gravitated toward Tandra, so I wasn't surprised when the elll cornered Tandra and me. We had spent the morning drifting around the island looking at colorful fish and giant clams. Then we planted ourselves on the Green Island beach near the pier.

Conn didn't waste words. "We've already got the four-body problem solved in this family. Are we going for five?"

"What?" At first Tandra didn't understand what Conn meant.

"Charley Hazard, I think his name is."

"Oh, is his name Hazard? I guess I didn't know," Tandra said. "He's a very attractive man—straight forward, hairy. It's fascinating how much hair some human men can grow."

Conn was beginning to heat up. "You're telling me this is nothing but a hair fetish?"

I had to laugh. "You're jealous, Conn. Again, after all these years. And you've got Lanoll. Can't Tandra have a human mate?"

"Neither one of you has any hair on your bodies," Tandra said.

It wasn't fair. Conn couldn't read between the lines, as I could. "Tandra, be nice," I said.

"Sorry, Orram. Yes, Charley finds me attractive, and I respond to such a man, Conn, but we've made it very clear to each other that we're not available. He is married to the sea, and my plate is full, as you should know very well."

"But? I heard a 'but' in that last sentence."

"Maybe Orram can answer better."

"I'll try," I said. "We have already solved the five-body problem. Charley will change our lives. He has already. I see Tandra now, more clearly, as the human woman she truly is, not just some universal feminine essence that released me from emotional bondage. She is my releaser, and she is your sacred tether, but we are not human. She is mate to neither of us, but this does not diminish our love."

"You sure can put out a pile, when you open your mouth, Orram my dear," Conn said.

After Green Island, we wandered south, enjoying the rich and peculiar life of the Great Barrier Reef but grieving for the extensive bleached remains of coral that hadn't survived warming.

The next day we turned north and circled out again to Michaelmas Cay. There we spent a full day on the white sand, enjoying a real picnic outing. We pried and pulled at the wreckage left behind by Dawson, and our imaginations soared as we reconstructed in our minds the scene that must have taken place when he opened the inadequate prison to find it stuffed with crushed aluminum and jammed with crates.

Charley added some vivid details from the eyewitness account of Dawson's crew. "They were so angry, they couldn't spit. Stormed around my boat as if they needed to stomp it to splinters. And, you know, I really believe their tantrum was about losing so much beer. They didn't give a hoot about what happened to Dawson."

Conn

The next morning Charley announced that his boat would pick him up from the Cay within the hour. "I'll have to say goodbye now," he said. "I do hope to see you in San Diego again some time soon." He gave Tandra a quick hug and went to the end of the Cay to await the boat.

"Maybe he doesn't like being a fifth wheel," Conn said.

"You should know, Conn. It's not unlike how loners feel at times like this." Tandra had tears in her eyes as she spoke, but she made no move to follow Charley.

He was not gone more than an hour when Orticon's radio call for help brought us sharply down to Earth—to the difficult life choices we would soon be forced to make.

"Your students have calculated the carrying capacity for the greater San Diego water conservancy," he told Shawne, "but there should be other limits." Orticon paused, as if he hated to continue. "Our progress is undermined by the Passage Foundation. There are no immediate obstacles to importing huge amounts of water from Alaska. The whole 'growth is good' paradigm is still alive and well in their circle."

"I have talked to Jeff," Shawne said.

"He could be a big help," Orticon said. "Otherwise, we're going to lose it to so-called progress."

"I can try again, Orticon." Shawne's voice was heavy.

It broke Conn's heart to watch her spirit sag. As she always had when her problems on Varok loomed too large, she went straight to the elll.

"Passage doesn't understand?" Conn asked. "Or is he devoted to boom and bust? Live it up today, to hell with the future?"

"Not that, Conn," Shawne said. "He thinks no-growth economics is pie in the sky—an ideal not possible for humans. People will struggle for power and wealth to keep their bellies full."

"A pragmatist."

"He doesn't like wasting resources or polluting water. He's all for selective technology to avoid overuse. He hates wasteful profiteering from selling non-essentials. He likes our orca farming idea."

"But he's a realist, right? He's making a good profit by giving people what they want."

"He's also giving me what I want, Conn. I'm human. I liked being with him on this trip to Australia. I'd do it again, even if you weren't in trouble."

"I'll be in trouble again, Shawne. There are more Dawsons out there. You know we can't stay here forever."

"How can I leave Jeff, Conn?"

"You've had an attack of pheromones. It will pass. You're just in love."

"But I do love him. The 'in love' rush is over."

"Nasty trick to play on humans, those brain chemicals. Wrenches your gut if you can't be with Mr. One-and-only. I'm sympathetic, Shawnoon. When Lanoll and I first met, I had an attack of similar hormones. Loners do, you know. Mother Nature's way of propagating—"

"Conn, what can I do?"

"We eells can school, the varoks can read thoughts as they go by, but all you humans have is trust—some intuition, true—but trust is what makes things work. Do you trust Jeff, Shawne *Aloon*?"

"Yes. He's always been honest with me."

"Then it's a clear situation, Love. Follow your heart."

Orram

Once we were settled again in San Diego, Stringer and Lanoll put out a call for all cetaceans interested in tuna farming. Nidok went back to work, flying messages out to the gray whales wary of oil and contaminants close to shore. Passage was helpful in reinforcing the human commitment to the effort.

Before the farming venture could go far, however, a major cleanup was needed. The effort at San Diego was impressive, and before summer the coastal waters were clean enough for the cetaceans to come closer in to shore.

Channel runs were established and the tuna harvest began, with orcas and gray whales acting as shepherds and taking their allotted share.

With the marine farming venture well launched, Conn began work on the waste concrete reefs. Human and dolphin volunteers helped him shape them into a natural park for divers and snorkelers.

Jeff Passage continued to see Shawne. Almost every day he walked her home from the School for Economic Longevity, and they hung around the pool until dinner time, when Conn would take pity on the man's hungry look and invite him for stew.

Carliano decided that a frank talk with Passage was overdue. "The demand for Alaskan water continues to grow," he said to Jeff as they sat by the pool, "in spite of San Diego's enthusiasm for Shawne's teaching."

"It's not surprising," Passage said. "People like it here."

"So you're shipping more water?" Shawne pulled herself up on the deck and sat beside him.

"Most of the demand comes from new businesses starting up," Passage said. "Nanochips for computers, expanding agriculture, nurseries. The city makes sure manufacturers recycle water, but they can't return all of it to the aquifers."

"There's value in the water reserves they degrade or draw down," Shawne said. "Does the price of computer chips reflect that cost?"

"People are happy to have the jobs new businesses bring in," Passage said, ignoring her question.

Shawne's brow pulled into a frown. "Jobs pull more people into the area. They wouldn't come if there were no water to drink or to make nanochips."

Passage passed a hand over the frown to smooth it. "People have to eat, too."

"It always comes down to population limits, doesn't it?" Carliano said.

"Now we're talking a total redo of lifestyle and personal life choices. It isn't going to happen." Jeff shook his head and tumbled into the pool, taking Shawne with him.

The rest of us converged on the kitchen, then moved out to the deck with a snack of urchin chips and ginger beer.

"Time is running out," I heard Shawne say to Passage. "You're help-ing rebuild another scenario for disaster, Jeff."

A great deal of splashing accompanied his next comment. "You need to face it, Shawne. You're beating a dead drum. Money and in-stant results motivate everything people do."

"Not any longer, Jeff." A bright laugh and more splashing. "We got the San Diego area council to consider a bill limiting further housing development."

Good. This felt much healthier than her earlier depression.

"She will have to keep winning these battles over and over again," Carliano said to me.

Passage must have overheard him. "Are you really willing to live a life of small victories here and there, watching the whole picture blow up again and again?" He sounded incredulous.

"Yes. Then picking up the pieces and trying again." Shawne sound-ed confidant, her voice steady. "People will eventually learn to care about the future."

Tandra, Conn, and I exchanged glances, then smiles—the kind unique to proud parents. Our interplanetary wildling was well rooted.

Jeff kept looking over at me. "On Varok," I said, not sure what good it would do, "growth of one market—or population growth in one area—is understood as a cancer that will destroy the whole if left unchecked."

"Then you think I'm totally wrong to believe economic growth is essential, Orram?" Jeff said.

"On the contrary. I think everything you've said is right—for a debt-based society or a rapidly growing population, until it becomes too large."

"So you think big change is coming?"

"Not soon. I think Shawne and her friends will have long lives of minor successes and major setbacks, but they will persist. They will continue to educate new generations in the basic ethics of conserving resources and having only one child to replace themselves, for they un-derstand that they are dependent on the finite resources Earth provides.

"Meanwhile, Shawne's students will remain absolutely credible. Everything they say will be supported by good evidence. Some day human history will tire of the recurring periods of overcrowding, scar-city, pollution and plagues, and enough people will preserve what is left to make a stable system work."

THE ALIEN EFFECT, 4086–4111 C.E. The human herbivores surviving the problems of the early 4000's were tired of their cycles of over-population, crowding, massive die-off, and recovery. Ellls and va-roks, always watchful on Moonbase, were there to remind the new herbivorous humans that such extreme cycling was unnecessary.

SHADES OF SUCCESS

Conn—weeks later

Conn tried to stay out of the lovers' debates since he was too tied in emotionally. He believed Shawne would waste her life if she stayed with Passage on Earth, working on what he now saw as a hopeless cause. He believed her teaching would wear her down and turn her bitter eventually.

Conn defended himself from grief at what he saw as Shawne's loss of life-joy by working at the marine park—a growing ecosystem that now encircled San Diego Bay.

With the water kept clear and free of motorized craft, he enjoyed cruising the jumble of concrete decorated with barnacles and limpets and anemones. He wore his isolation suit and stuffed the hip pack with samples and prize specimens, keeping records of the growing variety of sea life. Some corals had flourished from spawn they had brought back from Australia, for the Pacific waters this far north were now comfortably warm all year. Best of all, Conn liked the giant sponges that had taken up residence.

"Come into the water and look at this one, Nidok." Conn wrapped his arms around the ahlork's isolation sleeves over his carefully folded wing plates. "Ready? Breathe—or whatever it is you do."

"No time for insults, elll brother. Do it."

Conn laughed and dove, taking the ahlork with him. Nidok hated to be submerged, but he loved the weird sea life that grew in the crevices of the artificial reef. Moving slowly over the top of a barrel sponge, Conn pointed out a sea cucumber brilliantly decorated with the brights he knew humans called orange and yellow, then a sun star with many arms, and a starfish colored a solid dense cool blue.

When they surfaced, Conn looked puzzled. "I saw lots of those blue starfish in the reefs near Green Island, but never here. The dolphins didn't bring it in with their latest collections, did they?"

"They think we need one of each everything," Nidok grumbled.

"But they don't collect from very far away. Strange."

"Maybe it rode on pirate ship."

"What pirate ship?"

"Dawson's."

"Dawson was here? In San Diego Harbor? For how long?"

"Noon meal to sunset. No longer."

"When did you see him?"

"When I took message to orcas yesterday."

"I wonder what he was doing here."

Shawne—later, at the SCBA house.

That night Conn stayed out of the pool to talk with Passage. Shawne was delighted. Maybe Conn was coming around. Maybe she could tell him that she had decided to stay on Earth, that she would never give up (like her mother had—but she wouldn't say that).

"Have you heard or seen anything of Dawson or his rig, Jeff?" Conn asked.

"His boat was seen near the reef, but it left after a few hours," Passage said.

"What was it doing there?"

"No telling."

"I don't like it."

"We traced it earlier, Conn. It went into dry dock when it got back to Cairns and was re-converted for tuna fishing. Then it came north. Dawson himself is out of business. He invested everything in trying to trap you aliens. He lost credibility with his crew when you and Nidok escaped."

"Ha!"

Having heard Passage confirm Nidok's news, Conn disappeared into the pool and didn't come up until Passage was gone. Shawne was furious.

"You didn't give him a chance, Conn. He understands me and my work, but all you do is pick his brain for news. I'm going to marry him, Conn, so you'd better start learning to get along with him."

"Shawne. Shawnoon. I love you too well to see you throw your life away. New love for humans is like new wine. It's heady stuff, but it sours quickly. Take the tough lessons and run with them. Find yourself a varok that can appreciate your human qualities."

"You don't know all that much about humans."

"I can read, can't I? Romance novels keep me young."

"I'm being serious, Conn. You don't want me to stay on Earth?"

"Do you see any point in it? I'm not getting any younger. Let's take the next cruiser to Ellason. We won't have a better chance. I've longed to show you the bright lights of the northern shallows. I want you to see the hundreds of bioluminescent critters that ply those waters, the ones I loved to play with as a tad. I want you to know the grounding pull of gravity on a big planet, a hundred rich tastes from a huge ell-lonian garden—"

"I would love to show Ellason to Jeff."

"We'll take Jeff along," Conn said. "It would do him good to see how the other third lives."

She snuggled close, loving him for inviting Jeff. Though she knew it could never be, the thought counted. They tipped into the water to school away the tension between them. There they found Stringer and called Lanoll. Soon all of us, even Junah, Jesse and Orticon, were in the pool. It was a good time to review our options.

Orram—moments later

Before midnight a consensus developed within our team, with mixed feelings all around. Though Shawne's school might fail eventually with internal bickering, its educational infrastructure had blossomed into working groups on every continent. Local proponents of long-term sustainable economics were tailoring strategies to meet their regional needs.

Soon we would return to Varok. We couldn't know what Jeff might do. In any case, we would not leave until Shawne was sure she wanted to stay on Earth, alone, with or without Jeff.

"You stay only if you can be independent of Jeff," Conn insisted.

"Don't be a light-hopper-brain, Shawne," Stringer quipped. "He's not going to marry you. He doesn't want a rabble-rouser from outer space. He needs a corporate dolly to dress up for the CEO of Passage Enterprises—Growth For All: Lots and Lots of More and More."

"Stop it, Stringer. Stop it." Shawne jumped on her elllonian brother with a leg clamp over his backfin. He knew how to cut through to her. We older folks, and Orticon, got out of the pool in a hurry.

Conn loved it. We all sat with him on the deck, cheering Stringer on, then Shawne, one, then the other, until they were exhausted. When Nidok flew in and sat on heads, the game became "Drown the Beetle." Conn dove in, and we were thoroughly soaked as two green-plumed bodies, Shawne in smooth tan, and Nidok's flapping wings disappeared one last time together, then slid onto the deck.

The decision to leave Earth was reviewed once more over steaming cups of barley-wheat tea. Orticon believed they could find, if necessary, a director for the School For Economic Longevity. "Our efforts have found fertile ground", Orticon said. "Though it is clear that the growth paradigm is overwhelming, the School for Economic Longevity will go on as we have defined it. Come home with us, Shawne."

Conn—at the SCBA house pool

The next morning Shawne came to the pool, dove to the bottom, and swam back and forth over Conn, awakening him with her pressure signature.

He wriggled deeper into the muddy bottom close to Lanoll, but she pushed him toward the surface. "I would guess," she said, "that the prospect of staying on Earth without us has hit Shawne like sudden death."

Conn saw Shawne lounging in the *llaoon* grass at the shallow end of the pool. He joined her there. "So what to do, eh? There will be other Varokian expeditions, at least to the moon, to keep a watch on Earth affairs. If you want to stay, stay, Shawnoon. You might be able to come back to Varok. Give it your best shot here. Just don't expect any instant miracles. We've flapped our butterfly wings. Now its up to the unpredictable future to determine when and if our flapping has stirred up a thunderstorm way down the road."

"You are so comfortable with that, Conn. I wish I were. I feel overwhelmed. The school is holding to its values, but nothing really significant is happening there to stop the new rush to regrow and rebuild—to 'recreate the vibrant world that existed before the die-offs.' I feel that I've failed, and I hate it. You're right. I'm not the patient lobbyist, the collector of data, willing to make arguments over and over again all my life. I would hate every minute of it. What am I going to do, Conn? I can't leave."

"Earth hasn't defeated you, Shawnoon. You have no way of knowing what humans will do, not for another millennium."

His arms, always ready with soft green tiles, took her in. "If you feel you have to stay, you have to stay. If I could give you a parting gift, it would be that thing you call faith—faith in the natural processes of existence. Call it God if you like. It's all the same—faith in the beauty of roses and faith in yourself—faith in love and trust and all those emergent phenomena that give us consciousness. They also protect us from pain we can't bear."

THE ALIEN EFFECT, 4111–4113 C.E. After more than 2000 years, ellls and varoks returned to the habitable Earth and found sustainability ethics in place on the planet—adopted by the herbivorous humanoid populations. The planet was divided into ecologically distinct units, including the well-tended oceans and their flourishing elllonian hybrid coral reefs. By straw vote and volunteerism, populations spread according to the limits set for each ecological/geological unit by its carrying capacity.

The fisheries of Earth came under cetacean control, and the whales concentrated their care on the elllonian-coral symbiotic reefs. Eventually, the whales convinced six ellls and three varoks to stay on Earth as dispassionate observers and consultants. One of the ellls had a large collection of genes from his ancestor, Conn.

Revenge

Stringer—days later, working with Conn on the southern California coast

One morning in late September of 2070 C.E., when Shawne had gone off to teach a class in carrying capacity, Conn sat down with Lanoll and Stringer to begin a list of cetacean sounds. They intended to make demo tapes of dolphin languages, but disagreed on some sounds, so Conn talked Stringer and Lanoll into swimming out to the marine park. The dolphins working there could resolve the questions. They would also need to know that they were soon to be working with human volunteers to keep the park clean and healthy.

As the three ellls passed Alligator Head and swam south, Nidok joined them, flying low to keep them in sight through the deep fog still hugging La Jolla Bay.

"Don't take any chances flying through this pea soup," Conn hollered to the ahlork. "Stay right here on the end of the reef. We'll be back in one-half a light-period, Varok time."

Nidok agreed with a grumpy cough, acting sorry he'd come along. Then he sat on an exposed concrete block encrusted with sea life.

Conn led Stringer and Lanoll around the end of the inner reef near Goldfish Point. They swam through jumbled concrete alive with new corals and starfish and sponge variants more ancient than most of Earth's wild experiments in evolution.

Stringer loved the incredible menagerie living in the reefs, loved to identify them and test the quick reactions and defenses of each weird creature new to him. When he saw a flattened tail colored a lovely deep cool to his infrared vision (violet), he pulled it out of the crevice where it sought refuge. Before he could react, its small head whipped around, and sharp teeth sank deep into his arm.

He called out with an ultrasonic scream that brought Conn and Lanoll back to him. Within seconds the young elll's nervous system shut down. He was unable to swim.

Conn

Conn recognized the attacker when its whipping curves carried it swiftly away. It was a sea snake. He had studied Australia's poisonous sea life as a precaution when they visited there. The venom of the sea snake was one of Earth's most deadly, a paralyzing neurotoxin. Pearl divers who grabbed sea snakes by mistake and were bitten died quickly of suffocation, unable to breathe.

The sea snake had never been seen so far north before. How had it migrated up here so fast?

Conn thought of Dawson. Had he seeded the concrete reefs of San Diego with sea snakes? Could he have been so cruel? It was common knowledge that the reefs were a pet project of Conn's. The thought that his son had fallen victim to such vicious revenge sent chills of horror over his tiles.

Lanoll kept Stringer quiet, while Conn frantically searched for something to make a tourniquet. He pulled up sea grass and tied it around Stringer's arm, then he swam to the surface to look for Nidok. Thankfully, the ahlork sat exactly where Conn had left him.

"Back so soon? I haven't frozen to death in fog yet," Nidok said.

"We need serious help," Conn said.

"Slow down, Skipper. Use air bags you call lungs."

"Stringer. He's been bitten. Paralyzed by sea snake. Australian."

"They not be here."

"You saw Dawson's boat the other day."

"Harrahn hater dumped sea snakes?"

"Follow me. You've got to play egg beater for us."

"What?"

Conn didn't wait to explain. Nidok followed the elll's wake to the end of the concrete reef where Stringer lay under water. Lanoll had dug a soft spot for him in the bottom sand and lined it with sea grass.

"Is he getting any oxygen, Lanoll?"

She nodded and continued fanning a stream of fresh water over his gills in the hope that the gills would provide enough oxygen, if she could keep an active flow of water over them. The paralysis had shut down their normal pumping action.

"Nidok can keep the water stirred up, Lanoll. Can you keep him warm while I go for help? Are you all right? Of course, you're not all right."

He wrapped her in his arms and their pressure together in the water gave Stringer some schooling reassurance. When Conn resurfaced, Nidok was frantic.

"Are all ellls dead down there?"

"Use your worthless wings to stir the water. Stringer's paralyzed. Soon he won't be able to pump any water over his gills. You're his pump."

"I see it."

"Let's see you do it. You've got to keep his gills oxygenated. I'm going for help. Lanoll will keep him warm while he's inactive."

Eager to obey for once in his life, Nidok jumped in the water and vigorously stirred air into the quiet surface.

"Think of pushing air into the water. Try a circular, downward stroke. There. Wait! Stay over this spot. You're taking off like a motor boat."

"Picky, picky. Always nagging at ahlorks."

"My son's life is in your wing tips, Square Head."

"I told you. Ellls can't survive this Earth without ahlork."

"Truer words have never been spoken." Conn saluted Nidok by kissing the ahlork scar on his wrist, then he was off, swimming for shore.

Tandra and Orram came back with Conn in the survival dinghy. Stringer tried to cooperate as they pulled a full isolation suit onto his body. It was more than frustrating. With an oxygen line directed to his flooded helmet, he felt much better and let himself sleep. The family's vigil began.

Shawne—hours later

That same night Shawne, Orticon, Junah and Jesse arrived at the house from a long day of teaching and found a note, a cold piece of paper telling them that, once again, their lives were unraveling.

They motored out to the reef, and Shawne spent the night close to Stringer, surfacing only to take in quick breaths, like a dolphin on a mission of mercy. In the morning, thoroughly exhausted, she asked Jesse to take her out to the pier where Passage's tanker was berthed.

She found her lover having breakfast with his crew. Delighted with her surprise visit, Passage greeted her warmly and introduced her to the crewmembers she had not met. She tried to join them, but nothing tasted edible. They complained about the verbal attacks on the water-hauling business, and Jeff laughed it off, as if it didn't matter. Nothing they said resonated.

When at last the meal was finished and they were alone, Shawne hesitated, then made what felt like a demand. "I need to talk, Jeff. Now. Stringer's been paralyzed by a sea snake, possibly Dawson's doing. I'm wondering what we should do to protect ourselves. Soon it will be just Junah and me here, running the school."

He took her in his arms, and she was able to cry. "I'm frightened, Jeff."

As they moved to his cabin, she told the whole story, including the team's suspicions of Dawson's revenge. "The ellls can't stay any longer. The team has decided to return to Varok, all of them, all my family. Very soon they'll wrap up everything here and leave Earth."

"Probably a good thing."

"Good for what? For whom? What do you mean?"

"Look, Shawne. I can't talk right now. We've got to get this tanker moving and meet a schedule. When I get back we'll go out for lobster and talk all night if you wish."

"All night."

"Well, at least an hour or so. Business is picking up very nicely."

She looked at him and wished her feelings would all come clear, as they sometimes do when you suddenly see a person with a soul you don't recognize. She wanted to say, "Aha," and feel herself become a new person—more her own person, no longer a callow presence wedded to a dream. Instead, she felt empty.

She took Jeff's offer of a ride to the SCBA pier, and she came home to the silent lodge and a quiet pool. The water and the deep mud bottom and the water lilies gave her no comfort.

She tried to read the essays her students had spent hours researching. They would be waiting for her comments. Some might act on the ideas they had developed—some. But they would change nothing much. They would change too little too late. Jeff Passage and his ambitious business competitors would buy the store and sell it cheap, and the cycle would begin again.

When the security officer came in to announce a visitor, she expected to see one of her students, someone worried about their essay, but it was Charley Hazard.

"I hear your family will be returning to Varok soon," he said.

"You must have seen Passage."

"I was supposed to meet with his committee for North Mexican development. When he mentioned that the alien propagandists were leaving and the opposition to growth would soon peter out, I decided to come here and see what was going on."

"'Alien propagandists'? Is that what we are to him, Charley?"

"You're messengers of hope to me, Shawne. And don't think your teachings are going to peter out. He's dead wrong about that."

Charley put his hands on her shoulders. Tears were flowing but her jaw was set hard. "Look at me, Shawne. I've got to tell you something. You should realize how much water Passage's tankers are now providing to San Diego. As long as the water business continues to expand at such a rate, there is no hope for a consensus on the area's population limit."

"That means even my first pilot project is doomed," Shawne said. "Ironic, isn't it, that Jeff should be the one to shoot it down."

"I've tried to talk to Passage about it, Shawne, but he has no conception of a stable economic system. In his mind, growth is what people do, so why not him? He can't understand your students' attack on his business."

"Oh, I think he does, all too well." Her tears had dried up.

Charley moved into the living room and sat down, inviting Shawne to join him on the couch. "Was he right about your staying here? Are you not returning to Varok?"

The look Shawne gave him sent tears to his eyes.

"I don't know, Charley. Why should I stay? I can't make any difference here."

"What are you saying, Shawne? You've made a huge difference."

"I thought I was so smart coming to Earth to show them how to learn from their tragedy, but nothing has changed. The four solutions that are required for long-term survival are still anathema to most humans. They won't stop population growth, reduce consumption, redistribute wealth, or count real costs. Jeff brings in so much water from Alaska, everyone is convinced this is monsoon country, and they can wash the streets with pure water whenever they want."

She spoke with anger simmering hotter and hotter, then boiling over. "I can't do it, Charley. It's way too huge for me, this Earth and all its near-sighted profiteering. I've failed, pure and simple."

Charley took a deep breath. He spoke quietly, and slowly. "Tandra told me you understand complexity theory, at least some of its implications. Every time you open a student's mind to a new possibility, you are creating, not one, but many bifurcation points, forks in the road where new things become possible for human society."

"Yes, and that will have to do. I'm finished. I'm done." Shawne laughed as tears streamed down her cheeks. "You sound like Conn and Orram. I thought you were a fisherman, or a tour guide."

"A retired math professor, also," Charley said.

"Am I a coward, Charley? Look around. This is what life would be like, once my family is gone. Myself, in an empty lodge. What could cut through the loneliness, the hopelessness? Conn's faith? Faith in the unpredictable future of this miserably complex, dice-throwing universe?"

"Why not?"

She stared up at the golden-haired giant and saw in his smiling blue eyes a reflection very much like Conn's faith in Whatever.

"This planet will never be the same, Shawne, because you have been here."

She laughed and hugged Charley.

He looked down at Shawne with a skewed grin. "Forgive me for asking," he said, "but is there a chance your mom would consider staying here with you?"

The Alien Effect, 4113–4170 C.E. After much negotiation, Earth's branch of the Elll-Varok Concentrate was established with its center in San Diego, where the population of humans, ellls and varoks held steady at a sustainable 475,000.

Shawne and Her Dads

Orram—days later, at the SCBA house

Slowly, the snake's poison broke down under the onslaught of Stringer's defenses, and he was able to swim again. We moved him back into the lodge pool to complete his recovery. As he regained enough strength to travel, we began to make preparations for the jump to Moonbase and the long trip home to Varok.

When Shawne came to me in my home office one night, I assumed she wanted to talk about Jeff Passage and her decision to stay on Earth. She sat in the big reading chair next to my desk and looked at me without focusing. Her lovely blond hair was laying this way and that, as if she had been nervously twisting strands of it in her fingers. She smelled of sweet sweat. She had gone running with Junah on the beach south of the pier.

"Is Junah still determined to stay here and act as varokian liaison?" I asked.

She nodded. "As long as I stay." She looked at me with an expression I had never seen before and didn't dare invade with a patch reading.

"What is it, Shawne?" She had always found it a little difficult to open conversations with me. I suppose it was my role as the heavy in the family.

"Read me, Orram," she said. "I can't find the right words."

"I see that you are worried." I concentrated my patch sense on the flow of her thoughts, expecting them to be full of Jeff, or perhaps her fear of loneliness at being separated from the family. Instead, her mind was preoccupied with Charley Hazard and fear for me.

"What is this you're imagining?" I asked "You see me ousted by a human rival?"

"Orram, I've never asked about details, you know. I believed that your link to Mom had to include touch or you couldn't maintain the mind-link with her. I know your emotional health depends on this link—"

Tears began to flow down her cheeks. "Please Ramram, I know it's none of my business—Charley wants to go back to Varok with you." The words rushed out in a torrent, as if under pressure that needed release. "I realized Mom had seen Charley alone again. They were on the pier, talking very seriously one night."

"He kissed her, on the lips, as humans do," I said, as gently as I could. "And do you know how that made her feel? I do. I share her mind, Shawnoon, but I don't kiss her lips, because I am not human. I can't stir her hormones like Charley can, like Jeff has stirred yours, like Lanoll stirs Conn's."

"But you sleep together."

"Yes, and Tandra schools with Conn, and she puts on scuba gear and stays close to him on the pool's muddy bottom when he needs healing. Her contact with Conn has more genital content than her contact with me, because that's how ells relate, even in non-sexual ways. That's what has you puzzled, isn't it, Shawne? Genital contact."

"I've always assumed it didn't matter."

"But now you know it can. But it also can not, especially between different species. Think ells and daramonts, humans and horses. Think gray whales or dolphins who go out of their way for human touch or to save the injured. Our relationships, Tandra's and Conn's and mine, are not very different. But your relationship with Jeff is."

"Mom has said that many times: You give meaning to each other, or share it."

"It's all such a miracle, Shawne—life. Don't ever take a minute of your life for granted, and don't waste another second worrying about me. I've invited Charley to come to Varok and live at Orserah's lodge with us, if he and Tandra want to develop their relationship."

"But—"

"He understands our conditions, Tandra's and mine and Conn's. We are committed to one another. Top priority. Any sexual partner must accept that commitment and contribute to it."

"Like Lanoll."

"Exactly."

"So is Charley coming with you to Varok? Does he have someone's Replacement Certificate?"

"He was going to use Jesse Mendleton's, but Jesse has decided to go back to Varok, so Charley can use mine—but he'll have to make up his mind soon—and so will you. We would like to leave as soon as Stringer can travel comfortably. We're not sure he will ever be able to walk long distances again. He would like to complete his recovery in the Forested Sea."

Shawne—the next day, at the SCBA house pool

"I have to admit," Conn told Shawne as they cruised the pool's bottom, harvesting the last of the mud hoppers and *llaoon* grass, "Charley knows what sustainable practices mean. I can't fault the man."

Shawne pointed to the surface. She wanted to talk in air. Her clicking vocabulary and Elllonian were too limited for the questions she wanted to ask. "Orram has spent hours with Charley," she said, when they had surfaced. "He's got some good ideas for helping keep the Lake Seclusion area sustainable. Philosophically, we seem to be on the same wave length. And Conn, I love the way Charley treats Mom."

"Like she was made of star dust. He treats her like I wish I could."

"You've never treated Mom badly."

"But we've had our moments, haven't we?"

"You're not human, Conn. You've had to work out a lot of kinks between you. Orram too. And of all God's critters, it was Nidok who cemented it for all of you."

"Really? I guess so." Conn laughed and picked up Shawne's towel and rolled her hair in it. "Where's your brush?" He found it and started smoothing out the tangled waves, but she pushed his green hand away.

"I need you to be serious with me, Conn."

"I'm serious when I say life is too short to waste grumping around. I bet we'll have here a branch of the Concentrate, Concentrate Earth, run by great-fish, within your lifetime, instead of scifi-interstellar warfare and fights over resources and 'lebensraum.'"

"I wish I could buy your optimism, Conn. I'll bottle it. It should bring a huge price."

"Talk to Charley. He's real people. He's most people. He's the wave of *Homo sapiens*' future."

"I hope so. I have talked to Charley. You're right about him. I just wish Jeff would treat me the way Charley treats Mom."

THE ALIEN EFFECT

Shawne—one morning the week before the team leaves Earth

Orram looked as if he was about to give the speech of his life. Shawne had never seen him so nervous. "I owe you all the honesty I can muster. I don't want to leave you behind, Shawne," he said, "alone on a failing Earth. There, I said it."

She laughed. "I love you for that, RamRam. You know I'm trying to stay optimistic." She pulled her hair into a pony tail and gave Orram a smile she knew was not entirely honest.

Three days later, when we were nearly ready to ship out to Moonbase, Shawne called Jeff Passage. She motioned for Conn to stay close, and she put her communicator on speaker. He held his breath, and without shame, listened in on the conversation.

After an exchange of pleasantries with Jeff that nearly sparked a rude remark from Conn, Shawne said abruptly, "Jeff, I will be going home to Varok. My work on Earth is finished."

Conn whistled through his nasal gills.

"Gad, I'm sorry to see you go, Shawne," Jeff said. "I'm sure we can work something out. In a few months I'll be able to take a break from my business. Let me come see you on Varok."

"You'll be welcome to visit, Jeff," she said. "But don't plan on staying. I have only one Replacement Certificate for Varok, and I have other plans for it."

She tapped off her communicator and turned to face Conn, who reared back and gave her a double high five. "Take me home, Conn," she said, "then on to Ellason. I need a good dose of ellls to get my life back on track."

Orram—at the SCBA house, ready to go

"I've sold my boat," Charley announced. He walked into the SCBA house looking eager and hopeful, but a bit humble for all his red-blond hair and bulk. "Tandra tells me I can come along and give it a try."

"Glad to have you on board," Conn said, "if you'll excuse the expression."

The elll extended a warm handshake, and I saw Charley take a good look at the powerful be-finned appendage before he let go.

"Any lover of Tandra's is a love of ours," Conn added.

"I'm no lover yet, Conn," Charley said, calling his bluff. "Tandra and I have a hopeful start, and I'm the luckiest bastard this side of the moon—to be invited to come along with her to Varok—but I know enough math to be very respectful of five-dimensional complexities. No one's committed to me, nor I to you, yet."

"We'll keep our minds and our hearts open, Charley," I said. "Promise." Shawne gave him a hug, then helped me serve our last meal before we left Earth.

A yellow moon played with wisps of ocean mist decorating the darkening blue sky. Through the silhouette of tall Torrey pines, we watched the sun set over the Pacific Ocean. Far in the distance Conn saw a gray whale send a fine spout into the air, then another, as if in farewell.

THE ALIEN EFFECT, 4170–4202 C.E. AND BEYOND: The elllonian free-living corals that re-populated coastal waters shaped Earth's oceans into lush underwater gardens, where the fisheries thrived. When the World Association of Conversant Species was established, its members unanimously adopted the Human-Elll-Varok-Primate-Cetacean Plan for Earth. A consensus on an acceptable quality of life for all extant species was found. Steady state ethics held. The infrastructure for resource monitoring was set in place, mining quotas were auctioned, and humans began their adventure in sustaining the future for themselves and their fellow travelers in life.

APPENDICES

A. Principal Characters

The Oran-ElConn-Grey Family

Humans: born on Earth in the 21st century.

Tandra Grey	a microbiologist.
Shawne	a young woman raised on Varok by the Oran-ElConn-Grey family, originally adopted by Tandra on Earth in the 2040s.

Ellls: aquatic, playful, be-finned bipeds, native to Ellason. Emotionally volatile, loaded with senses, with logic-driven minds, focused on moment-to-moment experience.

Conn	a loner elll, lifelong friend of Orram, Tandra's first alien contact. Expert in Earth studies and lover of English slang.
Lanoll	Conn's elllonian mate, also a loner. An expert in Varok's ecology and recovery from Mahntik's treason in *The Webs of Varok*.
Stringer	a schooling elll, Orram and Lanoll's selected hatchling.

Varoks: durable but sensitive bipeds, emotionally fragile, senses easily overloaded. Open minds and mood reading ability, instinctively focused on the long-term stability of the planet Varok. Strong hormonal links triggered by mental compatibility.

Orram	a highly respected Master of Life Sciences bonded to the mind of the human Tandra Grey.
Orticon	Orram's son by planned procreation, now a teacher of local and global options to secure the future.

Other Characters

Humans: adaptable technological bipeds, emotionally variable, sensually inhibited. Intuitive minds, tend to focus on the self.

Jesse Mendleton the ellls' first human contact on Earth.

Bob Carliano astronaut befriended by ellls and varoks on their first visit to Earth in *A Place Beyond Man* (pending re-release as *The View Beyond Earth*).

Pete Dawson a fisherman and xenophobe.

Jeff Passage a young, ambitious entrepreneur and boatman.

Charley Hazard a former math professor, now a fishing guide to the Islas Revillagigedo, working out of Cabo San Lucas.

Varoks

Junah Orram's colleague, an expert in socio-political data taken by Elll-Varok Science at their Observation Base on Earth's Moon.

Mahntik the villain in *The Webs of Varok*.

Ahlork: semi-literate flocking insectoids living in the cliffs of Varok, covered with chitinous plates and possessing prehensile wing tips. Miners of the ancient urban ruins, with long-distance flight capability.

Nidok leader of the Greater Flock, bonded to the Oran-ElConn-Grey family.

Great-fish: marine mammaloids native to Ellason, immigrants to Varok. Larger than Earth's dolphins, with prehensile fin-tips.

Oleyall a Master of global health, immigrant from Ellason, recognized expert in holistic analysis of living systems. Respected for his wisdom.

Daramonts: mild-tempered ungulateoids of Varok, larger than camels of Earth, with heads resembling Springer Spaniels and kangaroo-like haunches. Committed to providing ellls with transportation.

Light Hoppers: tiny Varokian marsupialoids who love stories and thrive on imagination, ignoring reality unless threatened.

B. A History of the Archives

3631 *ir* **(Earth 5000** BCE) - Events recorded in *The Unheard Song*.[1]

3634 *ir* **(Earth 4962** BCE) – Amanok writes his memoirs.

4225.8 *ir* **(Earth 2020** CE) – Tandra Grey born on Earth.

4228 *ir* **(Earth 2047** CE) – Shawne Grey born on Earth.

4228.3–4228.4 *ir* **(Earth 2050–2051** CE) – Events recorded in *A Place Beyond Man*,[2] revised as *The View Beyond Earth*.[3]

4228.4–4229.5 *ir* **(Earth 2051–2064** CE) – Events in *The Webs of Varok*.[4]

4229 *ir* **(Earth 2059** CE) – Aman Telariahn (Amantel) publishes Amanok's memoirs as *The Unheard Song*.[1]

4229.8–4230 *ir* **(Earth 2068–2070** CE) – Oran-ElConn-Grey family events recorded in *The Alien Effect*.[5]

4229.8–4409.7 *ir* **(Earth 2068–4202** CE and beyond) – Biological Events recorded in *The Alien Effect*.[5]

4230 *ir* **(Earth 2070** CE) – Events recorded in *An Alien's Quest*.[6]

1. Penscript Publishing House, 2022. 2. Charles Scribner's Sons, 1975.
3. Penscript Publishing House, 2014. 4. Penscript Publishing House, 2012.
5. Penscript Publishing House, 2014. 6. Penscript Publishing House, 2016

C. Reprise: The Alien Effect

September 12, 2068 C.E. The first wave of nausea came without warning, and Conn lost everything he had eaten. It disappeared into the voracious sea. He swam hard, trying to escape the gnawing in his gut, then he could no longer swim. He drifted in a curled position, as if he were an embryo back in the egg. No pain he had ever experienced came close to this awful feeling. The ache surged, and surged again, and he hoped to die, anything to stop the pain. With explosive force, his waste voided and a sharp pain seared his cloaca. He saw the yellowish tinge of blood in the white excreta, then the worst of the pain was over. Feebly the ell worked his fins, trying to get to shore, then he lost consciousness.

2068–2070 C.E. As a precaution, Tandra had made sure that all alien waste was sterilized in the composting toilet of their temporary home. Like human waste, Conn's elllonian excreta contained useful microorganisms—useful to ells, that is.

Within the blood cells of ells, there lives a tiny creature somewhat smaller than Earth's bacteria, but more complex. It was free-living eons ago. Then it became an elllonian symbiont for a while. Now, it was as essential to the ells' cellular metabolism as mitochondria are to human cells. When Conn voided into the Pacific Ocean, huge numbers of the tiny creature—we'll call them Conn's Org—rode off in the blood cells from his poisoned stomach lining. Before a new sun rose over San Diego, voracious sea mites nibbled away Conn's protective cells. Thus set loose, Conn's Org struggled to find food and shelter. Many perished, but some found refuge in rotting debris caught in warm pockets of waste concrete on the ocean floor. There they reverted to their independent state.

Circa 2070 C.E. In rooting for food on the concrete reef, the large, flat gold fish of the San Diego coast 'inhaled' Conn's Org, and a few were trapped in their gills.

Feeling very much at home in fish gills, the little organelle/micro-organism from Conn's blood cells sought out a source of food and found easy prey in *Haemophilus* germs, which were giving the gold fish an irritating gill cold.

Conn's Org, full of nutritious *Haemophilus* bacteria, rode the fishes' coughs into the ocean, where it quickly found other fish gills in which to live. In those gills Conn's Org found other viruses and bacteria to eat, and the microscopic alien opportunist further developed the habit of gill hopping. The niche was wide open. Due to decades of human dumping in the oceans, the fish of Earth suffered from a large variety of disorders. Conn's org feasted and spread.

2070–2120 C.E. While the first human-orcan mariculture became established, the fish of the mid-Pacific grew healthier. Conn's Org was busy cleaning up *Haemophilus* in fish gills. The org had spread into deep waters where the sea bass and tuna enjoyed its benefits. The human population, recovering rapidly on a steady diet of healthy sea bass and tuna, didn't realize they were eating Conn's Org. Hearty opportunists that they were, a few of Conn's Orgs found the human gut and lungs fine places to live. There were *Haemophilus* germs to eat there, too.

2120–2220 C.E. As Conn's Org found comfy places to live in the gills of fish and the intestines of humans, chaotic change of another sort began. During the twenty-second century humans bred freely. Once again their populations reached stress levels. Hydrogen and hydro-electricity powered a mobile society similar to that of the twentieth century. Sewage and waste found its way into the Pacific Ocean.

Before a hundred years had passed, San Diego Bay and the North American shorelines became unsafe for swimming once again. The coral reefs went into another decline. In the re-polluted ocean, one strain of Conn's Org found a new source of food in the weakened cold-water coral.

2220–2416 C.E. As Conn's Org searched for sources of nourishment, it came upon the coral that had once overrun the concrete reefs of Conn's Marine Park. The weakened coral was vulnerable and tasty, while healthy reef coral adapted to warmer waters gave shelter to Conn's Org. Those corals that escaped being eaten found the waste products of Conn's Org quite nutritious. Eventually, both the coral cells and Conn's Org prospered in the warming ocean, and a symbiotic relationship was established between them. The human population was suffering another major die-off, so few people had time, health, or fuel to visit the reefs.

Circa 2416–2525 C.E. Conn's Org made itself at home in living coral cells, devouring the weaker ones, silencing some genes and releasing others, thus enabling the corals to thrive in northern waters.

As the decades passed, Conn's Org protected itself with intracellular membranes, until it became a resident organelle within the coral cells. The organelle gave the corals a huge reproductive advantage, and they colonized the entire west coast of North America. Fish found comfortable places to hide in the expanding reefs, and their numbers increased.

2525–2575 C.E. Along the northwest coast of North and South America, coral reefs were healthy again. Giant staghorn forests covered the ocean floor for miles. Brain corals flourished under their protection, and tiny crystal corals decorated with every color of the spectrum lay down carpets over the skeletons of older growth. The old growth provided small crevices for fish eggs to hatch, tiny caves in which the young could thrive, and large tunnels for safe refuge. As the fisheries recovered, so too did the human population, again—especially those immunized to *Haemophilus* courtesy of Conn's Org.

2575–3575 C.E. As the fourth millennium C.E. reached its mid-point, competition between elllonian-coral variants became fierce. The most vulnerable corals continued their age-old, haphazard method of spewing sperm and eggs willy-nilly into the ocean currents. But one particular mutant of Conn's coral hybrid found itself with a great advantage when it became free-living. The females sprouted a bright green receptacle with a yellow bioluminescent edge, and the males developed a primitive eye, thus enabling a more deliberate method of delivering sperm to egg.

3575–3625 C.E. Late in the thirty-sixth century, the Great Barrier Reef and the reefs of the South Pacific started their slow-moving dance across the ocean floors. Ever-changing, seeking out safer havens or richer waters, the reefs were dominated by the new elllonian free-living hybrid coral. Sea charts showing dangerous reefs were no longer valid for more than six months.

More slowly, the humans who had been infected with Conn's Org, hence resistant to the dangerous *Haemophilus* germ, began to out-number those unprotected.

3625–3827 C.E. Sixteen hundred years after Conn visited Earth, his free-living coral symbiont successfully rebuilt and extended the coral reefs all over Earth's oceans, providing rich environments for new fish populations. As food availability spread, the population of human beings, strengthened by Conn's Org, once again began to dominate their environment. These new people were unlike *Homo sapiens sapiens*.

Marine farming ventures were reestablished with orcas and with smaller dolphins. Whales declined to participate, so a dedicated group of people, with a long history of fighting for cetacean survival, set off into the oceans to find out why.

3827–3950 C.E. Someone among the whale preservationists was able to reconstruct the cetacean language Conn had taught hu-mans eighteen hundred years before. Using that ancient language,

three divers approached the whales with a plan for them to cooperate with humans in order to enhance the fisheries. They learned
that the humpback whales had done some reconstructive history
themselves. Laid bare was the long historical horror of slaughter by
humans for the sake of whale oil. The whales could understand predation for food, but not for oil, with the food wasted. They were not
about to deal with humans on any level. The gray whales—who had
been cheated out of their fair share of tuna in their early history of
partnering with humans—heard the story and agreed to the boycott.

In human society, the long-dead fossil oil economy was replaced by
ubiquitous solar, tide and wind energy sources, supplemented with
carefully rationed hydrogen. With the elllonian coral hybrid flourishing and the clean oceans filled with fish, the dominant humanoid
population once again took off into a period of nonlinear growth,
marked by an accelerated mutation rate.

3950–4052 C.E. With energy sources limited to the sun and wind,
various human populations learned to get along with local sources
of food, water, and shelter. As a result, when a population reached
stress levels, it tended to be self-limiting. There was no place to
go and no more to eat. This time the die offs were spotty, due
mostly to drought and epidemics from local water pollution. The
fisheries survived.

Conn's Org flourished in most humans, and its DNA had a heyday
recombining with the rapidly mutating human bacterial flora. No one
noticed when the recombinants took over the bulk of bacteria in the
human gut and started digesting the tough plant fiber, cellulose.

4052–4086 C.E. Since the local die offs did little to relieve the again
overpopulated state of human society, there was no relief from the
ever-changing epidemics and the scarcity of potable water. Only
one segment of human society seemed to thrive: the segment that
relished alfalfa salad.

4086–4111 C.E. The human herbivores surviving the problems of the early 4000's were tired of their cycles of overpopulation, crowding, massive die-off, and recovery. Ellls and varoks, always watchful on Moonbase, were there to remind the new herbivorous humans that such extreme cycling was unnecessary.

4111–4113 C.E. After more than 2000 years, ellls and varoks returned to the habitable Earth and found sustainability ethics in place on the planet—adopted by the herbivorous humanoid populations. The planet was divided into ecologically distinct units, including the well-tended oceans and their flourishing elllonian hybrid coral reefs. By straw vote and volunteerism, populations spread according to the limits set for each ecological/geological unit by its carrying capacity.

The fisheries of Earth came under cetacean control, and the whales concentrated their care on the elllonian-coral symbiotic reefs. Eventually, the whales convinced six ellls and three varoks to stay on Earth as dispassionate observers and consultants. One of the ellls had a large collection of genes from his ancestor, Conn.

4113–4170 C.E. After much negotiation, Earth's branch of the Elll-Varok Concentrate was established with its center in San Diego, where the population of humans, ellls and varoks held steady at a sustainable 475,000.

4170–4202 C.E. AND BEYOND: The elllonian free-living corals that repopulated coastal waters shaped Earth's oceans into lush underwater gardens, where the fisheries thrived. When the World Association of Conversant Species was established, its members unanimously adopted the Human-Elll-Varok-Primate-Cetacean Plan for Earth. A consensus on an acceptable quality of life for all extant species was found. Steady state ethics held. The infrastructure for resource monitoring was set in place, mining quotas were auctioned, and humans began their adventure in sustaining the future for themselves and their fellow travelers in life.

D. BIBLIOGRAPHY

Eco-Economy: Building An Economy For the Earth by Lester R. Brown. New York, W. W. Norton, 2001.

Enough Is Enough: Building A Sustainable Economy in a World of Finite Resources by Rob Dietz and Dan O'Neill. San Francisco, Berrett-Koehler, 2013. A concise text summarizing what is needed to convert to and maintain a no-growth economy and why.

For the Common Good: Redirecting the Economy Toward Community, the Environment and a Sustainable Future by Herman E. Daly and John B.Cobb Jr. Boston, Beacon Press, 1994. A scathing critique of classical economics and the moral implications of its faulty premises.

Hot, Flat and Crowded: Why We Need a Green Revolution–and How It Can Renew America by Thomas L. Friedman. New York, Farrar, Straus and Giroux, 2008. Important correlation between big money and loss of democracy and the need for America to lead the way to a sustainable future. But why does Friedman forget the "Crowded" part? He assumes growth is essential, giving too little weight to the fact that resources are limited, as is space for humane living.

Our Way Out: First Principles for a Post-Apocalyptic World by Marq de Villiers. Toronto, McClelland and Stewart Ltd., 2011. A sweeping analysis of how we can secure a better future with steady state principles; doesn't shy away from population problems, sharp critiques and difficult strategies.

Plan B: Rescuing a Planet under Stress and a Civilization in Trouble by Lester R. Brown. New York, W. W. Norton, 2003.

Supply Shock: Economic Growth at the Crossroads and the Steady State Solution by Brian Czech. BC Canada, New Society Publishers, 2013. A comprehensive analysis of the failure of classical economics and policies needed for a "Full-World Economy."

The End of Growth: Adapting to Our New Economic Reality by Richard Heinberg. BC Canada, New Society Publishers, 2011. Argues that we have no choice but to deal with the complex system of our current crisis — resource limits, environmental impacts and a failed financial system based on the fallacy of growth.

The Future: Six Drivers of Global Change by Al Gore. New York, Random House, 2013. Wastes no words describing the policy failures and blind denial that have bought us the likelihood of a miserable future; makes very clear the threats, the corrections needed, and the policy changes required.

The World in 2050: Four Forces Shaping Civilization's Northern Future by Laurence C. Smith. London, Dutton Penguin Group, 2010. Uses currently available data to make detailed projections to the year 2050 in a world moving northward.

E. GLOSSARY

Elllonian and Varokian Terms and Concepts.

adjustment. Intense schooling of ellls, in which strong pressure signals, electro-sensing, magneto orientation and ultrasonic messages are rapidly exchanged underwater so that accommodation may be made for the absence of a member of the school or for the addition of a new member.

aen (āĕn). One.

aen naran (āĕn närän). Specialist, Varokian educational degree.

aeo-o. Elllonian expression of intense pleasure.

aeyull. Elllonian expression of intense pain.

ahl (ähl). Source, life.

ahl ara (ähl ärä). Egg source, female sponsor.

Ahlkahn (älkän). Literally source line, the high-speed train connecting populated areas of Varok.

ahlleahnya (äläänyä). Mental consummation, joining (literally life peace).

ahlnat (älnät). Self-organization.

Ahlork (älŏrk). Ancient flying ones.

Ahlrialka tree. Huge spreading, plant-like growth on the hot acid plains of Varok; it produces dense, tasty reproductive lumps.

ahn (än). Three, balanced.

ahnye (änyĕ). Mists.

ahr (är). Deadly.

allahn (älän). Ocean.

aloon (älōn). Elllonian noun, usually used with affection to mean something like wet slob or water bum.

alyakah (ālyäkä). Desirable mate. Varokian word for a mature, well-integrated female who would be desirable as a mother or wife.

alye (älyĕ). Expletive, not desireable.

ar (är). Land.

ara (ärä). Egg layer.

backfin. The retractable dorsal fin of ellls, running from the neck to lower torso.

bayon. An encouraging sound used by ellls.

Callisto cycle. Varoks' reference to the cycling of Callisto around Jupiter. Callisto time: Moments when Jupiter's moon Callisto is visible from a locale, a Varokian township.

coalitions. Ecological regions on Earth circa 2060 C.E. that relate economically and socially, sharing common interests.

Concentrate. The institution of higher learning in Ahl Vior. See Varokian Concentrate.

consummation. Total mind link, achieved by varoks who develop complete subconscious emotional support and mind-sharing (See Release and Mind-link).

dan (dän). Poisonous, questionable.

dara (därä). Friend.

daramont (dârămänt). Literally, friend for riding. A large, four-legged beast of Varok, related to light-hoppers. Soon after their arrival on Varok, ellls recruited the semi-intelligent quadrupeds as transport, in exchange for the promise of protection. Their broad backs, concave shoulders, powerful necks, intelligence, and huge rabbit-like haunches make them ideal mounts for the speed-loving ellls. Their dog-like faces, enhanced with broad lips, give them an endearing quality. They will fold their front legs to invite ellls to race. They graze on web stalks, and are beginning to pass on their cultural habits and their devotion to ellls to their young.

dara vahn. Sire friend.

Directorate. Full title: Elll-Varok Lunar Base Directorate. The council of ellls and varoks at the EV base on Earth's moon. This group makes policy decisions on behalf of EV Science.

eefl. A large predator of Ellason, living in the cold waters of the Viortahk. It has primitive, pale gray eyes and a long whip-like tail on an arrow-shaped body.

ehl (ël). Rosy, blushing.

Ellason. A heretofore undetected self-heated planet in eccentric orbit around Sol, with aphelion just beyond the Kuiper Belt. Its gravity is equivalent to 1.4 Earth-gs. Lit by thirty volcanic moons, its continental masses are small, and the deep seas are enormous, glowing with ruby-red warmth from an extensive network of deep rifts and the bioluminescence of countless creatures.

Ellasonian. Adjective referring to the planet Ellason.

elll. An adaptable, aquatic, life-loving species of Ellason, equipped with a formidable array of sensory organs, covered with moss-like pressure-sensitive hexagonal tiles and feathery plumes on head and torso.

Elllonian. The system of throat sounds laboriously devised during the ancient first contact between varoks and ellls, spoken by both species in the varokian audible range in order to facilitate communication between those two species.

Elll-Varok (EV) Science. An organization of ellls and varoks that directs the scientific experimentation and observation conducted by those species. It acts as depositor, summarizer, and interpreter of accumulated knowledge and verifiable fact.

EV Lab. Observation station and lab of Elll-Varok Science on Ellason.

EV Moonbase. Observation station of Elll-Varok Science, set into the edge of a crater eleven kilometers in diameter, located northwest of crater Schlüter at 1.50° north and 89.5° west in the d'Alembert Mountains of Earth's only moon.

fan (fän). Run.

Generalist. A varokian academic designation, signifying the acquisition of thorough, detailed knowledge in a broad area of related studies, such as physics, chemistry, astronomy, and geology. Specialist is the first designation earned; Master is the expert designation.

gur (gër). Total, all.

har (här). Unbounded, great.

Harrahn. An expletive used by ellls and varoks; a legendary great-fish, symbol of nature's power, untamed evolution.

hex lines. Lines of tissue forming a meshwork around the skin tiles of ellls. Analogous to the lateral lines of Earth's fish, they house several of the ellls' many senses.

hoat (hōt). Sustainable.

hoats. A tangy, black edible root of Varok that sports feathery char-treuse leaves and tough nuts.

hork (hŏrk). Ancient.

ihn (ēn). After.

il (ĭl). Small.

ilara. A flocking creature of Varok, sometimes domesticated. It builds ground nests lined with moss for three or more eggs in group spawn-ing grounds. Its tiny wings are helpful in hunting web-crawlers, unripe berries and suckers, but it flies with difficulty. Though it is shaped like birds of Earth, it has an exoskeleton and a tiny-broad-toothed beak. Its pure song is a pleasant mewling sound of cascading tones that has a calming effect on ellls.

in (ĭn). Near.

integrate. An elllonian concept to describe the state of being when an individual of another species becomes a part of an elllonian school in a way that implies total acceptance of the ellls; in general, to accept oneself as part of a school.

integration. Activities to solidify knowledge after high-speed micro-volt implantation into the memory of established fact, non-interpreta-ble information, and thought techniques. During integration, students at the varokian Concentrate do Recall, Issues, Problems, and Projects in Creativity to apply the learned information to real problems.

ka (kā). Life.

kaehl. A delicate, easily tamed Varokian animal with silky, pink, branched hair that drapes in long strands about its tiny body and over its large, red nose, causing it to trip habitually as it attempts to run. It incubates its eggs in an abdominal pouch and protects itself with an acrid spray from its sour gland. The dried meat is tasteless but nutritious. Plural: *kaehll.*

kaehl-din. Elllonian invective. Din means fecal matter, kaehl spray. In general, any repulsive substance.

kaehloid. Literally, furry beast. The elll's nickname for species with hair.

kah (kä). Tough, bushy plant.

kahn (kǎn). Life, line, river.

laht (lät). Rover, wanderer.

landcom. Radio communicator.

leahnya (lāänyǔ). Peaceful place.

legh (lā). Plains, flat place, endless.

lial (lëäl). Trim, sleek, clever.

life-joy. The normal Zenfull awareness of ellls.

light-period. The period of time on Varok when the planet is facing Jupiter.

llaoon grass. A soft marsh plant of Ellason. It reproduces via spores.

Ll-leyoolianl (great-fish). A species of creative great-fish of Ellason who perceive the significance of experience and express it in a manner most easily understood by modeling clay representations of their ideas as progressively complex symbols. They have a smiling, triangular head and lateral fins with prehensile tips that dominate their six-meter length. Their sight is poor, they have no ultrasonics, no ear plaques, and a poor pressure sense. Ellls believe that they can penetrate their logical thoughts, and varoks believe they are mood-readers with holistic vision. Their narrow, prehensile, forked tail is a formidable weapon. They give live birth and converse amongst themselves with intricate wing-tip signals and readable thoughts.

lo (lō). Passage.

Loner. An elll who can stand to be away from the school for extended periods of time. Many prefer to be alone or to pursue individual interests.

L'Ran. The Elllonian word for the blue star-planet, Earth.

lu (lû). Sweet.

lur (lŭr). Quiet.

Lurlial. Varokian-built exploratory space cruiser, fourteen meters long, bat-shaped at full glide extension, with capacity to carry eight two-meter beings comfortably, eleven if necessary. The craft has an indefinite range, minimal noise, needs little landing space, and has an extremely low radar cross-section.

Master. Highest honorary recognition by varoks of expertise in a broad area of study, demonstrated by wisdom and restraint in integrating and in applying acquired concepts to real problems. Artellian is one of twenty living ellls to have received the honor; Orram, one of two thousand varoks.

mind-link. The patch organ function driving the intense desire for consummation—the bonding that allows male and female varoks to share thoughts and mood unrestrained, thus releasing their ability to experience emotion while functioning rationally.

Mutilation. The period of time in Varokian natural history in which the varokian species mutated from magnificent and normally sensual winged intellectuals to unduly sensitive bipeds incapable of experiencing strong emotion rationally.

nal (näl). Moving, rolling.

Nalkah (nälkä). Varokian-built land craft which rolls, climbs, or hovers as needed for rough terrain. This model was modified with lunar exposure seals, pressurized with an oxygenated atmosphere, and provided with heat shields. A crew of one to six can be transported in considerable comfort in its elllonian-designed couches.

naran (närän). Knowledge.

naran lu. Right, okay, reliable knowledge.

naranahl (näränäl). Varoks' patch organ (knowledge of the source).

nihr (nîr). Edge, cliff.

niloh (nīlō). Release.

-oon. Elllonian suffix implying water or moisture.

ork (ōrk). flying ones.

pallons. Elllonian unit of measure, about twenty-three meters, the length of an elll's arcing leap through the water from a fast swimming start.

patch organ. Round, featureless plate of tissue behind the ears of varoks which detects, amplifies, and interprets low frequency electromagnetic signals, particularly voltages produced by mental and nervous activity of nearby organisms.

ranat (ränät). Sailing energy.

Ranat. Thirty-meter varokian space cruiser designed to carry forty passengers over long distances.

reading. Sensing another individual's mood, emotion, or trend in thought. One function of the varoks' patch organs.

release. The ability to simultaneously experience emotion and to function rationally. An ideal state achieved by varoks with the aid of a mind-link partner.

rialka (rēǎlkǎ). Young, potential.

rialkahar (rēǎlkǎhär). Emergence.

school. Any number of ellls who inhabit a particular environs or locale and who relate by schooling. The ellls' normal social structure.

schooling. Functioning collectively and sharing awareness as if a group of ellls were one individual.

Sonics. The coded system of low frequency clicks made on the palate of ellls underwater for simple communication.

Songs to Life. Ancient varokian poems written anonymously during the Mutilation. The first verse of the poem translates as follows:

> *Though long denied Life's gracious gift of flowing free,*
> *In currents wild and lifting down, thrown tumbling,*
> *Lifted up, thrown down, and swept without control,*
> *Our minds unlocked, in gray mists swirling bright with crystal hue;*
>
> *Though elegance denied and flight subdued,*
> *We find Life's beauty in her gifts*
> *And take her favors where they fall.*
> *Though all our visions racked our minds with pain;*
> *Though sound grew dense and ruined quiet senses;*
> *Though mind-filling silence became unknown and unknowable;*
> *And new life came to us, imperfect yet yearning for consciousness,*

Heavily distorted, torn by savaged genes
And thrown upon misery to writhe in horror for years denied;

Though Life came not with joy or promise,
But used us for her mindless purpose-
Or too mindful—none can know—
We still survive, thankful for new strength,
Molecules still conscious in forms perhaps wiser.

Specialist. Varokian designation for those acquiring specific knowledge in one field of study, such as low temperature physics.

sponsor. An elll who has chosen a fertile el egg to incubate, to train as a tad, and to advise as an adult elll.

Stabilist. A person belonging, usually covertly, to a revolutionary group on Earth advocating any means to overthrow the World Federation in order to achieve a stable (steady state or no-growth) economy.

tad. An English word used by ellls to mean any young being or new life.

tahk (täk). Forest.

Two Big Stars. Elll's words for Jupiter and Saturn.

ultrasonics. Sound in the range above varokian hearing, used by ellls to echolocate and communicate. Their melons focus high frequency sound and bounce it off distant objects underwater, then receive information about shape and distance from the echoed sound.

uuyvanoon (-l, plural). Sleeping basins designed by and primarily for ellls. They are made of a tough, flexible synthetic imbedded with a thick growth of moss, shaped like a bathtub, and provided with a warm water inlet and a sealed cover for space flight. From Elllonian: u (go), uyan (beyond), van (knowledge), and oon (in water).

va (vä). Western.

vahin (vähēn). Brother.

vahn (vän). Sire.

Varok. A dense, barely habitable, hidden satellite of Jupiter, thought to be associated, at least visually, with the Great Red Spot. At its closest, it is less than 600 million kilometers from Earth; communications delay is at least 32 minutes.

varok. A degenerate species of the planet Varok, having lost its ability to fly and to tolerate emotion rationally. Varoks bear a striking resemblance to humans of Earth, except for the patch organs behind the ears, which at close range sense current thought and mood in other beings. The mind-link, achieved with the patch organ between male and female, is required for emotional expression and sexual contact without crippling loss of reason. (See Release.)

Varokian. Native language of varoks. Adjective referring to the planet Varok.

varokian. Adjective referring to the species varok.

Varokian Concentrate. An institution of Varok open to qualifying individuals of any species who are admitted as students to acquire, by high-speed microvolt implantation into the memory, established fact, non-interpretable information, and thought techniques. The integration and application of this knowledge is acquired at other institutions through continuing studies, leading to the designations Apprentice, Specialist, and Generalist.

Vior (vēōr). City, central place.

Warm Star. Mars.

waterfalling. An ellls' team water sport, like a mix of basketball, canoeing, and racing against the current.

wet-sweater. A shirt made of the most moisture-retaining, softest, and most delicious of Ellasonian mosses, kept alive by periodic moistening and feeding.

World Federation. A world government on Earth with limited sovereignty but growing enforcement capability, formed primarily out of economic necessity.

yakah (yäkä). Mate.

Carolyn A. (Cary) Neeper, PhD raised her family in the US Southwest with her husband and a friendly menagerie of dogs, fish and fowl. An avid proponent of sustainability and steady-state economics since the 1970s, she studied zoology, chemistry and religion at Pomona College and medical microbiology at  the University of Wisconsin–Madison. Cary paints landscapes and animals in acrylics, including the cover art for *The Archives of Varok* series.

The Archives of Varok

In an alternate 21st century Solar System, Earth learns that we have neighbors too intelligent, too nosy, and too near to ignore. . . .

The View Beyond Earth

Two offworld species, disturbingly human and altogether alien. Microbiologist Tandra Grey finds new hope for an ailing Earth and her own future when she makes first contact. Revised and updated from Neeper's 1975 classic, *A Place Beyond Man* (Charles Scribner's Sons).

The Webs of Varok

Silver medalist, Nautilus Book Awards 2013; Finalist, ForeWord's Book of the Year Awards 2012. Tandra leaves Earth for the ancient sustainable culture of Varok, with its promise of stability for her young daughter. But a genius with a hidden talent sets her eye on Varok's wealth — and Tandra's alien soul-mates.

The Alien Effect

Raised on the Jovian moon Varok, Shawne returns to Earth to help her devastated home planet build a new civilization — one that can thrive for millennia. She and her mixed family face unexpected lessons in love and personhood, unaware of the long-term consequences of their collision with life on Earth.

An Alien's Quest

Only two decades after first contact, even Earth's people know of Haralahn, the great-fish spiritual leader on distant Ellason. Shawne seeks his guidance in a quest for meaning that draws everyone she loves away to the Kuiper Belt and into a genetic mystery on the watery home planet of the ellls.

The Unheard Song

In this Archives of Varok prequel, a humanoid invader and aquatic native struggle to communicate in their race to ensure peace and a sustainable future for the wild seas of Ellason.

www.ingramcontent.com/pod-product-compliance
Lightning Source LLC
Chambersburg PA
CBHW022029240626
47154CB00007B/2333